Author's Note

This tale began with two questions: What would a new king mean to Owen Archer? That was simple to answer: He would be summoned to attend the coronation festivities as a member of the household guard of the king's mother. And what would a new king mean to the people of York? My mind already contemplating King Richard's coronation, I thought of the craft guilds in the city, that they would each rush to create something to present to the new king and thereby advertise their services. With that, a title sprang to mind, *A Lion's Ransom*, and the tale of the golden lion re-made (fictional) began to grow, with an already testy relationship among the goldsmiths brought to a boil when their valuable creation is stolen. But another issue loomed in the background, the tension in the realm arising from those competing for power in a new regime, and for that I added Sir John Neville and his ambition.

Sir John Neville, Baron of Raby, was King Edward III's household steward, a March warden, and Admiral of the North, as well as the head of one of the most powerful families in the north of England. In that latter role he worked hard for the enthronement of his brother Alexander Neville as Archbishop of York, who proved to be a very different sort of archbishop than John Thoresby, largely ignoring his duties in the north to seek preference from the king and the pope. Sir John was now eager to court King Edward's grandson and successor. Owen dreads Sir John's arrival in York in this precarious time.

Why precarious? With the death of King Edward III in June 1377, and the accession of his grandson Richard to the throne at the tender age of ten, England's enemies considered the realm ripe for the picking. The grandiosity of King Richard II's coronation in mid-July could not hide the fact that the people were worried, and with good reason. A few weeks before the coronation a force of French and Castilian ships burned the port of Rye, then went on to attack ports in southwest England. As King Edward's health failed in the last years of his reign, his son John of Gaunt, Duke of Lancaster largely ruled the kingdom for his father, and managed to keep its enemies at bay. He might have continued doing so as Regent for the young king until his maturity, but, unfortunately, during his time in charge Lancaster had so alienated the people, especially the citizens of London, as well as many nobles, that King Richard's mother, Princess Joan, and his late father's advisors felt it best not to allow Lancaster to continue in the role. England's enemies were taking advantage of the power vacuum and using the superiority of their navies to harry the English coast, disrupting ports and threatening shipping, going so far as to overtake and confiscate English merchant ships; hence Owen's concern about the ships owned by York merchants.

As much as Owen dislikes and distrusts Sir John Neville, he is well aware that the baron has experience the crown could use in this situation. As Admiral of the North, Neville had been in charge of the royal fleet for areas north of the Thames, and in 1372 had led a small army to Brittany on behalf of the king, holding Brest for several years. One of the two strikes against him in the Good Parliament was his inability to pay the troops in this latter service; Lancaster had experienced a similar disaster in France, unable to secure the money from Parliament to pay his troops, and one might have expected him to understand Neville's situation. But Lancaster gave Neville no role in King Richard's coronation, a snub that must have pained the ambitious man. This slight was the spark that set me thinking how he might use the threat to the shippers in York to win a commission from the king.

An unexpected thread in the story began much as Brother Michaelo's return to the series in *A Conspiracy of Wolves*: just as Brother Michaelo kept insinuating himself into scenes in that book, in *A Lion's Ransom* I found myself writing scenes in Owen's old friend Martin Wirthir's point of view, personal, thoughtful scenes, but perhaps beside the point. I decided to continue with this, exploring Martin's frustration with his ageing body and learning more about his past, though I had no idea what role he might play in the story. I trusted my instincts as a writer even when I didn't entirely understand them.

A LION'S RANSOM

A LION'S RANSOM

Candace Robb

**SEVERN
HOUSE**

First world edition published in Great Britain and the USA in 2026
by Severn House, an imprint of Canongate Books Ltd,
14 High Street, Edinburgh EH1 1TE.

severnhouse.com

Cover and jacket design by Nick May at bluegecko22.com

British Library Cataloguing-in-Publication Data
A CIP catalogue record for this title is available from the British Library.

ISBN-13: 978-1-4483-1317-4 (cased)
ISBN-13: 978-1-4483-1885-8 (paper)
ISBN-13: 978-1-4483-1690-8 (e-book)

All Severn House titles are printed on acid-free paper.

Typeset by Palimpsest Book Production Ltd., Falkirk, Stirlingshire, Scotland.
Printed and bound in Great Britain by TJ Books, Padstow, Cornwall.

The manufacturer's authorised representative in the EU for product safety is
Authorised Rep Compliance Ltd, 71 Lower Baggot Street, Dublin D02 P593
Ireland (arccompliance.com)

Praise for the Owen Archer
Historical Mysteries

'A story of love, danger, and political intrigue sure to
please history buffs'
Kirkus Reviews on *A Snake in the Barley*

'A highlight in a solid series'
Publishers Weekly on *The Riverwoman's Dragon*

'A melange of medieval political plotting . . . Sure to
please fans of historical mysteries'
Kirkus Reviews on *A Choir of Crows*

'Robb once again effectively blends crime with the politics
of 14th-century England'
Publishers Weekly on *A Choir of Crows*

'Recommended for fans of . . . C.J. Sansom, Ellis Peters
and Sharon Kay Penman'
Library Journal on *A Conspiracy of Wolves*

'A multitude of new and old supporting characters round out
the delightful cast and contribute to the twists and
turns of the compelling plot'
Booklist on *A Conspiracy of Wolves*

About the author

Candace Robb has read and researched medieval history for many years, having studied for a Ph.D. in Medieval & Anglo-Saxon Literature. She divides her time between Seattle and the UK, frequently visiting York to research the series. She is the author of fifteen previous Owen Archer Mysteries, three Kate Clifford medieval mysteries, and the Margaret Kerr Trilogy.

www.candacerobbbooks.com

Acknowledgements

Once again, I thank four wonderful women who support me, inform me, engage with me, and cheer me on throughout what is otherwise a solitary writing process. Early in the process, Dr Louise Hampson suggested the wax tablets for Costen van Peelt's itinerant art, and has answered questions throughout the writing as well as carefully reading the completed manuscript to ensure historical accuracy or plausibility. Dr Mary Morse also read for historical accuracy, and both have proved valuable proofreaders. My agent Jennifer Weltz once again pointed out an opportunity I had missed; I always enjoy tucking in those special moments. The fourth is my editor at Severn House, Sara Porter, who I met some years ago when she moderated an evening at the Leeds Library where I was in conversation with my friend Chris Nickson. Sara is a dream to work with. Thank you all, and the great team at Severn House.

I am grateful to my husband, Charlie, for his patience and skill in turning my list of locations into beautiful maps, and for cheering me on when I walk out of my office under a cloud of frustration. He and The Maggie, our fearless and imperious feline, have a knack for inspiring laughter on what seem the worst of days. Much love to you both.

I had just sent the manuscript of this book to my agent when the earth shifted beneath me with the news that my sister Gen had a few weeks to live. I rushed across country to be with her, truly one of the most important people in my formative years. As children we would rise early on Saturday mornings and raid the kitchen for treats to tide us over while we read until breakfast. When I needed a roof over my head, she took me in without hesitation. It was with her that I first travelled to England, and she encouraged my dream of graduate studies in medieval literature. It meant the world to me that she loved my books. My beautiful big sister, my good friend, is gone, yet with me still, and always.

It was Costen van Peelt, a fellow Fleming, a foreigner in a city anxious about foreign spies, who began to tie Martin into the plot. In time, Martin's relationship with Jasper opened into his delight in Owen and Lucie's younger children, inspiring his part in communicating with the street children. Suddenly Martin was a central figure, and I realised he was working towards his redemption.

But it all began with the king's coronation. Such is the nature of storytelling.

When the webs of the spider join,
they can trap a lion.
—Ethiopian Proverb

Owen Archer's York

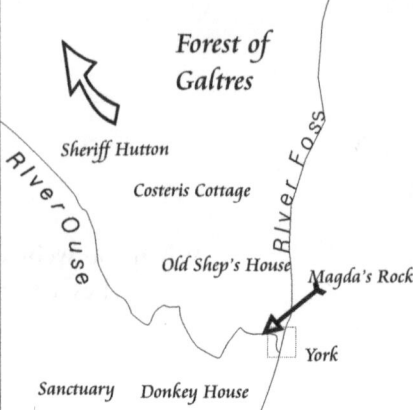

Forest of Galtres

River Foss

River Ouse

Sheriff Hutton

Costeris Cottage

Old Shep's House

Magda's Rock

York

Sanctuary

Donkey House

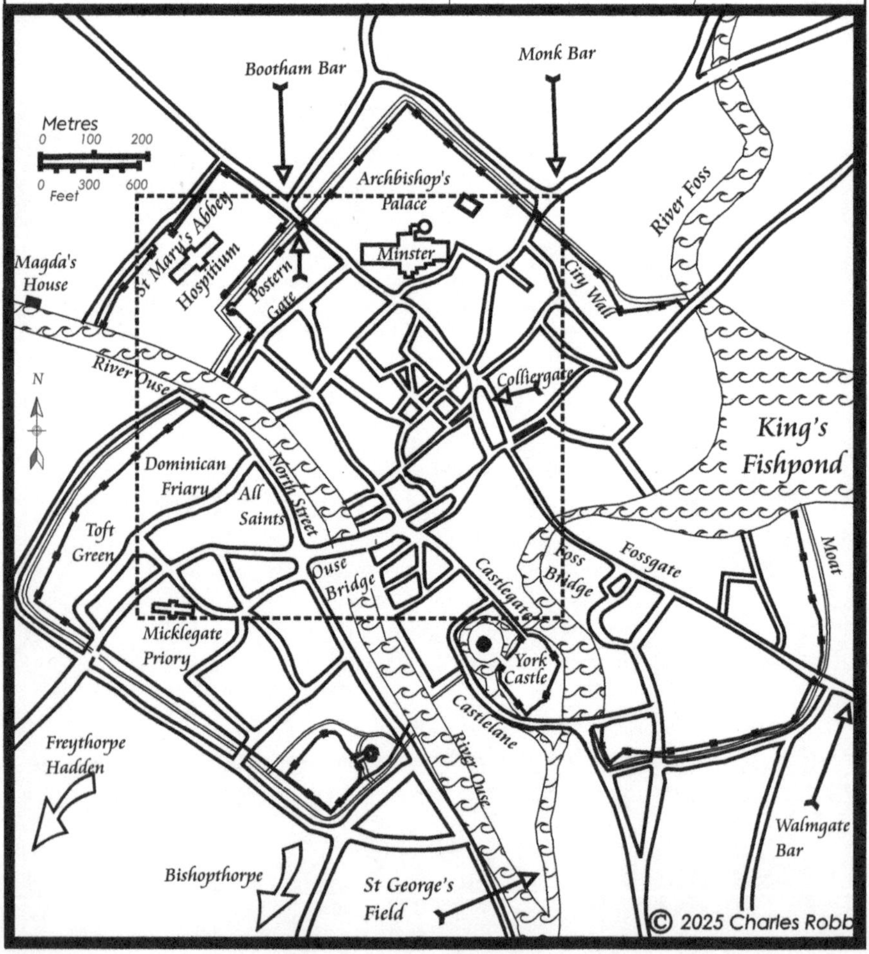

Bootham Bar

Monk Bar

Metres
0   100   200

0   300   600
Feet

Archbishop's Palace

River Foss

Magda's House

St Mary's Abbey

Hospitium

Postern Gate

Minster

City Wall

N

River Ouse

Colliergate

King's Fishpond

Dominican Friary

All Saints

North Street

Toft Green

Ouse Bridge

Castlegate

Foss Bridge

Fossgate

Moat

Micklegate Priory

Castlelane

York Castle

Freythorpe Hadden

River Ouse

Bishopthorpe

St George's Field

Walmgate Bar

© 2025 Charles Robb

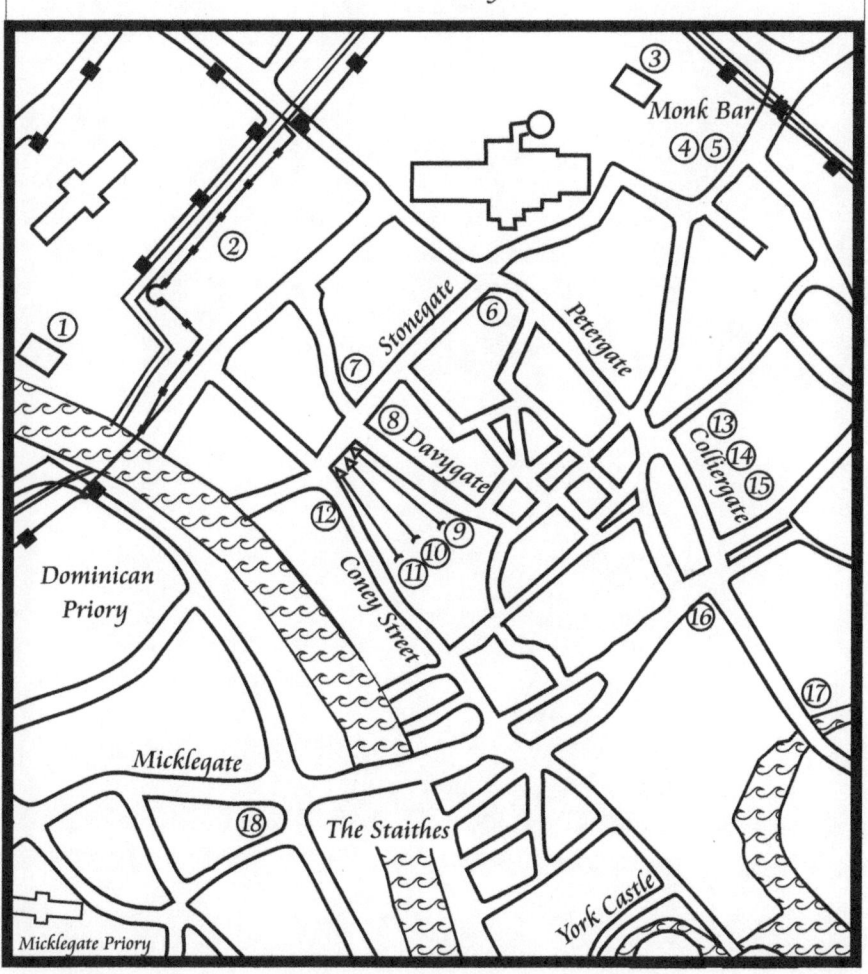

1. Abbey Hospitium
2. St Leonard's Hospital
3. Archdeacon Jehannes's house
4. Holy Trinity
5. Lady Row
6. Robert Dale house/shop
7. Bertram Harrigan house/shop
8. Celia Overton house
9. Owen and Lucie house
10. Lucie's Apothecary
11. York Tavern
12. John Scardburge house/shop
13. Costen van Peelt house
14. Wulf Gifford house
15. Rolo Creswick house
16. Peter Ferriby shop
17. Street children shelter
18. Bell Tavern

Monk Bar

Stonegate

Petergate

Davygate

Colliergate

Coney Street

Dominican Priory

Micklegate

The Staithes

York Castle

Micklegate Priory

ONE

The Boy King, the Goldsmiths, and the Flemings

York, September 1377
Saturday

For once, Robert Dale was grateful for his failing eyesight. The roomful of his fellow goldsmiths jabbing accusatory fingers at one another and spitting out insults wearied him, but at least he would carry only a vague visual memory of their display. Best of all, this was the last of the long, unpleasant meetings, for the golden lion was finished and tomorrow would be on its way to the royal court, carried by guildmaster Bertram Harrigan. Robert looked forward to returning to his usually peaceful life.

He had disliked the idea of the golden lion from the first, but for no reason he wished to express, so he had kept his own counsel, for the most part. It all began with a simple desire to create a gift for the coronation of King Richard that would reflect well on the goldsmiths of York. They would each contribute money, material – particularly gold coin to be melted down – time, and skill towards the project so that no one goldsmith could claim the glory.

But what to create? Silver goblets and dishes seemed too ordinary. A statue of the Christ child had excited them until someone worried that King Richard would take offence at being seen as a child, and they admitted that was rather the point. A silver salter in the shape of a ship with sails and ropes and edgings of gold, with small golden figures standing on the deck, had been a popular idea, until . . . he could not recall what had killed that idea – ah, yes, the difficulty of transporting such a delicate object. And then Bertram Harrigan's wife reminded him of a conversation when Archbishop Neville had dined with them about a golden lion, recumbent, crafted from a pound of gold, that the young prince – at that time Richard was still a prince – had loved, which was tragically lost when the family returned to England from Bordeaux. And they had all smiled at the thought of recreating the lost treasure for the king's coronation gift.

Work began in earnest, the gold coins collected – not quite sufficient to exactly duplicate the original pound of gold – the design sketched according to the image described by the archbishop, but before the mould could be created, they needed to ascertain whether the lion had been fierce or friendly . . . and then someone thought to enquire as to when Archbishop Neville had actually seen the golden lion, and Harrigan's wife said that he had not, but that it had been described to him in great detail. Nor had he said anything about the lion's countenance. Work stopped, and the goldsmiths began the finger pointing.

Robert had consulted his friend Owen Archer, who had recently returned from King Richard's coronation. As well as being captain of the city of York, he was in the service of the king's mother, Princess Joan, and had been summoned to aid in the security of her son during the celebrations. Hoping Owen might have some insight into the young king's preferences, he put the problem to him, though he felt rather foolish asking whether Richard would prefer a stern or a gentle countenance on the lion. But his friend did not laugh, understanding the delicacy of the matter, indeed saying that everyone at court was busy trying to discern the young king's preferences.

It was fortunate that Owen's wife, Lucie, had been included in the conversation, for it was she who suggested they ask their houseguest whether she had seen the original lion. Ermengarde, Lady Carlisle, who had travelled from the coronation in Owen's party and was resting for a few days before continuing on with her son, had been one of Princess Joan's ladies in Bordeaux. To Robert's delight she well remembered the golden lion, and spent several days consulting with the goldsmiths. One of Robert's apprentices, a talented sketcher, had drawn the lion's appearance from her description, working with her for hours to perfect the enigmatic smile – a garrulous woman, she was difficult to keep on point.

Now, almost two months into King Richard's reign, Guildmaster Harrigan was preparing to depart in a travelling company of merchants and clerics to present the goldsmiths' gift to the king. One hoped the insufferably proud man would be too in awe of the court to strut and brag and offend the king and the royal family.

The current argument concerned the carrying case for the lion. Several had been made, variations on a box lined in velvet and secured by a gold clasp, some made of fine wood, some of metal. Robert did not care which was chosen. The one he had made with a piece of beautifully patterned oak, smooth as satin, with a lion rampant carved on the top and the clasp shaped like a claw, would be put to use elsewhere if not for the king.

It was Lady Carlisle's memory of the box in which the lion had been stored that had inspired Robert. Indeed, he had made several of varying sizes, each with a unique clasp. A few of his fellows thought the simplicity of the box might have been the reason for the loss, someone in the household unaware of the value of its contents and leaving it behind. Robert realised they had not been privy to Lady Carlisle's musing that some in the household, including Princess Joan, had believed the lion stolen. He kept his counsel, merely noting that Princess Joan and her ladies would have ensured that everything was packed, but his fellows had gone on to vote on the more elaborate casings. He poured himself more wine and tried not to pay too much attention to the insults flying round the room.

So it was a surprise to hear on the final vote that his box had been chosen.

'I am honoured.' He took a deep breath and placed a hand to his heart. 'Truly.'

And immensely relieved that the meeting could now adjourn.

Early morning sun spilled through the garden windows, illuminating the long table in the hall at which Owen lingered with Lucie over fresh bread, cheese, and a bowl of pears and apples. A moment of peace after much travel for him – a month in London for young King Richard's coronation, a week home with

Ermengarde, Lady Carlisle as a houseguest for several nights, and then away to their manors of Freythorpe Hadden and Llŷnfield for a fortnight to confer with the stewards and celebrate the harvest. It felt a luxury to talk of the autumn chores in the apothecary garden, planning how he, Lucie, and their eldest, Jasper, would divide the work. Long ago, Owen had been Lucie's apprentice in the apothecary, the position now held by their adopted son Jasper, but he still enjoyed having a hand in tending the great garden that supported the shop. The pleasant conversation was often drowned out by the younger children's gleeful shouts as they chased the cat round and up the linden outside the long window. Ariela, fleet of paw, eluded them again and again, eliciting shouts and cheers from her pursuers. After a particularly long chase, Gwen, Hugh, and Emma tumbled onto the ground against the house, giggling and squirming as Ariela sought a warm lap on which to prop herself for a good cleaning.

'She always chooses you,' Emma whined. Owen could imagine the sweet pout of his five year old.

'Because I'm gentle with her,' said Gwen, her twelve-year-old elder. 'And patient with her fidgeting.'

'You think you're grown, but you're not,' said soon to be nine-year-old Hugh of the fiery hair, and, of late, temperament.

'Our new king is younger than I am,' Gwen said, 'and he's expected to rule all of England.'

'A boy king is trouble. Everyone says so,' said Hugh.

'I know.' Gwen sighed. 'Everyone fears that his uncle the Duke of Lancaster will take the throne. He's not only a duke, but the rightful King of Castile, and he could take advantage of his nephew's youth and inexperience to seize the throne here as well.'

Owen looked at Lucie, raising a brow over his good eye. She nodded.

'Where's Castile?' asked Hugh, an indifferent student of all but archery.

'Spain,' said Gwen. 'You should know that.'

'Would we need to learn Spanish?' Hugh asked.

'Castles in Spain,' Emma sang, 'castles in Spain.'

'We're talking of a city, Castile, not a castle,' Gwen snapped.

'Kings live in castles,' Emma said with quiet authority.

'If he's the King of Castile, why would he need to be King of England?' asked Hugh.

Gwen gave an impatient sigh. 'Because the duke claims the kingship of Castile, but there's someone already sitting on the throne.'

'Sitting on the throne, sitting on the throne,' sang Emma.

'I could be the duke's archer when he fights for Castile,' said Hugh. 'Like Da when he fought the French.'

'If he can wait that long,' said Gwen. 'If the duke doesn't win the throne of Castile, he will want the throne of England. You might need to fight for King Richard.'

Owen shifted uneasily. 'Perhaps it was unwise to permit the children so much time with Lady Carlisle?'

'Gwen's been fascinated by the king's youth since we mentioned it,' said Lucie. 'But you're right, they all heard much about the royal family from our talkative guest. Too much.'

On the journey north, Lady Carlisle had regaled the travelling party with gossip of the royal court gleaned from her many years attending Princess Joan as well as Queen Philippa. As they neared York, Owen suggested she be discreet in her conversations in the city, aware that the tensions regarding the French and Spanish navies harrying England's southern and eastern ports since the beginning of summer would have the city on edge. Part of Owen's duties as captain of York was overseeing the bailiffs, though he took active charge only in serious cases, such as murder, or danger to the realm, and at present his primary concern was the certainty that spies for the French and Spanish were in the city gathering information about merchant shipping in the North Sea. He did not need Lady Carlisle's gossip adding to the unease. To her credit, the lady had curbed her tongue in public, but not in his household.

'Lady Carlisle complicated things for us, to be sure,' said Owen.

'The children have promised to keep her tales among themselves,' said Lucie. 'Let us hope they keep their wits about them. Have you any news?'

'I'm meeting with the bailiffs this morning.' They had their men watching and listening, particularly around the staithes.

'I do not know whether or not to hope they have found spies.' Lucie rose. 'Will you dine with us after your meeting?'

'I plan to call on Peter Ferriby and thank him for recommending the new steward for Llŷnfield.' He also wanted to hear what members of the Merchant Adventurers guild were saying about the attacks on the English ports, and whether they had become more amenable to his recommendation that they arm their crews or, even better, carry a few seasoned soldiers on each ship. His advice had been unwelcome, the merchant traders fearing that doing so would invite the crown to seize their ships for the much-depleted navy. Peter Ferriby and his cousin Wulf Gifford were members of the Merchant Adventurers. They would know the current thinking. His friend and bailiff George Hempe was also a member, but too busy at present to attend meetings. 'But I will be home in time to dine with you.'

'I thought you planned to enjoy some time with Martin today.'

'Jasper says he left early for one of his walks about the city. I'll have the afternoon with him, and most of tomorrow, being Sunday. I look forward to it.'

A lifetime of hard living as a diplomat, pirate, and spy had caught up with their friend Martin Wirthir, weakening his heart. He had intended to return to Flanders and settle his affairs, but he was lodging with them for the nonce, too weak to travel, though sufficiently strong to walk about the city and manage his day-to-day activities. Owen had taken the opportunity while in London to engage a man of law to travel to Flanders in Martin's stead. Although the children loved him, and Owen and Lucie enjoyed his company, Martin had made it clear that he did not wish to outstay his welcome. Resolving his business in Flanders would afford him the means to find comfortable lodgings of his own in York.

Martin raised his face to the sun for a moment, appreciating the warmth that softened the autumn chill in the brisk breeze. Soon enough the damp cold of autumn in the north would complicate his efforts to help Owen, long hours of standing bringing a bone-rattling chill to his body that meant hours of shivering near a fire afterwards – he, Martin Wirthir, pirate and spy, invincible and untameable, was now humbled by time's predations. How bold and proud he had been, a necessary attitude for survival in the brutal world of his childhood. It was his memories of that time that had drawn him to Jasper de Melton, an orphaned boy abandoned on the streets, running from his would-be murderer. Owen and Lucie spoke of Martin's heroism in rescuing Jasper and bringing him to their home, and a priest had even called his action selfless, but it was neither heroic nor selfless, rather one of the most selfish things he had done, for he had seen his young self in the orphaned Jasper and resolved to do for him what might have saved him from his own life of outlawry. Whether he had been orphaned or abandoned, Martin had never known, his memory beginning when he was plucked from the streets of Bruges by a thief and murderer to do his bidding. Food and a roof over his head, cleaner clothes that almost fit, that had been heaven to him. He had not understood that his saviour was his undoing. Not until he left Bruges as a soldier, returning only once, to ensure that the monster did no more harm. Wirthir was the devil's name; after the man's timely death, Martin had added the name to his as a reminder of what he was, and why, and what he had done to survive. The origin of the name was something he had never confided in anyone, even Jasper. Now a fine young man and Martin's designated heir, a gift he was proud to be able to offer, Jasper need not know the unhappy tale. When Owen had asked whether the man of law should search for other members of the Wirthir family in Flanders, Martin had simply said they were all dead.

He had much to atone for. What he had done and would do on his death for Jasper was insufficient for Martin's redemption, did not begin to weigh the balance against his sins – violence, murder, theft, and betrayal – but it was a start, the beginning of the end of his embrace of outlawry. Martin had been welcomed into Owen and Lucie's home because they had witnessed his most honourable acts. He did not deserve Owen's friendship, or Lucie's, nor the children's love. But he meant to do everything in his power to redeem himself by using his ill-begotten skills to be of use to them.

At the moment that meant following the Fleming Costen van Peelt, a talented artist who moved about the city sketching buildings on large wax tablets while observing the people in the scenes. Martin meant to find out whether he was simply an artist or a spy using the sketching as an excuse for standing in one place and watching – in this instance the activity around the warehouse of several prominent merchants near King's Staithe. It was certainly an opportunity to study an assortment of people, but it was also a way to spy on business transactions or shipping information for the French and Spanish, currently the enemies of the realm.

Nothing about the wattle and daub structure seemed something to lure an artist, but the Fleming had spent a good hour sketching the warehouse while men delivered barrels from King's Staithe. Granted, the stone foundation and a window in the upper storey covered in waxed parchment gave it a richer look than the surrounding warehouses, but Martin suspected the sketcher was not so much interested in the building as in the men moving about it.

Just as the chill breeze had Martin itching to move for warmth, something distracted the Fleming and he stuffed his wax tablet into his sizeable scrip and started walking at a sharp pace towards Ousegate. As Martin hurried to catch up, he noticed that a raggedly dressed lad dipping in and out of the Saturday crowds appeared to be the person the Fleming was following. Martin kept an eye on both while maintaining a careful distance.

He was good at this, a skill honed in his decades on the run, and though he moved more slowly these days, so did his ageing target. Indeed, sketching in all manner of weather was taking its toll on Costen van Peelt, stiffening his gait. A left on Ousegate, a right onto Coney Street, up the side of St Helen's cemetery past the York Tavern and Lucie's apothecary to Stonegate. The lad slipped into the ginnel beside the house and shop of the goldsmith Harrigan. Martin was uneasy. The tidy storefront and fine timber-framed house behind suitable for the master of the goldsmiths' guild might prove of interest to the artist, but the boy's business at the house was worrying. Owen had instructed Guildmaster Harrigan to keep the golden lion secure in the minster treasury until his departure, its existence too well known throughout the city, providing too much temptation. Pray God the man had not been a fool, that the boy was not checking the place for someone, his Wirthir. While Costen chose a spot in a narrow, shadowed ginnel opposite and began to sketch and watch, Martin made his way round to study the boy. He was rewarded when a servingman opened the door to the boy and spoke with him, handing him something wrapped in a cloth. A brief exchange that Martin could not hear and the boy trotted off, the Fleming following. As Martin shadowed them, he wondered whether Costen was the lad's Wirthir. He hoped for the lad's sake it was not so.

The lad turned right into Petergate, left into Goodramgate, and left again into the churchyard of Holy Trinity, just visible behind Lady Row, a clump of simple whitewashed houses for the poor. Again, Costen watched the lad from a ginnel. Whatever the relationship of child and man, Martin thought Owen might find this of interest. It would have to do for the day. He had just enough strength left to make it back to his room over the apothecary.

It maddened him that he could not do more. He was paying the price for pushing himself beyond his physical strength earlier in the year, first on a long, late-winter journey in a fishing vessel in the Channel, then for a short while a prisoner of the English crown before escaping to the north, where he had found Owen in need of his skills and travelled to Beverley and back, tracking and catching a few of his friend's enemies. All might have been well had he not then been stabbed in the side by one of the Duke of Lancaster's men and lost too much blood. Thanks to the care of Magda Digby, the healer many called the Riverwoman, as well as Lucie and Owen, he had come far in recovering his health, but he began to understand that no amount of rest would entirely bring him back to his old strength. This seemed to be the extent of his usefulness now, short bursts of tracking on the streets of York, and he resented it more than he cared to admit. But so it was.

His curiosity about Costen van Peelt had begun innocently, noticing him sketching the great west door of the minster on a cold, drizzly day, seemingly indifferent to the weather. Not that Costen was not warmly dressed, with a fur-lined cloak, good boots, a wool hat that almost covered his ears, and fingerless gloves, yet to stand in such damp cold and create beauty seemed a remarkable feat.

'You are devoted to your art,' Martin had said as he joined the man, whose guarded gaze intrigued him, even more when his reply revealed an accent very much like his own.

'One cannot choose the weather,' the artist had said, returning his gaze to the minster's west door.

'Ah! A fellow Fleming, I think?'

Keeping his eyes forward, the man said, 'You're the one lodging with Captain Archer.'

'You are well informed.'

'I hear everything on the streets.'

'You would. Yes.' Silence. 'I'm Martin Wirthir,' he had offered. 'And you are?'

'Curious what you want of me.'

Perhaps he deserved that response. 'Do you use the sketches for paintings of York?'

'Why do you ask?'

'I might wish to buy one or more when I furnish my own household.'

Now the man glanced at him. 'You're likely to be doing that?'

'Yes.'

'Come find me then.' He'd returned to his sketching without offering his name.

No matter, Martin had easily learned it, but was left with many questions.

He had begun to walk on when he saw a younger child join the boy in the churchyard and receive the item wrapped in cloth the boy had been given at the Harrigan house. The young one opened it and, smiling, lifted a piece of bread to their nose, then tasted it. Food. He had begged food for his friend. But why at that house? And what had the servant told him?

Mingling with the people going about their business, Martin headed back to his room.

Owen's meeting with the bailiffs had been disappointing, though he was fain to complain about the city experiencing a peaceful stretch, knowing it would not continue. Tensions were high with the attacks on the southern ports and the unease about a boy king, and in a city such as York, a crossroads and a port, the troubles of the realm found a way onto the streets. The spies were about, he did not doubt it, and adept at avoiding discovery,

forewarned by the drowning of a suspected spy while Owen was
with the king and his mother. A group of staithe-workers had
taken it upon themselves to confront the man, chasing him into
the water, where he drowned. A letter in Spanish regarding an
unnamed mission and the reminder to maintain secrecy by
communicating with no one, waiting until his return to report,
and a small cache of gold were found in his room at an inn,
suggesting the men were right in suspecting him, but had they
left it to a bailiff to discreetly take him into custody they might
have learned more. Instead, the man was buried in a common
grave, his identity and mission with him, the incident putting the
city on edge and warning any of his fellows to have a care. As
Owen headed towards Peter Ferriby's shop, he gauged the temper
of the people going about their day as calm on the surface but
with an underlying tension that signalled potential trouble. Not
so strong that his blind eye prickled with warning, but there
nonetheless. It was no wonder.

As he reached the shop, a man stepped out, nodding to him.
'Morning, Captain. Fine weather.' Before Owen could recall his
name, he'd headed off towards the Ouse Bridge.

Peter Ferriby's shop, where he displayed the cloth and other
wares that were but a small part of his business, was a smartly
appointed building on the street just outside the gate to his home.
As Owen entered, Ferriby was showing a tailor who catered to
the wealthiest in the city the way in which a blue wool cloth
draped.

'Which is what one needs in a longer robe,' Ferriby said.

The tailor nodded. 'Yes. Graa will like this. With perhaps a
dark brown surcoat.'

'Such as this?' Ferriby snapped his fingers at his nephew. 'The
brown brocade.'

Belatedly, Owen realised the man who had greeted him on the
street was the prominent merchant Thomas Graa's secretary, an
efficient man whose job it was to know everyone's business in the
city.

Ferriby proffered the edge of an elegant yet subtle brocade for
the tailor to examine.

Shaking it to see the effect of movement, running the back of
his hand along the cloth, the tailor smiled. 'Quite. You have his

measurements for a robe and a surcoat. Send the lengths of cloth
to me.'

'As you wish,' said Ferriby. 'On Thomas Graa's account?'

'Yes.' The tailor took his leave with the air of one who wished
all to know he was a busy man, nodding sharply to Owen as he
passed him.

When the tailor was out the door, Peter said, 'I can see the
rumour now – Captain Archer paying a call on Ferriby's business, trouble brewing.' He chuckled, but his eyes had a worried
glint. 'Good to see you, Owen. I trust all is well with your
family?'

'Very well. That blue wool you showed him – a fine, felted
wool, I think?'

'You have a good eye. The finest wool, yes. You are thinking
of making a gift to Lucie?'

No wonder Peter Ferriby was successful, reading his customers'
minds. 'It's the very blue of her eyes.' A grey-blue, rare to see in
cloth. 'Have you enough?' It had been a while since Owen had
given Lucie an extravagant gift. Far too long.

'I do. Came in on the *Demeter* yesterday.'

The *Demeter* had been on Owen's list to arrive yesterday. Good
news that the elusive spies had not succeeded in delaying it.

Peter indicated Owen follow him to his office behind the shop,
shooing his nephew Luke out to watch for customers. 'Wine?' he
offered as he took a seat.

'That would be welcome.'

When they had settled with their drinks, Owen said, 'I attended
the harvest dinner at Llŷnfield a few nights past and couldn't be
happier with Murton's stewardship. I am grateful you pointed
him my way. He has made some timely changes and proposed
more. I am well pleased.'

The deep crease between Peter's brows smoothed. 'I am glad
to hear it. It's always a risk, recommending someone to a friend.'

'You need not worry on that front.' Owen sipped the wine.

'We've not talked since you were summoned to the coronation.
What was the mood in London and Westminster?'

How to describe it? Crowds in their best clothes, eager to see
and be seen, elaborate decorations adorning even the simplest
dwellings along the way of the procession and even far from the

events, but the chatter was a mix of mourning from those who had not been in the city for King Edward's funeral and anxiety about who would actually be ruling the realm – the boy, the uncle, the mother. 'Beneath the celebratory fittings and elegant clothes the mood was subdued, cautious. The crowd still grieving King Edward.'

'I mourn him as well,' said Ferriby. 'King Edward was sovereign all my life, and for much of the time he brought peace and prosperity.'

'All my life as well. He could be hard, unreasonable, imperious, but he was my king.'

'What was said of King Richard?'

Owen guessed what he was asking. His wife's mother, Lady Pagnall, had ties with Lancastrian nobles, and Ferriby agreed with her in favouring the duke as king, or at least regent, misplaced loyalties to Owen's mind. A memory of a tender moment with Princess Joan arose. *It should have been my Edward, King Edward IV. Confident, experienced. A bitter loss for us all. His uncle might have made a capable regent but that the people distrust him. My poor boy. I pray he is embraced with love and respect, but I fear . . . so much. I must protect him until he proves himself capable.* A mother's vow. Owen had promised to do what he could.

'Owen?'

'Forgive me. People were largely united in their regret that King Richard's father was not the one being feted. And they worry about Richard's youth, inexperience.' He paused, but he believed in honesty between friends. 'And they worry that Lancaster will wrest control of him. They underestimate his mother.'

'She is sufficiently strong to resist Lancaster?'

He thought of those clear eyes, the hand on her heart. She did not believe her brother-in-law wanted the throne, but she was nobody's fool. 'I have no doubt. She is keeping her late husband's most trusted men close.'

'I confess, I fail to see the benefit of that. Lancaster led us through the past several years with a steady hand. And now that our enemies see his power waning, they are encouraged. Why should he not be the regent?'

As expected. 'I have heard that argument,' Owen said, softly.

'I am loyal to my king, and I respect his mother and his late father's men.'

'So we disagree.' Peter nodded. 'And I should watch my tongue.'

Owen smiled. 'You need not watch your tongue with me, my friend.'

'Others might not be so understanding.' The crease reappeared between his brows.

There had been trouble, then. Owen finished the wine and set the cup aside, shaking his head when Peter lifted the flagon, suggesting more. 'Your business looks to be thriving, Thomas Graa's tailor coming to you.'

'He has been a loyal customer for many of his best clients,' Peter said, 'though not all trouble themselves to pay their bills in full.'

'In truth?' Was this the trouble? 'Lucie finds that the loftier the customer considers themselves, the less likely it is they will pay their bills fully and in a reasonable time.' Her apothecary was successful enough to bear the occasional losses, but more than once Owen had offered to have a word with a recalcitrant customer to ease her mind. She always refused.

'I am sure. In her case, they are now feeling well, and wasn't the physician clever – they likely pay him long before they pay their apothecary. In mine, once they have the clothing in hand they forget my part in it.' Peter poured himself more wine, sipped it, and sighed. 'One client, long a regular—' He shook his head. 'No. I should not speak of it. I am glad to hear Murton is working out.'

'You have trouble with this client?'

Peter glanced down at a note on the table beside him, nodded. 'He owes me a substantial sum, and it is he, I believe, who has spun a rumour out of a conversation he could not possibly have overheard. Where did he learn of it? I have been watching the servants, but I cannot believe they are the source.'

'I take it the rumour is meant to damage your custom?'

'Indeed. My Lancastrian sympathies. A worry right now, with the French and Castilian fleets wreaking havoc in the Channel and challenging merchant ships in the North Sea. Everyone is on edge, tempers are sparked by the slightest suspicion. How that will affect my trade . . .' He shook his head. 'The guilds advise us to avoid keeping our ships in English ports, which will prove costly, paying a crew to move round without cargo.' A fraught pause. 'And this person says they cannot in good conscience continue to bring their custom to me.'

'Or pay you what they owe you,' said Owen. 'Troubling that they have details of a private conversation. Is there anyone new in the household?'

'No. Although . . .' Peter glanced out the window. 'My nephew Geoffrey, Wulf Gifford's eldest, spends much time here. He and John are preparing for Oxford. But I cannot think why he would say anything, or to whom, except . . .' He paused, tapping his lip with a finger, frowning. 'He has made some surprisingly acute comments about the state of our navy and how it is the merchants who will pay, and my sons tell me some of that comes from the man Geoffrey follows about, trying to learn to sketch. They apparently converse at length. My cousin Wulf despairs of his son, idolising a Fleming weaver turned street artist.'

'Do you mean Costen van Peelt?'

Peter raised a brow. 'The same. You know him?'

'Not to speak with. But if he's feeding young Geoffrey such information perhaps I should make a point of talking to him.'

'There have been rumours he spies for influential merchants on their rivals.'

'I've heard that, but find it unlikely. How could he survive? Someone would have taken him down by now, as soon as a failure had them searching for the man to blame, would they not?'

'You have a point. Still, my nephew tends to say whatever occurs to him and regrets it later.' Ferriby sighed. 'Are you worried about the goldsmiths' extravagant gift for King Richard? All the city knows of it. I've heard you've had guards on Stonegate every night.'

'I have. But they've had no trouble.'

'That would worry me.'

'Rest easy. The bailiffs and I are worrying for you.' The most dangerous time, when the work was being done in Stonegate, was past, the lion stored in a safe place until taken south to the king. 'You say the guildmasters are advising keeping the ships out of port. And armed?'

'No, though more and more of us are urging them to agree to that. Why should we put the crews in danger?'

'Why indeed. I pray sense wins out.'

'When has it ever?'

TWO

A Theft

A quiet Sunday with the family had refreshed Owen. Monday dawned with a golden September sun and a pleasant breeze. Owen, Martin, Jasper, and Hugh sat on the steps to the backdoor of the apothecary before they all dispersed for the day. While the wood for his eight-year-old son's first bow was curing, Owen was teaching Hugh how to fletch arrows, with Martin providing encouragement. Jasper had stepped out of the apothecary workroom, where he was preparing cough tinctures for the autumn. Despite the warmth, the chill damp would soon sink into people's chests.

Hugh had his tongue curled over his upper lip as he snipped at a feather.

'Are you trying not to breathe?' his big brother asked.

Hugh ignored him, and Jasper was laughing when the shop bell rang.

'Be quiet and go back to work,' Hugh said, angry tears starting.

'I only asked because I remember doing that,' said Jasper. When Hugh continued to glare at him, he sighed and went to see to the customer. Lucie and Gwen had gone out after breaking their fast to forage in the woods with Magda Digby, so Jasper had charge of the apothecary.

'He takes his work seriously,' said Martin.

'That he does,' said Owen. 'He'll make journeyman this year.'

'Did Jasper really hold his breath?' Hugh asked.

Owen laughed. 'Until he was red in the face.'

Hugh grinned. Peace was restored. Until Kate – housekeeper, cook, children's nurse – hurried from the kitchen.

'Captain, you have a visitor. A lad, with a message from the mayor.'

Could the man give him no peace? 'I am coming.'

'Hugh and I will continue,' said Martin.

The messenger paced near the hall door, looking up with an expression of relief as Owen appeared. It was Tompkins, who had more than once told him he wished to work for him when he was old enough. 'The mayor asks that you attend Guildmaster Harrigan, Captain.'

'Harrigan? He's to leave today.'

'Er—' The lad bit his lip.

'If you would share what you know, I'd be grateful.'

After a slight hesitation, the lad nodded. 'The golden lion is missing, Captain. Stolen, most like.'

'From the minster treasury?'

'No, Captain. The guildmaster's shop.'

God's blood. After all their care. Owen had warned the goldsmiths that an extra night watchman walking Stonegate for the duration of the project as well as a guard during the day could only protect them to the extent they were careful. As Peter Ferriby had said, everyone in York – indeed everyone in the surrounding countryside – knew of the project. Owen had warned the goldsmiths never to speak about where the gold, and now the lion, were kept, which shop was doing the work on any one day, and that once their work was complete it should be stored in the minster treasury until the morning Harrigan departed. Now the worst had happened. Yet Owen concerned himself with crimes against the king's peace, not property thefts. 'This is a matter for the bailiffs.'

'The mayor says the guildmaster particularly asked for you.'

Of course he had.

Harrigan's clerk stepped aside for Owen to enter the goldsmith's office, which had a door off the ginnel so that visitors did not disturb the work in the shop.

'Master Bertram is in the workshop,' said the clerk. 'I will let him know you are here.'

Owen followed the clerk, curious about the mood of the apprentices and journeymen. The heat and the cacophony of hammers almost pushed him back into the quieter office, but the sight of Harrigan in his shirt sleeves bent over a table beating a square of silver into a thin, smooth sheet arrested his gaze. As the clerk passed the apprentices, they paused to glance round and the noise lessened until the only hammering was that of the goldsmith. All eyes were upon Owen, who nodded to the young men and motioned for them to go about their business. But they turned to watch the clerk bend to his master and say, 'Captain Archer is here,' in a voice that could be heard over the hammering. When Harrigan continued his work, the clerk repeated the message. At last the guildmaster paused with the hammer raised, turned towards his clerk, and nodded. A man, older than the apprentices, likely a journeyman, joined the master, saying something in his ear. Harrigan handed him the hammer and wiped his face with a dusty cloth. Owen stepped back into the office and settled into a high-backed chair intended for customers.

When Harrigan appeared he had donned a well-tailored tunic of good wool and slipped a comb through his hair, though his complexion was blotched from the heat, there was no shedding that. Like his workers, his hair, face, and hands glittered with gold and silver dust.

'Thank you for coming so promptly, Captain.' Grim-faced, Harrigan retreated behind a table strewn with boxes, some opened, some shut. Hoping he'd simply misplaced the valuable object? 'I know that you do not usually bother yourself with theft, but this is more than that. The messenger told you of it?'

'He did. But I would like to hear all of it, in your words,' said Owen, curious about what he meant by more than theft. 'I thought you had agreed to store the lion in the minster treasury until your departure.'

'We were to leave early, Captain, and I could not see—'

The clerk knocked, then entered with a flagon and two silver cups. Harrigan cleared a spot on the table for them, waited while the clerk poured and withdrew, then took a long drink and sighed as he returned his cup to the table.

'I believed it to be perfectly safe here,' Harrigan said. 'I cannot see how it could happen. I cannot.' He spoke without any of his usual self-important bluster. 'It was in a sturdy, iron-clad chest bolted to the wall. A chest for which I hold the only key. Yet it is gone.'

'Might I see this chest?'

Harrigan stepped aside and motioned to a corner behind his desk.

Owen crouched down to examine a large oak chest banded with iron, finding it well made. He tried to lift it. The bolt held. It would likely be too heavy for one man in any case, though two strong men might have wrenched it from the wall, taking plaster with it. Certainly not a stealthy process. But they had not. He ran his hand along the lock, felt an irregularity.

'Hand me the lamp.'

Harrigan did so, and crouched beside Owen.

'See these?' Owen indicated scratches on the lock and some small damage in the oak.

Harrigan crouched beside him. 'God help me.'

'Are these new?'

'Yes. Well—' Harrigan grunted as he stood up. 'I cannot with any certainty say when I looked at it so closely.'

'When did you last see the golden lion in here?'

'Towards evening on Saturday. I tidied up before opening a cask for the apprentices and journeymen – a celebration, you see, congratulating them on their hard work, tending to our regular business as well as all their work on the lion.'

'This celebration took place in the workshop?'

'Yes.'

Harrigan flinched at Owen's muttered curse. 'For this reason alone you should have stored the lion in the treasury. Are you certain nothing else is missing?'

'Nothing else.' He wiped his brow with a linen cloth, his hand trembling. 'I thought it quite safe. I have never had a problem.'

'All in the city have been fascinated with the lion for the young king. Far too many knew of it, and it required only one of them to guess where it might be stored. Hearing of the planned party—'

'I decided about the party only that morning.'

'And ordered the drink to be delivered?'

Harrigan reddened and lowered his gaze. 'Yes,' he said softly.

The man was a fool. 'Did you station someone in here to guard the chest?'

Harrigan took a deep breath. 'I barred the outer door in here, to the ginnel, and locked the door to the workshop.'

It was something, but not nearly enough. 'Who knew the lion was still here?'

'The few who were to accompany me to the treasury after our meeting on Saturday. John Scardburge, his journeyman Henry Wyman, and Sebastian Goring.'

Owen knew nothing against the three; they should have been trustworthy. But people are not always careful about who might hear them. 'What reason did you give for not taking it to the treasury?'

'The archbishop's clerics wished to depart early Monday and asked that I be at Micklegate Priory at dawn. I feared all in the minster would be at prayer and I might be late.'

'But the archbishop's priests were here to confer with the dean and chapter. Would they not also be at prayer?'

'Apparently not. Dom Paulinus and Dom Francis were quite clear when we dined on Friday that they wished to depart just after dawn.'

'Did you inform them of your concern?'

'I did.'

The clerics did not seem likely thieves. 'Did anyone else dine with you?'

'William Barlow represented the merchants in the travelling party. Just those three.' He frowned. 'Their servants did not sit at table with us, but they were in and out with messages and such.'

'They all heard your discussion about leaving the lion in the treasury?'

Harrigan frowned. 'I do not believe so. This was as we were departing. I was speaking to Dom Francis and Dom Paulinus. Their servants had already stepped out, and Barlow and his serving-man had departed as well. I think. I do not entirely recall.'

Owen had little faith at this point that Harrigan had taken care not to be overheard.

'Who else has access to the keys to the door and the chest?'

'My clerk knows where I keep them, in a locked chest in the house. He needs to ask either my wife or myself to open it.'

'You and your wife. No one else?'

A slight wince. 'All the household know what is in there. And we have on occasion entrusted the key to my daughter Elaine. Perhaps one of the older servants.'

'In short, your wife, your daughter, and one or more servants.' How did such a man rise to guildmaster?

'Well, yes. But last night, and all the while we have worked on the lion, my wife and I have been here.'

'I presume the lion was in a case of some sort?'

'Yes, an oak box, velvet-lined, with an elegant golden clasp. Robert Dale designed and made it.'

Dale was an old friend. Perhaps he would have some insights.

'I took great care with the lion, I assure you.' Harrigan looked about to faint. Doubtless his error had become clear to him.

'The bailiffs will talk to you and your employees,' Owen said.

'The bailiffs? Not you?'

'We work together. You will be in good hands, I assure you.'

'They will recover the lion?'

'They will do their best to apprehend the thief, or thieves, and recover the guild's property.' Owen moved towards the door. 'You should expect a bailiff to call on you by mid-afternoon.'

'That is it? That is—' Harrigan covered his face with his hands. 'I will be slaughtered.'

'That is unlikely.' His reputation would suffer, he would lose his standing in guild, but Owen doubted anyone would lay hands on him.

Stepping out into Stonegate, Owen thought perhaps he had underestimated the anger. A crowd of red-faced goldsmiths and others awaited him, demanding to know if the rumour was true, the golden lion stolen. He was not surprised by how quickly word had spread, nor that the coward Harrigan had quickly shut the door behind Owen rather than face the crowd waiting in judgement.

'I assure you the city will do all it can.' This was clearly going to be a headache until resolved. 'Bailiff Hempe will be in charge of the investigation.' George was the bailiff least likely to aggravate the tension. 'If you noticed anything out of the ordinary last night, I pray you speak to him.'

As Owen passed through the throng, he noticed the goldsmith John Scardburge, whom Harrigan had mentioned, standing back from the crowd, a worried expression on his face unlike the others – not mixed with anger, but fear. Curious, Owen approached the man, but he turned and hurried away past the apothecary and the York Tavern towards his shop and home in Coney Street.

He would mention it to Hempe.

Motioning to a lad standing at the edge of the crowd, one who often delivered messages for him, Owen told him to find his men Stephen and Alfred and have them meet him at Micklegate Priory. 'Tell them to prepare to ride out.' He would do this for Hempe, chase the travelling party, make sure one of them had not taken advantage of Harrigan's simplicity.

Stephen and Alfred had joined Owen while he spoke with the hospitaller at Micklegate Priory about the travelling company who had in the end left several hours after sunrise in order to attend mass and have a good breakfast before departure. His men now accompanied him to the stables at Micklegate Bar. While they chose the mounts and saddled them, Owen wrote a note to Hempe telling him to call on Harrigan and begin the investigation while he chased the travelling company. He handed the missive to a lad with a penny.

'How fast can you run?' Owen asked.

'I'm fast, Captain. I will find him before you leave the city.'

'I like your confidence.'

With a nod, the lad dashed off down Micklegate hill.

'You are fast!' Owen called after him. The lad lifted a hand without pausing.

'You'll have all the boys in the city following you about hoping to be chosen,' Stephen said as he handed Owen the reins to his mount.

'He already does,' said Alfred, 'all the young ones eager to be noticed and chosen. You'd think the scarred face and patch and that grim set to his jaw would have them running from him, but they count him a hero.'

It was good to share a laugh with his men on such a morning. Owen had known Alfred and Stephen a long while. He had been their captain in Archbishop Thoresby's household guard, and, since the archbishop's death, had employed them himself. Alfred was thoughtful and skilled with a knife, Stephen strong and formidable. They had seen much fighting together, their bond strong.

Finding the company of travellers was easy, and no surprise that they balked at having their baggage searched.

'We seek the golden lion, nothing more,' said Owen. 'Our search will be quick and efficient. Your choice whether we search here, or back in the city.'

The clerics quickly acquiesced, though they insisted on watching as Stephen and Alfred opened their baggage. When the merchants saw how quickly the matter was resolved, they agreed, with the same requirement.

None carried the golden lion.

'Have you checked the belongings of your friend Martin Wirthir?' the wine merchant William Barlow sneered as he strapped his pack to his saddle. 'He was a go-between for Goldbetter and Company, well known to be thieves.'

'Wool is what they wanted,' said Owen. 'And I was with Martin on Saturday evening and Sunday. Are you accusing me of theft, or just gullibility?' He sneered back and the man lowered his gaze, murmuring an apology. 'You were one of the victims of Goldbetter and Company?'

'That is neither here nor there.'

'Nor is Martin.'

'Are we in danger?' asked Dom Paulinus. 'Are there rumours we stole the lion? Might we be attacked on the road?'

'I heard no such rumours,' said Owen. 'But it is always best to be cautious on the road, particularly if you are carrying anything of value.' He had not noticed any such treasures.

'Letters of import to His Grace, Archbishop Neville, but nothing valuable to thieves,' said Paulinus.

'As you saw, I have a cask of fine brandywine,' said the merchant Barlow, 'otherwise a few contracts, valuable only to me.'

One of the other merchants nodded. 'Contracts, several letters, nothing more, as you saw. We are well rid of the goldsmith with his treasure.'

'I wish you luck in finding it, Captain,' said Dom Francis. 'I presume we are free to continue?'

'Just two more questions. Are all of the servants who attended you when you dined with Harrigan here now?'

Paulinus frowned. 'They are. As is Barlow's. Why? Oh.' His brows rose. 'You thought one of our servants might be the thief. I assure you that is not so, Captain.' He started to move towards his horse, then glanced round. 'You said two questions.'

'I did. Why did you tell Harrigan you wished to leave shortly after dawn, and yet in the end you did not?'

Paulinus glanced at Francis.

'The dean has wearied us with petitions for His Grace,' said Francis. 'We were eager to avoid his delaying us with more requests. And, in truth, we must take responsibility for asking Harrigan to avoid going to the minster treasury in the morning. It was selfish, and now, I fear, irresponsible.'

'Archbishop Neville is already disliked in York,' said Barlow. 'Now the guilds will have cause. Even worse that they then attended mass at the priory and ate a sumptuous breakfast.'

Francis, his face reddening, pointed a finger in Barlow's face.

'I wish you a safe journey,' said Owen, nodding to Alfred and Stephen, who were only too eager to escape the arguing travellers.

THREE

A Corpse

Foraging for healing plants, berries, and roots in the Forest of Galtres was a skill Gwen wished to learn, though it was not required for an apothecary's apprentice, which she hoped to be when old enough. Lucie had thought her daughter's interest would wane after a few hours accompanying the healer Magda Digby, but Gwen had surprised her, taking to the work with enthusiasm through the spring and summer. Today Magda had invited Lucie to accompany them, and after a time it was clear what her friend wished her to witness. Her chatty, earnest twelve-year-old softened and quieted in the forest, stepping silently and with care, listening closely to Magda's murmured instructions, asking questions in a hushed voice, smiling when praised for her attention. Dame Magda was a calming presence, but Lucie could see that there was more to Gwen's fascination as she watched her daughter tilt her head and listen to the sounds of the forest with her good ear, and the occasional silences, using what she had learned to creep forward or change direction, her face aglow when she showed the white-haired healer her discovery. In the apothecary and out here in the wood, Gwen was eager and quick. This was not a passing interest for her daughter, but a calling. The apothecary garden had not yet caught her interest, but Lucie now had confidence that when Gwen realised its usefulness she would take to it as she had to all her lessons so far.

She followed the two with a light heart, careful to observe, not interfere, intent on not disturbing their routine even though she itched to have something to do. But watching became wearying, and as they moved towards the river, Lucie sought out a place to sit for a while, finding a cool, dark space beneath an old willow where the bank cut in, as if the tree's roots had reached out to carve a trough and drink deep. An upthrust root invited her to sit, and she was easing herself down when something in the water caught her attention. Pale fibres rippling in the current, a more solid piece . . . She pulled back. The fibres were hair, pale hair. She turned away to breathe, deep, deep breaths, while she said a prayer for the dead. She wished she might walk away and leave this, not shatter her daughter's perfect morning. But it was not in her nature to step away from her duty. Turning back, she crouched at the edge of the bank to study the body floating face down.

'What is it?'

Lucie straightened and tried to block her daughter's view, but she saw by the widened eyes and the mouth shaped in a perfect 'o' that she was too late. She drew Gwen close. 'A drowned man, my sweet. I don't think he's been long in the water.'

Magda joined them. 'Ah. Mayhap it was his horse Magda found wandering yesterday.' She knelt down on the bank and reached out to the body with a long twig, gently pressing the flesh. 'Thou art right. Not long in the water.' She rose, dusting off her skirts. 'The horse may well be his.'

And the horse might provide the name of the dead man. 'Did you examine the saddle bag?' Lucie asked.

'There was none,' said Magda.

That was disappointing, but a search of the area might unearth it. 'We should go out to the track and find someone to fetch Crispen Poole.'

'Why him?' Gwen asked. 'Why not Da?'

'Crispen's the coroner of Galtres.'

'Then him and Da.'

Lucie had thought Gwen would be horrified, but she seemed her usual practical self. And she was right. 'Yes. Let's find someone to fetch both.'

Gwen looked back over her shoulder as they moved away from the bank. 'He's naked,' she whispered. 'Maybe he was bathing.'

'That is possible.' Though Lucie had noticed a dark area on the back of the man's skull, beneath the pale hair. 'Poor man.' She exchanged a look with Magda, who gave a little nod and led them up the path.

* * *

Hugh's fletching lesson finished, Martin offered to watch him and
his sister Emma in the garden while Kate prepared the midday
meal, as Lucie and Gwen were away and Jasper was alone in the
apothecary. In truth, he delighted in spending time with them. In
his peripatetic life, Martin had rarely been part of a household
with children and had forgotten what a joy they were at play, with
their powerful imaginations and easy embrace of what adults
considered impossible.

Today Hugh was a knight exhibiting his prowess in the hope
of winning Lady Emma. It was clear that he perceived 'winning
the lady' as becoming the first knight of the realm, slicing and
stabbing imaginary combatants with his wooden sword accompanied by loud cries, nothing to do with bedding her or even
gaining her affection. For Emma the story was about how hard
Hugh must work to please her – which included praising her
beauty and gathering the apples that fell as his sword knocked
them from the trees and offering them to her on bended knee.
She was quite firm about both requirements.

Martin's career had included fighting in various armies, never
as a knight, but that was part of the children's fantasy, that battles
were all knights fighting to impress ladies. He and all those with
whom he'd fought had strangely once been so innocent, so full
of chivalric nonsense, with never a thought to the fields of
slaughter, the likelihood that one's first battle would be one's only
battle, and, if not, the nightmares that would haunt one's sleep
at the edge of the field of the dying. Nor did they foresee that
the ladies – or the beautiful young nobles – for whom one pined,
whose colours one might carry, would glance away in horror at
one's injuries, place a silk to their noses at the stench of the
battlefield carried on one's person, and have eyes and sweet words
only for the leaders who had sat astride their horses ordering the
battle but not partaking.

He prayed that none of the children in this household ever saw
the truth of chivalry.

'Da!' Emma shed the haughty demeanour of the lady to rush
to her father as he entered the garden from Davygate.

Another man who knew the truth of war, his scarred face and
patched eye a warning the children ignored. Da simply looked
like that. He had always been so.

As Owen joined them, Martin noticed a grim scowl before his face broke into smiles. 'My sweetest!' With his powerful arms, Owen lifted his fair-haired daughter into the air.

She squealed with delight, and Hugh rushed to join them, telling Owen how Martin had praised his efforts with the fletching. Gently setting Emma on her feet, Owen ruffled his son's copper hair and joined Martin, settling down on the bench beside him.

'Trouble?' Martin asked, softly, although the children were loud enough to drown them out as they returned to the game that Owen's arrival had interrupted. He listened to Owen's account of Harrigan's costly mistake. 'The man's a fool. How did he come to be guildmaster?'

'Bought the votes, I'd wager. I caught up with the travelling company, searched their packs, found nothing.' Owen sighed and stretched out his legs. 'Tell me again about Costen van Peelt following the lad to Stonegate and then Holy Trinity.'

Martin did not like the question. 'You think one of them stole the golden lion?'

'At present I suspect everyone. The city has been excited about the goldsmiths' project.'

He had a point. Martin was repeating what he'd witnessed when they were interrupted by Crispin Poole, who stood at the gate into the York Tavern yard.

'We need to talk, Owen.'

Martin rose to leave, but Owen motioned for him to stay as Crispin came through the gate. Despite a slight unevenness in Crispin's stride from an old injury, and one empty sleeve tucked into the front of his tunic, the former soldier was a formidable presence, especially when glowering, as he was now.

'I don't like that frown,' Owen said as Crispin Poole approached.

'I don't like the cause. A body on the riverbank. In Galtres.' Crispin was coroner of the royal forest. 'You might want to come along. Lucie found it.'

Lucie. God help him. She had gone foraging with Gwen and Magda. Could the day get worse? 'Someone she knows?'

'I think not,' said Crispin. 'I'm sorry she saw it.'

'Gwen is with them as well.'

Crispin pressed his hand to his forehead. 'Even worse. Will you come?'

Owen glanced at the children.

Martin waved him on. 'I will entertain the little ones until Kate has a moment.' Though he could not entirely hide his disappointment, he nodded his assurance that he was fine with the arrangement.

'We did not invite you here to care for the children,' said Owen.

'We will argue that point later. Go!'

Crispin had thought to send a servant on to arrange a cart and awaited them outside Bootham Bar. They collected Brother Michaelo to record the details and headed into Galtres while they had several hours of light for the mission.

As they walked, Owen told his companions about the conversations with Harrigan and the travelling party.

'You do not believe in coincidence,' said Brother Michaelo, 'so I assume we are accompanying Poole because you suspect the drowned man was connected to the theft?'

'More because my wife raised the hue and cry, and my daughter is with her. But I do wonder.'

After finding someone on the forest track to send the message, Lucie had paced on the bank, guarding the corpse and rehearsing how to talk to Gwen about the experience, while Magda distracted her daughter by continuing the search for roots away from the river. Lucie tried to keep her eyes averted from the fish beginning to nibble on the body, and the growing drone of flies. She was not usually so squeamish, but the fish jostled the body as they fed and made it seem alive, as if they were feeding on a living man. When she heard Owen's voice, and Crispin's, she hurried towards them, almost tripping in her relief. In a moment she was folded in her husband's arms, her head against his chest, calmed by the steady beat of his heart, a comfort she'd not known she needed, not to reassure her against death, but against a world that threatened the innocence of her children.

When she had assured Owen she could bear to lead them to the body, he followed while quietly giving orders to his companions. Reaching the place where Lucie had paced, Brother Michaelo found a seat and drew out his wax tablet while Owen and Crispin continued to the bank. Lucie pointed out the possible injury to Owen, who checked to ensure Michaelo had heard. Such an unlikely pair, Owen, his movements those of a man at ease in a body honed by battles and the bow, his dark wiry hair hardly controlled by a felt hat, his Norman beard, high cheekbones, scarred face, the sharp, dark eye that seemed to see all; Michaelo with his smooth, almost ageless face, hooded eyes, willowy figure, moving as if floating, fussy in his tailored Benedictine robes, pale hair always freshly tonsured and tidy. One spoke with quiet command, the other ever with a hint of sarcasm overlaying a deep sadness. Yet they worked together seamlessly. Crispin was more like Owen, soldierly, battle-scarred, blunt-spoken, though he moved a little heavily in a body that was softening and expanding. Watching them steadied her and kept her eyes away from the poor soul in the water.

Magda arrived as Owen and Crispin were preparing to lift the body from the water, the latter using a belt round the ankles to lift with his one hand. 'Gwen is watching the cart,' she said to Lucie. 'Thou shouldst not worry. She is a strong young woman.'

Was her concern so obvious? 'I know her strength, but I cannot help wishing she had not witnessed the stuff of nightmares.'

'Of course.' Magda pressed Lucie's shoulder, then moved on to the men. 'Magda will assist thee.' She slipped easily into the water and took position to support the man's head.

Lucie moved back to the cart and embraced her daughter in silence. Gwen held tight to her.

They formed a solemn procession through the woods, speaking softly about the dead stranger – for he had not been long in the water, yet his features were familiar to none in the party. His much-scarred body suggested a life of soldiering or some other work that often led to violence. Part of one ear was missing and two fingers on the left hand were missing the first joints, both injuries long healed. There was indeed a serious wound to the back of his head, suggesting that he might have been dead before going into the water, or at least unconscious. Not likely an accident while bathing, then. Once they had moved him to the castle, they would examine him more thoroughly. Although his face had begun to bloat, and his eye sockets were empty, Lucie thought he might have been comely in life, with good bones.

She kept her arm round Gwen but did not intrude on her daughter's thoughts. She would have questions enough in time. When Owen said he was stopping at the stables outside Bootham, Lucie and Gwen left them to continue home.

Glancing at the corpse, the stablemaster crossed himself. 'You'll ruin my business bringing such in here.'

'We lifted the cover for you,' Crispin growled, 'we are not parading him outside. Do you look at him and tell us if you recognise the poor soul.'

Sweating, the man moved closer as one of the grooms joined him. 'I cannot say whether I knew him in life. The eyes!' The stablemaster crossed himself again and muttered something – prayer or curse, Owen could not tell.

The groom gave a little cry. 'Master, look.' He pointed to the entrance.

'Dost thou know this fine animal?' Magda asked, leading a horse into the stables. She had left the party to fetch the beast she had found wandering.

The groom nodded.

'Ah, that fine fellow,' said the stablemaster. 'Yes, I do know him. Belongs to a—' He looked back at the cart and crossed himself. 'I know him now. Stabled his horse here for a few weeks. Left yesterday, early. Walter, that was his name. May he rest in peace.'

Magda looked at the lad. 'Dost thou remember the man?'

The lad nodded. 'Just to hand him the reins.'

The stablemaster gently shooed the groom back to work.

'Had he stabled his horse here before?' Owen asked.

'Several times,' said the stablemaster.

'Same horse?'

A nod.

'Do you have any idea where he lived?'

'None. He said little, and I was fine with that. He gave me no trouble, paid what I asked and sometimes a little more for the grooms.'

'Companions?'

'Always alone, no servant, no one with him.' Glancing once more at the corpse, the stablemaster wiped his sweaty brow. 'A handsome man if not for the scars. I took him for a soldier come into some wealth. Now a merchant?' He shrugged.

A name, the fact that he had been to York before, missing a travelling pack, owned his own horse. It was a beginning. Owen thanked the stablemaster for his trouble and gave him some coin towards the horse's care.

'I cannot keep him forever,' the stablemaster warned.

Owen nodded to him and departed.

FOUR

Who Was He?

A damp wind sent dry leaves swirling in the castle yard as
the shadows lengthened, hinting at rain, perhaps by nightfall. Owen bent to examine the corpse, aware of people
pausing as they went about their business in the castle yard to
see what the cart held, then hurrying on with hands or cloths to
their faces. So far no one had come forth to identify the dead
man.

Seated on a low wall near the cart, Brother Michaelo glanced
up from his tablet. 'You have been quiet a long while. My last
note regards the torn skin on the knuckles suggesting a fight.'

Owen covered the corpse and stepped away, brushing his hands.
'I believe that's the last of the fresh injuries. A blow to the head
before throwing a man into the water does not always ensure
death. The water sometimes revives the victim. Not this time.'
He shook out his hat, raked a hand through his hair as he looked
back at the body. 'Why were you here? And why stripped and
murdered?' So far he saw no connection to the theft of the lion.

Michaelo set his things aside and joined Owen, gently touching
the damaged ear, the injured fingers. 'We have seen him before. I
am trying to recall when and where.'

'The stablemaster said he had been here several times, stabling
that same horse.'

'I am certain we have seen him before, and noted him. But it
would have been a while ago.'

That was it, the nagging thought Owen could not quite catch
and hold. 'You're right. But when? What was he doing here?'

'I will keep thinking.'

'Word will spread. Let us hope someone claims him.' He studied
the man.

A soft rain began to fall.

Michaelo touched Owen's shoulder. 'Come. We have done all we can for now.'

Owen's thoughts turned to Lucie and Gwen. 'I have an errand on the way home. Some cloth I bought for Lucie.' With a gift of the blue cloth he hoped to erase some of her pain in discovering the body and worrying that Gwen might be marked by the experience.

Brother Michaelo accompanied him to Ferriby's shop, keen to see Owen's choice.

'Exquisite,' Michaelo murmured, fingering it. 'The colour of her eyes, and so finely woven, of such quality.'

Peter Ferriby beamed. 'And there is something for you, Owen. A gift.' He gestured towards a brown brocade beside the blue. 'For court.'

'You need not—'

'This would make a fine jacket,' said Michaelo.

'Permit me the pleasure of this gift,' said Peter. 'I like to imagine you wearing it at court.'

A costly offering. But Owen could not in good grace refuse, and thanked Peter sincerely over cups of wine.

'Have you spoken to Costen van Peelt?' Peter asked. 'Or my nephew?'

'I've not had the opportunity. But I will.'

'Of course. The drowning.' Peter crossed himself. 'You have much on your mind now.'

'I will not forget,' Owen assured him.

As they walked towards Colliergate – Michaelo refusing the shorter route through the Shambles despite the rain, saying the butchering stench was more than he could bear – the monk spoke of the gift of accepting with grace.

'You saw how happy you made him.'

'Are you my advisor now?'

Michaelo laughed. 'Merely noting.'

'I am puzzled by his gesture of generosity. I cannot think how I deserve it.'

Michaelo made an amused sound. 'The citizens of York are grateful for your protection. I understand that you do not like to think you will be summoned to the royal court again soon and therefore need fine clothing, but it is the nature of your duty to our new king. He trusts you, which is no small thing. As does his mother.'

Owen could not deny that.

As they approached Stonegate, Michaelo sniffed. 'Your lodger waits to escort you home.'

Martin sheltered from the rain beneath the jutting first floor of a house at the corner, watching them.

'He said he would watch the area for anyone out of place, but I would have thought he would leave when the rain began,' said Owen.

'He means to impress you,' said Michaelo, bowing to them both and turning towards the minster gate.

Martin stepped out into the rain. 'The monk dislikes me.'

Owen shrugged. 'He gives most people that impression.' They turned towards home as the rain came down harder. 'Anyone lurking near Harrigan's shop?'

'Costen stood for a short while near St Helen's Church. No one else. They would be noticeable in the rain. He moved on to Holy Trinity churchyard and paused there, but did not linger. I found it odd.'

What was Costen watching for? 'Come. I've something I don't want to get too wet.' Owen picked up the pace.

'Captain!' Bertram Harrigan came hurrying out from his shop. 'The drowned man. Was it the thief? Did you find the golden lion?'

Owen looked away from the hope in the man's eyes. 'We have not found the lion. As for the man, we know little. No one has yet identified him.' He would keep the name to himself for a time. 'We know nothing of why he was here, whether he was your thief. But it is early in the search.'

With head bowed, Harrigan thanked them and walked slowly back to his shop.

'You need a strong stomach for your work,' said Martin as they approached the garden gate. 'People expect miracles.'

Owen nodded. 'And quickly.'

From beyond the fence the children's voices rose in what seemed a competition of screaming, and suddenly a ginger tomcat jumped up onto the fence, startled by and startling Owen and Martin, then leapt off and shot away. Martin opened the gate and stepped aside for Owen, who hurried over to the children crowded round Ariela, certain the tom would not have dashed out in the rain without cause.

'Did he hurt her?'

Emma looked up, grinning. 'No, Da! She hissed and spat and frightened him away.'

Crouching down, Owen ran his forefinger from the grey cat's pink nose up between her eyes. 'Our lioness.'

She rubbed against him, then bounded away, up into an apple tree. Giggling and talking among themselves, the children raced back to the house, where Kate bustled them inside, leaving the door open for the men.

Moving beneath the eaves, Owen gently closed the door. 'The man was wounded, then stripped to conceal anything that might suggest his mission before being tossed into the river. I don't like it.'

'More trouble for you,' said Martin. 'I will help in any way I can.'

'What I need is to remember where I've seen him before.'

'Not a complete stranger, then.'

'I don't think so. Michaelo agrees.'

'Harrigan rushing out to ask about him is good news,' Martin said. 'The city is talking. Someone will come forward to identify him.'

'Not if he's trouble, and killed by his fellows.'

'You're thinking ahead. You've said that's always a mistake.'

'It has been a long day. The wine merchant mentioned your connection with Goldbetter and Company, implying that it made you suspect.'

Martin laughed. 'Goldbetter. I have not heard that name in a long while. Greedy man, the type who would sell his dam if she brought a good price. Do you suspect me?'

'I know where you were Saturday night.'

'Otherwise?'

Owen laughed. 'We're neither of us saints. But you'd not be such a fool to steal something so infamous you could not sell it.' He clapped his hand on Martin's shoulder. 'Let's get warm by the fire.'

* * *

After the children were abed and Martin and Jasper had retired to their rooms above the apothecary, Owen presented Lucie with the cloth.

She lifted a corner of the blue wool, rubbing it between her fingers, smiling. 'For me? What is the occasion?'

'I saw it in Ferriby's shop, that it is the colour of your eyes. He was showing someone how it draped and I imagined you in a gown of this fabric.' He drew her close, kissing her, then leaned back to see her expression. Her eyes sparkled with tears. Happy or dismayed? 'Do you like it?'

'How could I not? It is so lovely. But I have a blue gown.'

She did. His favourite. In fact, she'd had one before that, which had been redone for Gwen. 'And now you will have two again.' Had he made a mistake? Would she prefer a different colour?

'I have never seen a blue like this. It's beautiful, Owen.' She hugged him and whispered, 'Thank you, my love. I cannot wait to take it to Claire.' The sempstress who made all her gowns.

He pulled her close again and bent to kiss her neck. She smelled of herbs and lemon, and her own wondrous scent. 'Should we go upstairs?'

She laughed. 'In a little while. Come. Sit by the fire and tell me about your day.' But she lingered by the package, lifting the brown brocade, then draping it round his shoulders. 'Surely this is not for me.'

'No. Peter thinks I need a new jacket for court. He added it as a gift.'

She smiled. 'It is a fine, rich colour. You will look elegant in it.'

'Do I need a new jacket?'

She tilted her head, her blue-grey eyes teasing. 'I am sorry to say it, but yes, you do. You seem to be called to the court with some regularity and you must be prepared.'

That was hardly a thought to entice him. But she was right, and Michaelo, too, that his role in the household of Princess Joan, her eye and ears in the north, had become more demanding the moment her son was crowned.

'I pray Brother Michaelo's letters suffice for a long while,' she said. 'You have much to do here. But it will make a handsome tunic or jacket. What did Michaelo think?'

'He agreed. I begin to suspect that you two communicate behind my back.'

She smiled as if amused by something far more interesting than his comment. 'You returned with Martin. Was he at the castle?'

'No. I met him in Stonegate. He's been following van Peelt, from St Helen's over to Goodramgate, Holy Trinity.'

'Is the sketcher making a study of the churches of York?' Lucie sighed as she folded the brown brocade. 'I am sorry all this is happening just as you've returned. You'll have no rest. I feared the theft of the lion would send ripples throughout the city.'

And beyond. Owen would see that Brother Michaelo sent a full accounting to Princess Joan.

They settled by the hall fire, Owen's arm round Lucie's shoulder. Here was peace. Refuge.

'Our Gwen seemed in good spirits,' he said. 'I pray she is not hiding her feelings?'

'She was quiet at first. As we walked home she wondered many things – why we feel so deeply for the death of a man we did not know, how the city will let people know of his death so that if he has someone who cares they will come for him, and, if he isn't known, whether the city will bury him. But she also spoke of how much she loves hunting for healing plants with Magda and how glad she was that I accompanied them today. You should have seen her with Magda. Just as engaged and attentive as she is in the shop. None of her usual chatter about the house, but a rapt attention. It filled me with joy to see.'

They were quiet awhile, but he could tell she was still troubled. 'What is it?'

'I've not told her the man was injured before going in the water. She thinks it was a bathing accident. But she'll soon hear otherwise.' A worried sigh. 'I pray she does not dream of the corpse in the night.'

'If she does, we will be there, my love.'

FIVE

The Sketcher, the Raggedy Lad, and Harrigan's Daughter

Nightmares haunted Gwen in the night, her first scream pulling Lucie from her own netherworld of shadows and rushing water and waking Hugh and Emma. Whispering soothing reassurances, Lucie soon calmed the two younger ones to sleep, but Gwen could not close her eyes without seeing the pale hair floating in the peaty water of the River Ouse. Only in bed between her parents did she dare risk sleep.

'We are magic,' Lucie whispered over her daughter's tousled head.

Owen put a hand on Gwen's shoulder. 'I wish I had the power to make her forget. But she of all people would not thank me.'

'No. Not our Gwen.'

Owen woke before dawn, easing out of bed trying not to disturb Lucie and Gwen. He carried his clothes out to the landing to dress, then padded down to the kitchen where Kate greeted him sleepily as she stoked the fire. Pulling on his boots, he went out to pace in a chilly mist, trying to recall where he had seen the dead man before. A scrap of memory teased him, a large crowd, in the minster, perhaps, a great space, a man with pale hair glaring at . . . What? Where had it been? Had he noticed the man's damaged ear and the shortened fingers? Did he approach him?

'Owen?'

Lucie stood beneath the linden holding out a cloak. 'Will you break your fast?'

'I woke you. I'm sorry.'

'Not you. Gwen turned and pulled the covers round her, leaving me shivering.' She smiled. 'Will you come in soon?'

'In a moment.'

She caressed his cheek, then hurried back to the warm kitchen.

He wrapped the cloak round him as he moved along the path away from the house. So many threads to follow. Which one led to the solution? He let them play out in his mind while he walked, finally turning to the kitchen with a clear purpose, to talk to Costen van Peelt and ask whether he might have noticed anything on Stonegate, whether Geoffrey Gifford confided in him – that would be tricky, as would asking what interested him about Holy Trinity. But Lucie's idea of a study of the churches might be a way to approach the latter. He hoped he might also get a sense of whether Costen did spy on merchants. He told Lucie of his plan as she handed him a bowl of ale.

'A bold move. Didn't you say he'd noticed Martin watching him? You might find him resentful.'

'I know it could be uncomfortable, but he might want to know why—'

'—and you will say Martin noticed him yesterday on Stonegate and you hoped he might have observed something of use regarding the theft. Yes.' An enthusiastic nod. 'Do you know where he lives?'

'Martin does.'

'You are not taking him—'

'No. I think that unwise. Isn't Costen's wife a customer of yours? Do you have any insights into his life?'

'Little from him, but his wife, now there's a tale.'

One can know a person for years, consider oneself connected to them, yet have no concept of how they move through their lives. Experiencing the rhythm of Jasper's day in the apothecary felt like a blessing to Martin. Dishevelled hair as he clomped down the steps in the early morning, eyes half-lidded as he swept the shop and unpacked items delivered late the previous day. Sometimes his stomach growled so loudly he tossed the broom aside and went next door to the kitchen, already warm and fragrant with Kate's cooking, and filled himself. Seeing how Jasper lived in the unexceptional moments rounded out Martin's understanding of the young man and filled him with a quiet joy. In helping him find this life, which treated him well, Martin had done some good.

On this morning it was Owen who caught Martin's interest.

He'd noticed him out in the garden before the others rose, pacing, seemingly talking to himself. His focus narrowed to his duty, Martin guessed, restoring peace to the city. A consequential theft and the stripped corpse of a stranger in the river, apparently murdered – both recent events were unsettling to the people of York and Owen felt it his responsibility to solve them. The dark, silver-flecked brows pressing together – he imagined the one beneath the leather patch, could see how the muscles moved to knit the brows together as the square jaw tightened, the one dark eye burning into the imagined scene before him. It amused Martin that this man who looked a threatening, battle-scarred soldier, albeit a handsome one, was the peacekeeper of the city, a man all the honest people trusted. God's inexplicable design.

Martin's welcome into the family, the intimacy they so gladly shared with him, the liveliness of the children, all this filled him with a desire to repay the gift in some significant way. He vowed to do all in his power to help Owen resolve the issues before him – while taking care to keep out of his friend's way. He'd been a thief, he'd been a murderer, he knew how such people thought. Surely he could use his dark past to help a friend.

Costen van Peelt and his wife lived apart, a mutually agreed arrangement. Anna van Peelt was housekeeper for Celia Overton, a wealthy widow in an elegant house on Stonegate, across the street from Guildmaster Harrigan. Lucie knew only unreliable gossip about what had caused the rift in the marriage – the lack of children, Costen's strange ways, the relative comfort of the Overton house, or a transgression kept private. Owen added his own possibility, that Anna was uncomfortable about Costen's spying on her mistress's friends, if the rumours proved true that the man's sketching covered a nefarious purpose.

Martin's directions led Owen to a two-storey house in Colliergate that leaned uncertainly like a man teetering home after a long night in the tavern. It sat behind a more substantial house and shop. A shutter on the one visible window hung precariously. The state of disrepair was a contrast to the inhabitant who dressed well, his person tidy, though his hair refused constraint.

On this morning a raggedly garbed lad sat on a barrel tucked beneath the eaves of the leaning house, still, watchful. Owen retreated into the shadows to observe the lad, who was no stranger. Perhaps a year past, Owen had caught him stealing items from a woman's basket as she left the apothecary, and had come to regret letting the boy go with a cuff to his ear and an apology to his victim, for the lad had been seen running from trouble many a time since then. He also fit Martin's description of the lad Costen followed. What was he doing here? Had he noticed Costen spying on him and decided to return the favour? Or did he work for the Fleming?

Circling round, Owen approached the house from the opposite side and quietly moved the shutter just enough to peer inside. One room down below, no one there. Unless Costen slept late in the day up above, he was likely out and about. There was another window on the opposite side, higher – perhaps why the lad sat on the barrel, so that he might peer in.

Discovering the lad at Costen's house lessened Owen's disappointment in not finding the man at home. He'd had a favour to ask him, to sketch the face of Walter, the victim, so that one of his men could show it to innkeepers and bawds. But that would have to wait. He'd sent out Rob, the brother of their housekeeper, Kate, to search the city for him. Separately, Rob's twin, Rose, was accompanying Crispin Poole outside the walls to search for information regarding the incident on the river. She knew many of the people who lived in the community of shacks along the riverbank and had offered to help Poole ask them whether anyone had seen the blond man go into the river, or whether anyone had found clothes and a saddle pack on the bank. Rob and Rose would leave word at the house if they learned anything.

Next on Owen's rounds was Archdeacon Jehannes's home, to find out whether Brother Michaelo had remembered where they had last seen the dead man.

Martin watched Owen turn round. Here was something he could do, continue following the raggedy lad.

Lucie stepped into the shop as Bertram Harrigan's daughter Elaine entered from the street. The young woman glanced over her shoulder as she approached the counter and did not respond to Lucie's greeting. How curious. Was she concerned that someone might overhear their conversation? Or that someone was following her? It would be understandable for all in the goldsmith's household to be on edge, but in the apothecary?

'Good morning, Elaine, how might I help you?' Lucie asked again.

The young woman started and turned towards Lucie. Up close, her eyes were red and swollen, the rest of her face too pale in contrast to her lustrous dark hair.

'Good morning, Mistress Wilton. I hope you can help.' She spoke softly, with some hesitation. 'I–I cannot sleep, you see. Nor can my mother. Since the theft.' A pause. 'Though I know that your husband is ensuring our safety,' she quickly added.

'I understand how it can be, the vigilance, no matter what the men promise,' said Lucie. 'I am glad to help. You want something to calm you at night, allow you to rest?'

Elaine managed the ghost of a smile. 'Yes. But Mother worries she will not wake if someone needs her.'

'My powder does not prevent that.' Lucie fetched a jar from the shelves behind her. When she turned back to set it on the counter, she caught Elaine wiping away tears.

'Your heart is heavy.'

'Oh, Dame Lucie—'

Hurrying around the counter, Lucie caught Elaine before she crumpled, steadying her, and leading her back to the workroom.

Jasper glanced up. 'What can I do? Shall I—'

'Measure out the sleep draught on the counter, enough for two, each night for a week,' said Lucie as she helped Elaine onto the bench by the door open to the garden. The cool air might help revive her. 'You are safe here, Elaine.'

'You are kind.'

Lucie joined her on the bench and took one of her hands. 'I am a mother as well as an apothecary. If you were my Gwen, I would encourage you to tell me what you fear, all of it. Saying it aloud draws it out of the shadows into the light, where the fear is less threatening.'

Elaine looked into Lucie's eyes for a long moment. 'The loss of the precious lion will ruin my father, Dame Lucie. And all of us. To collect enough gold coins to make a replacement is impossible. My mother says the guild will move against him, punish him for his pride. All my dreams vanished in a night.' She put a hand to her mouth. 'I did not mean to say that.'

'You can say that to me without fear of reproach.' Lucie had expected something more sinister. 'It is unsettling to be uncertain about your future. But I think it unlikely to be so dire. Your father has a reputation for beautiful workmanship.'

Elaine bowed her head and sobbed. Lucie sat quietly while she wept, handing her a linen cloth when the tears slowed, then fetching a cup of water, which the young woman gulped down.

'I feel so helpless. Women are useless.'

Lucie put an arm round her plump shoulders. 'Now that is not true.'

'But what can I do to help him?'

Lucie considered. 'Finding the thief would help your father. You may know what someone else might not. Did anything catch your attention that night, that day, or even a few days before that might be connected to the theft? It might not be obvious, just out of place, or puzzling.'

Elaine pressed her hands to her eyes. Lovely hands, plump, long-fingered, the nails remarkably clean. When she dropped her hands to her lap, she was nodding.

'My father treated the apprentices to a barrel of ale on Saturday night, as a celebration. They were all together, drinking, laughing, talking in the workshop. When I helped carry down the food, I noticed a few lads who did not belong, apprentices to other goldsmiths.'

'Do you think the apprentices have told Bailiff Hempe about this? He is in charge of the search for the lion and the thief.'

Elaine shook her head. 'They wouldn't want Father to know.'

'Why not?'

'It's not done, inviting apprentices from another shop into yours. They would be punished. Father frightens ours with his temper, so they would expect the worst, losing their apprentice-ships, and that would ruin their chances anywhere else. I think they'd fear the same for their friends.'

'And you've not told your father because you fear his temper as well?'

Elaine bowed her head. 'Yes.'

'Can you name the apprentices?'

'I don't know them by name, but I've seen them delivering messages, sometimes with their masters. At least some of them were from John Scardburge's shop. Henry Wyman, his journeyman, came to fetch them away.'

'That could be useful. Would you be willing to tell the bailiff about this?'

Elaine bit her lip. 'Could you tell him?'

'It would be best if he could ask you more questions, to tease out more details.'

In the end, Lucie convinced Elaine to return at midday to speak with Owen.

Rob had hailed Owen just outside the minster gate to tell him that Costen van Peelt was in the minster, in one of the chapels, praying. By the time Owen reached the nave, Costen was heading for the door, his heavy brows pulled together in a scowl, the large scrip in which he kept his sketching materials just visible beneath his voluminous cloak. When he noticed Owen approaching, he ducked his head and changed course.

Following him, Owen called softly, 'Master Costen, I hoped we might talk.'

The large man took a few more steps, then stopped and faced Owen, eyes wary. 'About what, Captain?'

The man's caution might mean nothing. It was common for people to avoid Owen when he was investigating, innocent people fearful lest their own secret dealings be exposed. 'I hoped you might help me. You have of course heard of the theft of the golden lion from Harrigan's shop, and the man found in the Ouse?'

Costen shifted his eyes from Owen's. 'I have.'

'As you move about the city sketching, have you seen anything or anyone in the past several days on Stonegate, at the river, or elsewhere in the city that stood out as unusual? Anyone out of place? Threatening? Stealthy?'

Costen's breathing had quickened while Owen spoke. 'Is it not rather that you suspect me?'

'No. It is as I said, I seek your help. As an artist you have a keen eye for detail, and I would guess you notice changes in places you have sketched in the past. Is it not so?'

By his cold stare Costen made it clear he did not believe Owen, and something in that stare made him wonder whether he should suspect the man.

'Forgive me if I have offended you. What about the lad I found guarding your home earlier? Is he often with you? Might he have noticed something?'

Costen blinked. 'Lad guarding my home?' The question echoed in the nave and he glanced round to see who might have heard.

'Shall we step into a chapel?' Owen suggested.

With a nod, Costen led the way, moving to the far corner of a vacant chantry chapel, beyond the flickering candles. 'What need for a guard have I? A weaver and sketcher, I own nothing of value but for my skills.'

'I would not know.'

Costen looked at the tiled floor, saying nothing. As he waited in the incense-laden space, Owen noticed a candle begin to sputter, sending curling ribbons of smoke up towards the vast shadowy ceiling.

His companion shifted a little and raised his head. 'Where was this boy?'

'Sitting on a barrel beneath your upper window.'

'You spoke with him?'

'No.'

'What does he look like?'

'Eight, perhaps older, skinny, dark felt hat pulled down almost to his brows, brown hair down past his shoulders, ragged clothes that look like they were made for someone larger and wrapped to fit him, tied with string.' He could see by the widening of the man's eyes that he recognised the lad by the description and, Owen thought, was surprised.

'I have wondered what he was about,' Costen said slowly. 'Flint is his name – or what he calls himself. The street children do not use their given names, if they even know them.'

'He works for you?'

'No. He approached me on the street to propose an exchange, work for drawing lessons. Showed me a drawing of a man's face on a broken wax tablet, said he'd done it. Good enough to recognise it as one of my neighbours.'

'What happened?'

'Told him I had no work for a lad. And he said everyone wanted information, that he heard much gossip on the streets. Cheeky chit, I've noticed him moving about the city, trading food for gossip. I told him I had no need of him.' Costen muttered a curse, his eyes haunted. 'So now he's watching my house. What does he want? Who hired him to watch me? Or is he—?' He gave himself a little shake. 'Thank you for the warning.' He closed his eyes for a moment, then faced Owen squarely. 'You asked whether I'd noticed anything unusual regarding the stolen lion. I was on Stonegate for a while the day of the theft. Scardburge is the only goldsmith I saw enter Harrigan's shop before they all gathered at the guildhall. He seemed angry.'

'Was he angry before entering or as he left?'

'Both. More so on leaving.'

'Anything else?'

'There were other customers, but no one I noted.'

Considering how hostile the man had been, Owen considered this a good beginning and judged it best to leave other questions for another day. 'Thank you for that. Forgive me for delaying you.' He stepped aside.

Costen did not move. 'I know you have heard the rumours about what I am actually doing as I sketch, that I hire myself out with merchants to spy on their competitors. An insignificant step from that to spying on the shipping for the French. I expected you to approach me long ago. Sending your Flemish friend to soften me so that you might demand I help you was a misstep.'

So that was the rub. 'I did no such thing. Martin goes where he wishes. He is curious about your sketches. And when he heard your speech, he—'

'You are no better than the others who shun me until they have need of me. For years I worked as a weaver, selling my wares at market. Fine cloth. Too fine for the guildmembers, so they decided I could no longer sell in the York market. Those same men came to me, as you have, asking whether I had noticed anything unusual, they were worried for their friend . . .' A cold laugh.

How quickly the peace dissolved. Feeling he had little to lose, Owen asked another question. 'What about the man who drowned in the Ouse?'

Costen stiffened. 'I know nothing of that.'

He did. Owen felt the prickle in his blind eye. 'I don't believe the rumours. When you sketch you are at ease, lost in the work. You are not worried about enemies finding you abroad in the city. Your skill is another reason I sought you out. I hoped you might sketch the drowned man for me, so that I might show it round the inns and brothels.'

Costen reddened. 'I do not do such work.'

'Geoffrey Gifford tells me you do excellent likenesses.' A lie. He'd not yet talked to the young man, but he noticed Costen relax a little.

'He's the one with that talent. Give him the commission.'

'I will do that. He's good, then?'

A nod. 'But he will do his duty to his family.' He looked aside as if considering saying something more, then gave a slight shrug.

'You mean Oxford?'

'Or go into trade to help his dam. His father's a drunkard, spending his days at The Bell.'

'Geoffrey told you that?'

'Yes. He seems frightened by it. Some trouble in Hull. I have not pried, just let him talk.' A nod. 'I've said enough. I bid you a good day, Captain.'

Owen followed him out of the chapel, but allowed him his privacy as he strode across the nave. Once he moved into shadow near the door, Costen paused, bowed his head and crossed himself, glanced behind and around, then continued out the door. Owen would ask the night watch to pay attention to Costen's home, and that of Celia Overton, the wealthy widow for whom Anna van Peelt worked.

Martin followed the raggedy lad to the house of an old clothes collector in Lady Row. The second one he had visited this afternoon. They spoke briefly, he bobbed his head to her, and hurried towards Monk Bar. Martin hesitated. He was tiring, and sensed rain on the way. But he wondered whether the lad might be searching for the drowned man's clothes, something that might identify him, so he resolved to follow the lad out the bar.

Late to join Lucie and the younger children for the midday meal, Owen found himself apologising for his growling stomach as he listened to Elaine Harrigan, who had come early, saying it was easier for her to explain being late for her dinner than needing to rush away. The benefit of his discomfort was that she came to the point quickly.

That Harrigan's treatment of his apprentices made them afraid to give George Hempe potentially important details about the celebration in the shop on the night of the theft had Owen silently cursing.

'I am grateful for this,' he said. 'I will tell Bailiff Hempe. He will find it useful in questioning the apprentices.'

Her brows knit together and her face flushed. 'He will not tell my father that I told you?'

'You need not worry.'

When at last Owen joined the family, he noticed that Martin was absent. He rarely missed this midday gathering.

'Is Martin waiting to dine with Jasper?'

'If he is, he did not say,' said Lucie. Once the children rushed off to play, she asked, 'Was Elaine helpful?'

'Indeed. What she witnessed that evening might be key to finding the thief. Hempe should talk to Scardburge's journeyman, Henry Wyman. Did she share with you her thoughts about how the locking of the door between the shop and the office might have made it easier for someone to hide in the office until the others left the celebration?'

'No.'

'She seemed unusually knowledgeable about how easy it is to pick a lock, but not for rowdy partiers.'

Lucie laughed. 'Unexpected talents?' Then she grew serious. 'Do you think Henry Wyman was involved?'

Owen had momentarily considered that. 'I doubt he would jeopardise his position as a respected partner – the guild calls him a journeyman for now, but Scardburge treats him like a partner because his designs sell. I think he intends to make him a partner as soon as the guild will accept that. For a foreigner, distrusted by many, it is the best he could hope for. I cannot think what would push him to risk everything.'

'If word spreads that he was there that night, his future is already at risk. I hope Scardburge defends him.'

'And I will do my best to keep this quiet until we know the truth.'

'Did you talk to Costen?'

He recounted their conversation. 'He knows something about the man you found in the Ouse. I will talk to him again. While at the archdeacon's house to see Brother Michaelo, I asked Jehannes about Costen's separation from his wife, wondering whether they brought it to the minster court. They had, and Jehannes advised them on their agreement. He assured me that Costen neither physically nor verbally abused Anna. It was his impression that she simply preferred Celia Overton's household and Costen agreed to her living there.'

'Yet you believe Costen is hiding something.'

'I am sure of it.'

From the kitchen, the children's voices rose in grievous complaint about a sudden downpour, drawing Owen's attention to the window. Rain came down in sheets.

'Where is Martin?'

'In his room? It's time I relieved Jasper. Walk with me and we can see whether he's returned.'

They did not find Martin in his tidy bedchamber, nor had Jasper seen him.

The lad headed down the road that led through Galtres. As he reached the first dense stand of trees, he chose an almost invisible path towards the river, glancing round often, clearly uneasy, perhaps sensing Martin or perhaps just wary. Near the riverbank the lad left the path, climbing over a large fallen tree, careful to avoid the thick branches that jutted up and out ready to trip or catch the unwary, then lifted a pile of debris and set it aside, revealing a leather pack, which he placed on the trunk. For a moment he fumbled with the leather tie holding it closed, muttering curses worthy of Martin's old companions, then drew out a shirt, leggings, a short cloak, and a pair of boots, all of which he lay one by one along the fallen trunk. Martin had no doubt these were the drowned man's clothes. But who had told the boy where they would be, and why had he first checked with the women who mended and resold old clothes? The lad was now digging round in the pack, shaking his head and muttering, then hastily stuffed everything back inside and, thus burdened, turned to retrace his footsteps.

The wind had picked up, now carrying a strong scent of rain. Any moment the sky would open. Martin took his chance, moving quickly.

'Drop the pack.' He held a dagger to the lad's throat and wrapped his handless arm round to pull the lad tight against him. As the boy wriggled and pushed, Martin warned, 'The blade is sharp enough to cause damage with the slightest nick.'

'Bloody cock wagger,' the lad growled.

With a clap of thunder the heavens opened and the rain sheeted down, startling Martin. His hand jerked. Martin felt wet warmth, and the boy slipped out of his grasp and ran off with the pack. In the moment before the rain washed it away, Martin saw blood on the knife's blade. He had injured the boy. How badly? Squinting against the driving rain, he moved along the almost invisible path in the direction the boy had taken, searching to either side, paying so little heed to what was ahead that he stumbled over the pack. He saw no sign of the boy. The leather of the pack was dark – with rain or blood? Some of it seemed too dark for rainwater. He cursed himself. Instead of helping Owen he had made more trouble, attacked a child. As he lifted the pack and straightened up, Martin felt a band tighten around his chest. It hurt to breathe and he sank back down, hugging the pack to himself and gasping for air. He deserved this. He deserved death.

SIX

Evasions and Clues

The York Tavern was busy mid-afternoon. Owen and Hempe headed to their usual corner table and settled in to await Henry Wyman. Hempe had sent a message to the journeyman, a summons for his eyes only, as soon as Owen told him of his conversation with Elaine Harrigan, desperate for any information that might help his investigation into the theft. While they waited, Owen recounted his conversation with Costen van Peelt.

'He's always behaved as if he cares not what people think of him,' said Hempe. 'I wonder what changed?'

'I believe he knows something about what happened to Walter. I want him watched.'

'More and more questions, precious few answers, and our men spread thin.' Hempe cursed under his breath.

'And you're worried about your own business, whether your shipments will arrive safely.' In the midst of the questions about the theft and murder there was the concern about the French and Spanish attacks on shipping, and the possibility of spies in York.

'I am. I've been less than cordial to the apprentices who waste my time with complaints.'

'Have you gleaned anything from them or Harrigan himself?'

'Only assurances that Harrigan's security is excellent and whoever stole the lion must be a magician.' Hempe stared into his tankard. 'You learned more from the daughter.'

'The other goldsmiths were confident about Harrigan's precautions?'

'For the most part. But they're also bent on protecting their guildmaster, the fools. They can't see beyond that to helping me recover the lion.'

As Hempe was talking, a newcomer paused in the doorway, a large man, plainly dressed.

'He's here,' Owen said.

Henry Wyman greeted Tom Merchet, then nodded as the taverner gestured to the corner where Owen and Hempe sat. After saying something further to Tom, he made his way through the tables, bobbing his head to several customers. He gave an oddly formal bow to Owen and Hempe before he took a seat. Bess Merchet hurried over with a tankard and a pitcher, asking whether he cared to eat.

'I would, yes,' said Wyman. 'I've not had a moment to myself today.' He shaped his words with a hint of his native German. After she moved away, he said, 'I trust you do not mind if I eat while we talk?'

'Not at all,' said Hempe.

Wyman took a long drink, eyeing the two of them over the rim of the tankard. Setting it down, he glanced at his sleeve, where some metal shavings caught the light, and gathered them as best he could, tucking them in his scrip. Surely that was not worth saving? Young Issy delivered a bowl of stew and a small loaf of brown bread.

'Good for getting up the juices,' she said with a dimpled smile.

Bowing to her, Wyman said, 'I am grateful for the recommendation.' After she departed, he tasted the stew, declared it excellent, then nodded to Hempe. 'You have business with me?'

'I've been told that some of the apprentices who lodge with you joined Guildmaster Harrigan's apprentices in celebrating the completion of the golden lion,' said Hempe. 'Unusual.'

Wyman raised a brow. 'Who told you that?'

'Is it true?'

Wyman took another taste of the stew, a drink of ale, likely thinking how best to frame his response, though he had already revealed his reluctance to speak of it, which raised more questions. Owen sat back, watching closely.

'I am responsible for the apprentices who lodge with me. When I realised several were missing, I listened to the others until I had a good idea where they might be, went there, retrieved them. They were out for some fun, nothing more. If I had spoken of it, they might have lost their places, their futures ended in shame.' His eyes were soft with concern for the young men.

'We need names,' said Hempe, 'and whether you found anything on them.'

Wyman looked from Hempe to Owen and back. 'You think one of them stole the lion? I assure you they did not.'

'Or a key,' said Hempe.

'I found nothing.'

'Did you shake out their clothes? Their scrips? Check their boots?'

The man straightened, clearly offended. 'I did not. I accepted their word.'

'Then we will check their belongings,' said Hempe. 'I'll need their names. And the names of their closest friends. We will not reveal the names of the innocent. They will not suffer for this.'

'Is this necessary?' The more uneasy the man became, the more his accent coloured his words. When both Hempe and Owen nodded, he asked, 'You will explain to Scardburge that they did nothing wrong?'

'You will tell him?' Hempe asked.

'I must.'

A man of honour, thought Owen.

'I will talk to him,' said Hempe.

Wyman drew a piece of parchment from his scrip. 'These are the lads.' He'd come prepared. Smart man. He took another mouthful of stew, washed it down with ale, wiped his mouth. 'These are close friends. They have no time for others.'

'A closed group, not friendly with the other apprentices?' Hempe asked.

'Friendly enough, but these five are always together.' Wyman had regained his composure and was using the bread to sop up the last of the stew.

'I've learned that John Scardburge went to Harrigan's shop on the day of the theft, and left looking angry,' said Hempe. 'Have you any idea what that was about?'

'I cannot speak for my master. You would need to ask him.' Wyman stood. 'Do you wish me to send the five to your house, Bailiff Hempe?'

'No, to their lodgings,' said Hempe. 'I will be there in a short while.'

'You will speak to Scardburge first?'

'He does not know of their attendance?'

'No.'

'I will talk to him before I come,' said Hempe.

As Wyman departed, Hempe studied the list. 'You were strangely quiet, Owen.'

'You were so thorough I saw no need to speak.'

Hempe grinned, bobbed his head. 'I will take that as a compliment.'

Owen left it to Hempe to organise a search of the apprentices' belongings. He itched to accompany him, but a messenger from Magda Digby awaited him in the apothecary workshop.

'What is this about?' Owen asked Jasper as they crossed the yard.

'He would not say until you were there, Da. It's one of Dame Magda's river lads.' These were boys from the families who lived in poverty on the riverside outside St Mary's Abbey gates who ran errands for Magda and rowed people across to her home on a tidal island in the Ouse when they had need of the healer. 'I told him he could trust me to deliver a message, but he stood firm.'

The youth rose from a stool with alacrity as Owen entered the workshop. 'Captain Archer. Dame Magda said to tell you that your friend Master Martin is recovering from a fall. He is resting in her home, and he wishes to speak with you. Urgent, he said.'

What the devil? 'A fall?'

'That's what he called it. Someone found him lying near the forest track all wet from the rain and helped him to Dame Magda's house.'

What had Martin been doing out there? 'Do we need a cart to bring him home?'

The lad thought about it, then nodded.

Owen turned to Jasper, but his son was already headed for the door.

'I will ask Tom Merchet if we can use his cart,' he said. 'And I am coming with you.'

'Good.'

*　　*　　*

The squall had left puddles in the open area between the road and the riverbank and the cart's wooden wheels clattered along the uneven ground, but Owen kept up the pace. He had seen how depleted Martin could become, and how quickly, one moment laughing with the children and the next slumped in a chair with a hand on his heart. Though he tried to hide those spells, all but Hugh and Emma were aware of it, and steered the two youngest away when Martin needed rest. Though Owen trusted Magda's skill, he was anxious to see his friend.

The boy, Drew, nodded to another lad who stood by Magda's coracle despite the soft but steady rain. 'I will take them to the Riverwoman's rock. You guard the cart.'

The other lad regarded the donkey with unease.

Jasper handed him a few apples and a carrot. 'Dole them out slowly and he'll be happy.'

The lad grinned. 'I can do that.'

Coming in out of the chill rain, Owen appreciated the warmth of Magda's house, and the scents of drying herbs and the mixture of woods that she used in her fire. She embraced Jasper and guided him over to where Martin sat close to the fire, draped in a blanket, bent over a bowl that steamed in his hand. Jasper sat on the floor beside him.

'I lost the boy,' said Martin, his voice thin and scratchy, 'but I believe I have the drowned man's things.'

'Boy?' Owen asked, moving a stool near Martin.

'The one I've been following.'

'Flint,' said Magda. 'That is the name he goes by.'

The boy seemed to be everywhere. 'What do you know of him?' Owen asked her.

'Many a time he has dragged himself to Magda's door with injuries suffered on the streets of York. Homeless, with a sister his only family, he has kept himself alive by doing errands for those who wish to conceal their business. When he fails them, he is beaten, and even sometimes when he succeeds. It is all he knows, and he is good at it.'

And this boy had come to Costen offering information. Had he been sent to get close to the man and glean what he could about his activities for another?

'He has a sister?'

'Works in a brothel at the edge of the Bedern. When here, he helps himself to things Magda did not offer him, for the sister or a friend. It is their way.'

Jasper leaned close to Martin. 'What happened?' he asked.

What had happened? Martin recounted what he remembered of the chase, the confrontation, the failure. 'I am not certain of his injury. It happened so quickly. The thunderclap, I jerked, he was gone. But the amount of blood that soaked into the leather pack would have me a murderer.'

'The boy did escape,' Magda noted.

'And how far before he collapsed? We've just not found him yet,' Martin said. 'I forget I have but one hand. After all this time, how is that possible?'

'You are more skilled with the one hand than most of the men I've fought beside,' said Owen. 'Do not berate yourself.'

'There comes a time when one should admit defeat,' said Martin. 'I promise I will make no more trouble.'

'Trouble? I do not count this as trouble,' said Owen.

'Why are you so determined to defend my stupidity?'

'We will argue about that another time,' said Owen. 'You say you followed him because you thought someone told Flint where to find the dead man's pack. Let's see it.'

Martin began to rise, but Magda gently pressed him back down and fetched the damp leather pack, handing it to Owen. Martin winced as his friend touched the dark stain. The boy was out there somewhere bleeding to death.

'Good leather,' Owen said as he drew out boots, a shirt, a tunic, a short cloak, leggings, stockings, and a leather hat.

More items than Martin had seen in the wood. 'Flint had not taken it all out.'

'Feeling around for something?' Owen suggested.

'A golden lion,' Jasper suggested.

'The clothes are well made,' said Owen, 'though not of the highest quality.'

A small leather pack held a comb, scissors, and a sharp knife with a four-inch blade.

'Weapon,' Martin said.

Owen nodded. He shook out the shirt. 'This would fit the drowned man.'

Considering the items, Martin had an idea, something he might do without causing more trouble for his friend. 'In my work I carried letters and documents that I had cause to hide in seams, boots, linings. If Walter was spying, it is possible he used similar means.'

He felt Owen and Jasper lean close as he lay the tunic on his lap, manipulating it with his right stump as he felt along the seams with his good hand. He found an irregularity in the stitching and a lump beneath. Not likely a document, but something worth hiding. He held out his hand. 'Knife.'

Owen handed him the sharp knife from Walter's kit. Martin used the tip to work out the stitches, then set it aside to pull out a piece of parchment folded around several coins. Groats. Not a fortune, but enough to help a man in a bad time. The parchment had some faded writing, illegible. Finding nothing more in the tunic, he picked up the left boot. Well made, good leather, not too worn. He felt round inside, searching for slits, irregularities, and found nothing immediately obvious. He examined the decorative tooling on the outside, a good place to conceal an opening, and found a small knife tucked into a slit. Now the right boot. Feeling inside, he grinned up at his audience. Working his fingers into a slit like the one with the knife, he caught hold of something, drew it out with care. A folded parchment with a damaged seal, perhaps an anchor. He handed it to Owen.

'Well now,' said Owen, turning it over in his hands, fingering a tuck. 'Folded so that it would stay closed.' He had to work it open, then silently studied the parchment.

Martin hoped it was worth all the trouble.

'Da,' Jasper said, leaning past Martin. 'What is it?'

'Numbers and the names of ships and barges,' Owen said. 'About half the list Lotta Hempe compiled for me.'

Jasper sat back with a satisfied sigh. 'Walter was a spy.'

'It would seem so. Well done, my friend.' Owen pressed Martin's shoulder. 'I am grateful.'

'There might be more.' Martin picked up the leather hat and

handed it to Jasper. 'Look at the lining. Too dark for me, but maybe with young eyes you can see any loose stitching, made easy to open and restitch if needed.'

Jasper bent to the task, moving the hat so the firelight illuminated the lining. 'I do. See here?'

Martin handed him the knife. 'Tease open the stitches.'

Jasper worked on it, brow furrowed, breath held. 'Ah,' he breathed out as the stitches unravelled so easily half the lining was hanging loose. And within, something white. He drew out another parchment, handed it to Martin with a grin and a nod.

Martin gave it to Owen, who opened it and held it for all to see, including Magda, who leaned over Martin's shoulder. It was a letter of safe conduct. The carrier was identified as Walter Bolton, representing Sir John Neville, Baron of Raby.

'Well, well, well,' said Owen.

'Neville's man carrying a shipping list?' Martin shook his head. 'Why? Does the baron own ships?'

Owen stared into the fire. Martin noticed the shadow beneath his right eye, the prominence of the scars radiating down from the patch over his left eye, signs of exhaustion. Yet towards the end of a long day he had come through inclement weather to collect Martin. The man always put his family, his friends, his city, his country before his comfort. It humbled Martin.

'Lancaster pushed Sir John to the side at the coronation,' Owen said quietly, almost as if to himself. 'His anger was clear for all to see. And now . . .' He rubbed beneath the patch as he continued to watch the fire. 'Neville's had some experience at sea, but Lancaster has his own plans for the king's navy. He might hope to present King Richard with a spy caught working in the city, a gift in exchange for consideration as admiral of the ships fighting the French. But I should think he would want the spy, not just a list. Did Walter Bolton catch a spy, and his prisoner killed him?'

'Why wouldn't the prisoner take back the list?' asked Jasper.

'He might have thought only of getting away,' said Martin.

'But who sent Flint to collect Walter Bolton's pack?' Owen wondered. 'Was it the same person who sent the lad to Costen offering information in exchange for drawing lessons? Did they think he was the spy?'

'He might still be,' said Jasper.

Owen frowned at his son. 'I don't think he is. But I need to talk to him.'

'I'm worried for the lad,' said Martin. 'What if he witnessed the murder? And watched the murderer hide the pack?'

'Whether someone told him where to look or he witnessed someone hiding the pack, I don't understand why he took the time to first check with those who collect rags,' said Owen. 'It doesn't make sense.'

Martin agreed.

'Maddening situation,' Owen muttered, 'sending out shoots everywhere.' He stood up, beginning to pace near the fire.

Martin cursed his failing body. He wanted to help.

'Why wouldn't Flint come to you?' Jasper asked Magda.

'If he recognised Pirate, he may know Magda is his friend.'

Pirate was Magda's name for Martin. He found no comfort in that answer.

'We need to search for Flint and talk to Costen,' said Owen, 'without giving him the name of the man who might have been spying on him, or his lord. Is Martin fit to ride back to my home in the Merchets' cart?'

A cart. God help him. 'I can walk,' Martin declared.

Magda fixed him with a steely gaze. 'Thy heart gave out on thee for a time, Pirate. Better to rest here for a day, but thou wouldst chafe to be away from the news. Magda will give thee something to ease the ride in the rain.'

A cripple. Weak. Bumbling. How could he bear it? Slowly, he rose, testing his legs. No wobble. 'I am ready.'

Owen pressed Martin's shoulder. 'I am grateful for all you've uncovered. You've proved a good partner. Take what Magda is offering so that you can continue to help.'

A reasonable request. 'Of course.' But after downing the warm liquid he moved on ahead, walking to the door and out with no assistance.

Leaving Jasper and Martin at the crossing into Stonegate, Owen headed towards Archdeacon Jehannes's house, hoping to find Brother Michaelo and have him make a few copies of the list found in Walter's boots for the mayor and the merchants involved in shipping. He would urge the shippers to be prepared for trouble and shift the schedules a day or two where possible.

To Owen's surprise, Michaelo's first concern was Martin. 'He will recover?'

'He will never completely recover his strength, but he will be well enough. As for Neville's man, it's likely he was killed by the spy in possession of the list. If so, where is the spy? If not, are we looking for another body?'

Michaelo crossed himself. 'I will listen for rumours in the minster close tonight.'

While Michaelo prepared the lists, Owen paced the garden and planned his next visits.

Owen escaped the mayor before he could push the work of informing the guilds onto him, heading for Lady Row in Goodramgate.

Goodwife Nan nodded as if she had been expecting him. 'You are wondering about the lad searching for a man's pack of clothes, I reckon, Captain. I hadn't seen it.'

'He interests me,' said Owen. 'Have you noticed him in the churchyard?'

'I have. Meets with people who always have a care to have their hoods pulled low over their faces, and brings food to some younger children, one in particular, delicate thing with a foul mouth. The clothes belonged to the drowned man?'

'That is what I would like to know. So does he meet any man regularly?'

She tilted her head, her eyes far away for a moment. 'No. The only regular is the foul-mouthed child. I'm sorry I cannot be of more help. Your daughter's green cloak brought good coin, Captain. I am grateful.'

Gwen had loved that cloak, but after a terrifying incident she could not bear to wear it again. She had taken it upon herself to follow a lodger she'd feared might be a danger to the family and had been grievously injured by the actual menace, a man who meant to destroy Owen and all he held dear. In truth, Owen was glad she had given away the cloak, an unwelcome reminder of a dark time. 'I am glad someone will enjoy it.'

'I've seen a slight young woman in it, a servant, I think,' said

Nan. 'How is Gwen's hearing? Any improvement?' Gwen had lost the hearing in one ear in the attack.

'She hears a little in that ear now. It has not slowed her down.'

'I saw her behind the counter at the apothecary. Will she apprentice to Dame Lucie?'

'That is her hope.'

'A fine tradition in the family, passing the apothecary down through the women. May God watch over you and your family, Captain.'

Back at his usual table in the York, Owen guessed by the gentle glow on Hempe's face that he had already downed a tankard. 'Lotta told me you were here. Did you learn anything from the annoying apprentices?'

A shrug. 'At first they were so frightened I thought it a waste to talk to them. But one of them mentioned that when Wyman pulled them from the celebration, he went to relieve himself in the ginnel beside the shop and caught a familiar street lad scurrying away. Wyman was holding a lantern and it lit the ginnel enough for the apprentice to see the lad's face. Said he knew him as Flint.'

The boy *was* everywhere.

'That seemed to loosen the tongue of another, who suddenly remembered seeing a stranger in the workshop. He said he could have been from another goldsmith, but too old to be an apprentice.'

'Did he describe him?'

'Said he wore a short dark cloak and a lighter-coloured hood. Thought he might have fair hair.'

Walter Bolton? They'd not found a hood. 'How was Wyman with them?'

'Quiet. Praised them for cooperating.'

'Do you believe they've told you all they know?'

'As much as they recall, yes. They admitted drinking more than usual. As for Wyman, I thought we might watch him this evening. No strong feeling about it, just a caution. I set Ned to watch.' A good choice, one of their best young men, who'd lived with Lotta and George for a few years. 'What did Dame Magda want of you?' Hempe asked.

Owen told him of Martin's discovery, the injured boy, the information found in the clothing, and the vague report in Lady Row.

'God's blood, that's a good afternoon's gleanings for Martin.' Hempe took a drink of ale and sat back, rubbing his bald pate. 'Walter Bolton, Neville's man. That's bad news. Are you thinking Sir John will come looking for him?'

'If he means to use the information to gain King Richard's favour, he might.'

Hempe drained his tankard. 'Fair hair. Do you think it was this Bolton who was at Harrigan's the night of the theft? Could he be the thief?'

'Why would one of Neville's men risk that, especially after cornering a spy? If that's what he did.'

'Neville surely wouldn't trust a spy and a thief.'

'It seems unlikely.'

Hempe raised a brow. 'But with a pound of gold he might go his own way.'

'A risk. But to be free of Neville might have been worth it to him.' Neville had a reputation for cruelty. 'We know too little to rule anything out.'

'Ah. Here is Poole.'

Crispin Poole took a seat, nodding his thanks to Issy for carrying his tankard to the table as he was holding his wet hat in his one hand.

'Did you learn anything in the shacks outside the wall?' Owen asked.

Poole nodded. 'Early Sunday morning, so the day after the lion was likely stolen, a few saw a man who might have been the drowned man arguing with Costen van Peelt on the riverbank, just beyond where the trees grow thick. Van Peelt grabbed the man and forced him deeper into the trees, so no one saw what happened after that.'

God help him. 'Costen and Neville's man? I don't like that.'

'Who's Neville's man? Not the one found in the Ouse?' Poole cursed at Owen's nod. 'Tell me.'

Once again Owen shared what he'd learned.

Poole's frown deepened as he listened. 'What the devil,' he breathed, and took a long drink.

'Did anyone see Neville's man after Costen forced him into the trees?' Owen asked. 'Or Costen?'

'One said they thought they saw Costen walking away,' said Poole. 'Another thought it was the other one. It was at a distance, so they were not confident.'

Walter Bolton might have survived that argument.

Poole took a long drink. 'Rose is skilled with questioning people, asking the questions that draw them out. They trust her. It was a pleasure working with her.'

Owen smiled. He had relied on Rose and Rob, her twin brother, as street spies since they were quite young. They never let him down.

'She's a pretty young woman,' said Hempe. 'Ned is lately awkward in her presence. Which has me thinking I need to give him more work so that he might afford his own household.' He winked. 'I've asked Lotta how he might help in our business and it's clear she likes the idea. But will he?'

They treated him as their son, which warmed Owen's heart. The young man had suffered a painful break with his father. 'I think he would be glad of it.'

'What next?' asked Poole.

'I'm going to ask Rose's twin to put out the word I'm looking for Flint,' said Owen. He had thought to warn Costen about the lad, that it was unclear for whom he was working, but after Poole's report of the Fleming being with Neville's man, he wasn't sure what to do. 'We have a watch on Costen. Make sure it's someone who can defend himself.' He pushed away from the table. 'I want to find Geoffrey Gifford, Ferriby's nephew, ask him what he and Costen talk about. And see whether he'd do a sketch of Walter Bolton.'

'A grim task, to be sure,' Hempe muttered into his tankard. 'He's surely looking less and less as he did in life.'

'It might encourage Geoffrey to talk,' Owen said, 'and it would be useful. I'll send word if I learn anything you need to know.'

For a man with the wealth to be a partner in several ships, Wulf Gifford had chosen a modest house on Colliergate and done little to make it a home. Geoffrey invited him into a hall sparsely and plainly furnished, with no fire and his boots calling up a mustiness from the rush-strewn floor. Geoffrey apologised for taking so long to answer his knock, he had been looking for a clean shirt. That and the fact that no servant answered the door for him suggested little to no staff. But then, as far as Owen knew, father and son had arrived just a few months past. Perhaps when the rest of the family joined them the house would become a home.

Yet there was the man Owen had seen rush from the ginnel between this house and the neighbouring one after his knock. For a moment he had thought it someone working in the garden and coming round to see who was at the door, but the man, pressing a hand down on uncombed hair, had hurried off down Colliergate with nary a backward glance. Hair much like Geoffrey's mop, Owen thought as he took a seat on a plain bench. He remembered what Costen had said about the young man worried about his father spending his time drinking at The Bell.

'Your father rushed out on an errand?'

A shrug. 'Don't mind him, he's worried about a shipment. No word of its arrival in Hull.'

'Out trying to learn more?'

Geoffrey began to say something, frowned, and nodded. 'Had you come to talk to him?'

'No. I hoped you might tell me about Costen van Peelt. I understand you've befriended him.'

'I've tried. Why? Is he in trouble?'

'I don't know. I'm not rushing to judgement, and you could help by telling me about him. What do you talk about?'

Geoffrey bit the inside of his mouth and shrugged. 'Everything. Life. God. Purpose. Beauty.'

'Does he speak of the French attacking our ships?' asked Owen.

'That?' Geoffrey nodded. 'He's said the French and Spanish are hurting the merchants' livelihoods, and calls it tragic that Lancaster didn't expect it and had no plan in place.'

'He thinks Lancaster should have foreseen the shipping fears?'

'He said that when King Edward died and people were adjusting to a boy king, it was an opportunity for our enemies to attack the realm in ways that weaken us and, yes, the duke should have known that. He believes there are spies for the French in the city and that some people – many, to hear him talk – think he's one. But he said they could not be more wrong.'

'How so?'

'I didn't ask. He might tell me to go away, and I like to listen to him. All the while he talks he sketches, and interrupts himself with explanations about how he trained himself to look closely, notice the telling detail that would improve a sketch. I respect him, and he doesn't treat me like a child. I feel I can learn a lot from just listening to him, and watching him work.' The young man's face brightened as he spoke of his admiration for Costen.

'Why does he think people suspect him of spying?'

'Because he's a foreigner, I guess. It isn't fair. He's a better man than most of them in the city.'

'I know what it's like to be the foreigner,' Owen said.

'I didn't mean to—'

'I know, Geoffrey, I know. I was agreeing with you.'

They talked a while longer, about leaving home for schooling, Geoffrey asking what it had been like for Owen to leave his home.

'Your experience is not likely to be like mine. I knew I might never return, never again see my family. I grieved.'

'Have you been back?'

'I have. But most of my family were dead by then.'

Geoffrey bit his lip. 'I'm sorry.'

'So was I. But you are not going so far, and you mean to return, do you not? You might find it suits you to be on your own for a while.' Owen rose to leave, but paused, remembering the other part of his mission. 'I have a favour to ask. It was Costen who suggested you for the task. A drawing of the man pulled from the Ouse yesterday. I'm keeping him in a shed in the castle yard.'

'Master Costen suggested me?' Geoffrey beamed.

'I warn you, he's not a pretty sight, and I'm hoping you might imagine what he would have looked like before going in. It's a lot to ask.'

'I'll do it, Captain. Be at the castle in the morning.' Owen was almost out the door when Geoffrey said, 'I hope you don't need to mention this to my father.'

'He would not approve?'

'Wasting my time, is what he thinks. So it's easier to say nothing.'

'He will not hear of it from me.'

About to head home, Owen changed his mind and headed towards Costen's home. It was near, and he was freshly curious about the man who so inspired Geoffrey Gifford.

SEVEN

Called Out in the Night

Through the window of the drunkenly leaning house Owen observed the fire burning, a cup of something on the table, a cloak and boots laid out by the fire, as if to dry. Warren, one of the bailiffs' new men, motioned to him from beneath the overhanging storey.

'He just left, Captain. I was not to follow, was I?'

In this case it would have been helpful, but only one of Owen's regulars – Alfred, Stephen, Ned – would have known to follow.

'Keep watch on the house until I return in the morning. I will be here just after dawn.' He meant to catch Costen asleep, or just waking. 'If you get drowsy, move about. Quietly.'

'I will, Captain.'

A shower of needle pricks in his blind eye pushed Owen to search nearby streets and ginnels, sensing danger, but he did not find the Fleming or anyone else out of place. He told the night watchman on the route to continue to keep an eye on van Peelt's house.

The watchman led Owen, lantern held high. *Found Warren Frost in the doorway of van Peelt's house, not moving,* he'd said, *and a smell of blood through the shuttered window. I did not open the door.* Winding down the ginnel, Owen was glad to see Hempe crouched by Warren, who had been propped up against the wall, and Ned beside them. A faint light shone through the shutters.

'We just arrived. No sound from the house. Have not gone in,' said Hempe.

'How is Warren?'

'I'll live. I'm sorry, Captain.' He pressed a hand to the back of his head. There was a smear of blood on his upper lip, no blood elsewhere that Owen could see. 'He came from nowhere. Knocked

me down with a punch and hit me on the back of the head with
something hard.'

They were good, whoever they were. Or Warren had fallen
asleep, not unusual on a night watch.

'How long after I'd left?' asked Owen.

'A while. Enough time that I'd done two or three walks round
the house, with waits in between.'

'Sit here. We'll get you home after we look inside,' said Owen.

'You came here last night?' Hempe asked.

'I did. Let's go in.'

When Owen knocked, the door swung open. Taking the lantern
from Hempe, he told the watchman to wait with Warren and
motioned to Ned and Hempe to follow him. Once within, he held
the lantern high as he turned his head this way and that – the
curse of seeing with but one eye. A feeble light came from the
fire circle in the middle of the room, embers, but enough to illu-
minate the chaos around the fallen man to his right. Paper, parchment, pieces of wax tablets were strewn over and around Costen
as if his murderer meant to bury him in his work. The large
vertical loom lay on its side across the room, dangerously close
to the fire. Owen righted it, then knelt to the dead man, who lay
on his chest, head turned to one side, a bloody gag in his mouth.
Blood was soaking into the packed earth floor beneath his head.

'They stayed a while, to do all this,' said Ned, kneeling next
to a pile of splintered wax tablets.

How much time had passed since Owen left Costen? Six, seven
hours? And Warren had had time to walk round and take breaks.

'See whether you can find another light,' said Owen.

'I have one here.' Hempe handed Owen an oil lamp. 'They
didn't bother with that area.' He nodded towards a long shelf
beside the door that held some dishes and a few more lamps.

After lighting the wick, Owen handed the lamp to Ned. 'Search
for anything that seems out of place. And a knife. I think his
throat's been slit.'

Ned started to rise, then paused and pointed down. 'Look at
his hands.'

Hempe joined them.

Owen moved the lantern along Costen's outflung right arm,
near where Ned crouched. Two fingers looked out of joint. And

the wrist had swollen around a leather tie, now cut but still embedded. 'He was bound and tortured, I think. Gagged all the while.' He removed the gag. 'Help me turn him over.'

'But the coroner—' said Ned.

'He would do the same,' said Owen. 'We need to see how he died.'

Their work unsettled the debris scattered over Costen. Noticing glints of glass, Owen warned the others to have a care.

'His neck,' Hempe said.

It was as Owen had guessed, the neck a yawning wound, blood still oozing from it. When they cleaned the blood off Costen's face and body they would likely find bruising. Whoever had done this had taken their time. All this would require at least a pair of attackers, one of them strong enough to snap a wrist. He felt sick, witnessing such brutality, the point far more than ending Costen's life. They had wanted him to suffer. What could Costen have done to them? Were they friends of Walter Bolton's and thought the Fleming had murdered him? Had he?

'Over here.' Ned stood in a corner in the back, holding up a shovel and an axe. 'They dug up the floor.'

There were several shallow pits in the packed earth, and above one in the very corner was a jagged hole in the wall, dark against the white paint that brightened the interior. 'Look behind you,' said Owen. 'They opened the wall as well.'

'Digging for treasure,' Hempe said as he joined them.

Had they followed Owen here? He should have set Stephen or Ned to guard, men with experience. But one against how many?

'What are you thinking, Captain?' Ned asked.

'You know about the lad, Flint, who watched Costen?'

Ned nodded.

'And who the drowned man was?'

'Neville's man. Master George told me. And that Costen was seen arguing with him.'

'I came here to ask Costen about that, but he was away. Meant to see him early this morning. Had the men thought Costen had Bolton's clothes, the groats, the list, the letter?'

'And they thought he'd buried them?' Hempe nodded. 'All this took several hours. They were confident they would not be discovered.'

'Or they were ready to defend themselves,' said Ned.

'We don't know what they sought,' said Owen. 'It might have nothing to do with Bolton. Listen for rumours about what Costen might have hidden.' He rubbed his scar. The needle pricks. Had he misjudged the warning? Had Costen's murderers been near? 'I'll send for the coroner. And I need to tell his wife before she hears it on the street in the morning. Are you all right to stand watch, Ned?'

'I've a knife, and know how to use it.'

'That you do.' And it was unlikely the murderers would return. 'Trust no one. As much as possible, leave everything as it is until morning, when we can sift through it. There might be information in what they broke, what they dropped over him.' He turned, remembering the cloak and boots drying by the fire. Gone. Perhaps the murderers thought he'd taken the time to hide the items in his own clothes.

As Owen moved towards the door, his boot connected with something that clattered. He crouched down, picked up a wooden box, hinged, with a clasp. It was open, nothing in it but a velvet lining. He tucked it into his scrip.

Hempe joined him. 'I did not like the man, but no one deserves such a death.'

'Someone thought he did.'

'Do not blame yourself.'

'Easily said.'

'I know. If you see to Anna van Peelt, I'll summon the coroner and fetch someone to help Ned watch.'

With a nod, Owen walked off into the night, feeling cursed.

An erratic sleeper in his old age, Martin had heard the pounding on Owen's door, a murmur of voices. Perhaps he could be of help. But when he put his feet down on the cold floor he found no strength in his legs for a moment. He cursed himself. He'd been an old fool to chase after the lad. Or had he? What he'd found might prove useful. Breathing, calming himself, trying again, he rose, but had to clutch the wall beside him to stop wobbling. God in heaven, was this how it would be, he would fade away, a cripple unable to help himself, dependent on others? He eased back down and took more deep breaths.

Someone knocked on the door of his chamber. 'Martin? Do you need something?'

He must have made more noise than he'd thought. 'No, Jasper. Troubled sleep, nothing more.'

'Might I come in?'

'Yes, of course.' Martin sat up to light the oil lamp beside his bed and tugged a blanket round him.

Jasper padded across the room in his bare feet and slumped down beside Martin, rumpling the hair already sticking out on one side from sleep. 'I dreamed I was back on the street and a cart came rolling towards me and I couldn't find my legs, I couldn't run or even throw myself aside, and it came right over me, the noise, the clanging and groaning, and the pain . . .' It was a memory from his childhood, but changed so that Martin did not pluck him out of the path of the woman's wagon in time. Jasper took a shuddering breath.

Martin put an arm round him. 'I am sorry you have bad dreams about that moment, what might have happened. Those terrors stay with us. Haunt us in our dreams. They remind us to be grateful.'

'I am. I have so much.' Jasper touched his right cheek, where a long scar, white, not puckered, told a tale of an even worse memory.

'Do you dream of her as well?' Martin asked.

Jasper nodded. 'Not so much as I did. The dreams of her are more about John's death.'

The Merchets' groom at the time, who had betrayed Jasper, but then saved his life from a woman determined to silence him.

Dropping his hand to his mouth to cover a yawn, Jasper asked, 'Do you have bad dreams? Things that almost happened?'

So many to enumerate his companion would fall asleep long before Martin finished, bored by the long telling. 'I do. The ship that was sinking, the arrow that just missed my heart, the sword I saw just in time, the other sword I could not prevent slicing off my hand, killing that boy today.' He did not speak of his own violent deeds.

'You don't know Flint's dead. You might have died out there yourself.'

A fitting end? Many of his enemies would say so, or they

would laugh at his pathetic decline. He patted Jasper's hand. 'We push all that away when we're awake. Don't want to think of it. But something in us needs to walk through it now and then in our sleep, to remember.' Some of the actual moments replayed in sleep as well – his tormentor's death, the slice of the blade through his right wrist, the comrade almost cut in two. How was he yet alive?

'So we're grateful,' said Jasper.

'For the sake of our souls, though it's difficult.' Penance, Martin thought, effectual penance for a questionable life.

As if hearing Martin's thought, Jasper asked, 'What's keeping you up?'

Martin almost laughed and asked, 'How could I possibly sleep?' but then he recalled the immediate cause of his wakening. 'I thought I heard someone pounding on the door. Not here. At the house.'

'The watchman came for Da?' Jasper crossed himself.

Piety often irritated Martin, but not Jasper's expression of his faith, being so much a part of the remarkable young man.

'I think so,' he said. 'I heard voices. So I lay here wondering who was in trouble and thinking about how devoted your father is to this city, rising in the middle of the night and hurrying to their aid, ensuring their protection. Most captains of cities enjoy the benefits of the office, dine with the wealthy merchants, let their underlings do all the work. But not your father.'

'No.' Jasper rose and went to the window. 'They came to the kitchen door?'

'No, it sounded farther away. The hall door.'

Jasper turned from the window, leaning on the sill. 'Usually when it's the middle of the night someone's died, or badly injured. The watchmen won't go into the house if it sounds like trouble. They wake one of the bailiffs. But if Da was roused, the watchman must have thought it was very bad.' Jasper yawned.

'Go to sleep. You don't want to be late opening the shop.'

Jasper shrugged, raked his hand through his hair, and straightened. 'You're right. Mother will be up waiting for Da to come home. I don't want to give her more worry.'

Martin watched him leave, marvelling at the easy grace of youth even after waking from dark dreams. The talk had calmed him. Once again he tested his legs, and now they held him. Fickle old body. With a sigh, he lay down and let sleep take him.

The home of Celia Overton stood tall and proud in Stonegate beside St Helen's Church, with a stone undercroft and a timbered hall. As Owen approached, he noticed a light shining through the shutter of a window in the overhanging upper storey. Someone might yet be awake.

As soon as he knocked, he heard a woman's voice up above call out, 'The door!' In a few breaths he heard footsteps approaching and the door swung open revealing a woman carrying a small lantern. She was wrapped in a colourful shawl, a white coif covering her hair.

'Who knocks at this unseemly hour?'

'Dame Anna van Peelt?'

She lifted the lantern towards Owen and gasped. 'Captain Archer. Is there trouble? Is it Costen?'

'If I could speak with you inside.' Already a light shone from the house next door.

'Oh, yes.' Anna stepped aside, then closed the door behind Owen. 'Come into the kitchen.'

Owen followed her through the long, dark hall, moving with care. In the kitchen the fire had been stoked. 'You rise early.' It was a few hours before dawn.

'Dame Celia often wakes in the night and wants hot spiced wine, so I keep the fire going.' Her voice trembled as she spoke. 'Would you like—'

'Perhaps you should pour yourself some wine,' said Owen.

Dark eyes stared up at him. 'Mother in heaven, has Costen been attacked? Why else would you be here? At this hour?' She sank down onto a stool.

Owen sat near her on a bench. 'The watchman came for me when he noticed trouble at your husband's home. I am sorry to tell you that Costen is dead.'

Her hands flew to her mouth. 'Dead? My Costen dead? God have mercy, I had not thought.' She took a breath. 'Dead.' She looked at the floor, shaking her head. 'He is dead,' she whispered. 'What will this mean?'

'What is this?'

Owen had not heard the other woman approach. Like Anna, she wore a white coif and was wrapped in a woven shawl of bright colours.

Anna had risen to go to her, explaining in a soft voice, 'This is Captain Archer, Dame Celia.'

'Of course it is. I am not blind,' Celia Overton said.

'He's come with terrible news. My husband.' Anna took a breath. 'Costen is dead,' she whispered.

Celia Overton looked to Owen, pale eyes unblinking. 'Your bringing the news tells me he's been murdered?'

'Yes.'

She gave a brisk nod. 'May God rest his soul.' To Anna, she said, 'You ask what this will mean? It means you are free of him.' Anna had begun to cry, lifting a corner of her shawl to scrub at the tears. Celia put an arm round her. 'Do not waste your tears. It is my turn to fetch you mulled wine. Go up to bed. I will bring it.'

When Anna began to protest, Celia gave her a little push.

'One question,' said Owen. 'When did you last see your husband, Dame Anna?'

'Just this morning. He came to — apologise. After all these years, he asked my forgiveness.' She peered up at Owen. 'Did he guess it was his last chance? Oh, Costen,' she moaned.

'Forgive me for asking, but for what was he apologising?' Owen asked.

'For my unhappiness. He said it was his fault, that he had not loved me as he should.' Her voice broke on the last words.

'Enough, Anna,' Celia said sharply. 'Off to bed.' She turned to Owen when Anna was out of sight. 'Thank you for bringing the news, Captain. Anything else can wait until after dawn, can it not?'

'Might I just ask why your mind went straight to murder?'

She gave a little laugh. 'The apology, of course. And, as I said, why else would you show up in the middle of the night?'

'Nothing else?'

She raised a brow. 'Are you asking whether Costen van Peelt was a man who invited death? Oh yes. Every breathing moment he was inviting it, watching people, drawing them. They all feared he was spying on them.'

'Was he?'

'Yes, no, very little if he's been honest with Anna. She begged him to be more discreet, but he is' – she crossed herself – 'was a stubborn, stubborn man. Now if you would leave me to calm her.'

'My wife offered to come if you've need of her.'

Celia had gone over to a shelf where she poured wine from a flagon. 'She would be welcome in the morning, Captain. After sunrise.' She turned towards him, the flagon still in her hand. 'Anna will insist on preparing his body. And to see how he was found. Will it distress her?'

'It will. He met a violent death.'

A nod. 'If Dame Lucie could bring something that will help her sleep for the next several nights, that would be a blessing.'

'I will tell her.'

As Owen left Celia's house, a glance at Harrigan's shop across the way reminded him of the cloth-lined box he'd found at Costen's and he drew it out of his scrip, turning it round in his hands, wondering whether it might be the case in which the golden lion had been placed for presentation.

After preparing some mulled wine and setting it close to the fire to stay warm, Lucie had covered herself in a blanket and sat by the garden window awaiting Owen's return. She'd soon fallen asleep. Now she woke to his kiss on her forehead. Blinking in the soft light from the oil lamp, she guessed by the prominence of the scar radiating beneath his patch that what he had found at Costen's house had shaken him.

'Dead?' she asked. He nodded. 'Murdered?' Another nod. 'Oh. Do you think it was the same person who murdered Walter Bolton?'

'This feels different. Furious. Determined to destroy all trace of the man.'

She ran her hands down his arms, found something clutched in his left hand. 'What is this?'

'Something I found.' He let it slip onto her lap as he sat down beside her. 'By Costen's door, lying open. I believe it would be the right size for the golden lion. They did seem to be searching the house for something.'

While she listened to his account of the terrible scene, she examined the small wooden box, finely made, a lion carved into the lid, closed by a delicate metal latch like a claw. When Owen paused his account to pour some of the mulled wine, Lucie opened the box and fingered the velvet lining.

'You say things were crushed and scattered everywhere, and this box was lying open on the floor. Yet there is no dust on the dark velvet. Or grit. I don't understand. Everything clings to velvet.'

Owen looked at the box more closely. 'You're right.'

'Where was it?'

'Just inside the door.'

'Might they have brought it with them and dropped it as they left, to make him out to be the thief?'

Owen rubbed his good eye. 'And where, then, is the lion? And what did they seek buried in the floor or hidden in the walls?'

She had not thought it through. 'Let's take the wine up to bed.'

Later, in the darkness, Owen said, 'I went to tell his wife. Widow. Her mistress, Celia, asked that you bring Dame Anna something to help her sleep for the next several nights.'

'Yes. She will need it. Poor woman.'

'He had gone to her yesterday morning to apologise for making her unhappy.'

Her heart fluttered. 'He knew he was in danger.'

'Or he meant to run. I should have taken a seat and waited for him to return.'

She kissed his cheek, stroked his arm. 'You could not know he was in such danger. Shall I go to them early, talk to them, and then, if Anna wishes, escort her to you at Costen's house?'

'I would be grateful. I did not feel welcome there.'

She imagined Owen's courtesy, and Celia's sharpness in response. 'Celia is not accustomed to answering to men. In the morning you might give me a list of questions to ask.'

EIGHT

Pieces of the City

Lucie had expected tears, the heaviness of grief, but Anna van Peelt seemed distracted rather than devastated, fidgeting and frowning, her eyes hardly focused. Perhaps Costen's death was not yet real to her. They awaited Celia, who was still dressing.

'She refused my assistance this morning,' said Anna. 'Your husband was kind to come last night.' She fussed with a piece of cloth in her hand, twisting it and then smoothing it out on her lap, over and over. 'I apologise if Celia snapped at him when I left the room. Is that why you came in his stead?'

'I planned to come in any case to offer you some comfort from the apothecary, so I suggested I speak to you while he met his men at the house. They will be searching for clues as to what happened last night.'

'The captain will have questions to ask me.' Anna could not quite meet Lucie's gaze.

'I can guess most of them. Shall we talk before we meet him there?' Lucie had told her that it would help Owen were she to go to Costen's house and see whether she noticed anything unusual. Although Anna had explained she had not been there in some months, she had agreed, raising her voice against Celia's protest.

Now she gave a shaky sigh. 'We will see if I know anything of use.'

'Was there anyone who might wish to harm Costen? Someone strong enough to overpower him?'

Anna crossed herself, then bowed her head and returned to twisting then smoothing the cloth on her lap. 'If any had come to know what he did some years ago for a few merchants in the city who had threatened to cause trouble for us should he not cooperate, what he was really doing when he sketched their places of business and their homes, they might. But he swore he had stopped that a while ago.' She rushed over the words as if she did not want to linger over them. 'I have no knowledge of what he had discovered, if anything, nor can I name the merchants for you. I did not want to know. But why would they wait for years to attack him?'

A good question. 'Is that why you lived apart? He feared for you?'

She looked Lucie in the eye at last. 'No. He was not a loving husband, and I was happier here. As soon as he agreed with me that we might live apart, I left. I hadn't been to his house in some months, as I told you, and your husband.' She gulped air, glanced away.

'You can name none of the merchants who hired him?'

Anna shook her head. 'I see – saw – him now and then about the city and I did my best not to notice who or what he was sketching.' She paused, then said softly, 'But I did find him working by the apothecary this past summer. I did not like that, and I told him so. He said he had no patrons, that he was just drawing a fine building.' She sighed. 'He had talent. For a time he was pushed to use it for ill.'

Lucie had never heard the apothecary called a fine building, but she remembered how lovely she had thought it when she married her first husband, Nicholas. There were intricate carvings of leaves and vines in the supports for the first floor, and they had recently made improvements while expanding the building. She remembered herself. She had no time for such thoughts. Celia might appear at any moment. 'Costen came to York as a weaver, did he not?'

'Was a weaver when we wed, yes. He made beautiful cloth. My mother did not like me marrying a Fleming, but I thought I would die if I could not have him. He said he loved me. He was hand-some then.'

As was Anna, Lucie guessed, her iron-grey hair still lustrous and curly and her eyes a strange pale hazel.

'Did a clothier bring him here?'

'Yes. He came with another weaver who was brought here by Will Overton, so Will took him on as well.'

'He was brought here by Celia's late husband?'

'Christian de Bruges, his partner, was the one with the contacts in Flanders, but yes, it was Will Overton's business. He wanted to promote York cloth and brought in several fine weavers. But he died before he realised the success he had hoped for.'

Lucie chose her words with care. 'Was it after Will Overton's death that Costen started selling his cloth himself?'

'Yes. He quietly sold to the wealthier families until the mercers decided he was too successful. I had left him by then.'

Probably the cloth merchants in the powerful Merchant Adventurers guild, Lucie thought. 'Do you have a list of his clients?'

'No. I remember the Graa brothers, their families, the Gisburnes, several of the goldsmith families.' Wealthy indeed, and influential. 'It was not a great deal of trade, he was but one man, doing all his own work. I could not understand why anyone cared. But none of them would have cause to have him murdered.'

'I agree that's unlikely. Yet my husband says it's impossible to guess what detail will be the very thing that leads to the murderer. Do you know who reported him to the guild?'

'Peter Ferriby initiated the suit.'

'Peter Ferriby?' Lucie was surprised.

'His fellows with shops Costen's customers had patronised in the past then supported the suit.'

The Graa and Gisburne families alone would be valuable customers. Yet, as Anna had said, Costen could not have produced a great deal of cloth, and merchants like Peter Ferriby sold costly Cotswold wool as well as silks, velvets, brocades. It seemed a petty complaint. 'This was some time ago?'

'Several years.'

'Had he mentioned anything to you of late about any trouble?'

Anna glanced to the side, then shook her head. 'No. But he wouldn't. He knew I did not want to hear.'

'And you last saw him yesterday?'

'Yes.' Anna went quite white. 'Yes.'

'Forgive me. I know this is painful—'

'I want Captain Archer to find his murderer.'

'When was the last time you saw him before yesterday?'

Anna took a deep breath. 'We last exchanged more than just a greeting a few months ago, when I found him sketching your shop. He told me he was doing some weaving for a patron, and if it worked out he would do more of that and less of the sketching. And he had sold a painting he'd done of the abbey grounds.'

'The abbey grounds?'

'I never knew him to go there. When I asked who'd wanted that, he said he did it for peace of mind, but someone saw it and offered him money, and he thought he could always paint another.' Her voice caught. 'But now he cannot.' She hugged herself. 'I did not mean to stop loving him.'

When Celia finally joined them, Lucie was holding Anna while she wept.

A crowd of neighbours called out questions as Owen arrived at Costen's house in the morning, and he took the opportunity to ask whether anyone had heard or seen anything out of the ordinary in the night.

'I thought I heard voices,' said a man, his dusty apron suggesting a stonemason or baker. 'But my wife heard naught.'

'Do you live near?'

'Just there.' He pointed to a small house tucked close to Costen's.

'Voices? Anything else?'

'Nothing.'

'Did you look outside?'

'What's to see in the dark?'

'A fair point. I am grateful.' Owen lifted his voice to ask if anyone else had heard anything unusual.

A woman stepped forward. 'I woke in the night, told my husband I heard a cry and to check, but he saw nothing when he looked out the window. Is it a madman loose in the city? The one who pushed the man into the river?'

'The two deaths do not appear to be connected,' said Owen.

'So there's more than one murderer loose in the city,' a man grumbled.

'Or they have fled,' said Owen.

'I would,' said a man. 'Wouldn't want to face you in a dark ginnel.' That generated nervous laughter.

'There's a bad smell coming from the house,' said another woman.

'I understand,' said Owen. 'We will soon have it clean. Anyone else?'

When no one else stepped forward, he assured the crowd that his men were guarding the area and doing all they could to find the murderer, singular, though he was quite certain more than one person had descended on Costen in his house the previous night. He saw no benefit in adding to their fear.

'Dame Anna, Costen's widow, will be here soon. I pray you, leave her in peace to grieve.'

As the crowd talked among themselves and began to disperse, Owen noted a pair, perhaps husband and wife, exchanging looks, and hesitating until most were gone. By their dress he guessed them to be servants – tidy clothing, but worn, faded, an air of deference in their postures and expressions.

He approached them. 'Do you have something to tell me?'

The man nodded to the woman. 'We were heading home through the ginnel last night – we don't lodge with the couple we serve, you see – and we saw what looked like workers carrying tools. They noticed us and stopped, and we hurried past.'

'What tools were they carrying?'

'A shovel and something else,' said the woman. 'Axe, I think.' She looked to her husband, who nodded.

'Did you happen to look back to see where they went?' Owen asked.

They exchanged a glance, and he nodded. 'I looked to see if they were following us. They were peering into van Peelt's window.'

'Two of them,' said the woman. 'I did not see the third that time.'

'How late was this?'

'Very late,' she said. 'Almost midnight. We'd been cleaning the hearth.'

'God forgive us for not going for the night watchman.'

Owen wanted to shout, *No, it's unforgivable.* But was he any less guilty for not staying at the house until Costen returned? And there was no guarantee the night watchman would have frightened off the attackers. 'Can you tell me anything about their appearance? Their voices? Language?'

'Three men. One dressed better than the other two, wearing a short cloak and a hood. He did not carry a tool,' said the woman. 'One might have limped, or it might have been the tool making him walk oddly. Could not see faces. And they said nothing.'

'You have been most helpful. If you recall anything else, please tell the men on guard here. One more thing. How is it that you are not at work this morning? You came here to tell me what you saw?'

The woman shrugged. 'We did. But when we saw the crowd, I said we should come later.'

'I understand. If you have any trouble with your employers, send them to me.'

The two bobbed their heads and hurried away.

Owen cursed them, himself, the three men. But it was done, and now he must find the murderers.

Although the house boasted two windows, the taller houses crowded round it blocked all the light. Opening the shutters of both and the door did little but blow the debris about and make the firelight dance, yet no one suggested closing them because of the stench of violent death – blood, urine, and stomach contents.

Alfred, crouching near the corpse, looked pale and unsettled. 'God help him, he must have suffered.'

'Butchers,' Owen muttered, more to himself than the others. The brutality sickened him. 'Help me shift the loom out of the way.'

Alfred jumped up, clearly relieved to move about. As they placed the loom against the wall, the light revealed that the partially completed cloth was stained – with blood, Owen imagined – and dusted with debris. It was strangely comforting to begin restoring order, though he could not restore Costen or his beautiful creations.

He was dusting off the loom when Michaelo arrived.

The monk lifted a cloth to his elegant nose. 'I am glad I brought incense.'

'Bless you, so are we,' said Alfred. 'Have you come to give him the sacrament?'

'I have.' For Brother Michaelo's good work among the poor, Archdeacon Jehannes had obtained permission for him, though not a priest, to administer last rites to the dead, something the monk felt a kindness among the poor who slept in the minster yard, often dying alone, unnoted. Michaelo knelt beside Costen now and began to pray, a figure of calm in the chaotic house.

Owen drew Alfred and Ned aside to ask what they had noticed so far about the debris.

'Pieces of the city, that's what the murderer poured over him,' said Alfred. 'A corner of a staithe, a bit of a warehouse, a fine house with a garden, walls, windows, doorways . . .'

'And St Mary's Church on Castlegate, I think,' said Ned. 'But most of it's hard to reckon. Alfred's better at this than I am. I hadn't noticed his trick right away. He showed me. With the ash.'

Owen had been about to chide Ned for dirtying the evidence, but then realised what he was doing, sprinkling ash on the pieces of wax tablets, shaking them a little, then blowing, revealing lines that had been too faint to decipher.

'Pack it all up for me,' said Owen. The coroner had come by earlier, so Costen's body could now be moved, the house cleaned. Owen would take the pieces home and see whether he could get a clearer impression of what Costen had been sketching, which might suggest who had committed this crime.

'Do you think he was killed for his drawings?' asked Alfred. 'Something he recorded that his killer did not want others to see?'

'A possibility. If nothing else, we might learn where he's been of late.' There were a few parchments with drawings as well, which Owen rolled up.

As Michaelo rose from the body to join them, Ned nudged Owen.

'Dame Lucie and the widow,' he whispered.

Lucie stood in the doorway, Anna and Celia behind her. Celia had her arm round her housekeeper. As Owen approached them, Lucie gave him a little nod. Good. He need not question Anna.

'Brother Michaelo has just given your husband the last rites, Dame Anna,' said Owen.

She looked startled. 'I thought he died in the night.'

Michaelo joined them. 'He did, Dame Anna, but I believe the spirit remains for a time, and I wished to give him ease.'

'How kind,' said Celia, her tone dismissive.

Anna approached the monk. 'Bless you for your kindness, Brother Michaelo. I am grateful.' She cast a look round the interior of the small house and moaned. 'Oh, what a horror. Costen's beautiful drawings. Someone destroyed them all?' Her legs seemed to give out beneath her.

Owen caught her by the waist and helped her to a bench near the door, Celia following, making worried noises.

'It is the stench,' Owen said. 'Some of us are more accustomed to it. Brother Michaelo's incense helps, but cannot fully dispel the odour.'

'Bless Brother Michaelo again,' said Anna. She made space on the bench for her mistress.

As the two sat, Lucie stepped aside with Owen and told him what she had learned from Anna.

'Helpful?' She searched his face for a clue.

He marvelled at the calm in her blue-grey eyes. 'Yes. You say merchants were threatening Costen and Anna?'

'In the past, yes. Thinking he threatened their livelihoods or reputations? She did not say, but they must not have realised that in Celia Overton's employ, Anna was no longer dependent on him. I wish I had asked more.'

'Unless at the time they had still been living together,' Owen said. 'Now that I know about it, I will find a way to ask more. I am grateful.' He glanced at the newly widowed woman.

Catching his eye, Anna straightened, brushing tears away. 'It was a momentary weakness. I am quite capable of standing now.' She rose. 'We might walk round, Captain, and I will try to answer any questions about what might be missing.'

Keeping a hand beneath her elbow, Owen began at the shelf near the door. 'What was usually kept here?'

'An oil lamp. And the large scrip with his wax tablets and tools ready to hand as he left the house.'

Owen looked at Alfred and Ned. 'Have we found Costen's large scrip?'

Both men shook their heads.

'Did he carry anything else in there, Dame Anna?'

She frowned. 'Tools for drawing, as I said. And he might carry gloves or a hat, but he took great care with the tablets so that the impressions were not damaged before he reached home. What they did, murdering him and destroying the beauty he created . . . They killed him twice over.' She wiped at tears with her sleeve.

He understood. The drawings were part of Costen, evocations of his spirit, the skill with which God had blessed him. It was meant to hurt him. Had they done this before murdering him, made him watch, and then, after butchering him, covered him with the debris?

Moving past the covered corpse, they came to the shovel and axe propped against the far wall.

'His tools?' Owen asked.

She was looking back at the blanket-covered form and did not answer.

'Dame Anna?'

She crossed herself and turned back to him. 'I have not seen them before.' Her voice was breathy.

He gestured to holes in the packed earth floor along the far wall. 'Had he buried something?'

'Merciful Mother,' she breathed. 'This is where the loom stood when not in use. He had buried a chest of coin beneath it.' She glanced up. 'I'd noticed the loom was moved. By you?'

'We found it thrown down.'

'How would they know to search there?' She took a trembling breath. 'All this for a little coin?' She reached out towards the hole hacked into the wattle and daub, touched the edge. 'I do not know why they would do this.'

'Had he hidden anything else in the house?'

'I cannot imagine what else. Or why.' She glanced back at the covered form. 'I must see him.'

'Are you certain? Perhaps first you might step out into the fresh air for a moment?'

'No. I pray you, I would see my Costen now.'

As they moved towards the centre of the room, Celia hurried over.

'Not now, my dear. Wait a while.'

'No. Now,' Anna said firmly. She nodded to Owen.

He crouched down by the top of the blanket and paused. 'It is not an easy sight.'

'I will see him.' Her tone made clear her annoyance with the attempts to protect her.

He peeled the blanket down to Costen's chest.

She gasped and dropped to her knees. 'My husband. What have they done?' Her voice broke. She bent close to kiss Costen's forehead.

Owen was grateful they had cleaned the blood from the man's face.

'May you walk in God's presence,' she whispered, waving away Celia's efforts to help her up. She ran her fingers along her husband's damaged hands, touched his torn throat. 'Oh, Costen. Who hated you so?' Now she allowed Celia to lift her up, enfold her in her arms, and murmur comfort as Anna wept.

Joining Owen, Lucie quietly asked, 'Has she seen all you need her to see?'

He nodded.

'Brother Michaelo and I will escort them home.'

'That will be a great help. I will have Costen's body brought to them.'

Lucie told the women of the plan and was walking with them towards the door when Anna turned round, a puzzled look on her face.

'Costen told me of a large piece he had woven and hoped to sell, invited me to come and see it. He said it took up most of a wall.' She glanced round. 'Perhaps he had already sold it?'

'We found nothing like that. We will be checking the debris to see whether anything that large might have been cut up. Was it a scene, like his drawings?'

'Perhaps, or an intricate weave. He did not say, and I did not come to see it. I did not come.' With a hand to her mouth, she turned away, her shoulders shaking. Celia and Lucie each had an arm round her, guiding her out.

Brother Michaelo paused by Owen. 'Poor woman, the stench of a violent death is surely a taste of hell. Shall we meet when they are finished with me?'

'If you would come to the house,' said Owen. As Michaelo departed, Owen thought of what he'd said. Sadly, he'd become accustomed to the odour.

NINE

Helpers and a Hero

Seeing Brother Michaelo on Colliergate, Martin asked whether Owen was still at Costen's home.

The monk looked down his long nose at Martin, but instead of his usual arrogant sniff, he merely nodded. 'He is. The brutality . . . You might wish to spare yourself.'

Martin was no stranger to horrific cruelty, and had performed his share. 'I should like to see, to understand this new weight on our friend's broad shoulders.'

Michaelo solemnly bowed. 'Go with God, Martin.'

The exchange cast a shadow over the day, not so much Michaelo's warning, but his use of Martin's name, something he could not recall the monk doing before. He was so shaken by what he'd found in Costen's home that he had shed his shield against the world.

On the threshold, Martin winced at the stench. Owen knelt beside Costen's body, glancing up as Martin cleared his throat.

'Might I be of help? I'm familiar with most forms of torture.' Too late, he thought better of the grin he had thought would soften the words.

Owen glowered, but motioned him over. 'You have the stomach for it. Tell me what you see.'

Martin crouched down, taking in the mangled hands, the face, the final release of the slit throat. His stomach clenched, remembering how Wirthir had lain in his blood and urine, torn and broken. He had deserved such suffering. But Costen? No, Owen would have recognised such a monster in his city. 'I cannot think he deserved this.'

'I cannot think of anyone who would,' said Owen.

Fortunate man, to be able to say that. Martin pointed to the cuts behind Costen's knees, on his heels. 'Ensuring he could not run away. This took time. Death came as a relief.' He crossed himself, remembering the pain of his own torture, the brutal severing of his right hand. 'He suffered for an hour, or more. It must have felt an eternity,' said Martin.

'I think that was the intent.' Owen sounded weary, depleted. 'And the ones who did this are likely still in the city.'

'I cannot think what he had done to inspire such hatred. I know some thought him a spy, but this suggests something far worse.'

'Or a murderer with a twisted soul,' said Owen.

Martin touched his friend's shoulder. 'You need to come away from this. Breathe, move about. I will stay awhile, if I may.'

Owen glanced towards the doorway, where a newcomer shifted foot to foot, clearly ill at ease. 'It seems I have another visitor. See what you can glean, Martin.' He rose.

'What is your business here?' Owen demanded, then recognised the newcomer. 'Geoffrey.'

The young man held out a parchment roll. 'The drawing you asked for, Captain. I went there first thing.'

The drawing of Walter. Owen had forgotten. 'So prompt. Thank you.' He motioned him outside, feeling the need for fresher air. He'd not needed Martin to tell him that. 'The castle guard gave you no trouble?' He had neglected to send word of what he had asked of the young man, so focused on the torture and murder he might have prevented.

'When I explained my task they left me to my work,' said Geoffrey. 'Was he murdered, Captain?'

'The man you sketched?' Owen asked as he unrolled the parchment.

'No, Costen.'

Owen glanced up, noticed the young man's clenched hands, his eyes dark with sorrow. Of course. Geoffrey had admired Costen.

'Yes, he was murdered. Sometime in the night.'

'He was right, then? People didn't trust him? Thought he was a spy?'

'I don't know the why of it, Geoffrey, nor can I name the murderer. Not yet.'

'He was a good man.'

'This drawing . . .' Owen was staring at the lifelike image. 'You have seen past the corruption to the living man. Remarkable.'

Geoffrey relaxed his hands. 'The truth is, Captain, I'd seen this man walking about. I didn't know it at first, but as I studied him, trying to make out the bones beneath, that's what Costen taught me,' a hitch in his voice, 'I realised I'd seen him before.'

Owen was interested. 'You remember him? Where? What was he doing?'

'I've tried to remember. He was walking past me. Another time I think I saw him outside my house – no, the Creswick house next to us. So it was here, on Colliergate, not back in Hull.'

Creswick. Owen tucked that name away. 'If you remember, let me know. This is most helpful. I should pay you.'

Geoffrey threw up his hands. 'No, Captain. I am glad to be of help. You said Costen recommended me to you?'

'He did.'

A sad smile. 'That's payment enough.'

After the dim, dusty, odorous house, the sunny morning had Owen blinking against the brightness. He had left Alfred to guard Costen's house until the body had been removed and was heading home to help Ned with the bundles of fragments collected from the death scene. But as he turned into Stonegate and began to pass Robert Dale's shop at the corner, he remembered the wooden box in his scrip.

He found Robert pacing in his office behind the workshop.

'Owen, my friend, we are ruined. Ruined by that lackwit braggart. He told us he was taking the lion to the minster treasury until he departed. Swore to us. We should have insisted on escorting him. Better yet, we should have taken it to the treasury and arranged to deliver it to him on the day. His damnable pride. He cannot hear anyone but himself. I warned them, and advised that another guild-member should travel with him. How could they not see? Yes, yes, they argued that he would be travelling in a company of clerics who were accustomed to carrying valuable documents and items entrusted to them. But why would Harrigan suddenly listen to clerics?' Robert stopped, and slumped down onto the high-backed chair behind the desk, head in hands. 'Forgive me. I am distraught. We cannot replace the lion. We are too short of gold coin.'

'Feel fortunate you lost only money, Robert,' Owen said as he dropped onto a chair and helped himself to the wine the clerk set before his master and guest. The clerk had scuttled away as if fearing for his life. As if his gentle master would ever lift a hand to him.

Robert winced. 'Forgive me. I heard the news. You must have just come from the home of the murdered man. Was it terrible?'

'I pray you never see the like, nor any of your family,' said Owen, downing the wine. 'Perhaps I should come back another time. I am not fit company.'

'No. It is good you came. I was frightening my workers with my foolish outcry. How might I help you, my friend?'

Owen set the box on the desk. 'I found this in Costen van Peelt's house last night.'

'The artist who was murdered.' Robert picked up the box, holding it very close to his eyes, and ran his fingers along the wood, the clasp, the velvet lining, lowered it to his nose to sniff. 'Curious. I made several boxes for the lion. Different clasps, hinges, some lined in velvet, some silk. This is one of the boxes I discarded. You found this in van Peelt's house?'

'Yes. Had you sold any of them? Given them to anyone?'

'No. No, they were on a shelf in the workshop.' He paused, tilted his head. 'However, my journeyman, Louis, had taken one to Harrigan to test the size, but the lion was in Scardburge's workshop that day. I wonder. Did Louis return with it? I have a vague memory he did not.' He crossed to the workshop door and called for his journeyman. When Louis appeared, his brown hair sparkling with silver dust, Robert held out the box. 'Is this the box you took to Scardburge's shop for sizing?'

Louis leaned close, brushing the box with remarkably long fingers. 'It is, Master.' He gave Owen a worried glance. 'Someone found it? I don't know how I misplaced it. But it wasn't in my scrip when I returned.'

Robert grunted. 'I remember now.'

'You thought you put it in your scrip in the workshop?' Owen asked.

'Yes, Captain.' Louis glanced between Owen and Robert, his face crinkled in worry. 'What is this about?'

'Did you stop anywhere on your way back from his shop?' Owen asked.

The man reddened. 'I might have slipped into the York Tavern for an ale and some food.'

Owen could not imagine a thief successfully operating in the York, not under Bess Merchet's keen eye. 'Did you encounter anyone on the street?'

Louis closed his eyes, and tapped a finger on his temple as if stirring his thoughts. It was apparently successful, for he looked at Owen and nodded. 'A boy. Beggar type. Asked me for a penny. He pushed at me as I walked away.'

Owen described Flint.

'That's him.'

Had the lad been at Costen's last night? Perhaps arriving after the others had gone, which was why the velvet was clean. Or it fell from his clothes as he was carried or dragged away. Owen was worried about the boy.

The clerk knocked and entered the office. 'My apologies, but I think Captain Archer will wish to see who is walking down Stonegate, Master.'

Gwen and Hugh were part of a small group walking down the street, his daughter with her arm round a younger girl with bowed head, his son and another boy gripped by the children's assistant schoolmaster, one boy to either side of him.

'God's wounds,' Owen muttered, made his apologies to Robert, who had followed him to the door, and strode off to find out what had happened.

Owen nodded to the assistant master, who brought the little procession to a halt. Gwen kept a protective arm round the little girl, whose eyes were red, her lashes wet with tears, her lower lip trembling. Hugh faced his father with straight-backed pride. The other boy had a blooming black eye.

'Captain Archer, your son punched Edwin Scardburge,' said the assistant master, jutting out his fleshy chin as if to ward off an attack. 'We cannot have that.'

'H–he was defending me,' sobbed the little girl.

'He called her father, Master Harrigan, a thief and a liar,' said Hugh, 'and then called her a lying little cheat.'

'All because Pippa corrected Edwin's Latin translation,' said Gwen.

'Be that as it may, rules are rules,' said the assistant master.

Owen felt all the tensions of the morning easing as he regarded his children's earnest faces. He felt himself grinning at the self-important assistant master. 'I presume you are escorting them to Master Harrigan's shop so that Edwin can apologise to him and Mistress Philippa, and then my children will return to their lessons while you escort Edwin home and report to his father,' he said.

'Apologise to . . .' The man turned a dangerous shade of crimson. 'I . . .'

'Of course you are.' Owen erased the grin. 'That is the right course of action. Young Scardburge is in the wrong.'

'Your son . . .'

'Defended Mistress Philippa's honour.'

'But he injured the boy.'

'Young Scardburge will remember not to resort to insults and false accusations when embarrassed by a correction.'

The assistant master looked round him as if seeking supporters, but the few paused onlookers offered no comments.

'I—Yes, of course, Captain.'

Gwen grinned at Owen and he winked at her.

'Mistress Philippa, will you lead the way to your father's office door?' he asked, giving Edwin Scardburge, who was digging in his heels, a gentle nudge.

'We were not needed,' Lucie said when Owen expressed surprise to find her in the hall at home with Brother Michaelo and Ned. 'Anna, Celia, and the two servants have it all in hand.' In fact, they had almost been rude in their eagerness to have them away. But Lucie did not like to mention it to Owen until she'd given it more thought. He had enough worries. Although . . . at present he looked the opposite of worried, indeed he seemed pleased with himself. 'What happened?'

'I just encountered two of our children with their assistant schoolmaster.'

'You went to the school?'

'No . . .'

She listened in amazement to his account of Gwen's motherly

protection of Philippa Harrigan, Hugh's chivalric behaviour, and the thin-skinned bully Edwin Scardburge, exchanging surprised looks with Brother Michaelo all the while.

'When I sensed the assistant schoolmaster's reluctance to have the boy apologise to Harrigan and report Scardburge's bullying to his father, I thought it best to accompany the group,' said Owen, still grinning.

He had clearly enjoyed himself. 'How was the apology received?' she asked.

'Bertram Harrigan controlled himself in chastising Edwin while holding Pippa and smoothing her hair.' Owen smiled. 'The miscreant's own father was not so restrained, and the entire workshop jumped at his explosion. I don't expect the lad to be seen abroad much for a while, until his eye heals and his father cools.'

'Gwen will talk of it for weeks.'

'She did not witness that part. I encouraged her to return to the schoolroom from Harrigan's office while we continued. I trust she will explain it all to the schoolmaster before his assistant can complain.'

'That was wise,' said Michaelo.

'Poor young fool,' said Lucie. 'Doubtless Edwin has heard complaints about Harrigan and the lion and believed he would be respected for bullying Pippa. But Hugh punching him. I am not easy about that. We don't want him to think that's how the world is set right.'

'I suggested that kicking Edwin in the shins might have left less of a mark,' Owen said. When she did not smile back, he grew serious. 'I will talk to him.'

She relented, a little. 'I am sure that the class and certainly the Harrigan family will consider him a hero. Was Hugh injured?'

'Not a scratch. He seemed surprised that Edwin did not hit back.'

'And Gwen?'

'She is proud of him.'

Lucie could not deny that had been her own first reaction.

'Your son is mirroring his father, the protector of the city,' said Michaelo with a wry smile.

Owen looked discomfited by the comment, as if it had not occurred to him.

Seeing that, she said, 'I trust you let them both know you were proud of them.'

'I did. But you are right, Hugh needs to learn to pause and consider the least violent way to achieve the same end.'

She stretched up to kiss his cheek. 'Did Hugh return to the classroom as well?'

'He did. Expecting to be praised and feted, I imagine. But I am sorry that the children are being drawn into my work.'

'It is not your doing, my love. Children hear their parents talking and take on their opinions. It has ever been so. I dare to boast that we are raising our children well.'

Owen scratched his beard and considered her comments. 'Perhaps it does reflect well on us.' He looked tired, the scar on his cheek standing out, his eye red from interrupted sleep. Rolling his shoulders, he made a move towards the kitchen door then stopped, looking towards the corner of the hall where Ned was arranging the bags of flotsam and jetsam from Costen's house. He had recruited a few lads to help carry the bundles – the fragments wrapped up in bedclothes found in the house – and seemed to be trying to make the pile as compact as possible. 'More of my work crowding our home.'

'I confess I was taken aback by the number of bundles,' said Lucie, 'but he is doing his best to contain them, and we do have the room to spare.'

Owen looked relieved.

Lucie considered the piles. 'The children will stay away from it, but the cat might reorganise the piles from time to time. We might cover it with a cloth at night to dissuade Ariela from carrying away pieces that entice her.'

Brother Michaelo, who had discreetly withdrawn to the garden window, asked, 'Is Dame Magda waiting for someone?'

Lucie had forgotten. 'It's you she came to see, Owen.'

TEN

A Missing Lad, Puzzles

As Owen went out to join Dame Magda on the bench beneath the linden, Lucie turned her attention to Ned, who had begun to arrange a few piles of fragments on the end of the long hall table. She could not imagine when Owen would have the time to try piecing it all together. Brother Michaelo had offered to assist, but Owen might need his help in searching for Costen's murderer.

'I might try my hand at this.'

Lucie had not heard Martin join them. 'It will be tedious work,' she said. 'And possibly of little use.'

'All the better that it be undertaken by a man searching for purpose.'

Lucie turned to look at their houseguest. He was gaunt and pale despite his hours walking the city streets or sitting in the garden, with shadows beneath his expressive eyes. Yesterday's mishap in the rain had undone him, yet he had been out again this morning. 'You already do so much.' He often assisted Kate by watching the children, walked Gwen and Hugh to and from their lessons, and gifted Jasper with his company in the evenings.

Martin gave a sad smile. 'You are kind. But I think I might enjoy this. I was curious about Costen.'

'Have you a theory of who might have killed him?'

'That is Owen's gift. I could make an argument for far too many and have no way to sort them.'

'If so many feared that he was spying on them, how had he not been confronted long ago?'

'I wondered the same. Perhaps few among the merchants believed the rumours, and the ones who did hired him for their own ends – or tried to.' Martin grinned. 'He could be difficult to approach.'

'He lived among us, we passed him in the streets, but we did not know him.' She regretted that.

'I tried.'

'You did.' She looked at the piles. 'If you are determined to work with this, I would ask you leave half the table clear for the family to use.'

'I will.' Martin went over to talk to Ned.

Brother Michaelo followed. 'Perhaps I might help as I wait for the captain.'

Magda sat on the bench beneath the linden lifting her face to the sun. Ariela was curled in a tight ball on the healer's lap. 'This is welcome after the rains.'

Owen settled beside her, stretching out his legs. The sun did feel good. He allowed himself a moment of quiet, then told her about Hugh and Gwen.

Magda chuckled. 'A fiery lad, thy son Hugh.' She placed a finely veined hand on Owen's forearm. 'But thou art troubled.'

By so many things. 'I don't want Hugh to think violence is the way to peace. Or honour.'

'That will not happen, not with thine example, and Lucie's.'

Owen breathed deep. 'Thank you. Poor Pippa Harrigan. Her father's troubles are now hers.'

'The goldsmiths are worried, their fine reputations tarnished by the theft, and those who felt they were grasping for royal favour enjoy their failure. The city will dine on this for a long while, and Harrigan will carry the blame.'

'Unless I find the lion.'

'Yes. Thou hast claimed this thy task even as thou art bowed down beneath the weight of two murders and Flint's danger.'

'You know me well.'

'Very well, Bird-eye. Thou wilt worry at all this until thou hast restored calm to the city.'

A winged insect, tiny, delicate, landed on Ariela's ear. She twitched the ear, but the insect stayed. Again. The insect rose and resettled. Now the clawed paw came up and swiped the delicate thing away, and Ariela resumed her nap, undisturbed. Had it been him, he would have questioned what he'd done, let it gnaw on him all day as he paced and argued with himself.

He had not asked why Magda had come. 'Have you heard anything of Flint?'

'No. But the Swan might.' Her name for Michaelo. 'The child sometimes sleeps in the minster yard. He will know the monk tends the people there and might seek him out.'

'Or avoid him.'

'That is so.'

'Anywhere else?'

'The street children find hidden places and huddle together for warmth and safety. He might be anywhere.'

Jasper might have become one of them, if not for Martin's care. Owen rubbed his scar. 'Costen van Peelt's murder was brutal.'

'Magda heard. Art thou thinking the boy might have done it?'

'What was done to Costen took far too much strength for one lad.' He told her about the velvet-lined box he had found at the scene. 'Do you think Flint is a violent lad?'

'He does what he must to survive. But Magda senses no murderous passion in him.'

Meaning he might have assisted, without true malice. A chilling thought that such a young one might measure his choices in such wise.

'That disturbs thee.'

'Everything about Costen's murder does.' Owen rubbed the cat's soft ears, listening for a moment to her purr, a comforting sound. 'I went to Costen's house last night.' He told her about the conversation, his later call to the house, and described the scene.

'Thou art sick at heart.'

'If only I had protected Costen.'

'Had he asked thee for protection?'

'No.'

'Even so, thou didst set a watch.' She patted his hand. 'Thou art good at keeping the peace, but thou canst not protect all in the city.'

'The violence of the act, torturing him before cutting his throat, destroying his art, digging up his floor, opening the wall . . . this was both a passionate deed and a search for something of value. I believe there were at least two attackers, but I would wager the anger is confined in one of them.'

'A dangerous man.'

'Yes.'

'Thou wilt learn the truth in this.'

'I don't know how you can be so certain.'

'Magda knows thee. But have a care, Bird-eye. Thou art being warned. Whoever did this does not fear thee. Do not be reckless in proving them wrong.'

The warning gave Owen pause. He glanced at Magda, who had lifted her wrinkled face to the sun, her white hair glimmering in the light. 'You think me proud?'

She lowered her head and met his gaze with her steady blue eyes. 'Of course thou art. Thou shouldst be. But thou knowest enough about the world of men to know thy limits. Magda feels thy doubt, she knows thou art ever fearful that thou wilt fail those who trust thee. Do not let that fear lead thee.'

If he had not been unsettled before, he was now. And she was right, he did worry – he would not call it fear – that he would fail the goldsmiths, and Costen. Perhaps Flint as well. And Neville, damn the man. He would send someone to search for Walter Bolton.

'Did you know Costen?' he asked.

'Not well.'

'What do you know of Anna van Peelt?'

'A neglected wife who found solace with her mistress.' Magda smiled. 'Neither were happy with their mates. Celia benefited handsomely from her late husband's wealth and enjoys sharing it with Anna.'

He remembered the similar brightly coloured shawls. 'Anna and Celia, like Ambrose and Martin?' A perfect way to live together without comment, as housekeeper and mistress. It might explain Celia's protectiveness, her lack of sympathy for Costen. But that might be true even without a sexual aspect.

'Magda does not pry.'

'No. That is my task.' His interactions with the pair since Costen's death piqued his curiosity. Something was not being said.

His thoughts returned to the missing boy. 'I hope Flint goes to the minster yard tonight.'

'Do not spend too much time searching for him. He would not thank thee.'

'He's in danger. Bound to be.'

'It is always so for him, and for all the children who live by their wits. To go about the city asking if he has been seen would endanger him.'

'I meant to do it through his fellows.'

'Have a care.'

'Do you have any sense of who might have stolen the gold lion?'

'Thou wouldst have Magda do thy job?' She chuckled. 'Thou art the searcher, Bird-eye. Magda is the healer.' She rose from the bench, took his hands in hers. 'Hugh dreams of being a hero like his father. It is a great compliment.'

'I do not know how to feel about it.'

'Be pleased, Bird-eye. Thy son loves and admires thee.'

Owen lingered in the garden after Magda departed, thinking about what she had said. He was proud of Hugh, and Gwen, how she had supported Pippa.

'I am glad to see you smiling,' said Brother Michaelo, settling beside him. 'I would guess Hugh's valour is the cause.'

'And Gwen's maturity. She saw Pippa's distress and comforted her.' Owen watched Lucie cross from the house to the workshop. 'But I dislike how my family is being pulled into the city's troubles once more.'

'Dame Lucie understands that is the nature of your work.'

Of course she did. But did she wish it otherwise? 'Magda says Flint sometimes sleeps in the minster yard. Would you watch for a lad with an injured neck?'

'There are so many young ones, and most keep to the shadows. But I will look out for him and let you know if I learn anything. Should I write to Sir John Neville about his man's death?'

Owen had forgotten. 'Another matter that the night's business put out of my head. And I must clarify that it might have been murder.'

'Of course.'

'I trust you to come up with the right words to soothe and flatter him while delivering such unwelcome news.'

'The late archbishop sent many such messages. I know what to do.' Brother Michaelo rose. 'You will need to sign it.'

'You've not yet mastered my signature?'

'I had no need.' A secret smile.

'No need to use it yet. I see. We'll send it to Raby Castle. If he's not there, they will know where to forward it.'

'Do you think he will wish his own retainers to investigate?'

'Unfortunately, I do. Or he might decide to do it himself, depending on his relationship to Bolton.'

'God help us,' Michaelo whispered.

'Indeed. Pray for us.'

After Lucie, Brother Michaelo, and Ned departed, Martin studied the piles on the table before him, pieces of cloth on the left, pieces of wax tablets in the middle, pieces of other assorted materials on the right, all small mounds at the moment, only a taste of what was in the various sheets and packs. To the far right were several piles of wax tablet pieces that Ned and Alfred had already sorted. He moved over to study those in the largest pile. When fitted together they revealed a sketch of a building, perhaps a house, with a stone ground floor and wooden upper storey. He was shuffling through the middle mound of wax tablet pieces to see whether he could complete the sketch when a little hand tugged on his sleeve.

'Good day to you, Mistress Emma.'

'Gwen and Hugh are still in school.' She sighed as if her world were in shambles.

'Are you here to help me sort this?'

'Will it be fun?'

'With your help, yes.' He plucked her up and sat her beside him on the bench. 'Do you know what these are pieces of?'

She knelt to see better, her soft brown hair masking her expression as she shifted several pieces the size of her little palms. 'Wax tablets. Were they for school?'

'No, a man drew pictures on them.' He told her about Costen sketching the city and showed her the almost complete sketch of the building.

She considered the house, her mouth scrunched to one side. 'Animals are the hardest to draw. Are there animals?'

'That is one of the things I hope to learn by sorting these.'

She pointed to the building sketch. 'Some of the lines are black on that one.'

'Alfred showed Ned how to dust them with ash to help them stand out.'

She looked down at the stump of his right forearm. 'I could fetch ashes for you. I have two hands.'

Her blunt practicality made him laugh. 'Perhaps we should leave that until later.' He did not want to be responsible for ashes everywhere. 'Let's see what we can see as it is.'

While they worked, he told Emma a tale his mother once told him, about a witch who punished those who made fun of her. She would sneak into their homes at night and wreak havoc while the people slept under her spell. They would wake in the morning to their belongings in shreds. If they publicly apologised and said they had been wrong to laugh at her she would restore it all. Almost all. She would leave just enough tears and chips so that every day they would be reminded of what she had done, and why.

'I hope they learned their lesson,' Emma said when he was finished.

'Why do you side with her and not the people?'

She tilted her head to one side while continuing to sort the scraps into piles. 'She was a powerful witch, to tear everything up and then put it all back together. But maybe she just wanted to be friends. Maybe if the people weren't so mean she would have used her power to help them.'

It was the longest speech he had ever heard Emma expound, and so wise. Martin kissed the top of her head. 'You have hidden depths, my child.'

'Houses. Churches. Gardens or trees.' She indicated three piles. 'We need that witch to help us, don't we, Uncle Martin?'

'That we do.'

'I hope we find some animals.'

'So do I.'

'The witch that made this mess made a mistake.'

For a moment Martin was puzzled. 'What do you mean?'

'She killed the man who made her angry. Now he can't ever be her friend.'

He frantically thought back to what he'd said to her, relieved that he'd made no mention of murder. But the child knew.

ELEVEN

Guilds, Ships, a Will, a Splinter

While Brother Michaelo retired to Jehannes's house to write the letter to Sir John Neville, as well as a summary of all that the night and morning had revealed, Owen called on George Hempe, who was interviewing the last of Harrigan's apprentices and servants in his home. Away from their fellows and their master, Hempe hoped they might be more willing to talk than the others had been.

When Owen arrived, his friend was pacing and muttering to himself.

'He's completed the interviews?' Owen quietly asked Lotta Hempe.

'Almost. He was interrupted by our guildmaster's clerk, instructing him to have a care taking sides in another guild's troubles. How dare they tell him how to do his job.' Her eyes flashed.

'Now, love, they were telling all the members, not singling me out,' said Hempe, putting an arm round his wife as he joined them. 'But I do not like that all the guilds are watchful and wary. The Merchant Adventurers, well, you've heard they're advising members to keep their ships off shore to rob Lancaster of the chance to seize them. And of course everyone is watching the goldsmiths, wondering how they will survive this disaster, some whispering about how wealthy they all are, that they could easily gather sufficient gold coin to make another.'

'I very much doubt that,' said Lotta. 'Though I have heard they're fighting among themselves.'

'And their children are listening,' said Owen. He told them about Hugh, Pippa Harrigan, and Edwin Scardburge.

'Dear Hugh,' said Lotta, 'but poor Pippa.'

'We need to quiet their fears or there will be trouble,' said

Hempe. 'It takes but one argument turning into a row in a tavern and we have trouble atop the mess we're already facing – theft, drowning that might have been deliberate, torture and murder, a missing injured lad, rumours of spies.' Hempe raked a hand across his almost bald head. 'I do not like the temper of the city. A foreign merchant was followed across Ouse Bridge by lads heckling him, calling him a spy.'

'Sweet Jesu.' Owen wondered about Martin as he walked about the city. Was he next?

'Come, sit down, have a cup of ale and calm yourself, husband. You, too, Owen.' Lotta herded them to the chairs by the hall fire circle.

As they settled, Hempe spoke of the apprentices and servants he had interviewed. 'Frightened, every one of them, fearing they will say something to make us think they stole the lion. Most of the apprentices drank too much too quickly and remember little of that night. A handful recall seeing someone who sounds very like the drowned man, and the servants are willing to admit they saw some lads from another shop. An apprentice and a servant admitted to witnessing Wyman arriving and gathering his sheep, herding them off.'

'Did any of them speak to the man who looked like Bolton? Notice what he was doing? To whom he spoke?' Owen asked.

'Only one pointed out a fellow apprentice to whom the man seemed to speak, but that lad remembers little, and his fellows have said he fell asleep in the shop and when they tried to move him he lost everything in his stomach and had to be carried to bed.'

'Anything unusual about the apprentice to whom he spoke?'

'He's an Overton, nephew of Celia Overton's late husband. But nothing else.'

A link perhaps to Anna van Peelt, who worked for Celia, but a weak one. 'I will talk with Dame Celia in a few days, if we're still floundering.'

'Floundering.' Hempe growled the word. 'We are doing all we can.'

'With nothing to show for our efforts but more problems.' Owen saw no point in avoiding the truth.

'You learned much from the documents Martin found on

Neville's man,' said Lotta. 'I understand the shipping list was almost as complete as mine.' George's wife kept a close watch on their shipping and that of their partners, having done so for her first husband.

'Half as complete. I thought perhaps the ones omitted fit a pattern,' said Owen. 'But I've found none so far.'

'But you now know that someone in the city is spying on the shipping for the French,' said Lotta, 'and that Sir John Neville wanted that information.'

'It would seem so. And that's another mystery. Where did Walter Bolton get that list? Surely he would have known the spy was the more important part? Had he already sent him running? How did he find him before we did? Have we been so blind?' Owen raked a hand through his hair. 'I trust you to keep this to yourself, Lotta.'

George grunted.

'You know I will, Owen Archer. My George is bailiff and shares all manner of things.'

'Forgive me.'

Lotta reached over to pat his hand. 'You have much on your mind. It is no matter.'

Dinner was one of Martin's favourite times of the day in the household, especially when all the family were gathered round the table, Lucie and Jasper able to close the shop for an hour, Owen not too busy to take time in the middle of his day. On this occasion Lucie presided over the group with calm authority, particularly needed with Hugh and Gwen teetering towards an argument, he loudly proclaiming his gallantry and she warning him that pride might tilt him towards being a bully like Edwin Scardburge, while Emma sang songs about the bits and pieces she was helping Martin organise. All the while Lucie reminded them to eat and Owen noted that the volume of their argument threatened to wake the dead in the cemetery across from the house, while Jasper desperately tried to steer his father away from that as Gwen's one great fear was that the inhabitants of the cemetery were not truly at peace.

The biggest revelation in all this was Owen, whom Martin had known as a cunning former soldier, skilled archer, his size, strength, and scarred face marking him as such. Yet he was equally a fond father and devoted husband. He had glimpsed Lucie and Owen together when he'd brought Jasper to them, but their own children had yet to be born. He had not lived with them, seen how they shared responsibility and with what affection they held each other. He'd glimpsed Owen's compassion in his unhesitating care for Jasper and his grief for Lucie's father, Sir Robert D'Arby, who had died on pilgrimage to St David's in Wales, but all these were fleeting glimpses. Even in York, Owen's reputation was as the captain of the city and a trusted servant of the young king; the gentle father and husband was a private Owen. As the children were excused, hurrying out to the kitchen to concoct a game for a rainy day, their father watched their departure with a fond smile, an expression a world apart from the glower with which he gazed on his prisoners.

'A moment of peace for us, but not for Kate,' said Lucie.

'Emma has been a help with sorting the pieces from Costen's house,' said Martin. 'I might try recruiting Gwen and Hugh as well.'

'Tomorrow, perhaps,' said Lucie. 'This afternoon they need to play out their differences. Have you discovered anything in the debris?'

'At this point I am simply sorting the pieces of sketches into buildings, gardens or fields, and water,' said Martin. 'I fear many pieces are too small to be of use. But I think I may recognise the building in a fairly complete drawing.' He invited them to the end of the table and showed them the large piece of a wax tablet and some smaller pieces he and Emma had discovered. 'And one of the paintings or drawings on parchment is based on the sketch.' He unrolled it.

'It's familiar,' said Owen. 'Not in the city, I think.'

'No. I don't recognise it,' said Lucie.

Martin could not help smiling at Owen. 'I trust you have been to Sheriff Hutton?'

The Neville property at the north end of the forest of Galtres, just miles from the city.

'I have, and I believe you're right. They're building a castle there now, but this is the old house. So Costen had been there.' Owen glanced up at Martin with delight. 'This could be the link between him and Bolton.'

Gratifying. But he must tell them what he'd discovered about Emma.

'While I worked with the little one I discovered that she knows Costen was murdered.' He watched for surprise in their faces and found none in Lucie's. In Owen's he saw only a flash of sorrow.

'God help us,' Owen muttered.

'None of that, love,' said Lucie. 'We know how little escapes them. They are clever children and very good at listening. And sharing with one another what they've heard.'

'I am astonished by Emma's quiet wisdom,' said Martin.

Lucie smiled fondly. 'We all underestimate her. Because she's the youngest.'

'And the singing,' said Owen with a chuckle. 'But if one listens to what she's singing, it's clear she's taking in all that's going on.'

Proud parents. Martin was relieved.

A conversation with the sheriff, Sir John Constable, soured Owen's mood as he crossed the city to sign the letter to Neville that Brother Michaelo had prepared.

'That is one of Sir John Neville's men,' Constable had sputtered when Owen showed him Geoffrey's drawing. 'I remember him from one of Neville's visits. For his brother the archbishop's enthronement. Kept him close, as I recall."

Of course. That is where Owen had seen him, during the ceremony in the minster, and at the archbishop's palace.

'This is terrible news,' Constable had whined, then frowned up at Owen. 'And you waited a day to tell me? Why?'

'I was following some lines of inquiry that I hoped might help me understand what had happened to him.'

'The French spy murdered him, that is what happened,' Constable snapped, with his usual knack for oversimplifying.

Owen knew it pointless to correct him. He would not like being reminded that there might be multiple spies, or none, which meant the murderer might live among them. He said only, 'That is possible.'

'Possible?'

And so it had gone, with Constable wanting Owen's assurance that he would bring Neville to him if he came to the city.

'But he will surely come straight to you,' Owen had said. 'Sir John Neville is not a man to knock on the door of a city captain.' That had calmed the sheriff, petty little man.

'Catch the spy before Neville arrives, Archer,' were Constable's parting words.

The sheriff's secretary had been more helpful, remembering Bolton from a tavern near the castle. The taverner told Owen he believed Bolton had been there a few times, drinking quietly in a corner. Guildmaster Harrigan also thought he recognised him after squinting closely for a while.

'I can't think where, when. I will let you know if I remember anything.'

It seemed Bolton had been good at blending into the city. Neville had chosen well.

The sun had disappeared behind glowering clouds, and he smelled rain in the air. A matter of moments. The drizzle had begun by the time he reached Archdeacon Jehannes's door. He knocked more loudly than he had intended.

'You come trailing storm clouds,' said Brother Michaelo as he opened the door. 'But do not despair. Dom Jehannes has some information that might cheer you.'

'The golden lion? Costen's murderers? Bolton's spy?'

'Information about Costen. A will.'

Owen was momentarily disappointed, but reconsidered. The will might provide him with more information about the man's affairs, perhaps a hint of what someone thought he might have hidden in the house.

Michaelo led Owen into Dom Jehannes's parlour, where the archdeacon stood at the window watching the rain, heavier now. With a sigh, Jehannes closed the shutters and turned to Owen and Michaelo.

'A pity. It was a beautiful day.' The archdeacon nodded to Owen. 'Brother Michaelo says Costen made a will?'

'Yes. One of the clerks who handles merchants' wills remembered it because it might mean much to Archbishop Thoresby's lady chapel. I had a clerk bring it from the minster.' Jehannes indicated a roll on the table beside him.

The minster lady chapel had been meant as the late archbishop's legacy. Owen felt a tingle of excitement. A clue at last? 'How long ago did he prepare it for Costen?' he asked as he chose a seat where he might see both of his companions.

'About five years ago, when Costen was certain that Dame Anna meant to remain living apart from him.'

'Have you read it?'

'Skimmed it, to see whether it might be helpful.'

'I am interested. Did he leave Dame Anna anything?'

'He did, yes. He wished to be generous to her, considering himself to have been in the wrong. He left her his loom and many of the furnishings of his house, which he lists, as well as any of the wool he had not yet sold. The will stipulates that Dame Anna may claim any of his wax tablets, sketches, paintings, wall hangings, and cloth that might be of interest to her, to keep or to sell. Whatever coin was left he wished to be added to what he had already given Archbishop Thoresby for the lady chapel. Dame Anna apparently knows where he kept it.'

'She does. It was dug up last night.'

'Oh.' Jehannes's shoulders sagged. 'A pity. Someone else knew of it? Murdered him for that?'

'I feel in my bones it was more than that. The brutality suggests a crime of passion, not ordinary greed.'

'I see.' Jehannes's eyes were sad.

'I am curious about his gift for the lady chapel,' said Owen. Thoresby's vision was for as many of the past archbishops of York as possible to be reinterred in the minster's lady chapel, where he would join his fellows in the fullness of time. But King Edward's war and the pestilence had slowed work on the project, and it remained unfinished at his death. 'Do you recall seeing him with Archbishop Thoresby?' he asked Michaelo.

'I do not. I cannot account for it.'

Brother Michaelo had run the late archbishop's household and known of every visitor, their rank, their relationship to Thoresby, their purpose in calling on him. It would be remarkable if Costen had circumvented him.

'He might not have felt it necessary to inform the archbishop,' said Michaelo. 'A quiet donation.'

'Shall I read the will to you?' asked Jehannes. 'I will translate the trickier legal phrases.' He donned his new spectacles and opened the roll, pausing to look over at Owen. 'I share this only because the details of the furnishings, which I understand might have been stolen by the murderer, might assist your investigation.'

'Yes, thank you.' Owen helped himself to a cup of wine and settled back to listen. Most interesting was that the donations to the lady chapel had been intended to contribute towards the redemption of Costen's soul, forgiveness of his sins. For ordinary sins, or transgressions that led to his violent death?

When he had finished, Jehannes set the will aside and took off the spectacles, rubbing the bridge of his nose. 'I hope that will prove helpful.'

'A valuable tapestry is missing. In the mounds of scraps, I have seen no evidence of one,' said Owen. 'The rest, the sketches, difficult to know whether any survived. And of course the coins are gone.'

He was still pondering Costen's sins as he skimmed Michaelo's diplomatic letter to Sir John Neville. There was, of course, no mention of Costen van Peelt in the letter, but he wished he knew what had taken Costen to Sheriff Hutton. Perhaps if Neville descended on the city Owen would find out. Though he would rather discover it in some other way. Any other way.

Kate's younger sister Rose took up the assignment with enthusiasm, wrapping her reddish-brown hair atop her head and donning a coif. 'I know just the house to watch from. Mistress Felice, an old friend of Mother's, lives with her sister across from Holy Trinity churchyard.'

'You will not tell her what you are about?' Owen asked.

She looked at him as if to say he knew better. 'I will tell her I've been trying Ma's patience and need a project. I will find something to fix, a task that will take some time. If I remember rightly, there's a shutter needs mending on the front of the house. I should be able to watch anyone entering or leaving the yard. We'll find the boy.'

Satisfied, Owen moved on to Costen's house to take a closer look at the digging and the hole in the wall. Stephen stood by the door, greeting Owen with relief on his strong-boned, well-fleshed face.

'Too quiet here. I start hearing things.'

It was a lonely spot, tucked behind buildings, little reason for most to walk past. And yet the couple had done so the other night.

'When was the last time anyone came past?' asked Owen.

'Seems a long while. Hours. I took up the guard a while past dawn, and it's now afternoon.' Stephen pulled on his ear, thinking. 'In all I've seen five people. A mother and her little girl, she offered me a hunk of bread still warm from the baker in thanks for protection, a man with a hand cart filled with plants he was keen to assure me came to him honestly, two men arguing about which one of them had misplaced a new spade. I reckon all live close by, certain the mother and girl do. Cannot think why else anyone would come through otherwise.'

But Owen remembered all the people crowding round earlier in the day for news, the few that had heard voices. They might still find someone who had noticed the three men. Owen would have Alfred go round and ask.

Stephen's stomach growled.

'Get yourself some food and bring Alfred when you return,' said Owen. 'I will watch till then.'

Stephen shrugged. 'I could stay.'

'I need you sharp, and I need Alfred.'

With a happy nod, Stephen strode away.

A slow walk round the house revealed little – the place where Warren had been attacked, his hat still on the ground near the wood pile. The window shutters had not been damaged, so Costen's murderers likely came through the door, which was also undamaged, suggesting that he'd either known them or had not locked the door.

Stepping inside, Owen almost choked on the unpleasant stew of odours, the fading incense doing little now to mask the blood, sweat, urine, and faeces that had soaked into the packed earth. An argument for tiled floors, such as in Owen's hall, and the stone floor in the kitchen. But even in his home a violent death would leave a lingering stench. He opened the shutters and crouched to stir the ashes in the fire circle with the tip of his dagger, the remains of the fire Costen had laid sometime yesterday. His blade met another piece of metal. Owen plucked it out. A buckle, too small for Costen's belt. From a harness? A boot? He tucked it in his scrip and went through the ashes a second time, but found nothing more. The debris left round the body had been ripped, torn, sliced, not burned. It seemed the point was not to destroy evidence, but to destroy the beauty Costen created.

Costen had believed people suspected him of spying. But that was no motive to torture and kill a man. Or was it?

Owen stepped outside for a moment to escape the stench. Thinking a good fire might dispel some of it, he filled his arms from the stacked wood and set about laying a fire, lighting it from the lantern Stephen had left shuttered near the door. Once it burned well, he took the lantern with him to inspect the hole in the wall, feeling round it, looking for a further hole, a hollowed-out area that might have held a treasure, but he found nothing. He examined the holes in the packed earth. Both his feet pressed together would fit into the largest one, and the depth could cover a fair-sized box or chest. Another was almost as wide, but shallower. Bending closer, he found a splinter of wood the size of a small finger, jagged, partly stuck in the earth. Easing it out, he noticed one side was smooth, as if polished. He examined the axe and spade handles but found no gouges the size of the splinter, nor were the wooden handles so polished as the one side. He tucked the splinter into his scrip and continued to examine the holes that pocked the floor. The rest were small, shallow, and contained no debris.

He climbed up to the bed tucked under the eaves. The white-washed walls were plain, no line of flowers as down below. A nail near the bed held a fragment of cloth, green wool. Part of a wall hanging, something Costen liked to look at in bed? A chest in the corner held a clean linen shirt, braies, stockings, and a long wooden box containing pens and jars of ink, the wood no match for the splinter he had found. Nothing the murderers wanted.

Down below he settled by the fire, which was beginning to mask the stench a little, and looked round the room, wondering about the life of the solitary inhabitant. What had torn apart his marriage? Who had hated him so much to torture and kill him, then destroy the beauty he created and toss it on his corpse?

Not all the beauty had been destroyed. A tapestry was missing, and possibly the large piece Costen had mentioned to his estranged wife. Taken as payment for the deed, along with the coin?

Where were Costen's torturers today? Toasting each other in a tavern here in the city? Or riding out to report their deed to their master? Riding northeast, towards Raby Castle? Neville's men would be experts in such violence. The thought chilled him. But to what purpose?

On his way home for the evening, Owen stopped at Robert Dale's shop to show him the splinter of wood he had found at Costen's. The silkiness of the wood on one side reminded him of the boxes for the golden lion. Could it be?

Robert took the splinter in hand, not even bothering to look down at it as he ran a finger along it with care. After a moment, he smiled up at the ceiling. 'My work. One of my boxes. But larger than the one for the golden lion.' A sigh. 'Now shattered. It would take a strong tool to do this much damage to the oak.'

'A spade or an axe, I think.'

He nodded. 'One of those would be sufficient, used with some force.' Robert put the piece aside, never having glanced at it. More and more he behaved as if completely blind.

'You are a goldsmith, but you take pride in these oak boxes.'

'I can no longer do the delicate work with which I made my name. My journeymen and apprentices do that, with my guidance. But I can still work with wood. It is a matter of feeling along the grain, feeling how it wishes to be carved. I can fit the pieces together. It is remarkable what one can do with the hands. Quite delicate work. So, yes, I take pride in them.'

'How long ago might this have been made?'

'Difficult to say. Even when my sight was far better I took pleasure in making the presentation boxes.'

'Do you recall making one for Costen van Peelt?'

Robert coughed, his face flushing. 'This was one of the items smashed by his murderer? I am sorry.' He tilted his head, frowning. 'But it was a gift for another. I cannot think why it would have been in his home.'

'A gift for his wife?'

Robert cleared his throat. 'A woman, but I am quite sure not his wife. I did not pry, but his insistence on secrecy, some of the things he said, suggested a lover.'

'Could you tell me what the item was?'

A shrug. 'I see no harm. A silver plate, an oval, with a golden swan at the edge. He provided the gold for the swan.'

A swan, a symbol of mating for life, for a woman not his wife. 'I see.'

'Yes. Puzzling that the box was in his home. Perhaps he kept it after presenting the plate. A pity.' Robert shook his head. 'The catch was a gold swan feather.' He smiled.

'Could you tell whether it was a romantic gift?'

'I assumed so. I recall a tenderness in his voice, a sparkle in his eyes, and joyful anticipation. I miss being able to read so much in a face, though I still hear quite well, and it is surprising how much one can sense in a voice. Such as that I have frustrated yet excited you.'

A good description. 'I am no stranger to the heightening of some senses when one loses half of another.'

'Of course. Your left eye. Then you do understand. You asked how long ago, and I would say at least five years, when my sight was still sufficiently good to enjoy the work, though one of my journeymen assisted with the swan. I told him nothing of the customer. I hope this is of help.'

'It raises new questions, which might be the very ones to lead me to the murderer. I am grateful for your time.'

TWELVE

A Spider, a Witness, a Rumour

The drama played out above Owen as he lay in bed shrugging out of the night's dreams, his worries rushing in to set his heart racing. Buzzing about, the fly seemed invincible, with its speed and ability to walk sideways and upside down. But then, from the corner of his good eye, Owen noticed the spider on her web, moving slyly, slowly, spinning it out to the edge of the fly's path, then creeping away, just far enough, and waiting. The fly spun, climbed, dipped, and touched the edge of the sticky web. It felt the tug and tried to pull away, only to make it worse, now a delicate wing stuck, now another leg. Fluttering, fighting, worse and worse.

With a curse, Owen looked away. Is that what had happened to Costen? Had he danced too close to the web, thinking himself invisible, invincible? Martin had said that spies were spiders, spinning webs, catching the unwary, a dirtier business than pirating, which was bold and honest. Owen had laughed. Piracy honest? But he understood.

Had Costen been caught by the spies? Perhaps not. The brutality of his murder suggested something more personal. The destruction of his art, mauling his hands . . . Owen glanced up at the web. In the place of the struggling fly was a wrapped bundle, a meal set aside for later.

At this fraught moment the realm was likely full of victims who had flown too close to the spies' webs, and some of them must be in York. But perhaps not Costen. As much as the man's murder haunted him, Owen had other concerns that might point to trouble for the young king. Might the theft of the golden lion be a warning? Bolton's murder seemed so. Were they connected?

Spiders. Flies caught in webs, sticky, their squirming costing them their freedom. Squirming. Harrigan had squirmed yesterday under Owen's and the assistant schoolmaster's regard. What did he fear? That Owen might ask him whether the accusation was true? But with all on his mind, Owen had neglected to ask Hugh or Gwen what exactly Edwin Scardburge had said about Pippa's father. He must remedy that.

The morning was dry but cold, with a sharp breeze that rattled the late-summer plants and blew Hugh's red hair round his face as he concentrated on holding a heavy piece of wood straight out in front of him, practising the exercise that would strengthen his arms for the longbow. His eyes flicked to his father coming down the garden path, but he moved nothing else.

'Da,' he said through clenched teeth.

'A tight jaw does not help, son. If you clench your teeth whenever making an effort, you'll be toothless when you're half my age.'

Hugh did not move.

'Have you broken your fast?'

'I do this first.' He glanced at Owen with a worried expression. 'Why?'

'I wanted to talk to you.' But clearly not regarding whatever Hugh was expecting.

Face reddening to match his hair, Hugh glanced again at him, this time the distraction causing his arm to wobble. 'I didn't step on Emma's doll. It wasn't me.'

Mystery solved. 'I know nothing about that. I need to know what Edwin Scardburge said about Bertram Harrigan. Just as you remember it. The comment that upset Pippa.'

'Oh, that.' Hugh lowered his arm, breathing hard while frowning in thought. 'He said his da said, "The goldsmiths wonder where Guildmaster Harrigan got so many gold coins that the lion was one quarter his." And something like, "We did not know he had such a brick trade."'

Owen tried not to smile at his son's error. 'Brisk trade?'

Hugh shrugged. 'I think he was calling the guildmaster a thief.'

'I see.' When Owen escorted Edwin to his father, Scardburge
had asked nothing about what his son had said to upset Pippa
Harrigan, but took him to task for talking about things that were
none of his business and being unkind. He knew, or guessed, his
son's insult. 'Good lad. Now eat something before your muscles
weaken with hunger.'

With a nod, Hugh set aside the piece of wood and headed into
the house.

As Owen walked through the gates into the minster close, he
considered the implications of Scardburge's comments. A quarter
of the lion – no wonder his daughter felt they were ruined. A
few had claimed to have seen Bolton at Harrigan's shop the night
of the apprentices' party. Had they some dealings? Had Neville
given Bolton gold to buy assistance and Harrigan had benefitted?
But that would not explain Bolton's presence at the party for the
apprentices – he would have been with Harrigan. No, it seemed
more plausible that Bolton was not just a spy catcher, but also
a thief.

But that left Owen with the gold Harrigan had accrued. He
did not like to think the guildmaster was taking money from a
spy for the French or Spanish. The man irritated him, but he'd
thought him honest.

'You are making a habit of arriving in a thunderous mood,'
said Michaelo when he opened the door and stepped aside to let
Owen enter.

'My mind is in knots.'

'This does seem a complex web.' Michaelo motioned Owen to
a chair by the hall fire.

Owen repeated what Hugh had told him, and his thoughts
about it.

Brother Michaelo listened with a growing expression of despair.
'If Bolton stole the golden lion, and a second thief killed Bolton
for the gold, we may never recover it.'

'I know.'

Michaelo frowned and shook his head. 'But I find it difficult
to understand why someone so favoured by Sir John, and poised
to prove his worth by catching a spy, would have taken the risk
of stealing the golden lion.'

'Many a heretofore wise man has been felled by greed.' Owen took off his hat and ran a hand through his hair. 'Constable reminded me that Bolton accompanied Neville to his brother Alexander's enthronement.'

Michaelo paused to gaze up at the ceiling for a moment, then nodded. 'Yes. I recall him now.' He poured Owen some wine. 'Despite your frustration, you are making progress. Perhaps Lord Neville will enlighten you further. I found a messenger to carry the letter to him at Raby Castle. He left a while ago.'

Owen took a drink. 'Your efficiency astounds me. I pray he finds Neville there.'

'I have thought of that. You might wish to send a messenger to Sheriff Hutton.' In the northern part of the Forest of Galtres. 'I overheard Crispin Poole talking with fellow merchants about Sir John Neville's building works there, and that he has the king's permission for a market and fair at the site. It is possible that someone at the works might know whether Sir John is at Raby.'

Owen thought of Costen's drawing of the old manor house at Sheriff Hutton. 'How did you hear this?'

'I had gone to Poole for his signature on letters I had prepared for him.'

Brother Michaelo offered his services as a scribe for select people in the city, primarily clerics, as well as Archdeacon Jehannes and Owen. Jehannes had suggested the arrangement upon Archbishop Thoresby's death, which had left the monk with a choice of returning to St Mary's Abbey, where the abbot made it clear he was not welcome, or finding another Benedictine community willing to take him.

'I might go myself if things are calm at the staithes.' A long ride might give Owen time to sort his thoughts on the theft and murders. The more he considered it, the better it sounded. 'If we leave by mid-morning, we should be home at nightfall.'

'We?' Michaelo looked anything but enthused.

'While I'm at King's Staithe with Hempe, you might arrange for two horses at Bootham Bar. I should not be there long.'

'Why choose me to ride with you?'

'You will remember all you hear, and notice what is left unsaid.'

Michaelo raised a brow. 'You become skilled in the art of persuasion.' He nodded. 'I will await you with the horses at Bootham.'

On his way to the staithe, Owen called on John Scardburge. The shop had not yet opened for the day's business, and Owen found Scardburge breaking his fast in his hall. When young Edwin caught sight of him, he covered his black eye and backed away from the table.

'I am not here for you. I hope to talk to your father.' Owen nodded at John Scardburge. 'Might we have a word in private?'

'Of course.' The goldsmith led him out to his office behind the workshop.

'Despite your reassurance to my son, for which I thank you, I imagine this has to do with him?'

'Not him, but what he said. I would like to know why you questioned where Harrigan acquired sufficient gold coin to boast that a quarter of the golden lion was his.'

'Merciful Christ, he said so much?' Scardburge pressed his forehead. 'I had no idea he'd heard.' Owen noticed a slight glitter to the man's fingers in the lamplight, the mark of a goldsmith who kept a hand in the actual work in his shop.

'According to my son, he did. I ask about it because I am investigating two murders and the theft of the golden lion at a point in time in which I'm also concerned for the security of our shipping. Spies often buy information, some in gold coin. You see why I need to know more. And why I ask you not to repeat this conversation.'

'Spies buying information in gold coin. I see. Yes. That is clear.' Scardburge's dark eyes sought out Owen's with a plea. 'I cannot vouch for the accuracy of what I am about to say. Which makes it all the more troubling that my son repeated it.' He shook his head. 'They hear everything.'

'My children as well. I am not here to judge.'

'It's known in the guild that Harrigan pads his accounts to keep his place at the head of the guild. But in fact his business has not grown. He hasn't the benefit of artistic talent such as Robert Dale or a talented journeyman such as my man, Henry Wyman, and he has lost clientele to us.'

'Is there more?'

'It's said he's met with men late in the evenings, when the apprentices are finished for the day. Not guildmembers, and one a merchant for whom there is little respect in the city.'

'Any names?'

'I would rather—'

'You are helping the crown in talking to me.'

'Of course. The young king's mother. Yes.' Scardburge steepled his hands and pressed them together, then released them to his sides. 'I know only two. Rolo Creswick. You are aware of his reputation?'

'He had quite a loss, a shipment—'

'Only the most recent failure.'

'The other name?'

'Wulf Gifford. A newcomer to York. Though a guildmember, he's a shipper, not a goldsmith.'

Geoffrey's father, Peter Ferriby's cousin. That troubled Owen. 'Your source for this?'

'I do not wish to involve them. The household has suffered a loss . . .'

Owen could guess. Celia Overton's house looked out on Harrigan's; her companion had suffered a terrible loss. But he preferred to be certain. 'I repeat, you are helping the crown. Your source will have no trouble from me. But you will if you do not tell me.'

'My wife's godmother, Celia Overton.'

'Dame Celia found this worth mentioning?'

An embarrassed shrug. 'She is ambitious for her goddaughter's husband. Believes I would make a better guildmaster.'

She might be right. 'One more question. A witness noticed you at Harrigan's shop the day of the theft, looking angry. Did you two argue?'

Scardburge closed his eyes for a moment. 'So it's come to this, all spying on one another?' He shook his head, then looked Owen in the eye. 'I told him he was a fool to keep the golden lion in his shop, that he must heed your warning. I am sorry I was so right. *You* were so right.'

'Much trouble might have been avoided, yes,' said Owen. 'Thank you for your help.' As he took his leave, he paused. 'Your son's black eye. Has someone examined it?'

'The Riverwoman assures us that it will heal well.'

'I regret my son's tactics.'

'Edwin was in the wrong. But you might warn your son that I intend to give Edwin a lesson in defending himself.' Scardburge grinned.

Owen chuckled. 'I will do so.'

'I appreciate your asking after him.'

The staithe was buzzing with activity. Owen and Hempe stood back, listening to the chatter of the workers moving barrels and boxes off Graa's ship and stacking them on the landing. A calm sea, no trouble, all good news. Not so pleasing to the workers was the news that the ship would depart in the evening, meaning they must rush to unload and then reload before sunset. Clearly Graa and his partners were following the advice to keep their ships out of the clutches of Lancaster.

'No one unexpected on the staithe,' said Hempe, 'except for the young woman pacing off to the side.'

Owen had noticed her. She wore a green cloak that reminded him of the one Gwen had loved, stained in the ordeal that had robbed her of most of the hearing in one ear. Though Kate had cleaned the cloak and mended the tears, Gwen had never worn it again. He wished the woman more joy in her green cloak, though at the moment her uneasiness as she paced and watched the men's movements seemed to consume her. Curious, he approached.

'I could not help but notice that you seem worried,' he said. 'Is there someone you need to speak to?'

She took a step back from him, glancing round, shaking her head. 'I am to tell my m—master when the ship is reloading. But no one seems to know, so I wait.' She spoke with an accent much like Martin's.

Close up, the cloak was not Gwen's. It was worn, with a tarnished clasp, likely passed down from the family for whom she worked. 'Your master has items being loaded today?'

'Why else would I be here?' She averted her eyes.

'Who is your master?'

'Rolo Creswick,' she said, then bit her lower lip and glanced behind her, as if fearing punishment for misspeaking.

A curious coincidence, to encounter the man's maidservant after Scardburge mentioned him. His lost shipment explained his concern, but why send a serving woman? Owen sought out the captain's mate and asked when the reloading would begin.

'I'd say three hours. It will take that long to offload, Captain.'

Owen delivered the message to the woman, who hesitated, as if unsure whether she trusted him, then thanked him and hurried off.

A shadowy figure separated from the crowd to follow her. A woman, he thought, by the way the person moved, though the cloak concealed her skirts. And now he noticed Martin in the crowd, watching the women with interest, moving to follow them. He would ask him about it at home. For now, Owen returned to the captain's mate and asked whether they had encountered any problems on their journey.

'None to speak of, though we slipped away from one ship that seemed to be looking for trouble.'

'Well done.'

The mate nodded. 'The crew deserves a rest, but we're ordered to reload and head back out. I'm sure you know why.'

'God speed to you.'

When he rejoined Hempe, he asked about Creswick, mentioning his conversation with Scardburge.

'You're right about the lost shipment. It happened almost a year ago now, I think. Lotta knows more. Why? Does that woman work for him?'

Owen told him what she had said, and mentioned her accent.

'I am not surprised. Her mistress is from Bruges, or at least that is where Rolo Creswick met her. Left for Bruges a widower, returned wed to Christine, apparently from a merchant family. Lotta says she's been a good mother to his children from the first marriage, and given him another son.'

'She has been in York for a time then?'

'Seven, eight years, I think. They are a quiet family, not very active in the guild, neither he nor his father ever in the city government. So, you talked to Scardburge about Harrigan. Not my investigation now?'

'I have begun to think the theft might somehow connect to the two murders and perhaps even the spying, so we need to work together. I'm heading out to Sheriff Hutton now with Brother Michaelo. I hope to learn more about Bolton. I will keep you informed. You do the same.'

'Always, Owen, you know that.'

THIRTEEN

Sheriff Hutton and a Fearful City

They heard the building works before they saw them, hammers, saws, men's voices calling orders. As the trees thinned, a high wall rose before them, extending so far it was clear this was the wall for the outer ward. Owen and Brother Michaelo dismounted and led their horses through an unguarded gateway into the heart of the works, an internal wall with two square towers at the corners, and beyond a motte on which stood the original keep, small and out of place now with the fine new walls and towers.

'Sir John assured the merchants that this would remain a modest castle.' Michaelo sniffed. 'Modest relative to Raby, perhaps.'

The York merchants would see this as threatening competition. 'They'll doubtless replace that baily with a larger, more imposing keep.'

Men moved about on scaffolding, others stood down below with chisels and hammers, and lads rushed about with buckets and tools, shouted warnings and orders filling the air.

'Who can tell what's meant for them?' Michaelo wondered.

Hearing voices beyond this inner wall, Owen led his horse over a low, unfinished part into what seemed to be the main stoneyard with piles of cut stone separated into general sizes and benches littered with dusty tools. Three men near the base of the motte were speaking in raised voices and gesturing sharply. Two of them looked as if they had been swimming in stone dust. The third and loudest of the trio was clearly someone of higher rank. One of the dusty pair said something and pointed towards Owen and Michaelo.

The loud one turned and narrowed his eyes to study them for a moment before approaching. He walked with a slight limp, and a scar partially closing one eye stretched down to his chin.

'Captain Archer, I think, though we've not met.' The man

glanced at Michaelo, back to Owen. 'I'm Colum, steward of Sheriff Hutton.'

'I am Archer, and this is Brother Michaelo.'

Colum frowned at Michaelo. 'I'm in need of a priest?'

'Not that I know of,' said Michaelo.

'Dame Magda sent me in her stead to see to your man,' said Owen. The canny healer had met them outside Bootham with the request and Owen had not hesitated to grant it, though how she had known he was headed that way was a mystery she merely smiled about when he asked, noting that Colum would be indebted to him, a good position to be in. He had, of course, agreed. 'Brother Michaelo sees to the injuries of the poor in the minster yard. He's here to assist me if necessary.'

'The old healer couldn't come herself?'

'She is at a birthing. Children do not wait.'

Colum nodded. 'Then I'm grateful to you, Captain. My man had a hard night. Come this way.'

They moved forward into the busy yard, Owen's horse shying as they passed a man splitting stone with a chisel and mallet. He patted his mount, murmuring reassurance.

'I should have thought to tell you to leave them out beyond the wall,' said Colum. 'Ours are accustomed to the noise.'

The horse had calmed. 'I prefer to have them near,' said Owen. 'Extensive works. It looks as if Lord Neville means this to rival Raby.'

The steward laughed. 'Nothing like the great Raby. But with an inner and outer court and a larger keep, it will be impressive.'

Outside a small house tucked into trees bordering the wall Colum indicated where to tie up their horses. 'They'll not be bothered. My man's in here.'

Owen stayed him a moment. 'I've sent a messenger to Raby with news for Sir John, but perhaps he is here?'

'Not here now, but Lord Neville sent word he might be riding to York soon and I should be ready for an inspection. You might see him in the city before he comes here. Have you any word of Walt Bolton? He left for York some weeks ago.'

Owen was glad he had taken the time to ride out here. 'I do. You know him?'

'He's my second. Lord Neville pulled him away on some mission. Was to be gone but a week. It's been three. I could use him back. Did he get himself into trouble? Always likely with him.'

'He was found floating face down in the Ouse.'

The scarred eye twitched. 'Drowned? How did the bloody fool manage that?'

'Not drowned. By the gash in the back of his skull he was dead, or nearly, when he went into the water.'

'Murdered?' He looked away a moment. 'Is this the news you sent to Lord Neville?'

'Yes. You say you don't know what Bolton's mission entailed?'

'That is right.' Colum stepped into the house.

The one room was furnished with simple benches, two box beds in opposite corners, and a pallet by the fire circle on which a man lay beneath a pile of hides. His face was white as death.

'I thought it best to keep him with me,' said Colum. 'It's not much, but more comfortable than the old manor house, where the other workers lodge, and he's not keeping them awake.'

'His name?'

'Alan.'

Owen crouched beside the pallet, quietly introducing himself, explaining that he was here to set his bones and make him more comfortable. Alan's eyes flickered. With care, Owen peeled the hides away, eliciting groans. Beneath, the man lay naked, the flesh of his left arm and left leg purple and swollen.

'When did this happen?'

'Yesterday, as the sun was setting.'

'The limbs look as if you attempted setting them?'

'His brother tried, but he couldn't bear the howling.'

Owen rose. 'I'll need two men to hold him when I'm ready. Do you have brandywine?'

Colum glanced at a shelf. 'We've plenty wine.'

'This will be agony for him,' said Owen.

'Bloody— Of course. Brandywine's to the left.'

Michaelo fetched a stoppered flagon.

While laying out the supplies Magda had provided, Owen asked, 'Why wouldn't Sir John explain what he wanted from Bolton?'

'It's his game. Playing his men against each other. Thinks it keeps us awake, on guard, eager to please him.' Colum's expressive face dripped with disgust. 'He should pray he never need depend on any of us to save his life. But Lady Maud, I would give my life for her.' Lady Maud was Neville's wife.

'She is an admirable woman,' said Owen. 'Would it surprise you to learn that Bolton was hunting for French and Spanish spies in York?'

'Spies? He is clever with languages, that is true. Was. Did he ask for your help?'

'No. I did not have the pleasure of meeting him.'

'He was there three weeks and didn't seek your advice?' Colum shook his head. 'Arrogance. Held himself apart.' He frowned. 'But then how did you know who he was?'

'I found Neville's letter giving him safe passage.' Owen looked to Brother Michaelo, who gave a slight nod. That is all they would share about what they had found.

'What would French and Spanish spies want with York?' asked Colum.

'Information about shipping,' said Owen. 'They're seizing our ships at sea.'

'Doubt he knew much about shipping, but I don't suppose he'd need to. Who killed him?'

'That is what I need to discover. Had he any enemies in York?'

'Not that he said.'

Owen poured a powder into the bowl of brandywine Michaelo held. 'Now I need that pair to hold him down.'

'Of course. You'll want to return to the city before nightfall.'

Later, once the bones were set and Alan was asleep, Colum offered them bowls of brandywine in thanks, and apologised if he had seemed disappointed that they had come in Magda's stead.

'I should have trusted that she would not fail me. But shouldn't you be searching for Walt's killer? And the spies?'

Owen stretched his legs. 'I am. I thought I might learn something of him here. What more could you tell me about him? Why did Neville favour Walt Bolton?'

'He thought him clever. Proud of his bastard? Who can say with Lord Neville.'

Michaelo had sniffed at the word 'bastard'. Yes, worse and worse. Neville would be particularly angered by the murder of his son. 'You said you didn't know of enemies in York, but anywhere else?'

'Course he made enemies. The way Lord Neville plays us, we're all jealous of each other. But not enough to kill him. A husband cuckolded? He was one for the ladies, with a weakness for married women.'

Owen doubted such a man would strip Bolton before dropping him into the water. Unless, of course, his wife had learned of Bolton's parentage and he did not want Neville sniffing round. Still, unlikely.

'Did you meet Costen van Peelt when he came to sketch Sheriff Hutton?'

'Meet Costen? I commissioned him.' Colum turned towards a series of sketches of the building works nailed to the wall behind him. 'He was sketching the old baily and I asked whether he might do some work. Haven't seen him for a fortnight or more. Why? You don't think he killed Bolton?'

Owen ignored that question for now. 'He comes regularly?'

'Weekly for a while. It's rumoured he has a place tucked in the wood between here and York. Where he comes with his mistress.'

That was very interesting. 'Did he know Walt?'

'Couldn't say for certain, but it's likely he would have seen him about.'

'Have you ever met Costen's mistress?'

'I do not pry.'

Owen thought of the silver platter Robert Dale had made for a woman other than Costen's wife.

Michaelo had been moving about the house as he sipped his brandywine, touching the few items while glancing out the windows. 'Where did Walt Bolton lodge?' he asked.

'Here. With me. He'd lived in the village for a while, but one of the husbands discovered him with his wife and . . .' Colum shrugged.

'This is not far from the village,' said Michaelo.

'Far enough.'

Owen slapped his thighs and rose. 'Do you have any idea where Costen's hideaway is?'

'No. I saw no need to pry.'

Brother Michaelo picked up the pack of medical supplies. 'I will take these out.'

Owen gave Colum instructions for mixing the powder for Alan's pain, then took his leave. He found Michaelo talking to a young man.

'You will see the Devil's oak, and a track leading to the water. Not far along it,' the man was saying.

Owen waited until they were mounting beyond the outer wall to ask, 'Costen's cabin?'

'Yes. I believe I noticed the Devil's oak on the way, part of it blackened by lightning. It is halfway through Galtres.'

'Let's find it.'

Tucked into the trees, the dwelling Costen had shared with his mistress was comfortably furnished, a large feather bed draped in a thick green worsted painted with exotic birds and vines dominating the one room. Displayed on benches and shelves were acorns, mossy stones, the skull of perhaps a squirrel, other treasures from the forest. Owen walked around within, carrying an oil lamp lit with the lantern he had brought in case they were late heading home.

'The home of someone who loved the forest,' Michaelo said, touching a stone with the tip of his finger, his voice soft with some emotion Owen could not fathom.

Or perhaps he could. It was the house, cradled by the forest, and the forest brought within. Even the oil lamps had been chosen for their pleasing shapes. A length of silk lay across the bed, a costly deep-blue wrap. Who was his lady?

Satin slippers beside the bed and a woman's rabbit-lined cloak on a hook by the door beneath a man's plain wool cloak were the only personal items. They had left no documents, no clues, except, perhaps, for a wall hanging, a painting on cloth of a small flotilla of ships in front of a city wall. Owen did not recognise it, nor did Michaelo.

'I will take this.' Owen removed the nails that had fastened it to the wall, rolled up the painting with care. The cloth was dark green, like the piece Owen had found above Costen's bed. But he found no tears in this hanging.

'A pity to think all this will rot now he's dead,' said Michaelo.

'Unless the mistress comes to collect what they left behind,' said Owen.

'Will you tell his widow of this place?' Michaelo asked.

Owen glanced round. 'No. It's worth little, and would cause pain. Let's head home.'

As they rode, Owen brooded over Neville's imminent arrival, interfering in the complexities he was juggling. A son's death, albeit one he did not publicly acknowledge, would be considered a personal attack by such a man. He would demand retribution to the extent of the law, intending to ruin the family of the murderer. But with Owen's primary suspect a spy who might be far from York by now, he would be frustrated. The only other man he might name as a possibility was Costen, but his death had rendered it all but impossible to prove his guilt. Perhaps that would not matter to Neville. Anna van Peelt would be ruined. Fortunately, she had Celia Overton's support. Unless Neville threatened her as well. Or had Neville's men already avenged Walter Bolton's death by torturing and murdering Costen? Was he wrong about it being more personal, merely the order of a lord for whom it was so?

'You are thinking of the troubles facing you in the city?' asked Michaelo.

They were about to ride out from beneath the cover of the trees, the fires of those who lived up against St Mary's walls visible in the distance as the sun set. 'Are you not?'

'They are not mine to own. But I will do all I can to help you.'

By the time Owen parted with Brother Michaelo by the minster gate, the streets were dimmed by twilight shadows. Walking down Stonegate, he came upon Martin hurrying along, his cloak wrapped tight round him as he glanced back over his shoulders. Owen felt it, too, eyes on them, unfriendly eyes.

'Has there been trouble?' Owen asked.

'People are unsettled. I am glad you made it home before dark.' Martin's voice was subdued.

'What happened?'

'I'll tell you in the house.'

Owen thought back to the morning at the staithe. He had not put too much importance in how people watched Martin. He should have. 'I would make this right.'

'They are frightened, Owen, for good cause. You cannot change that.'

He could. By finding a spy, any spy, and showing him off to the city, a victory that so far eluded him. 'Did you follow the young woman I spoke with?'

'No. I'd been a fool to linger there, where all are fearful of spies. I noticed people moving away from me, but not before I heard the whispers about my being a Fleming, not to be trusted. I should not have gone there.' Martin looked aggrieved as he glanced back on the street, then opened the garden gate. 'I took myself off to the abbey. A beautiful day should not be squandered, and no one there suspected me of being a spy for the French.'

Lucie met them at the kitchen door. 'I am glad you are home, Owen. And you, Martin.'

He sensed new trouble. 'What has happened?'

'A barge shipment expected in York this afternoon did not arrive,' said Lucie. 'Suddenly people are seeing spies everywhere. Several came to the shop to report their neighbours.'

A panic would make his work all the harder. 'Had I found the spy—'

Lucie caught his shoulders, waited for him to look her in the eye. 'You are doing all you can. You and your bailiffs are not to blame for these difficulties. You can never hope to fix every unhappiness experienced in York. Rest tonight. You've had a long day.'

'And tomorrow will be no easier,' said Martin.

'You were followed?' he asked.

'We will speak of it later.'

Moving towards the welcome warmth of the kitchen fire, Owen sank down onto the settle beside the napping cat and closed his eyes, willing his mind to quiet. A small, furry paw touched his hand, then Ariela crawled into his lap, turned three times before settling. He managed to take the bowl of ale Lucie held out to him without disturbing the cat, and afterwards a bowl of stew and bread, her purring warmth reminding him of the pleasures to be found even in the midst of troubles. His peace was not broken until the children tumbled in to say goodnight, and that was a shattering of quiet that he welcomed.

Once the children were abed, Owen noticed Martin's unease, how he could not sit still, strumming his fingers on the seat beside him, tugging at his ear, glancing out the window time and again. At last, he rose to take himself to bed.

'Before you go, I would know what has you so unsettled, Martin. I think something happened just before I caught up to you on Stonegate.'

Martin nodded. 'As I was moving through Bootham in a small crowd, a man behind me loudly told his companion that I have spent much time at the staithes of late, lurking, and called me a Frenchman. Others hissed and someone threw a clot of mud. God be thanked it was not worse.'

Why would they turn on Martin? People had seen him for months and knew he lived with them. Had one late ship erased their memories? He thought of the staithe this morning and saw the truth of it. Today's worry was not the beginning, but had taken a trouble that had been simmering and brought it to a boil. He had been too busy to notice the warning signs. 'I think you should stay in the house until I've resolved the murders,' he said.

Martin let out an explosive breath. 'You would make me a prisoner?'

'You know that's not my intent.'

'Tilde would love to see you at Freythorpe Hadden,' said Lucie. 'It's a beautiful house. With plenty of land to walk.'

'Run away from the place where I mean to make my home in my last years? That would be a bad beginning.' Martin raked his hand through his white hair and sighed. 'Yet there is wisdom in your suggestion. I am grateful for your concern. I will sleep on it.' He wished them both a good night and departed.

As autumn approached and night came on earlier, a larger crowd of sleepers descended on the minster yard than in summer evenings. Brother Michaelo wended his way among them, a basket of bandages and salves on one arm, a lantern in the other hand. He paid close attention to the boys moving about, looking for one with a bandage round his neck. He thought for a moment he was being led to Flint when a young girl asked him to come help her friend who was bleeding, but the injured child was younger than Owen had described Flint, and he had a gash in his leg, not his neck. Michaelo soon had it bandaged and moved on, catching up to an elderly woman who made it her business to

keep track of the people in the yard. He knew she might be trusted
to be discreet.

'Do you know a lad named Flint?' he asked as he helped her
stick the pole into the ground from which she nightly draped a
tattered blanket for shelter.

'Who doesn't know Flint? He is ever asking for what none of
us can spare, and taking when he can. In trouble is he? But when
isn't he?'

Her face was webbed with wrinkles and her eyes were cloudy
with age, her back bent, but the woman's mind was keen and her
hearing keener.

'He may be badly injured. His throat cut. If you hear of his
whereabouts, or condition, I would like to know.'

'I will listen for word, Dom Michaelo. Anything for you.'

Only when they were in bed did Owen fully recount his day to
Lucie. He'd been reluctant to add to Martin's unease with the
news of Neville's imminent arrival and his relationship to Walter
Bolton.

'Neville's natural son. That complicates matters,' said Lucie.
'It's a pity he's coming here.'

Owen would use stronger language.

'Costen's mistress – I wonder who she might be. Together a
long while, you think. So not an unmarried woman, surely. A
married woman who can slip away into Galtres . . .'

'Any possibilities come to mind?'

Lucie chuckled. 'Are you hoping I keep a tally of married
women seeking love potions?'

He smiled into the darkness. 'I had not considered that. Do
you?'

She laughed. 'No. But I would look for an unhappy marriage,
or an infirm husband.'

He sighed. 'I have other more immediate concerns. I talked to
Scardburge. Magda's seen to young Edwin's black eye. He will be
fine. He mentioned Rolo Creswick and Wulf Gifford visiting
Harrigan at his shop after hours. What do you know of Wulf
Gifford?' Emma Ferriby, Peter's wife, was Lucie's close friend.

'Emma does not care to have him in the house. His wife took
the younger children and went to stay with her mother until he

learns to control his drink. Coming to York was meant to get
him away from bad companions and give him a chance to right
himself. Geoffrey's with him only because he's sharing a tutor
with John and Ivo, and Emma and Peter promised to look out
for him. But it seems Wulf's found new drinking companions. I
cannot guess what business he would have with Harrigan.'

'Nor I. And Rolo Creswick? Do you know anything of him? I
saw his wife, Christine, on the staithe this morning.'

'I do know her. She is a regular customer for my bruise salve,
the strong one with frankincense and woundwort. It is possible
what she has said, that she bruises easily. But a woman seldom
admits to being abused.'

'You think her husband beats her?'

'I thought it possible. It is unusual for a merchant's wife to be
at the staithe, is it not?'

'As far as I know.'

'That is curious.'

In the night Gwen woke them, crying out with another
drowning nightmare. Lucie rose to calm her as well as Hugh and
Emma, telling Owen he needed his sleep. He was grateful.

When Owen went down to the hall in the early morning, Martin
already sat at the head of the hall table, organising pieces of wax
tablets and torn cloth from one of the packs.

'You could not sleep?' Owen asked as he approached.

'Well enough, but I woke early and could not resettle. It
appealed to do something useful with my time.'

Owen reached for a scrap of green cloth that might be part of
whatever was torn from the nail by Costen's bed. 'I hope we can
piece together what this was part of. I believe it was something
important to him. He hung it by his bed.'

'I will pay particular attention to cloth that seems to go with
it.' Martin rose. 'Come. I'll break my fast with you.'

FOURTEEN

Burial, Blood, Slander

The lad who had lingered in the doorway while Lucie saw to a long-winded customer stepped aside to let the elderly woman depart, bobbing his head to her with respect. The woman sniffed and hastened her exit as if to escape his grime, firmly shutting the door behind her.

The boy approached the counter with measured steps, his eyes darting this way and that, his lips moving though Lucie heard no words. Perhaps he rehearsed his request. She guessed him to be a few years older than Hugh.

'How might I help you?' she asked.

'I have coin to pay for what I need,' he said, his eyes hard, likely expecting her to shoo him away. He lifted a coin to show her.

'That is reassuring.' Seeing the shape of the hand, then looking more closely, Lucie realised this was a girl who dressed as a boy. For her safety, no doubt, though the street children were never truly safe. 'What do you need?'

The child tucked in her chin to roughen her voice. 'Something to dry up a cut. So it stops bleeding. And something to put on it so it pulls together and doesn't open up again.'

'That sounds serious. Where is this cut? On you?'

'No. It's on . . .' A frown, eyes wary. 'What difference where it is?'

'Some parts of the body are more sensitive than others. A salve for a leg wound can be harsher than one for the face.'

'It's close to his face.'

'Does it need stitching? I could come—'

'No.' She shook her head. 'I will do it.'

'Was he cut by something clean or dirty?'

'I don't know.'

By now Lucie had little doubt the patient was Flint. 'I can give you something to pack into the wound to encourage the bleeding to stop, and a salve to put on it. Some clean bandages as well. How long is the cut? Is it a clean slice or was some skin removed?'

The girl wrinkled her nose at the last question. 'Clean,' she said, a bit breathless. 'What does it mean to pack a wound?'

Lucie had started to set jars on the counter, but put them aside and lay down her left hand, palm up, separating her second and third fingers a little. 'Say this is the cut, gaping like this.' She pointed to the 'v' shaped opening between the fingers. 'You would tuck the mixture into it and ease the edges together, then put the salve over it and bind it, just tight enough to hold it all in place. Do you understand?'

The girl tilted her head, as if reviewing what she'd heard, then nodded.

As Lucie measured out the packing and the salve onto waxed parchment she asked again, 'How long is the cut?'

The girl spread her hands out about four inches. 'That's what's open. Some of it's just a long scratch.'

Lucie flinched. 'Poor boy. Is the injury in a place that will be easy to wrap? You know, wind it round.' She gestured wrapping something around her neck, then her forehead. 'Or something more difficult, like a chin?'

'Easy to wind it round.'

'Good.' Lucie picked out a long, clean cloth and laid it beside the two waxed parchment bundles. 'Clean the area, including the wound, before you do the packing, and dry it off with a cloth. A clean one, of course.'

'He kicked me when I tried to clean it. I thought he was weak, but he knocked me down.'

'But you're not hurt?'

'No.'

'Does he have a fever?'

'He's sweating and shivering. And hot.'

'Can you find water? Ale? Anything for him to drink?'

'I snatched some wine for him.'

She ignored the confession and fetched feverfew. 'Put a pinch of this in a cup of wine.' She demonstrated a pinch. 'And have him drink, morning, midday, night.'

The girl made a face like Hugh did when complaining that something was too much work.

'I know this sounds like a lot to do, but tending to an injured person takes patience. And he will be grateful.'

'Doubt it. But I don't want him to die if I can help it.'

'He's fortunate to have such a friend. That will be a penny.'

She took a few coins from a small bag beneath her shirt, fingered them, placed the penny on the counter. 'I thought it would be more.'

'Come back when you're ready for a clean bandage. In a day or two.' Lucie handed her the items wrapped together in a piece of cloth she might use to clean the wound.

'Thank you.' The girl bobbed her head and hurried off.

Lucie stepped into the workshop. Jasper had paused in his work, listening.

'Should I follow him?'

'Her. Though she tries hard to look and sound a boy. Yes, follow her. Do not try to engage her, or the lad she's helping. Just see where they are.'

'You think it's Flint she's helping.'

'Don't you?'

Jasper was already heading out.

The early-morning sun shone gently on the cluster of Costen's mourners in St Helen's Churchyard. Not so gentle were the hisses and loud complaints by the people standing on the street to either side of the cemetery, near the guildhall on one side, Stonegate on the other.

'Murderer!'

'Spy!'

'Why should such a sinner be buried among our dead?'

'They judge him without trial,' said Brother Michaelo. 'I will speak with them.'

As he walked away, Geoffrey Gifford took his place beside Owen.

'They're wrong. He was a good man,' Geoffrey said through clenched teeth. 'No one gave him the credit due him.'

'You did,' said Owen.

Geoffrey gave a little shrug. 'I wanted something from him.'

'You saw his talent and you asked him to teach you. That is the greatest compliment you might have given him.'

For a moment, Geoffrey's face cleared and he smiled. But his joy was brief as voices rose, protesting Brother Michaelo's attempts to calm the onlookers. Michaelo returned, lips pursed, jaw tight.

'Ignorant fools,' he muttered.

As the priest spoke his final words over the grave, Anna van Peelt leaned against Celia Overton and wept. Her companion's eyes were dry, but reddened, speaking of an earlier, more private grief. A few neighbours stood behind them. Owen led Brother Michaelo to where Geoffrey had retreated. In the overhang of a house across the churchyard from Owen's home stood a cloaked figure, the size and shape suggesting a woman. He wondered whether it was Costen's love.

As Anna knelt above her husband's grave, her weeping grew louder and Geoffrey bowed his head and wiped his eyes.

The woman in the shadows crossed herself and withdrew down a ginnel. With a nod to Michaelo, Owen took off after her, dodging a cart trundling down the lane between the churchyard and the ginnel, rushing into the darkness. He paused in there, listening for footsteps, but heard nothing, nor did he see her when he stepped out into the next street. She was gone.

The girl walked fast, dodging people and carts as she headed down Low Petergate, around Christchurch, down Colliergate, then ducked left into a ginnel. Jasper managed to keep up, wondering how many customers would be asking him who he'd been chasing. The girl wound her way between houses towards the Foss, finally entering a falling-down shack close to the riverbank, behind a house that looked little better. Jasper waited a few minutes to see whether she had just ducked in there to lose him. A loud moan drew him closer. He peered in through a gap between the roof and a partially collapsed wall. A lantern illuminated a pile of rags on which a lad lay beneath a tattered blanket that fluttered as Jasper watched. The boy was shivering, but sweat glistened on his face. Fever.

The girl crouched down beside him. 'I brought medicine, Flint. See? The lady apothecary was nice. Showed me what to do for you.'

Flint's eyelids fluttered.

Jasper took a good look round so that he could find the shack again, then ran back to the shop.

As he approached the churchyard across from the apothecary, he saw people standing round a fresh grave, and his father and Brother Michaelo moving away. Costen's burial. He crossed himself and went to meet them.

'You look like you've had a good run,' said Owen.

'It's Flint, Da. He's fevered. I think he's dying.'

'Where? How did you find him?'

'A girl came to the shop – she dresses like a boy, but – Ma found out all she could, enough that we guessed she was talking about Flint. I followed her. I can take you.'

'Fetch the Merchets' donkey cart,' said Owen. 'I'll fetch what we might need.'

Jasper hurried on to the York Tavern.

Tupper, the Merchets' groom, led the donkey cart, following Jasper, Owen, and Brother Michaelo. The plan was to stay back and let Brother Michaelo try to convince the girl that Flint needed the abbey infirmary. Owen and Jasper would watch through the gap in the collapsed wall, ready to carry Flint to the cart – or go to Michaelo's aid if he encountered trouble.

Owen could smell the infection from where he stood, and noticed Michaelo pause by the opening, not really a door, to lift a scented cloth to his nose for a moment. Trust him to have one tucked up his sleeve.

'That's her, the one who came to the apothecary,' Jasper said of the child kneeling by Flint, who lay quite still. 'Is his stomach bleeding?'

Owen had wondered why she was pressing a cloth to the lad's stomach rather than packing and binding his throat. The stench alone should speed her to finish the task. He leaned closer, trying to see what she was doing. A tattered blanket had been pulled away and a shirt lifted. Her hands were dark with blood. She was trying to staunch the flow from a more recent injury that still bled. God help the child. Owen motioned for Michaelo to step in. 'Now!' he mouthed. The festering neck, the fresh wound, the loss of so much blood, the boy was in a bad way. Owen fought the urge to rush in, but if she delayed them too long . . .

The girl glanced up with red, swollen eyes as Brother Michaelo entered the hovel.

'Go away!' More a sob than a shout.

Michaelo made the sign of the cross over the two of them. 'I am Brother Michaelo, the monk who sees to the people who sleep in the minster yard. I heard that you might need help.'

'Did she send you?' the girl asked. 'The lady apothecary?'

Brother Michaelo did not answer, kneeling to the shivering Flint and touching his forehead. 'He is burning up. And the neck wound is foul with infection. But what is this?'

'Someone . . . While I was away . . . We're good at hiding. I could swear no one knew we were here.' The girl barely paused for breath. 'I was only out a little while, getting him some food and medicine. And now he's dying. Flint's dying.'

'I came with one who has seen to such wounds on the battle-field.' Michaelo lifted his head and called out for Owen. 'He can help.'

The girl's eyes grew large as Owen stepped through the door. 'The captain.'

He bowed to her. 'My wife told me of your friend. I feared it might be bad. Might I see him?'

The girl looked to Brother Michaelo.

'He knows how to tend such wounds and wants to help.'

When she nodded, Owen crouched beside Flint, bending to sniff his breath, then the neck wound. The boy teetered at the edge. Owen glanced up at the girl. 'You are a good friend to Flint. I have been worried about him. As are you, I see. His stomach – that happened while you were out?'

'Yes.'

'Might I examine it?'

She nodded.

Michaelo offered Owen a rag from the basket Lucie had packed and he lay it over the wound to soak up the blood. Gently lifting it he found a long, deep gash in the stomach. Losing so much blood when already weakened with infection from the neck wound greatly lessened the boy's chance of survival. Owen felt sick at heart.

'I am going to try to stop the bleeding and sew him up,' he told the girl. 'And then we need to get him to St Leonard's.'

'No! They will keep him in the orphanage.'

'I could go for Dame Magda,' said Jasper.

'The Riverwoman. Yes,' said the girl.

Owen fought his impatience with the possible delay. 'I understand. What is your name?'

The girl looked down at her hands.

'Dame Magda calls me Bird-eye.'

She glanced up, eyes widening, and her mouth twitched, though tears fell. 'I'm Robin,' she whispered.

'My son will fetch Dame Magda, Robin. But if she is not available, I will take Flint to St Leonard's and make certain that once he's healed,' which Owen thought unlikely, 'he will be free to leave. I promise you. On my honour.'

Robin bit her lip.

'He will die if we don't get him someplace warm, where they know how to care for such wounds.'

She nodded.

Owen turned, looking for Jasper.

'He's already left to fetch Dame Magda,' said Michaelo.

'Good. Where is the salve that Mistress Wilton gave you?' Owen asked the girl.

She handed him the waxed parchment package.

'I would like you to talk to Flint while I am working on him. Tell him what I'm doing, and that he will soon be sleeping in a comfortable, warm bed. Speak right into his ear. Can you do that?'

'But he's not—'

'He may be able to hear, Robin. He needs reassurance.'

She nodded and scooted closer to Flint's head. Owen motioned for Michaelo and Tupper to be ready to hold down the lad's arms and legs if he began to flail. It took all the salve to create a paste across the stomach wound. Flint licked his lips. Owen noticed a liquid in a small wooden bowl.

'Is that wine?' he asked.

Robin nodded. 'I borrowed some for him.'

'I don't care where it came from. Did Mistress Wilton give you a feverfew powder to put in it?'

She nodded and scrambled to fetch it. Owen sniffed at the powder – feverfew, poppy, valerian. Bless Lucie. He added four pinches to the wine and handed it to Robin. 'Help him drink this.'

'Mistress Wilton said one pinch.'

'What I'm about to do requires more.'

Michaelo offered her a small spoon. 'Drip it into his mouth.'

The blood was caking on the boy's stomach. A shame to disturb it, but moving him without stitching the wound could cause bleeding the boy could not afford. Lucie had added a needle and thread and some milk of poppy to the basket. At the time, thinking of the neck wound, Owen had not been sure his fingers could work so delicately as that would require. But a stomach had more fatty flesh, even in this slender boy. He asked Michaelo to add the poppy to the wine while he wiped the caked blood from one edge of the wound and threaded the needle.

'Time to hold him,' he said, nodding to Robin to keep spooning the medicine into Flint's mouth. It was a good sign that the boy was swallowing. Owen prayed he drank enough, and quickly, to dull the pain he already suffered and that to come. He worked as quickly as he could while battling the renewed bleeding, though the salve had slowed it. At first Flint flinched and feebly flailed, then, towards the end, went limp.

'He is in a faint,' said Michaelo.

'Perhaps for the best.' Owen was working against time. When he had done all he could do, he sat back on his heels and crossed himself. He noticed Robin frantically trying to get Flint to swallow more of the drink, whispering encouragement. 'He's had enough for now, Robin. You've done well. Now we will carry him to the cart. Do you want to come?'

The girl wiped her nose and nodded. Her eyes were red and swollen. Such devotion to her friend. Suddenly she looked behind Owen. 'The Riverwoman!'

Magda and Jasper hurried towards them. Owen showed her what he'd done, and the neck wound.

'Thou hast a steady hand for such stitching,' she said, touching the boy's forehead, bending close to sniff his breath, then the neck wound. 'He needs Magda's care, but the journey to her house is too far for the child. Come. Magda has a friend at St Leonard's.' When Robin began to protest, Magda took her hand and looked into her eyes. 'Magda will watch over him this night, and visit often so long as he must remain there. When he is able to choose, he can walk away, Magda promises.'

Robin nodded.

Owen tore off a door dangling from a hinge and he and Jasper shifted Flint onto it, then Michaelo and Tupper helped them carry him to the cart. They were a solemn procession through the streets.

Robin paused in her pacing and glanced up as Owen stepped out of the undercroft of St Leonard's that housed the children. 'Can the Riverwoman save him?'

'She will do all she can for Flint. He's sleeping now.' Magda was unsure the boy would make it through the night, and had suggested he should die with a friend at his side. 'You might stay with him if you like.'

Her face brightened. 'I would—' She looked down at her legs and shook her head. 'Can't.'

'They will say nothing about how you are dressed, Robin. They'll understand it's for protection.'

She looked up, her dark eyes searching his face. 'You knew all this time?'

'My wife told me.' He did not want her to fear her disguise was not good enough. 'It would have taken me some time. Would you like to be with him?'

She nodded. 'He's always good to me.'

'Before you go in, I need to know more about what might have happened. I want to find whoever did this to him.' He held out a bowl of ale. 'Drink?'

The girl took the bowl. 'The throat or—'

'The more recent wound, while you were away. That was intended as a mortal wound.'

'A slit throat is a faster kill.'

She was so young to know that. 'Was it just the two of you in that shed?'

'During the day. At night more come in. We all share.' She took a long drink of the ale, nodded. 'That's good.'

Owen watched her drain the bowl while he considered his next question. A number of the street children stayed in that shed. Any one of them might have been coerced into betraying Flint. 'Have you noticed anyone following you? Standing about?'

'I swear I wasn't followed when I went to the apothecary. Swear it.'

Owen gently touched her skinny shoulder. 'I did not mean to suggest that. I'm hoping you might have seen the person who hurt Flint and not realised it. Have any of your friends? The ones who sleep in the shed?'

'No one said so.'

'Costen van Peelt said that Flint came to him offering information. He thought someone sent your friend to him. Do you know anything about that?'

She bowed her head. 'Master Costen is dead,' she said softly. 'Murdered.'

Costen's death had disturbed her. 'Yes.'

'Do you think someone thought Flint killed him? That's why they hurt him?' She glanced up, her eyes frightened.

He thought of the velvet-lined box. 'Perhaps that he was a part of it. Or that he witnessed his murder.'

'Flint would never have hurt Costen. He was good to all of us.'

'Then you have suffered a great loss. But the attack on Flint might have had nothing to do with Costen. Do you have any idea what information your friend might have been offering?'

She shook her head.

'I want to keep Flint safe. If you remember anything, or if any of the others do, will you leave a message for me at the apothecary?'

'I will.'

'Come within. You'll be warmer sitting with Flint, and I'm sure Dame Magda will make certain they give you something to eat.'

Owen had stopped in the shop to let Lucie know how it had gone with Flint. Now he sat by the kitchen fire with a bowl of ale and a purring cat on his lap, stroking Ariela and thinking of Flint, the hollow belly that he had stitched closed, the amount of blood lost, the pain the boy could not endure. Had he done enough? Too much?

'I've killed him,' Martin said, slumping onto the settle beside Owen. 'I've murdered a boy.'

It took Owen a moment to pull out of his thoughts. 'You're wrong. Magda said the neck wound was not deep and would have healed easily had it been cleaned and bound right away. But the stomach wound is deep and caused much damage. Someone meant to kill him. He may die, yes, but not by your hands.'

'A small blessing. But I weakened him, rendered him vulnerable.' Martin said nothing else for a while, though he shifted and muttered as if agitated. He suddenly turned to glare at Owen. 'You went without me. I should have been the one to go to him. Why did you say nothing to me?' His eyes burned.

'I thought only of getting there as quickly as possible. What more could you have done?'

'I need to go to him, sit with him, tell him I will do penance for what I did to him for the rest of my days.'

God help him. That would be the worst thing for the lad. Owen risked putting a hand on Martin's shoulder. 'I understand why you want that, but it's not best for him. If he wakes and recognises you, he will be frightened. You know that. Besides, his friend is with him.'

Martin began to pull away, then stopped, shaking his head. 'You're right, damn you. Why should he trust me? I am thinking only of myself.' He turned to stare at the fire, head in hands. 'It was bad enough to be useless. But to harm a child – I am worse than useless.'

The despair Owen saw in Martin's eyes troubled him because he knew how that poisoning of the soul pushed a man into desperate deeds, risks that welcomed death. 'You are helping me piece together what Costen's murderer destroyed. I might not have known he'd been to Sheriff Hutton but for you. You found Walter Bolton's clothes with the hidden list and the letter identifying him as Neville's man.'

'And in doing that I injured the boy.' Martin's voice was flat.

'Flint harmed himself. Instead of standing still, he chose to risk being cut.'

Martin rounded on Owen. 'I am not one of your children, to be soothed with half-truths.'

Owen had no time for this. But he could not leave Kate and the children with a volcano about to erupt.

'They are not—'

'Uncle Martin, I have a garden with a wall,' Emma said from the doorway to the hall. 'Come see.'

Martin's face softened as he turned to her. 'I will be right there.'

In that moment Owen realised what he needed of Martin. 'I have a favour to ask of you. If I show you where I found Flint, would you go there at twilight, see whether you can befriend the young ones who shelter there for the night, try to learn something, anything about who might have wanted to harm him? Who they worked for?'

Martin turned halfway to where Emma waited. 'Another attempt to soothe me?'

'No. My men are stretched thin, I need the place watched, and you have a gift with children.'

As Martin glanced back at him, Owen could see the truth of it register in his eyes.

A sharp nod. 'Let me see what Emma has found, then we'll go.'

While Owen waited for Martin, Kate's sister Rose arrived to report that she had not seen Flint in Holy Trinity churchyard.

'I was about to come and tell you we found him this morning,' said Owen. 'Dame Magda is caring for him. Do you know anything about one of the street children, Robin? Dark-eyed, wears boy's clothing?'

'I don't. But I can try to find out.' Rose grinned. 'What's she done?'

'She tried to save Flint. But someone attacked him again when she left him alone for a while today.'

'Do you think this girl was paid to leave him alone?'

'I believe she thought he was safe, but I'd like to be more certain.' Rose gave her sister an apologetic look. 'I am in no hurry for this. Stay a while with Kate. Coax her to sit by the fire.'

The sisters had their heads together, laughing and talking over each other, when Martin came out to the kitchen. Owen hastened him out the door.

'Beautiful and dangerous,' Martin said under his breath as they started down Davygate.

'Rose? I do sometimes worry what I've unleashed on the city with her and her brother, but especially her. He's a good tracker, but she has a way with people, making them feel special so they tell her all they know.'

'Poole said much the same. I will watch my tongue with her.'

'You've no need.'

They'd not gone far when Martin asked, 'You are serious about me and Flint's friends? Last night you wanted me to stay in the house.'

'I think you're safer out and about at night, and that's when I need you. You easily befriended my children and I'm hoping you can do the same with them. I can't think how else we might coax them to talk.' He recalled why Martin had been delayed. 'What had Emma found?'

'A drawing of the abbey grounds, I think. When I invited her to help me I did not expect her to have a gift for this. She goes quite still and moves pieces about, finding patterns. I was not aware that such a young child could do that.'

Neither was Owen. 'I'm a little jealous that it was you who discovered it.'

Martin laughed. 'If she needs protection it is you to whom she would run. And you whom she loves. I am merely new.'

'And that is exactly what might bring the street children to talk to you.'

'Shall I confess to them that I've been a pirate?'

'I would be disappointed if you didn't.' They had arrived at the falling-down shed. It was deserted for the moment, though the smell of blood and the fevered wound lingered.

'Go on with your day,' said Martin. 'I will look round, then go back to work with Emma while I think how to dress, how to approach them this evening.'

FIFTEEN

A Petty Man, Gold, a Puzzled Goldsmith

Owen left Martin studying the area, deciding where he would set up the watch at dusk, and continued on to Peter Ferriby's shop. On arriving, he found Peter instructing his nephew Luke as to the lengths to cut and wrap for a customer, rich reds and a gold brocade, as well as a dark velvet – brown, perhaps, though there was a greenish sheen to it.

'Have you decided you need more elegant cloth for your court clothes?' Peter asked with a wry smile. Owen guessed from his good spirits that business was going well.

'I fear that will come,' said Owen, 'but my immediate need is information. Might we talk in your office?'

'Come this way. Luke, while you prepare that, watch for customers.'

Peter motioned Owen to a high-backed chair in the office, something comfortable for customers spending good coin on fabric. 'How might I help you?'

'It's about Costen van Peelt.'

'Costen.' Peter crossed himself. 'The family prayed for him when we heard.'

Owen did not like what he needed to ask, but he must know. 'Forgive me, but according to his widow you were the one who reported Costen to the guilds, which resulted in his losing the few customers he had for his cloth. I do not believe it.'

Peter gave a soft cry and shook his head, his face reddening. 'That old rumour. It's a lie. It was a lie then and it is now. I never reported him. Why would I? He was an artisan producing his own cloth and could never have sufficient stock to compete with me.'

'I wonder how Anna van Peelt came to think that?'

'Because someone signed my name to the letter they sent to the guildmaster. Or rather the scribe put my name to it. And the guildmaster waved away my protest saying if I had not reported him I should have. That was not the point!' He pounded the arm of his chair, his face red, eyes on fire. 'A damnable business.'

'A horror for you. Forgive me for bringing this up.'

Peter gathered himself and waved away the apology. 'I understand why you would ask. And I thank you for not believing it.'

'Did you see the letter?'

'I did. And I told the master that was not the hand of the scribe I employ. But he wasn't interested.'

'Do you have an idea who did this? And why?'

'I searched for the scribe, but no one would own the work.' Peter grunted, looked down at his hands with a sigh. 'I have an idea who was behind it, but I do not like to say.'

'Costen was brutally murdered, Peter.'

'It's not good business to point the finger.'

'And if someone else is murdered?'

Peter wiped his brow, glanced out the small window that opened onto his own garden as if checking whether he might be overheard. 'You will not spread the word?'

'You need not ask that.'

'Forgive me. Creswick. Rolo Creswick. The customer who cannot in good conscience pay what he owes me.'

The Creswicks again. 'He's a member of the Merchant Adventurers?'

A short, sharp guffaw. 'Yes, if you can believe it. He failed at the trade, but was kept on the rolls by our soft-headed guildmaster. Creswick fails at all his endeavours. They say it's his wife's money that funds them.'

'Why say that you were the one who complained?'

'His word is clearly worthless in the guild.'

'And his refusal to pay you what he owes, and spreading lies about you?'

'A man in a corner will do anything to bring others down with him.' Peter sighed. 'I can think of no other reason. I have never crossed him. My fool of a cousin befriended him when he moved here, in the house next to Creswick. They drink together at The

Bell in the late afternoon, according to Geoffrey, where fellow guildmembers won't see them in their cups.'

Scardburge had connected both men to Guildmaster Harrigan. Time for another visit.

The guildmaster of the goldsmiths was in a temper when Owen arrived.

'My fellow goldsmiths are convening a meeting tomorrow to vote me out. Put Scardburge in my place, I've no doubt. That my fellows would so betray me. By the rood, I will not stand down without a fight!'

'I am sorry to hear of your trouble,' said Owen. 'I could return later . . .'

'No. Forgive me, Captain.' Harrigan wiped his brow. 'This is not your problem to solve. Is it about the golden lion? Have you found it?'

'No. But questions have arisen in the course of our investigation of the theft.'

Harrigan had collected himself, his face returning to its normal ruddiness. 'How might I help?'

'I've been informed that both Wulf Gifford and Rolo Creswick have had business with you after hours.'

'You've been informed?' Harrigan's momentary calm evaporated and he shot up from his chair and pounded his fist on the table. 'Spying on me, are they? Who told you that?'

'I am simply gathering information, not attacking you.' Owen kept his voice calm and waited for Harrigan to take a few breaths. 'Is it unusual to meet with clients after the shop is closed?'

'No.' He shrugged. 'Though rare, I admit. And inconvenient. Still, I cannot imagine why someone would mention it.' The unease in his eyes belied that comment.

'Why don't we sit and discuss this?' Owen took a seat at the table and waited while Harrigan resumed his with much fussing about the drape of his sleeves, clearly embarrassed by his outburst. 'I remind you that I am investigating two murders and the theft of the golden lion, representing the crown, the city, and you.'

'Yes, of course.'

'What is your business with Wulf Gifford?'

Harrigan cleared his throat. 'He came to me Monday evening,

after hours, as you said, offering me gold coins, thinking we would be replacing the stolen lion. In exchange for silver coin. I told him I was not in the market for more.'

'More?'

'He was my source for much of the original gold, his offer, which I had gladly accepted.'

'I see. But there has been no discussion of a second lion?'

Harrigan shifted in his chair, moved a tally stick a few inches, wiped his brow. 'The guild cannot afford to create another.'

'How much gold did Wulf Gifford originally sell you?'

'More than half my share.'

'And you claimed a quarter of the stolen lion was your gold.'

'Did I?' His colour was rising again. 'Well, you know, I am the guildmaster and need to set an example. But I might have exaggerated.'

'How much is he offering now?'

'It sounded as if the same amount again.'

Where was Gifford accruing so much gold? 'Did he seem eager to trade it?'

'He approached me. I did not go to him. I don't know him well, though I know his cousin, Ferriby. I've done nothing wrong, Captain.'

'As I said, I am gathering information, nothing more. How did he respond when you refused to purchase more?'

'I would say he was annoyed, implying I was ungrateful, insulting me. He reeked of ale, so I tried to appease him, telling him I understood, that silver is much more practical in day-to-day exchanges, not everyone has the coins available to provide the change. But I could not help him. I called for my journeyman, fortunately working late in the shop, a large man, asking him to fetch some wine, and at the sight of him Gifford excused himself and hurried off. Much to my relief.'

'A most unsettling encounter.'

'It was not my journeyman who told you of it?'

'No.' It sounded as if Gifford was in trouble. Perhaps he was trying to rid himself of gold that would raise questions about his trade. Who was paying him in gold? It was nothing Harrigan could answer. 'And what of Rolo Creswick? What was his business with you?'

'His visit was more of a puzzle. Not after hours, but before the shop opened the following morning. He described a silver plate to me, decorated with a golden swan, wanting to know if it was my work. It was not familiar to me. He seemed disappointed when I would not say who might have made it.'

Costen's gift, Robert Dale's work. 'Did he say why he wanted to know?'

'I presumed he was in the market for a similar item, but he said he was merely curious about it. He meant trouble. I could feel it. And to wake me for that.' He muttered a curse.

Owen remembered Lucie's advice about Costen's mistress, that he should look for an unhappily married woman. Christine Creswick? Had her husband noticed the plate, and was trying to trace whoever had commissioned it? If so, he may have given himself away as one of the men who murdered Costen. 'Anything else?'

'He warned me against trusting Wulf Gifford, informing me that his son Geoffrey has been sneaking visits to my daughter Elaine.' Warning Harrigan against his drinking partner. Curious. 'I didn't know what to make of it, and what that had to do with the silver plate. But coming the morning after Gifford's visit, I wondered how they might be connected.'

Owen wondered as well. 'I know Geoffrey. He's a good young man.'

'I agree. I had not known about him and my daughter, but I am not alarmed by it. Well, perhaps a little, considering the father. But I cannot fathom Creswick's purpose. He seemed to expect gratitude. I did not ask him to spy on my daughter, or my business. I told him to see to his own concerns.'

'How did he leave you?'

'With a curse. I'd heard of his troubles, and that he'd likely brought them on himself, and I believe it now. Who would wish to trade with such a man? A shrew in men's clothing.'

'You have been most helpful,' Owen said as he rose.

'Have I? Gifford surely did not steal the lion. He's trying to rid himself of gold. But Creswick . . . Do you suspect him?'

'I do not yet know what to think of all this. And I would ask you not to speak of this conversation with anyone.'

'Of course, Captain, of course.'

Gifford and Creswick. Had they cooked something up while in their cups at The Bell? And then Creswick thought to turn on Gifford? It made no sense. But perhaps it would in time.

Owen had noticed the shop next to the Gifford house on Colliergate when calling on Geoffrey, but not the house behind it, a tidy two-storey with a linden sapling shedding its leaves by the front door. The maidservant with whom Owen had spoken at King's Staithe responded to his knock.

'Captain Archer, sir. The master is not at home.'

He had counted on that. 'Perhaps I might speak with your mistress?'

'I will see.'

He turned to study the shop, a wax chandler, which explained the strong scents of beeswax and tallow. He glanced over to the Gifford house, its front garden neglected. Wulf spent none of his gold on his home, that was plain.

'Captain?'

Christine Creswick stood in the doorway. She had dark, deep-set eyes, a wide mouth, brown hair caught up in a simple crispinette. The sleeves of her green gown were protected by cloths and she wore an apron. Not too fine to participate in the housework.

'Forgive me. I have interrupted your work.'

'No, I pray you, I would enjoy a moment away from it. Come in, Captain. I am sorry Rolo is away.' Her speech was more accented than either Costen's or Martin's.

The fire circle was cold, and with shutters open to let in what little sunlight shone down between the surrounding houses there was a chill to the hall. She led him to a pair of high-backed chairs near a shelf holding an oil lamp, motioning him to sit.

'I will tell Maud to bring some wine.'

'That is not necessary.'

'Not for you, perhaps, but for me. And I dislike drinking alone.' As she moved towards a passage to what Owen guessed were the kitchen and storerooms, a boy about Emma's age ran to her. She caught him up in her arms and said, 'Shall we see what your sisters are doing, my prince?'

He saw no sign in her of a woman humiliated, possibly beaten by her husband. Instead, she seemed calm, steady, assured. But one might practise such a demeanour.

When Christine returned with Maud, who carried small bowls and two flagons, she had removed the apron and sleeve protection. 'I will pour,' she said, dismissing the maidservant. Owen noticed she added a little water to her cup. 'Is this about my presence at the staithe?' she asked as she sat back.

Owen added a little water to his wine as well while he chose his words. 'No. I can think of no graceful way of asking this. It concerns Costen van Peelt.' He stopped, interested by the change in the woman's expression, from open and friendly to closed, wary. 'Forgive me, but his murder is of course a worry to all the city, and I am gathering as much information about him as I can. In the course of it, I have learned that your husband was the one who reported to the guild that Costen was selling his own wool cloth.'

'Oh.' Her expression softened. 'Oh, that.'

'He signed Peter Ferriby's name to the letter. I was curious whether there was some history between your husband and Costen.'

Touching her temples, Christine closed her eyes for a moment, gave a little nod, then looked at him with a wry smile. 'You were wise to approach me with this rather than my husband.' She folded her hands and Owen sensed that the words that followed were chosen with care. 'Rolo claimed that Costen van Peelt had stolen his customers and ruined him.'

'But surely Costen could not produce sufficient cloth for that to be true.'

'No. It is only one of the litany of things outside his control that have ruined every business venture my husband touches. And why I have taken over what little trade we still have.'

Owen began to understand. 'Which is why it was you at the staithe.'

She inclined her head.

'Why put Peter Ferriby's name to the letter?'

'Jealousy. He believes men who marry into noble families need not work, that wealth is bestowed on them by marriage. He's a fool, Captain, and I am sorry that others suffer for it.' Owen could not help but raise his brow at her blunt lack of affection for her husband. 'You think me unnatural. But were you forced to live with him, you would understand.' She touched her cheek as if checking for a blush. 'Have you any idea who killed Costen? Van Peelt?' She quickly added.

'I have ideas, but nothing definite. It is clear that one of his attackers had a violent temper.'

Her eyes were dark with imagined pain. 'You believe more than one attacked him?'

'I am certain of it.'

She averted her eyes as she crossed herself. 'The poor man. He seemed a kind, gentle soul. Who would do that to him?'

'It is my task to find out,' said Owen, rising.

'I was sorry to see the unfriendliness towards your friend Martin Wirthir on the staithe. As I, too, am from the Low Countries, I wonder how safe I am. And my children. Perhaps I should take them to my father in Bruges.'

He heard a false note in this, an attempt to shift attention from her. 'We are doing all we can to find any spies in the city.'

'I am grateful, Captain.' The lack of emotion in her voice confirmed his suspicion.

As Christine Creswick led Owen to the door, she paused and touched his arm. 'A warning, Captain. Be discreet in any discussions concerning Rolo. He has a sharp, cruel tongue.'

'Slanderers do not trouble me. But thank you for the advice.' As he reached the door, he asked, 'I noticed the Giffords are your neighbours. Geoffrey, the son, admired Costen van Peelt. He wished to learn all he could about his drawing technique.'

Christine glanced away. 'Did he? How sad for the young man, to lose his teacher.'

'Do you know them, Wulf and Geoffrey Gifford?'

'My husband talks to Wulf. I have not. And the boy is too old to play with my children.'

He found it a curious, careful response. He turned towards the Hempe residence with questions for Lotta, particularly about any connection between Christine and Costen. The conversation had increased his interest in the Creswick family.

SIXTEEN

Street Children

Coming up to his room over the apothecary to change his shirt after spilling an oil, Jasper glanced through Martin's open door and saw him bent over a pile of clothing lying on the floor next to a leather pack.

'Are you going somewhere?'

Martin glanced up. 'Preparing my costume for this evening.'

'I thought you were going to talk to Flint's and Robin's friends.'

'I am. If I look more like a pirate than a merchant they might be more likely to talk.'

Jasper laughed. 'You're good at this.'

'I hope I am.'

'Emma thinks you are. She's changed since she's been helping you, grown more confident.'

Martin picked up what Jasper had thought a leather pack. He shook it out. A jupon, worn, but it was still handsome, with finely worked leather. 'What do you think? Could I look less like a citizen of this fair city?'

'I've never seen a merchant in such a jupon. But Da has one.'

'I know. He looks better in his than I do in mine. But with my hair tied back, this and leather leggings and boots, and missing a hand – they might find me interesting.'

'Don't stay too late. I'll be waiting to hear all about it.'

Before settling at home for the evening Owen called on Anna van Peelt, thinking she might be glad to have the painting of the harbour. At first there was no answer to his knock. Stepping back, he noticed no light in Celia Overton's window onto the street, but perhaps she had not yet lit the lamp. He knocked again and a young woman opened the door just far enough to peer out while holding a lantern up towards his face, a foolhardy approach to self-protection. An intruder determined to enter would have yanked the lantern from her hand and in her confusion pushed her inside. He shook himself from such thoughts.

'I have something for Dame Anna.'

'The goodwife and the mistress are out.' Also foolish, announcing that she was alone.

'Do you know when they might return?'

'I could not say.' She retrieved the lantern with some difficulty, clearly not the one who usually answered the door.

'If you would just tell her that Captain Archer has something of her late husband's to give her.'

'Yes, Captain.' And with that she shut the door.

Twilight on the day of her husband's funeral seemed an odd time for Anna van Peelt to be away. Perhaps she and Celia were with friends, or in church.

'The mistress is up with Gwen, giving her something for her stomach,' Kate said when Owen asked where everyone was. 'I think she might be with her a while. Hugh and Emma are telling her tales to calm her.' She grinned. 'Dragons and ghostly tunnels, Master Martin's tales with their own favourite additions.'

Owen smiled to think of the merry sickroom and decided not to add his worry and gloom to it. 'Does Gwen have a fever?'

'No. She was in the apothecary workroom mixing a powder and laughing so hard at Jasper's japes that too much mallow root went up her nose.'

Owen surprised himself by laughing. Mallow was a mild purgative in small doses, which for a child were very small. 'She will have a mighty hunger tomorrow.'

'I will go out to the baker at first light for the finest pandemain to have with honey.'

'Suitable for a queen,' said Owen. 'And easy on the stomach.'

'Sit by the fire and I will bring you ale and something warm to eat, Captain.'

He put his feet up before the fire and gathered the threads twisting round in his mind. Once again Lotta Hempe had proved a valuable source of information. Christian de Bruges, the cloth trader who brought Costen van Peelt and his friend to York in partnership with Celia Overton's late husband, was the uncle of

Christine Creswick. At some point Celia Overton's late husband took over their sponsorship, a curious change.

Or perhaps it was not so mysterious. Christine might have met Costen through her uncle. She clearly felt something for Costen, an affinity she was keen to hide. Was she his mistress? If so, and the silver platter with the golden swan was his gift to her, it would explain Rolo Creswick's interest and her effort to disguise the connection. Another thread that might connect with Costen and Christine was Walter Bolton. If Bolton had seen them together in Galtres, they might have felt threatened by his presence in York. It might even explain the confrontation on the riverbank, Costen trying to ensure Walter Bolton's silence. Whether that was motivation for murder, he could not say. And he might be too eager to tie this up neatly.

Martin moved through the twilight shadows, reaching the shack without trouble from the townspeople. Hearing nothing within and seeing no flicker of fire, he moved on past it and settled on a low wall near the river. While he waited he wondered about the property, whether the shack and wall were the ruins of a house and garden or a business, perhaps a warehouse. Odd that in the crowded city it stood vacant, unused except by the homeless children. It was a cruel world for them, cold, uncaring. He pushed aside his pity, remembering the pride with which he held himself when on the streets, disdaining those who expressed sympathy but wanted him away. It was quiet on the river at this hour, no traffic moving up or downriver in the dark and the tide not yet rushing out. The church bells, so loud where he lodged, seemed farther away. An occasional splash or flutter in the river below him hinted at the fish and waterfowl who doubtless took advantage of the peace to hunt for food. He wondered whether the children who gathered together in the shed appreciated the peace of this place. Peace was not something he'd thought about as a child, indeed rarely as an adult.

Sensing movement behind him, he turned to see small, shadowy figures moving into the shed, and suddenly a fire bloomed in the stone circle in the middle. The young ones spoke in hushed voices as if fearful they would be told to move on.

Someone approached, put a foot on the wall beside Martin.

'The shed is ours. We want no trouble here.' The speech was delivered with strength and the lower pitch of an older boy.

'I come in peace to bring word of your friends Flint and Robin, and a warning,' said Martin. 'Might I speak to the group?'

'Where are they? Why should I trust you?'

'They are safe at St Leonard's Hospital. Flint was attacked here this morning while Robin was fetching medicine for him. Stabbed in the stomach. He lost much blood and is very weak. The Riverwoman is caring for him.'

'How do you know this? Who took him there?'

'I would prefer to tell all of you at once. Would you ask?'

'You're the one the Riverwoman calls Pirate.'

His reputation preceded him. Martin smiled into the dark. 'I am.'

'I will ask.'

Martin watched him join the others. In the firelight he recognised the youth as one of Magda's river lads who took turns guarding her coracle on the bank and rowing people out to her rock at high tide. He'd thought they all belonged to families in the shacks outside the walls. This was fortunate. He watched as the others bent their heads close to listen to him. Some bobbed their heads, one fled the group, disappearing back into the darkening city. A few more moments and the older lad approached.

'They want to hear the tale,' he said. 'The Riverwoman's friends are our friends.'

'I feel the same.' Martin followed him into the shed, where he was offered an upturned half barrel to sit on.

He looked round at the shadowy faces, gaunt for the most part, a mix of ages, perhaps a dozen, only three obvious girls. 'Your friend Flint was badly injured today. It was lucky that the apothecary Mistress Wilton was worried the injury Robin described might be more than a friend could handle, and asked her apprentice to follow and see how bad it was. When Jasper saw the stomach wound freely bleeding, he fetched help.'

'Stomach,' someone whispered.

'Nosey,' another said.

'My friend Captain Archer did all he could for Flint, and then they took him by cart to St Leonard's with the Riverwoman. Robin is with him.'

'Will he live?' asked a long-haired waif that might be a girl, at least by the voice. Which would make it four girls.

'I will not lie to you. Dame Magda does not know. That's why she invited Robin to stay.'

'His neck was bad, but this sounds worse.'

Martin flinched at the mention of the neck wound, but nodded. 'Right in his belly,' he said. 'Deep. He lost much blood.'

'Who did it?'

'That is what the captain means to find out. I came to ask for your help. To learn whether you have noticed anyone watching Flint. Following him.'

'The captain of the city doesn't care about one of us,' said the older boy he'd first talked to.

'I think he proved he does with his actions today,' said Martin.

'Why is Captain Archer a friend to a pirate?' asked one of the girls, older, with fierce eyes.

Martin chuckled. 'That is a long story that I will be happy to share another night, if you like. But I am here tonight to help find Flint's attacker, and to warn you to watch yourselves.'

'We always do,' said the older girl.

'Until we find out who attacked your friend and why, you might be in more danger than usual. Whoever hurt him might want something they think you have.'

'I see,' she said. 'I do see. Flint's not always careful. I saw him talking to the man who was murdered in his home, the one who draws the city.'

'He was Robin's friend,' said one of the lads.

Several nodded and murmured agreement.

'And there's a man who always wears a cloak and hood who asks about him,' said a boy.

Again, several agreed, but the group argued about whether the cloaked person – none of them had heard them say much – was of the merchant class.

'It's a fine cloak,' said the older girl.

Before Martin headed home, bone weary, he told them a tale about Owen's skill as a bowman in Wales, and about the time they walked through a haunted tunnel. They invited him to come again.

※   ※   ※

Owen turned from his study of the kitchen fire as someone opened the door, sending the flames dancing. It was Martin, dressed as if ready for travel in a leather jupon, slumping down onto the bench just inside to remove his boots. His face was red from the wind, rain, and exertion, but it did not mask the shadows beneath his eyes. He might still fit into his old clothes, but he was no longer the man who had worn them.

'Come join me,' said Owen.

'Some stew?' Kate asked as she handed Martin a bowl of ale.

'Thank you,' said Martin, 'but this is sufficient for me. I'm soon for bed.' He eased down by Owen and set the bowl aside to warm his hands near the fire.

'Forgive me for sending you out in such weather,' said Owen.

'They had a good fire, and offered me ale. I did not suffer.'

'Did you learn much?'

'No, but I pray I convinced them to come to you with any information. Some did say that Robin and Costen were friends.'

'Friends. But she did not seem to know anything about Flint offering Costen information.'

'Or does not care to tell you. What have you learned?'

'I'm not certain.' Owen shared his thoughts about the connections.

'I would count that a good day's work.'

'But I've nothing on the golden lion, except that Gifford is hoping the guild will make another. I would love to know why Creswick has turned on him.'

'Sounds like the sort who turns on all, given time.'

Owen would not argue with that.

Martin tilted back his head to drain his bowl, then rose. 'I am for bed.'

'Thank you, my friend.'

Martin grinned. 'I enjoyed it. I promised them I would return to tell them the tale of my unhanding.'

'Make it bloody and cruel.'

'It was. And I will admit to it being my fault.'

'I disagree. The man who cut off your hand believed people in power would permit him to express his delight in cruelty.'

'But I pushed my way into his home.'

'You have carried that weight all these years?'

'One should never forget profound lessons. And now to bed.'

'Thank you again. I hope to talk to Robin in the morning.'

When Martin had gone to his room above the apothecary, Owen finished his stew and went up to see his ailing daughter. He found the three children and Lucie, her arms round Gwen, sleeping peacefully. Pulling the bedclothes up to keep them all warm, he slipped out.

Sometime in the night he woke to Lucie slipping in beside him.

'Gwen's stomach has quieted?'

'Yes. Poor thing, she learned a valuable lesson about laughter and powders today. I am grateful it happened with something harmless.'

He kissed Lucie and pulled her close. 'I forget the dangers of your profession.'

She touched the scar beneath his blind eye. 'The threats are less visible than in yours, but just as deadly.'

'And now two of our children are embracing it. God help me. I may never sleep again.'

SEVENTEEN

A Missing Child and an Unwelcome Visitor

The building housing the children at St Leonard's was well away from that for the adults, tucked into a corner where their play would not disturb those in the main hospital. Owen and Michaelo arrived while the children were breaking their fast, so the only people rushing about were the lay brothers and sisters at their chores, and one boy about Hugh's age squatting near the door using sand to scrub a large bowl.

'Are you a kitchen helper?' Owen asked.

The child frowned up at him. 'No. I dirtied it, I clean it.'

'You're doing a fine job.'

The boy shrugged and bent to his work and Owen thanked God his children were free to be children.

Brother Michaelo put a hand on Owen's shoulder as he knocked on the door. 'Whatever the news, you did all that you could for Flint.'

'I know. I'm most worried that Martin will believe he's the cause of Flint's death.'

The door was opened by a young woman in simple garb and coif. 'Captain Archer, Brother Michaelo, benedicite. Dame Magda said to lead you right to her.' She smiled. 'The boy made it through the night. I thought you would want to know first thing.'

'That is good news.'

Flint lay in a small, plain room. He looked tiny and pale as death, but his breathing was far better than when Owen had left him the previous day. Magda was stirring something in a small pot over a brazier.

'Where is Robin?' Owen asked. Kate's sister Rose had caught him at home earlier, eager to tell him what she'd learned of the

girl. Robin and Flint were close, often worked together, and he
gave her pretty things he'd collected, which she was said to hide
in various places in the city. The others teased her about her
hoards, but respected her as the best one for slipping into houses
unnoticed. Having learned that Robin and Costen were friends,
Owen was even keener to ask her whether she dropped the velvet-
lined box at Costen's after his murder, or whether the small buckle
he found in the fire had been hers.

'She sat with him through the night but would not stay past
the dawn,' said Magda.

Owen cursed himself for not coming sooner. 'Do you know
why she left?'

'Magda sees that look in thine eye. The child may have noticed
as well. Guessed thou wouldst have questions for her.'

'And doesn't want to answer them.' Fearing the murderers
would find out she had talked.

'Thou wilt see her soon enough,' said Magda. 'It will be difficult
for her to stay away. How else will she know if he is healing? For
now, he needs peace. And Magda.'

Brother Michaelo had been praying over Flint. Owen crouched
beside the pallet to look at the neck wound. It was clean and not
so angry as the previous day, nor as rank.

'Bless Lucie for sending Jasper to follow Robin to Flint,' said
Michaelo. He looked up at Magda. 'And bless you for your skilled,
loving care.'

She chuckled. 'Save thy blessings for those who find them
comforting.'

'When might Flint talk?' Owen asked.

Magda's clear blue eyes burned into him. 'He will talk when
he will. Thou knowest such healing cannot be hastened. In a few
days he might answer simple questions. But the wound on his
throat festered. His voice might not be as it was.'

'Martin will be grieved to hear that.'

'Say nothing to Pirate for now. Youth are hardy.' She reached
for Owen's hand, pressed it. 'Thou shouldst know, John Neville
is in the city.'

Too soon. 'Do you know where he's lodging?'

'No, but thou wilt hear. He will want to know everything about
the death of his man.'

'It is worse. Bolton was his son. Unacknowledged, but he favoured him.'

'This thou heard at Sheriff Hutton?'

Owen nodded. 'I have an idea who might have murdered him, but no proof. Do you tell me this because you have some insight?'

'Magda can sense thy frustration. Do not doubt thyself. The baron believes there is power in making noise. But there is none. Do not bend to him.'

'Like Thoresby.'

Magda smiled. 'In the end Old Crow wore his power lightly. Neville expected great honours after holding Brest so long as the old king's steward. Now he must start afresh with a child king who does not value him.'

'How do you know this about him?'

'Magda listens.'

A shower of needles over his blind eye had already begun while Owen sat in the kitchen, intensifying when Kate hastened to answer the knock at the hall door. Now it was a torrent. Standing over the end of the table where Martin had been working, his back to Owen, was a tall man in a finely tailored cloak, a felt cap with the fashionable drape round the neck covering much of his silvering dark hair. Magda had warned him, but not that John Neville, Baron of Raby, would appear in his hall unannounced, and alone. As Owen had entered the room a tremor had gone through his guest and he had lifted a gloved hand to his brow. Emotion? Had he just learned of his son's death?

'Lord Neville,' said Owen in a softer tone than he might have used a moment before.

Sir John turned. 'Archer.' The shadow of his beard accentuated his lack of colour. He gave a slight nod, his expression blank. 'What is this puzzle?' He had a low, resonant voice.

'Debris from a murder scene.' Owen drew a cloth over it and motioned the baron to a seat by the fire. He did not like that he had shown up in his home without forewarning, without an escort from the mayor or sheriff, and with no lackey to see to his needs and protection.

Since Neville had arranged for his brother Alexander to become Archbishop of York, the baron had done what he could to assist the city in keeping the king's peace; but if that were his purpose he would have gone first to the sheriff and the mayor, and either or both officers would have sent Owen word that Neville wished to talk to him. He had not, and his well-tailored but modest attire – Owen had never seen him in such muted colours and fabrics – suggested Neville did not wish it widely known he was in York. Or not yet. He had guessed the moment of emotion correctly. This was about his son. Personal.

Kate entered with refreshments. Owen set a small table near his guest and took the tray with thanks. While pouring wine, he mentioned seeing him in London during the coronation festivities in July.

'The festivities, yes,' said Neville with a bitter sigh. 'You were privileged to lodge with the king's mother throughout. I was afforded no role in the ceremonies.' The Duke of Lancaster had taken up the office of steward for the coronation proceedings, which placed him in charge of choosing who would fulfil the numerous ritual offices or roles. He had afforded no place in the ceremonies to John Neville, Baron of Raby, who had glowered throughout the celebrations.

'I was honoured to serve our king,' said Owen, 'but those of us keeping the peace had little sleep.' He had often been roused to investigate rowdiness or escort the young king to an unscheduled meeting, and when he had the leisure to lie on his pallet, the day's impressions would tumble round in his head, the competition among the nobles for the young king's attention, Richard's petulance, his mother's unease, and an overall sense that the kingdom was on the edge of a precipice with no clear commander taking charge. Knowing Neville's reputation for cunning and ambition, Owen wondered now whether some of that unease was fomented by the late king's former steward. He settled where he might see Neville with his good eye. 'I was unaware you were in York.'

'I am on my way to the building works at Sheriff Hutton.' He searched Owen's face as if expecting surprise.

That suggested he did not yet know of Owen's recent visit there. 'I heard you'd received a licence for a fair at the old castle.'

'A Monday market and the feast of the Holy Cross.'

'September. A good time.'

'Next year.' Neville sipped the wine, sampled the cheese, gave an appreciative nod, though his eyes were haunted. 'I hear the Fleming Martin Wirthir is lodging with you.'

'Is that why you've come? King Richard has given Martin permission to bide here in peace. We consider him part of the family.'

'I am aware, and I've no problem with that.'

'Was it my letter? Can you have received it so quickly?'

Neville was quiet a moment, studying Owen as he sipped the wine. Again a tremor moved through him, his expression darkening, jaw set. He put the wine aside and leaned forward, as if to impart a confidence. 'I received no letter, but I know you can guess why I have come to you, Archer.' His voice was quiet but strained, as if tightly controlled. 'It is about the murder of my man, Walter Bolton. I expected to meet with him, but the sheriff tells me he is dead.'

He had already spoken to the sheriff, yet called on Owen unannounced. He meant to catch him off his guard. Perhaps he blamed him. What had the sheriff implied about it? 'We believe it is him. Did you view the body?'

'I did.'

'Is it your man?'

'Yes.' A glitter of emotion in the usually cool eyes.

'Why did you not have the sheriff send for me?'

'I preferred to speak with you alone. You have Walter's belongings?'

'I do.' Owen did not have time for this dance. 'But before I give them to you, I need more information. Your son arrived in York carrying a letter of safe passage, yet he did not make himself known to the sheriff, the mayor, or myself. Why?'

Neville had grunted at the word 'son'. 'My bastard. How did you know?' He had lost some control over his voice, the volume increasing.

'I spoke to Colum at Sheriff Hutton.'

'Why would you go there?'

'As I explained, I wanted to know why your son was here. I ask again, why did he not make himself known?'

'I do not answer to you,' Neville snapped.

'I disagree. I am captain of this city and retained by the king's mother to protect the north. Your man Bolton – your *son* – carried a letter of safe passage and introduction, yet he did not make himself known to the city or shire authorities as is the law. We found in his clothes a list of ships, sealed, incomplete, but some of those ships have met with trouble. Where did he acquire that list? What did he mean to do with it? What happened to the person from whom he acquired it? If he caught a spy, where is he?' Owen did not flinch as Neville rose from his seat to lean into him, a threatening posture that served only to stoke his temper. 'Bolton had no prisoner with him when he retrieved his horse. And why in God's name did he not simply ask if he might be of help in our watch for spies? Why the secrecy?'

The usually cool eyes burned in Neville's now crimson face. 'I will not tolerate your questioning my son's actions.'

'You came to me here, in my house. You are welcome to leave.'

Neville stepped back with a chilly grin. 'How do I know you did not discover him and put him aside?'

There it was, his suspicion. 'It was my wife who discovered him, floating in the Ouse.' He paused. 'If he was on a mission to catch our enemies' spies, he would have had my help – had he asked.'

'Pah.' Neville's face twisted and he turned away as he resumed his seat.

But Owen had seen the emotion. He had cared for his son, no matter that he could not acknowledge him. 'I wager you don't know why he did not make himself known,' he said softly.

'You mentioned a letter,' Neville said in a more measured tone.

'I wrote to inform you of Bolton's death, and that I intend to find out what happened to him. A messenger carried it to Raby and I took a copy to Sheriff Hutton, thinking you might be there.'

Neville watched the fire, not meeting Owen's eye. 'He was murdered. Someone in your city murdered him.'

'That I know. What else can you tell me? Where might he have lodged? Did he know anyone here? Why would he attend a party for the apprentices of the master goldsmith?'

Neville turned back to him, his eyes narrowed. 'Goldsmiths? Have you found the golden lion? The meddling Lady Carlisle's inspiration?' He muttered the last part, a curious comment.

'No.' Was that relief on his face? 'We have not. You do not think the golden lion an appropriate gift for the king?'

'I could not say,' Neville said with impatience. 'I am here about Walter. You say he attended a party for the apprentices?'

'In celebration of the completion of the king's gift. It was held for Harrigan's apprentices at his shop, the very one from which the lion was stolen, likely that very night.'

'You think he attended the gathering intent on stealing the piece?'

'It crossed my mind, and it may have occurred to someone else. His murderer.'

'You are eager to condemn him.'

'I want answers. I want to understand what he was doing here, why he chose to act alone, how he came to possess the shipping list, and if he took it from a spy, what he did with him. Why he chose to attend a party where he could not hope to be overlooked. Did he expect the spy to attend?' Owen paused for a response, but when none was offered, he added, 'I cannot rule out the possibility that Bolton stole the golden lion. Nor that he was killed by the spy he thought he had cornered.' Owen sat back. 'Were it my son, I would want answers.'

Neville steepled his ringed fingers and closed his eyes for a moment. 'He wanted to prove himself worthy of a more important position in my household.' He spoke quietly now, keeping his gaze on his steepled hands. 'I'd heard rumours there were spies in York gathering information about our shipping for France and I wanted to seize them and present them to King Richard.' A fleeting smile as he finally looked at Owen. 'I have experience in naval battles, and I have proposed myself for the counteroffensive. But King Richard prefers his late father's men, and Lancaster, well, he prefers his own, so I am in need of something to offer the king, to catch his attention, convince him to consider my proposal. Walter proposed he would precede me to York and gather evidence, and when I arrived we would catch the spies. Together.'

'Had he some experience? Did he know anyone in the city?'

'No to your first question. He was to ingratiate himself with Constable,' said Neville. 'I had provided sufficient funds for him to buy the sheriff's cooperation. I fully expected Constable to involve you, but with the understanding that you were working for me.'

Had Walter Bolton followed his father's plan, Owen might have but one murder to solve, perhaps none, though so far he did not see how Costen's murder might have been connected. Even if he had killed Bolton, who would have avenged his death by murdering Costen, and with such passion?

'Are you certain he was alone here?'

'That was the plan.'

'No servingman travelling with him?'

Neville snorted. 'He was a bastard, not a baron's heir. You say you talked to Colum at Sheriff Hutton? Had he mentioned a companion?'

'No.' But Owen had not thought to ask. He cursed himself for that. 'It would appear he had his own plan about how to handle his work for you.'

'Yes. And in his arrogance he managed to fail me and get himself killed, is that what you're thinking?'

'I want answers, that is all. I want to know whether the spy, if he took the list from a spy, murdered your son and then fled the city.' But there was too much wrong with that.

Neville watched Owen. 'You don't think that's what happened.'

'Why would the spy strip him and hide his clothes without searching them? He might have acquired the letter of safe passage as well as the list.'

Neville grunted. 'I understand a Fleming was seen arguing with Walter at the river on the day he died. And that he's now dead.'

'That is true.'

'A theft and a pair of murders and no spies caught.' Neville leaned forward, and in a quiet voice said, 'Tell me this, Archer. You call yourself captain of the city, and I know that the king's mother has to all effect entrusted the north to your care. Yet in a time when our navy is key to the protection of the realm, and spies are clearly in York to learn what they can to use against us, you are gentle with these people, no house searches, no detainments. Our king depends on you to find the spies and stop them. And if that requires entering homes and searching, that is what you must do. Is your connection to the people of York hobbling you? Can you not perform your duty?'

A cool thrust of the dagger right to the gut. 'Your son's secrecy complicated my investigation.' Owen rose. 'I will bring you his things.'

'You have all of them?'

'All that he had with him on his departure. His horse is at the stable outside Bootham Bar. Will you be staying in the city?'

Neville had the good sense to look away. 'I'm riding to Sheriff Hutton today, but I will return tonight and stay until I have some answers. I am not a patient man, Archer.'

Not trusting what he might say, Owen went to fetch the pack.

Neville was standing by the hall door when Owen handed him Bolton's things.

'I am not finished with you, Archer.' Neville strode out without a backward glance.

EIGHTEEN

A Tale of Two Tempers

Owen stormed through the kitchen and out into the garden, walking swiftly to the shed, where he plucked up the axe and headed to the woodpile. He rubbed his hands together, lifted a cut log to the chopping block, raised the axe, and brought it down so hard the wood jumped as it split, a piece falling onto his booted foot. With a few more logs he worked up a sweat in the warm morning sun and paused to shed his shirt before continuing. He fell into a rhythm, his mind emptying, able to see the damning truth in what Neville had said, the truth he'd spoken. As much as he blamed the man for entrusting his inexperienced son with a serious mission, he might be right in pointing to Owen's reticence. He *was* hesitant to search homes and question those he distrusted, but with the realm considered vulnerable under a boy king, all must do their utmost to prove that wrong, to ensure its safety. What was he waiting for? He turned his mind to the threads of his investigation, what he had connected last night, what he had learned from Neville. The pile of split wood had grown to waist height round him when, as he raised the axe, he heard a voice behind him.

'What is it, Owen? What has happened?'

It was Lucie, keeping a safe distance, her eyes wreathed in worry. 'Stripped to the waist and flaunting your muscular back and arms would enchant me if I had not seen the fear in your children's eyes. They say you stormed through the kitchen without a word, rushing out the door.'

He set down the axe, knocked the piece still there off the block, and sat, raking his sweaty hair from his face. 'A plague on the Nevilles. He handed his bastard a task for which he had no experience, providing him with sufficient funds to do harm, and now he questions my ability to perform my duty to the king.' He wiped his brow. 'And some of what he says is right.'

'Ah.' Stroking his hair, Lucie leaned down to kiss his cheek. 'Put your anger to a better purpose than splitting wood. We now have sufficient to see us to Advent. And do it for you, the city, and Princess Joan, not for the Nevilles. That family does not care what you think of them.'

'I blame myself for my too cautious approach. But I begin to see a way.'

'As you always do.' She took his sweaty hand. 'Come sit with me on the bench and tell me all that was said. It will help you decide your next step.' She smiled. 'And put on your shirt so that I might think more clearly.'

He did not deserve her. Catching up his shirt with his free hand, he followed her to the bench. She offered him a cloth to dry some of the sweat before dressing, teasing him with an account of how his habit of removing his shirt to cut wood had tormented her with desire before they were married. He felt himself calming.

'Now we can talk,' she said when he was dressed. 'Tell me all that was said.' She watched his face as he recounted the conversation, her eyes worried, then angry. 'How dare he,' she muttered when he spoke of Neville's criticism of his caution. 'The mayor and aldermen offered you the captaincy because of the care you take never to storm into someone's house and accuse them based only on rumour or desperation. You are trusted. Respected. How dare he presume to tell you what to do.'

'There was some truth in it. I am careful. Perhaps too careful in this instance.' He scraped back his sweat-tangled hair. 'Yet now I need to act before he does something to endanger the innocent. And I need to keep before me the danger we all face with the world's perception that England is weakened by King Edward's death, that King Richard is too young to protect it. Neville's forced my hand, but the urgency is deeper than that. And, in faith, he should be in the south offering his services to the king. We need him. But he won't leave until he has answers.'

'I see. Do you have ideas?'

'Gifford and Creswick are trouble. Both Creswicks, I think.'

She touched his forehead between his eyes. 'You feel it here? What Magda calls your third eye?'

Magda believed that his partial blinding awakened an ability in him, clear-seeing, she called it. With her guidance he had learned to trust it. 'I do.'

'Then you see your path.' She shifted on the bench, but stopped. 'An odd comment about Lady Carlisle. Meddling. Did the golden lion mean something to Neville?'

Owen thought back to the odd relief. What had he just said? That he had not yet found the lion. 'He was relieved I'd not found the golden lion in his son's pack?'

'Perhaps it meant something to Walter Bolton.'

Owen encountered a group of goldsmiths climbing the steps to Robert Dale's home behind his shop, overdressed in finery for the warm morning, their faces flushed, the feathers in their hats limp from the heat. Bertram Harrigan stood at the foot of the steps urging each man as he passed to remember all the good he had done in his time as guildmaster. It had come to this. But for Owen's purpose, it was a timely gathering. As long as Robert Dale was not already upstairs.

To his relief, Robert greeted Owen at his office door and welcomed him in.

'We are about to meet to discuss whether Harrigan should be replaced. They chose my home so that his family need not serve the men who might be voting against their head. It all smacks of school-boys taking sides in a schoolyard argument.' He motioned Owen to a chair. 'I am hiding here until Harrigan joins them upstairs.'

'The meeting is well suited for my purpose,' said Owen. 'I will be quick. I would like the guild to offer a ransom for the golden lion, or information that leads to its recovery. A sum sufficient to encourage someone to step forward.'

Robert shook his head. 'We all stretched our budgets to create the gift for the king. I cannot imagine anyone being comfortable with your proposal. And to reward a thief?'

'I did not say you would hand over the money – at least until it was recovered on the strength of their information. But it might inspire someone to speak up.'

'Why now?'

'Because Sir John Neville is here, angry about the murder of his man, and I want to resolve the troubles before he inspires more.' He could be honest with Robert, to a point.

'Ah. So we would offer a large ransom, but you would take over from there. Would we indicate that those claiming to know something should come to you?'

He had considered that, but deemed it too threatening for most. 'No, to Archdeacon Jehannes.' Who was not entirely delighted by the prospect, but had agreed.

Robert frowned down at his hands, then nodded. 'I will think how to bring this up. But I cannot promise they will agree.' Someone knocked three times on the outer door. 'My daughter's signal. I must go up.'

Owen stepped out with him, wondering whether his friend was about to become guildmaster. They could not choose a better man. 'I hope the meeting is cordial.'

'And brief,' said Robert with a weary smile. 'I will send word of our decision.'

As Owen stood in Stonegate considering his next step, he was hailed by Peter Ferriby who was hurrying towards him with a companion wearing a hat too large for their head on this warm morning. Peter himself was sweating, his hair sticking to his damp face.

Owen was annoyed by the interruption until he saw Peter's expression. 'What happened?'

Peter was not so distraught that he did not glance round, then ask whether they might talk in the house. Owen led him back down Stonegate.

Once within, Peter's companion plucked off the outsized hat.

'Geoffrey.' Owen peered more closely at the younger Gifford's face. 'Were you fighting?' He led them to the window seat where he might see the extent of the young man's injuries. 'Would you like my wife to see to this?'

'I would be grateful.' Peter answered for the so far silent young man. 'But might we talk first?'

Owen settled on a bench so that he could watch Geoffrey. 'Go ahead.'

Geoffrey looked to Peter.

'Wulf went into a fury and hit Geoffrey so hard he fell against a wall,' said Peter. 'As you can see he has a great bruise blossoming on the side of his head. Wulf did this. To his own son!'

Wulf Gifford. Owen had been on his way to find out more about the man at The Bell. 'Why? Did he say why, Geoffrey? Can you talk?'

Geoffrey nodded. 'I can. It's just— I don't want to get my da in trouble.'

'I'm just listening,' said Owen.

'I don't think he knew what he was doing, he was in such a temper.'

'About what?'

'He heard that it was my drawing of the drowned man that your men are showing round the city and—' A sharp exhale. 'He started to shout about the baron of Raby and bringing attention to us and being ruined and that I was a wretch and should never have been born.' His voice broke on the last words.

'What did you do?' Owen asked softly.

'I tried to calm him. I said Lord Neville wouldn't know I'd drawn it. And if he did, that would speak well of us, we were helping him. He shouted that I was a fool and kicked me, then punched me in the face.' Geoffrey touched his bruised cheek and forehead. 'I fell to the ground and he . . . He spat on the floor and rushed out, kicking stools out of the way and calling me a cursed bastard, no son of his.' Geoffrey bowed his head, as if in disgrace.

Owen grasped his hand. 'I am sorry my request created this trouble for you.'

Geoffrey looked up, frowning. 'No, Captain. He's in the wrong, not you. He's gone mad. Maybe the drink. Maybe he's done something . . . He promised my mother he would not touch drink, that he would build a good life for the family in York and prove his worthiness. And he was good for a while. Until Creswick started coming around.'

'Rolo Creswick?'

Geoffrey nodded.

Owen felt more and more certain Creswick and Gifford were at the bottom of much of this. Why else would Gifford attack his own son? He thought about what Geoffrey had said. 'You moved here to start again?'

'We did. My mother did not want me to come with Da, but I was going to study with my cousin, and . . .' He sighed. 'He was doing well. The guild accepted him, and he was feeling redeemed. And then Creswick befriended him and pulled him back to the tavern. He hasn't done any work for weeks, and this past week I've felt I'm living alone. If he's not at The Bell, he's sitting by the window to the back garden staring out, or walking circles in the hall muttering to himself. He's frightened off the servants. His factor is doing what he can with the trade, making excuses for him with the guild, but he's said he won't continue for long.'

Leaving it all on this young man's shoulders. And he had said nothing until now. Loyalty his father did not deserve.

'I'm sorry to hear this.'

'I can't stay with him, Captain. Not now.'

'Of course you can't,' said Peter. 'He came to us after Wulf stormed out of the house,' he said to Owen. 'We promised his mother when they first came that we would take him in if need be, and we're happy to do it. But there is clearly something very wrong there. I don't know what to do.' He reached for Geoffrey's hand, held it protectively.

Owen was glad to see that. 'Is it all about the drink, Geoffrey, or something more? You thought he might have done something?'

'I don't know. I don't even know if he sleeps. He's sitting and staring when I go to bed, and he's there when I wake up. I stoke the fire, make some food, but he won't eat.'

'It's been like this for a week, you said?'

'Did I?' A shuddering breath.

'I cannot force you, but I can't help if you don't tell me all you know,' said Owen.

Geoffrey glanced at Peter, who motioned to him to speak.

'I was at the Ferribys until late last Saturday. When I got home he was pacing round the hall muttering to himself. He told me to go to bed. To let him be. He's not been himself since.'

Saturday. 'He still goes to The Bell with Creswick?'

'Yes.'

Likely there now. Owen had much to do. 'Geoffrey, do I have your permission to search your house?'

Peter sat back, looking at Owen. 'What aren't you telling me?'

'Permission to search?' Geoffrey asked. 'Why? What do you expect to find?'

'I want to rule out your father's involvement in the troubles of late.'

'You think he's a spy? Or a thief?' Geoffrey's voice rose to a cry.

'I don't know what to think at this point. Do you?'

'God have mercy,' Peter muttered. 'What should we do if Wulf comes demanding Geoffrey go home with him?'

'Tell him his son is injured and you are caring for him. If Gifford causes any trouble, find me or one of my men. Before I go, I'll ask my wife to see to you, Geoffrey. Wait here.'

Peter followed Owen to the kitchen door. 'It's that cur Creswick. He's poison.'

'Is it just him? Why did Wulf move his business away from Hull? It's the centre of the shipping. Why move upriver to York?' The shift in Peter's posture, from worried to defensive, was telling. 'You have dreaded this question.'

Peter wiped his brow. 'There were whispered accusations, never to his face. Two of his ships came back – late, missing some goods, but they returned, while several others gone missing at the same time never returned. He drank more and more, became belligerent when approached about it, spewed his own accusations. Finally, Mary, his wife, told him she was taking the children to her family in Sussex and would stay there until such time as he was able to prove himself sober and trustworthy, and that if he had anything to confess he must do so.'

'She thought the accusations might have merit?'

'She did not know what to think. Some friends, still loyal, suggested he come to York, offered to help, say nothing of why he was here.'

'You were one of the friends?'

Peter winced. 'I was. His wife is a good woman. I wanted to help keep her family together. You are thinking he is a spy.'

'I think it is possible.'

'I begin to think I was wrong to support him. But his wife—'

Owen pressed his shoulder. 'You were not ready to believe he might betray the realm for profit. Who would believe that of a friend, someone they had always trusted? Geoffrey is fortunate to have you. Take care of him.'

* * *

Martin had gone to the kitchen for a cloth. Rose was there, telling Kate she had important news for Owen about Robin. He'd been resting in his room above the apothecary when Neville and Owen met, awakened by the axe coming down with force over and over again, then watched the children in the kitchen while Owen talked to Peter Ferriby and Geoffrey Gifford. He guessed that his friend would be out in the city following up on a flood of new information. He could help.

'He's away right now, and I wouldn't expect him back soon,' said Martin. 'Might we work together?'

The clear eyes studied him for a moment.

'You can trust it to Master Martin, sister,' said Kate.

'The girl's been hiding in the room of a man who's been missing for a week. The old couple lodging him say he's French, has paid good money for the room.'

'Take me there.'

NINETEEN

Discoveries

Owen paused at the Giffords' door. Geoffrey's description of his father's behaviour and the timing both pointed to the possibility that he was somehow involved in the theft and perhaps Bolton's death, maybe Costen's as well, and beginning to lose his courage. His family and the Ferribys were close; if what Owen suspected was true, they would be devastated, and worried about their own standing in the city. He must move quickly but with care, Neville be damned.

With a grunt Hempe pushed open the door. 'We don't want to leave Alfred and Ned so long in The Bell that they forget their mission.'

A feeble fire burned in the stone circle in the middle of the echoing hall, the furnishings a few benches and stools, the latter kicked over as Geoffrey had described, and one high-backed chair placed by a window looking out towards the separate kitchen and a tall yew. A large bed was tucked into one corner behind fine wooden screens.

'I'll search here, you take the solar,' said Owen.

With a nod, Hempe headed for the outside steps.

Clothes, a wax tablet and a box with a quill, ink, a few pieces of parchment – Owen was looking at Wulf Gifford's bed and belongings. The bedclothes were smudged with dirt, possibly dried blood, and smelled of sweat. Owen pulled them off and carried them into the light. Definitely some dried blood. A shirt had some as well. Beneath the straw mattress he found a small wooden box, and within red sealing wax and a seal – like the one on the list found in Bolton's boots.

Hempe joined him. 'I would guess it's the lad sleeps up there. Tidy. Nothing to see.' He lifted the shirt. 'Is this blood?'

'It is.'

'There might be some at the bottom of the steps. Dirt kicked around to cover it, but someone missed a spot just at the foot.'

Owen followed him out and examined the stained soil. 'Could not swear to it being blood.'

'No.' Hempe sighed. 'Anything else?'

'Wulf must keep his shipping accounts at the warehouse, which would make sense if his factor has been handling most of it. Yet he keeps this hidden in the bed.' Owen opened the box with the seal.

Hempe bent to look closely and then grinned up at Owen. 'We have our spy.'

'I think so.'

'Ferriby won't like this. And Wulf's son—'

'I cannot believe Geoffrey had any idea.'

'Kitchen?' Hempe suggested.

They found little food in the kitchen, and nothing of interest.

Owen stepped out into the yard, looking back at the window where Wulf had placed the high-backed chair, and felt a sharp shower of needle pricks in his blind eye as he wondered about the placement. It faced a kitchen garden in need of weeding and pruning, and beyond it the tall yew. As Owen walked towards the tree the pain in his blind eye grew more insistent. He glanced back at the window, crouched down, noticed loose soil, a good-sized area disturbed recently. Shaded by the yew, it was no place for a new bed of plants. He thought about the smudges of dirt on the bedding, and wondered whether Wulf rather than one of the now-departed servants had been digging here, and had then watched the area from the house.

'We need to find a shovel,' he said.

The work was just what his body hungered for after Neville's visit and the fear in Geoffrey's eyes. Digging down, heaving up, he worked up a good sweat, while Hempe worked with a hoe, the only other tool. They were a few feet down when Owen felt something shift as he lifted a shovelful. An arm stuck out of the loose dirt.

'That's a nasty bit of gardening,' said Hempe as he used the hoe to scrape away sufficient dirt to expose a shoulder. He stood back. 'How long do you think it's been there?'

'Not long. No more than a few weeks, probably less. Fetch some men and a cart.'

Someone gasped. Owen spun round, dagger in hand. It was Geoffrey and Peter. He slipped the dagger back in its sheath.

'We came to collect some of his things,' Peter said softly. 'God help me, a body.' He reached out to prevent Geoffrey from moving near, but the young man shrugged out of his grip.

'What has he done?' Geoffrey moaned.

'Fetch your things and go to the Ferribys, Geoffrey. Stay there,' said Owen.

'But—'

'Now.'

Geoffrey caught Owen's arm, brought his face close as if to force him to see his distress. There was no need.

'I know nothing more than what I've found here, Geoffrey. Your father will have a chance to explain.'

'My da is not a murderer, Captain. I can't believe it.'

The truth was, one might know a man well and vouch for him as a man of peace, yet discover that in a moment when cornered and threatened he defended himself by taking a life. Was that not what they had all done in battle?

'You must go to the Ferribys, Geoffrey. You can do nothing for your father here.'

Peter pulled Geoffrey away and led him into the house. In a while, they shuffled out with Geoffrey's things bundled in a blanket.

Owen turned back to the grave, scraping enough soil away from the face and the torso to find the likely cause of death, several stabs to the gut, angled up under the ribs to the heart. Experience taught that angle. The dead man looked strong enough to defend himself from most men. The killer would need to be strong and know how to ensure a knife reached the heart. Gifford was a large man, but as far as Owen knew he'd not been a soldier.

But when he took him he would be ready.

'What is this? Oh, Blessed Mary and all the saints,' a woman gasped.

Still crouched beside the body, Owen looked up into the frightened eyes of a woman carrying a baby. Her coif was limp with sweat and her cheeks overripe from the heat.

'Who is that? What has happened?'

Owen rose and drew the woman away from the grisly sight. 'I am sorry you saw this, Goodwife. I am Captain Archer—'

'I know who you are. Is this that drunken man's doing?' Pinched lips and the lines to indicate she disapproved of much in a day contrasted with the serene face of the babe in her arms. He thought it pointless to ask her not to speak of it, but there was always a chance she might listen. 'I advise you to take the child away from this and to say nothing to anyone about what you have seen here. I do not yet know how the man came to be in this yard, or even who he was. Unless you might recognise him?'

'Me? I do my best not to look over here, though that poor young man, Geoffrey, he is a good one. I worry for him. He deserves better.'

'Dame Alice, have you had some trouble?' Christine Creswick approached, holding out her arms. 'Oh, baby Janet, shall I hold her while you talk to Captain Archer?' She looked from him to the overheated mother and, as if just realising there was more going on, glanced over to the gravesite. She gasped. 'God help us. Is that why he was digging there?'

How quickly she moved to point a finger. Or was he simply wary of Creswicks? 'You saw someone digging here?'

Her hand to mouth, Christine Creswick shook her head. 'I did not mean to say that.'

He thought she had. Better she had a limited audience. Owen looked to the woman with the child. 'If you would leave us, Dame Alice. And remember what I said.'

With a sniff, the woman removed herself and baby Janet to her house.

Owen turned back to Christine. 'A man was murdered and buried here. If you witnessed this, I would know. Or the sheriff will call you to court.'

A slight step back, as if she had not realised the serious nature of his discovery. 'I did not see much of use to you.'

'Tell me what you know.'

'What I saw . . .' She paused as if gathering her memory. 'I was searching for one of my children and saw Wulf Gifford kneeling on the ground beneath the tree, smoothing over the earth as if he had been planting. I asked him whether he had seen young John, and he looked at me as if I'd attacked him, stumbling up and backing away, shaking his head. I took that as a no and went on. Young John was my concern.' She sighed. 'Wulf Gifford is a troubled man.'

Troubled by her husband, it seemed. 'Do you recall what day it was? When you saw him digging?'

'It would be Saturday. That was the day I found young John at Dame Alice's, playing with her dog.'

'You say he is troubled. What do you know of Wulf Gifford?'

'Perhaps I misspoke. I know only the few things my husband says about him, his unhappiness, how he misses his family. He is not in the habit of talking to neighbours. He keeps to himself. I've greeted him, but he is not one to respond. His son is well spoken and friendly to my children, but I do not pester him with questions about his father. Now I must find that boy. He's on the loose again.'

Owen watched Christine Creswick walk away, straight-backed and brisk with purpose. Like her husband with Bertram Harrigan, she was keen to point the finger at Wulf Gifford. He would find out why.

Rose led Martin to a ramshackle house where Robin had been hiding. It was tucked away between a tavern on Micklegate and the Dominican Priory, the couple wizened and eager to tell Martin all they knew of their missing lodger. Which was little. French, most likely, though he spoke God's language clear enough for them to understand most of what he said. 'God's language' was a curious expression that Martin had grown accustomed to in the city and surrounding countryside. The man's name was Jean. He had paid for a month, more than they had asked with the understanding that he was buying the gift of being left alone. He said he had lost his family and was visiting the religious houses in the city to find one that would accept him as a lay brother who might eventually take vows. He was away most of the day and never had visitors.

In the lodging, a comfortable room with a high-backed chair and a box bed, lit by an oil lamp and, in daylight, a shuttered window looking out on the Dominican Priory, Martin found nothing that would seem to have belonged to Jean, neither clothing nor a pack – nothing. The couple said they had not seen him in days, which was not unusual, but that they would have expected him to tell them if he were leaving for good. They thought perhaps he would return. Martin wondered whether Robin's visits had been spent confiscating anything worth selling. When he asked the couple whether they had seen a child lingering around the house, they looked bemused, said a child had not been on the premises for years, since their grandchildren died of pestilence. All the while the woman spun and the man petted an old, notch-eared cat. Returning to the room, Martin asked Rose to help him move the box bed, a piece too heavy for the child to shift, and too noisy. He pulled up a loose floorboard beneath it and found a leather sack of gold coins.

'Quite a treasure,' said Rose. 'Do you think it was Jean's?'

'No way to know for certain, but they said he had been their first lodger in several years and there's no dust, so it is likely.' Martin removed it to take to Owen. 'It's important we find Robin as soon as possible. How did you find her before?'

'She was hiding by the children's quarters at St Leonard's,' said Rose. 'I think she hoped to hear about Flint without needing to go see him. I will search again and come straight to you if I find her or learn anything.'

Hempe returned with the men, the cart, and a message from the sheriff, that he wanted a full report when Owen returned to the castle with the body.

'He expects you at once.'

No doubt. Constable wished to be ready to answer to Neville, likely unaware that the baron was visiting the works at Sheriff Hutton.

'He will wait. We have more important business.'

Once the men had loaded the body on the cart and headed back to the castle, Owen and Hempe washed off the sweat and dirt with a pail of water in the kitchen and moved on to The Bell. Stephen had gone ahead to position himself where he could watch and come to assist if Gifford gave them trouble.

The Bell crouched across from Queen's Staithe, sagging in one corner but recently given a fresh coat of paint. The new taverner hoped to improve the tavern's reputation, the former proprietor known to harbour thieves and others hiding from the law. It would take time to dissuade the old crowd; though at first glance Owen did not find Alfred and Ned out of place, he noticed a few slip out when he and Hempe entered and looked around. Wulf Gifford was at a table in the far corner staring into a tankard while Rolo Creswick talked.

Owen and Hempe settled at a table cleared by a pair fleeing their presence, situated so that Gifford and Creswick would need to rise to see them, but Alfred and Ned were clearly in view and had subtly acknowledged them. From past business at the tavern Owen knew the layout, that Gifford and Creswick were near the door to the kitchen, where they might flee through an outer door – at present guarded by Stephen.

Doubtless wishing to reassure the captain and bailiff that they were welcome, the taverner himself approached their table.

'When you bring our tankards, bring something for yourself and we'll talk,' said Owen.

The taverner was a large man with a shock of curly pale red hair, pale brows and eyelashes, pale eyes. 'Am I in trouble?'

'Not you, but there might be a little scuffle when we're ready. Before we proceed, we'd like to know more about the pair we're watching. So, our ale? Go at your usual pace. We don't want to cause any alarm.'

The man did as Owen requested, looking for all the world like he was just proud to have some new custom and eager to please them. A younger man took over the refills as the taverner rejoined them with two tankards and a bowl for himself.

'It's not Merchet's ale, but my wife has a knack for it, I think. My name's Roland, but you know that. And you're Captain Archer and Bailiff Hempe.'

'We're interested in Wulf Gifford and Rolo Creswick, sitting towards the kitchen.'

A wince and a nod. 'I guessed they were trouble. The big one, Gifford, is a sad lot, needing the pretty one to guide him home. Wouldn't make it otherwise. They leave when I refuse to serve him more. I should stop him sooner, but sometimes Creswick drinks his own.'

'Most of the time Gifford drinks Creswick's share as well?' Hempe asked.

'He does. His mate encourages it. He's after something, Creswick. Has a reason for getting Gifford drunk, that's what my good wife believes, and I think she's right.'

'Does it take many tankards to topple Gifford?' Owen asked.
'No.'

'Strange for such a regular, wouldn't you say?' The ale was weaker than Tom Merchet's.

'I never thought about it, but you're right,' said Roland.

'When we leave, put Gifford's and Creswick's tankards aside for me. Do not wash them.'

'You think Creswick's putting something in Gifford's drinks?' asked Hempe.

'I want to see what my wife thinks,' said Owen.

'The apothecary,' said Roland. 'I see. I will take care with them.'

'Do they ever meet others?'

'Not that I've noticed. But they've been watched. The drowned one, Lord Neville's man, he was in here a few times watching them. And a dark-haired fellow who hardly spoke – I reckoned him for a foreigner who did not want me to guess – he sometimes sat near them. When he did, Gifford would leave early. Without Creswick.'

'The foreigner would stay?'

'For a short time.'

'And Creswick?'

'He would leave soon after the foreigner.'

The corpse was dark-haired. 'Straight, trimmed dark hair, full mouth?' Owen asked.

'Sounds like it might be him. But I haven't seen him for a while.'

'Can you recall when you last did?'

The man fluttered his pale lashes, pursed his lips. 'Saturday, I'd say. Midday. It's the last time I saw the drowned man as well.'

'Were they here at the same time?'

Roland closed his eyes for a moment. 'The foreigner sat right here, Neville's man over there.' He indicated a table in the opposite corner.

'And Creswick and Gifford?'

'They were not here yet. You'll be taking them?'

'We will see. I thank you for your help.'

Watching the taverner pause at a nearby table and motion to the younger man to fill the tankards there, Hempe leaned close. 'Both?'

'Do what we agreed. Let's see what Creswick does when Gifford is removed. I told Alfred to linger outside, follow him.'

They rose, made their way through the now curious crowd to Gifford's table. Creswick reared back, sober and alarmed.

'Captain Archer. Bailiff Hempe.' He elbowed his companion.

Wulf Gifford raised his head, blinking at them, his mouth slack with drink. 'What's this?'

Owen put a hand on Gifford's shoulder. 'If you would come with us.'

'No!' The man rose too fast, stumbling against Owen, who held him firmly.

'What are you accusing him of?' Creswick asked with wide-eyed innocence. Feigned, Owen was sure of it. But he needed more to take him.

'We need his help with an investigation,' said Hempe.

'I am his friend. I will come along.'

'No.' Hempe stepped close to prevent him from rising.

Creswick sat back with hand raised in submission.

As they moved away with Gifford, steadying him between them, Owen glanced at Alfred. Ned would remain for a while after Alfred departed behind Creswick, watching the reactions. Already a few were slipping away, worried about their own secrets.

Rose lifted her head, listening, motioning to Martin to stop, her jaw tightening.

'Trouble. A group of men waiting to catch you. They've been drinking and they've decided you're robbing the couple. Call you the Fleming pirate.'

God's blood, why now? Martin took a deep breath and held out the bag of gold coins. 'Take this to Owen. I will distract them with a good chase.'

'But your—' She bit her lip, took the scrip. 'God speed,' she whispered as she retraced her steps to the house and around it, disappearing.

Martin smiled. A remarkable young woman, confident, discreet. He could well guess she'd been ready to argue about his heart, that a chase might wreck him, but she had respected his offer. In truth his heart reminded him almost constantly of its fragile state. But he would not lie back and let the world harm his friends if there was anything he might yet do. Surely a few drunk men did not mean to murder him, only to humiliate him for a lark. And if he was wrong and needed to defend himself, he was armed, and far more experienced in self-defence than they were likely to be. He took several deep breaths and turned his mind to the streets around him. This was not a part of the city he knew well, but he recalled a ginnel across Micklegate that led down towards the river. He doubted his taunters would follow him so far. Pray God that was so, because he did not trust his ageing body to run a long distance.

When Wulf Gifford saw the corpse in the castle yard, he struggled to break from Owen's and Hempe's grasps, but to no avail. They brought him close so that he could not avoid seeing the man he had buried. 'God help me,' he groaned.

'Who is he?' Owen asked.

'The devil. My devil. But I did not kill him.'

'We found him buried in your garden.'

'I did not kill him.'

Men were moving towards them, curious, eager for gossip. Owen and Hempe led Gifford away and into the castle. Brother Michaelo should soon be joining them to record his confession. Stephen had gone for the monk as they left The Bell.

The large man stumbled on the steps in the dark, not his first tumble in his inebriated state. Hempe hurried forward to help, but the steps were too narrow. Owen held Gifford securely and guided him down without further mishap as he muttered over and over, 'I did not kill him.'

In the cell, Gifford sank onto a bench and covered his face with his hands while Owen answered a knock on the door, expecting Brother Michaelo. It was the sheriff's manservant, uneasily shifting from foot to foot.

'Sir John Constable wants to see you at once.' He blinked at Owen's frown and added, 'Captain.'

'Tell him I will report to him after I have completed questioning a prisoner.'

'But, Captain—'

'You have my answer, now go. My secretary is here to record the confession.' With a curt nod, Owen swept the just-arrived Brother Michaelo through the door and closed it behind them.

'Is it wise to keep the sheriff waiting?' Michaelo asked. 'Lord Neville might be with him.'

'Gifford's confession is my priority.'

With a nod, Michaelo glanced round and began to arrange a seat close to the one lantern.

Owen straddled the bench beside Wulf Gifford and Hempe brought a stool near.

'Start from the beginning,' Owen said.

'Neville's here? Here in the castle?' Wulf asked. 'It was his man killed Jean. His man.'

Owen glanced up at Michaelo, who raised a brow.

Once he had whipped out his dagger and threatened them, the three had avoided touching Martin, but they continued to follow him, shouting that he'd stolen from the elderly couple and was a spy for the French. Rose was right, they had been drinking, their words slurred, but people on the street as he crossed Micklegate seemed to be hissing at Martin, not them, fools that they were. Once in the ginnel Martin moved more quickly, dodging round rain barrels, debris, stray dogs, and children tossing a leather ball. The children briefly followed along, adding their shrill voices to the men's, but all were falling behind Martin, and after he climbed over an abandoned cart, he seemed to lose them. God be thanked, for his lungs were screaming and his heart beating fast and irregular. He did not like that. Finding a quiet alcove, he sat down and rested a while. Crazy old man, he had been mad to come. But he had found the gold coins. He smiled at that. He had done something.

TWENTY

Apprentices and Some Answers

The unexpected warmth had Lucie regretting her plan to prepare a stock of unguents containing wax, the oil lamp she used to soften the wax adding to the temperature of the workshop despite having the door and shutters open. When Jasper stepped in to tell her that Elaine Harrigan was in the shop, with a group of apprentices who wished to talk to her, she gladly snuffed the lamp beneath the bowl and told him to guide them out, round, and through the garden gate, where she would meet them.

Four lads followed Elaine into the garden, eyes ablaze with purpose as they nudged each other forward. Two were younger than Jasper by a few years, the others a little older, so not lads but young men. All wore solemn expressions, as if on a mission.

'Dame Lucie, you might have heard that the goldsmiths are meeting today in Robert Dale's home, pushing to replace my father with a new guildmaster.' Elaine's eyes were pained, yet she was much more self-possessed than on her last visit.

'I had not.' But she was not surprised. 'I am sorry to hear that. How might I help you?'

'My father's apprentices have information for Captain Archer.'

'He is not here.'

One of the older ones stepped forward, carrying himself with some importance. 'We want to help our master. He's a good man and doesn't deserve to be brought down.'

Lucie guessed that they worried about the worth of their apprenticeships, knowing from experience how parents weighed the prestige of a master. She'd had difficulty finding an apprentice when her husband Nicholas died and she was permitted to replace him as apothecary.

She motioned to them to take seats on the low wall by the workshop. 'How do you propose to help him?'

As the older apprentice sat forward, his already tousled hair lifted in a sudden draft and covered his eyes. He raked it back with irritation. 'Master Harrigan did not know we invited some of Master Scardburge's apprentices to last week's party.'

'And that will help him how?' Lucie asked.

'He meant it only for his apprentices and journeymen,' said a doe-eyed young man with a soft voice. 'He didn't invite the dead man. We don't know how he knew of it.'

'By the dead man you mean Walter Bolton, and you saw him at the party?' Lucie asked.

Four timorous nods or shrugs.

'Did you talk to him?'

'I did,' said one of the younger ones, whose prominent upper teeth seemed in conflict with his tongue. 'I was trying to keep him from talking to anyone else. I knew he was trouble.'

'And you are?'

'Harry Overton.'

So this was Celia Overton's nephew. 'I had heard—'

'I know. It's true I can't drink. I always think just one sip won't hurt. But I did my best as long as I could.' His lisp grew more noticeable as he hurried through his words, but he was determined to spit them out.

His fellows did not interfere or try to hurry him. Lucie liked them for that.

'How did you know he was trouble?'

'My aunt Celia told me that he'd been sniffing around her house on Stonegate, asking questions about her housekeeper's husband . . . and about the goldsmiths. She warned me to watch out for him.'

Celia had said nothing of this to Owen. Lucie wondered whether Anna van Peelt knew of Walter Bolton's interest in her late husband, whether she had warned Costen.

'Why was he interested in the goldsmiths?'

'Everyone knew about the golden lion,' said the lad who had not yet spoken. 'But Harry was worried about something else, weren't you?' He elbowed his companion.

'I didn't want anyone telling him – Bolton – that sometimes the master forgets to lock the doors to his office, where he kept the lion. I didn't know if the master remembered that night, and I couldn't check while Bolton was there.'

Even these lads, so eager to protect their master, realised he needed protection from himself. Lucie managed to smile at him. 'A loyal apprentice.'

'I don't know how helpful this is for my father,' said Elaine, 'but I thought the captain should hear this.'

Indeed he should. Sooner would have been helpful. 'Why did you lads wait so long to say all this?' Lucie asked.

'We didn't want to get anyone in trouble,' said the leader of the group. 'But now our master's in trouble.'

'Can you tell me anything else? Anything you noticed. Take a moment. Think through the evening.'

After a long drink of water and a few perambulations of the cell, Wulf Gifford appeared more clearheaded. Now Owen brought out the seal and wax and Hempe leaned forward with interest, Michaelo giving a surprised sniff.

Gifford blinked as if not believing what he saw, his face reddening, eyes hot. 'How did you get that?'

'I saw this seal on a partial list of ships expected at our staithes with their shipping dates,' said Owen. 'Did you create that list?'

'I'm in shipping. Of course I have lists.' He glared at Owen. 'Did you search my house?'

'Why seal the list? And how did it come to be in the possession of a murdered man?'

'You have no right.' Gifford grabbed at the seal, but Owen held it away from him.

'It was Geoffrey, wasn't it?' Gifford growled. 'Betrayed by my own son.'

'Geoffrey had nothing to do with this,' said Owen. 'But why do you consider yourself betrayed if, as you say, all shippers have lists?'

Gifford blinked. 'But you said . . .' He stopped. 'You said the murdered man had it.' He was not so drunk as he had seemed. 'Of course Neville's man had it. He took it from the devil himself.'

'You said before that Neville's man killed Jean, whom you call the devil, so is that how he came to possess the list?' Owen asked, making certain he understood. 'You'd given it to Jean?'

Gifford looked away. 'I'll hang for this, won't I?'

'Hanging is for lesser crimes. I'm assuming Jean was spying for the French. You were the one who prepared it, and handed it over to a spy, which is in itself spying. You are a spy, Wulf, and spying is treason, a most serious crime. So, no, you will not hang for this.'

'Not . . . This was ransom, not spying,' Gifford growled. 'My customers trusted me. I rescued most of their goods.'

'I call it treason to ransom your ships by providing information about your fellow guildmembers' ships to the French. Your fellows would agree, don't you think?'

Gifford grunted.

'The man you buried in your garden was your French contact, Jean?'

'I'll say no more.' Gifford turned away.

'Tell me why I shouldn't also charge you with the murders of the man in your garden and Neville's man, Walter Bolton.'

'I'm not a murderer,' Gifford said through clenched teeth, 'but what does it matter? I'm dead already.'

'You are. But if you help Sir John Neville find out what happened to his man, he might ask the crown to make allowances for your family. Not forfeit all your property.'

'My family.' Gifford clenched his hands, his jaw tightening.

'You must have known your family would suffer for your crimes.'

'Not a crime to work hard for a living.'

'Honest work. Not spying,' said Hempe.

'Not spying. Ransom.'

'You have convinced yourself of that lie,' said Owen, 'but not me, nor anyone else in the king's service. Or your fellow guildmembers.'

'I was protecting my customers' ships!' Gifford shouted, lunging towards Owen, who put out an arm to unbalance him so that he fell to the ground.

Owen rose to look down on Gifford, cowering on the floor. 'You left Hull when people began to talk about your unnatural luck. You knew you had grievously transgressed.'

Fear and doubt flickered on the man's red, sweating face.

Someone knocked on the door. 'What now?' Hempe grumbled, going to answer it.

'I have something for Captain Archer.'

Rose's voice. Owen went to the door.

'I have this for you, Captain.' Rose reached past Hempe to hand Owen a leather bag, heavy with what felt like coin. Ned stood behind her, looking winded.

'Stay with Michaelo and Gifford,' Owen told Hempe and stepped out into the corridor, closing the door behind him.

'It's from Martin Wirthir,' said Rose. 'He feared the men waiting for him would snatch it and he told me to bring it to you.'

'The men waiting for him? Is he out in the city?' Martin had promised to stay in during the day. Bloody fool. Owen did not have time to be worrying about Martin.

'I came for you and he offered to help,' said Rose. 'And he did. I would not have thought to move the box bed. That's where we found the coins. The men must have seen him and thought he was robbing the old couple. Let me explain the rest, then I'm going back to find him.'

She told him about the lodging of the Frenchman, Jean, how she had found it by following Robin. 'We found nothing belonging to him except for these gold coins. I think Robin helped herself, but couldn't move the box bed to find what was hidden beneath. I'm off now. I'll find him, Captain.' She hurried away, Ned looking after her with longing.

'And you?' Owen nudged Ned.

Ned turned back. 'The Bell was abuzz after you left with Gifford, right enough, and Creswick talked to two large, rough men, not familiar to me, then some others, then left. Alfred followed him. Mostly people were sharing ideas about what Gifford had done – spy, thief, murderer, all mentioned. Sounded like Creswick had told some of them that Gifford fled Hull under a cloud. Nice friend. But many seemed to like Gifford and didn't believe it until today, when we came for him. Seems no one trusts Creswick. And when I asked the taverner about the two men he talked to, he warned me away, said that they're trouble.' Ned was almost dancing from foot to foot.

'Would you know them again?'

'I would, Captain. I'd like to catch up to Rose, help her find Martin.'

Owen nodded. 'Go on.'

Ned hurried off, practically galloping by the time he reached the steps up to the yard.

When Owen returned to the cell, Gifford had resettled on the end of the bench and was gulping down the water left in his bowl. Owen took it from him and set it aside.

'Tell me about Walter Bolton and Jean.'

Sweat curled Gifford's hair and dripped over his red-rimmed eyes. 'Will you do what you can for my family if I talk?' At last he seemed to understand he could not wriggle out of this.

'Yes. I cannot promise anything, but I have the ear of the king's mother.'

Gifford looked down at his hands for a moment, then nodded. 'My son trusts you.'

'And I trust him.'

'Did I hurt him badly?'

'Worse than I like to see. My wife took care of him and he's at the Ferribys now.'

'Good. He's better there.' Gifford shrugged his shoulders as if preparing for an ordeal. 'A week to the day, Jean left my house and Neville's man, Bolton you say, was waiting in the ginnel. Must have been. I'd seen him in The Bell and told Creswick he was following me, but he said no, no, that was the drink talking. And then there he was. Waiting for the devil.'

'Jean.'

Gifford nodded.

'You witnessed their meeting?'

'Jean had just left me. I was round the corner of the house, making sure he moved on.'

'And what did you witness?'

'Neville's man pressed Jean against the wall, a knife to his throat. Jean offered him a trade. His life for the list of ships and information about a treasure that would set Bolton free from the bastard taint. A golden lion that would afford him a new life anywhere he chose. "The golden lion for the king?" Bolton asked. Jean said yes, told him Guildmaster Harrigan was a fool, keeping something so valuable in a chest in his office, and that the apprentices would be drinking that night. Easy to take advantage of that. Then someone cried out and I heard him fall to the ground. When I looked, Neville's man was gone, and Jean was lying there, bloody and not breathing.'

'And you think Bolton killed him?'

'Who else? They were the only two there. Of course he killed him. And likely stole the golden lion.'

That was how he came to be at the party that night. But Owen did not understand why Bolton had given up his success in tracking down the spy for a handful of gold. Pleasing his father, the powerful Neville, would have gained him his father's respect and surely a comfortable position in his household, or by his side fighting for the king. Why would he abandon Jean's body, and that future, to chase the gold? Had he expected the body to lie there all night? Was it more important to him to chase the chance of breaking free from his powerful father? Owen put that aside for later. Right now, he needed to learn all he could from Gifford. 'If you had nothing to do with Jean's death, why did you bury him in your yard?'

'What else would I do? I didn't want Geoffrey to find him. Or Creswick. He'd see the body in the ginnel and come asking for money to be quiet. He'd threaten to put it all over York that I'd murdered a French spy.'

'People might cheer you.'

'But Jean's men in Hull would hear of it and I'd be dead.' Gifford rubbed his face. 'God's blood, I'm dead anyway, and Geoffrey will know what I've done. Jean and his men sent me down this road months ago.' He bowed his head for a moment, then straightened, looking Owen in the eye. 'Beheaded? Is that my fate, Captain?'

Drawing and quartering is what young King Richard had mentioned as the only death suitable for traitors. Owen had wondered which of his tutors had given him that idea. But he would not mention it now. 'That will be for King Richard to decide. But I will write to Princess Joan about your family. Is there anything else you can tell me? Did you see Bolton again? Did you go after him the next day to claim the golden lion?'

'No. Would that I had, and kept running, taking my family and sailing away.' He shook his head. 'I buried the devil and drowned myself in ale, hoping it would all go away while I slept it off. And then I couldn't peel myself away from the house, watching the grave, expecting the devil to rise out of the ground and point his bony claw at me.' Gifford covered his face with his hands.

Elaine and the four boys were filing out of the garden when the fair-haired one paused and took a few steps back, almost toppling Harry.

'The big Fleming who draws the city. I think I saw him the night of the party, standing across Stonegate, keeping to the shadows. I could not swear to it, but I thought it at the time, no question.'

'Thank you,' said Lucie. 'Any small detail might help.'

He glanced over towards the kitchen door, where Hugh had come out to see who was there. 'Master Hugh! Mistress Pippa's champion!' he called out.

His three companions turned round and cheered Hugh, who grinned, rose up on his toes and took a bow.

'Go on now,' said Lucie. 'More of that and he will be impossible to live with.' But she was glad to see their mood lighten. 'You've done a good thing for your master.'

'Pippa worships Hugh,' said Elaine. 'And the family appreciates how he stood up for her and my father.'

Lucie hoped her son had not heard that. When she turned to him, he was lifting a thick branch, preparing to work on his strength.

He looked up at her, biting his lip and frowning. 'Were they laughing at me?'

Her heart went out to him. 'No, love, they admire you. Did you not hear Pippa's sister? She said her family appreciate how you stood up for Pippa and her father. You did the right thing.'

He smiled and flexed his arm muscles.

'Except for punching Edwin in the face.'

'Oh.'

Martin strained to hear whether it was safe to come out from hiding and head home. His mouth was so dry. He would do anything for a sip of water.

'They're gone,' a soft voice said.

He looked round and discovered a child in a pale hood far too large crouching nearby. Girl? Boy?

'You're Pirate, the captain's friend.'

'I am. Are you Robin?' he guessed.

'I might be.'

He could hear now how she forced her voice low. It was a fine hood. Hadn't Owen said something about Walter Bolton's hood? That it had not been with the rest of his clothes? 'You say the drunkards chasing me are gone?'

Robin nodded. 'Back to the tavern to boast how they chased you into the river.'

'Well, that is quite a day's work.' Martin used the wall to assist him as he rose, standing slightly bent over for a moment, allowing his legs to remember how to straighten and support him.

'Are you old?'

Oh, the pain of her question. 'I am, dear Robin. An old pirate, good for little more than telling tales of my younger self round a fire. Might I inquire as to why you are wearing that hood on such a warm day?' He could smell his own sweat, and hers.

She touched the cloth. 'Someone gave it to me.'

'Someone special.'

A nod.

'Such a finely tailored hood. An expensive gift.'

'He found it.'

'Down by the river, perchance? Last Sunday?'

She frowned at him. 'Were you there, too?'

'No. No, I was not, alas. Would that I had been, so that I might tell my friend who it was that murdered Lord Neville's man. I believe that was his hood.'

Robin touched the hood and, before Martin could say aught, she was gone.

Mad old man, now look what he'd done.

TWENTY-ONE

A Roundup

Despite the cold damp in the bowels of the castle, the large man was still sweating and gulping water as if desperate to drown in it. Too much ale or wine and no food might create a terrible thirst, but they had brought him here in late morning. Surely he had not had sufficient drink. Once again Owen eased the now empty bowl from Gifford and put it aside. A few more questions and then he had much to do.

'What did you do with the gold coins Harrigan would not buy?' Owen asked.

Gifford wiped his mouth with his sleeve. 'Harrigan told you?'

'Answer the question. I know Jean paid you for information with gold coins. Where are the ones you couldn't trade for silver?'

A shrug.

'Judas money goes to the king,' Hempe growled.

'And what of my family? What are they supposed to live on?'

'Had you truly not understood what you were doing?' Hempe asked, his tone incredulous.

Owen motioned for Hempe to stop needling the man. 'I told you I will ask the king's mother to intercede on behalf of your family,' he said. 'But only if you cooperate.'

'Why should I trust you not to keep it for yourself? Why wouldn't you?'

'Because he is an honourable man,' said Brother Michaelo. 'And you yourself said that your son trusts him.'

Gifford turned, clearly having forgotten his presence, and considered Michaelo for a moment, then wiped his brow. 'I buried the gold coins under the cook's pallet in the kitchen.'

'Buried it. Like Costen van Peelt buried his chest of money,' said Owen.

Gifford scratched his chin and gave a weary shrug. 'I wouldn't

know anything about that. Didn't like that he was encouraging
Geoffrey to spend his time drawing when he needed to be studying
for Oxford, but that's all I knew of the man.' He looked away
with a curse. 'I've ruined everything for my son. Everything.'

'You never spoke to Costen?'

'No. I didn't like the way he watched me.'

Owen studied the man as he spoke and decided he was telling
the truth. This was not Costen's murderer.

'What about Creswick? Did he know Costen?'

'Creswick.' Gifford spat. 'He talks about him sometimes. Seems
to hate him, but he hates most in the city.'

Owen looked to Hempe for anything he'd forgotten. Hempe
shook his head.

A wave of dizziness came over Martin and he pressed himself
against the wall to stay upright. Hot, thirsty, tired, he closed his
eyes and took a few deep breaths, focused on quieting the throb-
bing in his ghost hand, the pain that too often now came before
he collapsed. Dame Magda said it was like Owen's ruined eye,
a ghostly warning of danger, like the shower of needle pricks in
his friend's eye when trouble was near. The pain was not the
message, it was the warning. Martin must breathe deep and move
with care. Cursed old body. The wall was rough against his
stump, warm where the sun beat on it. He squinted against the
brightness as he moved out of the shadows. No, that was a
mistake. He moved back into the shadows and crept down the
ginnel. He recognised this place now. Up ahead was The Bell,
and then the staithe and river. Might he risk stopping in the
tavern for a drink? Through the buzzing in his ears, another sense
Dame Magda said was not what it seemed, not true sound, he
heard voices raised in argument. Two men, near the tavern
kitchen. He crept closer.

'I don't trust him to pay us. Let's take the silver plate and run
for Hull. We can find work there. Or sell the silver and go down
to London. Plenty work there.'

'And if he's there when we fetch it?'

'Martin!' Rose stood behind him.

He put a finger to his lips. 'Listen.'

But too late. The men hushed, moved slowly towards them,

then came at a run. Martin reached for his knife and lay open the cheek of the largest of them, who raised a hand to his ruined cheek and kept coming. Like an ox. They needed Stephen here, as large as Owen and as powerful. Martin dropped to the ground and kicked up at the ox, but the man simply threw himself on him, the blood that dripped from his face blinding Martin. God help him. He put all his strength into bucking and rolling to dislodge the man, who was howling, cursing, and pummelling with one hand. Martin kept up the movement as he felt his strength leaving him. The ox began to roll, and then he was gone. Martin blinked, wiped at his eyes. Stephen? Had he conjured him or was he so weak he was seeing things? But he could swear his attacker now lay limp beside him and Ned knelt to tie his wrists while Stephen and Rose held down the other man.

Martin slowly rolled to one side, caught his breath, and struggled to sit up against the wall. Several men hurried over from the tavern kitchen asking what was happening. Stephen rose and yanked up the one clutching his bleeding cheek. It *was* Stephen, blessed Stephen. All would be well now. Martin closed his eyes.

Owen, Hempe, and Brother Michaelo arrived at The Bell to find the tavern room emptier than earlier, and the few remaining customers crowded by the kitchen doorway. From beyond came a chorus of voices, sometimes all seeming to talk at once.

'Stabbed. Two of them.' One of the onlookers said to his question.

'One of them brought down by a woman,' another said with an almost toothless grin.

They made way for Owen and his companions to enter the kitchen. Martin sat slumped on a bench, head back, eyes closed, the taverner's wife, Helen, as Owen recalled, holding a wet cloth to his forehead. A man sat on a stool by the door with a bloody bandage round his head, Stephen standing over him brandishing a cleaver clearly borrowed from the kitchen. Rose, her hair tumbling out from a plain crispinette, face smudged, held a damp cloth to a cut on her hand.

'Martin opened his cheek and the cur tried to crush him,' said Ned. 'Stephen pulled him off, then helped me and Rose with the other one.'

Owen hadn't seen Ned sitting to the right of the doorway with a knife held at the neck of a scowling man.

'God bless Stephen,' said Martin, eyes still closed.

'Drink some of this now.' Helen held a bowl to his lips.

'These are Creswick's lackeys,' said Ned. 'I think we have enough to take him to the castle, Captain.'

'Rolo Creswick?'

'Indeed,' said Martin. 'Come sit by me and I'll tell you all about it. And what I learned from Robin.'

Rose and Brother Michaelo escorted a disappointed Martin back to the apothecary with the tankards for Lucie to examine. The more Owen thought about Gifford's thirst, the less certain he was that Creswick had put something in the ale, now suspecting that Gifford started drinking when he rose in the morning and continued until he lost consciousness at night, empty pitchers with sticky residue in the kitchen suggesting how he hauled it home, but it was worth checking. Martin had told him of the exchange between the two men before the attack, with extra detail from Stephen before he and Ned escorted the two to the castle. Now Owen and Hempe approached the Creswick house. If he had headed here, they should find Alfred standing watch. And there he was, beckoning to them from behind a barrel in the ginnel.

'He's in the house now,' said Alfred, straightening his lanky form with a grateful sigh. 'But he took a pile of things to Gifford's kitchen as soon as he came from the tavern. You might want to see what's there before you question him.'

That might be helpful. The pair Ned and Stephen were taking to the castle had not confessed to helping Creswick murder Costen, but they had said enough to suggest they were expecting to be paid from the items taken from the Fleming's house.

Alfred joined Owen and Hempe in Gifford's kitchen, indicating a chest by the wall. There was little inside, but Owen pointed out how it stood a little out from the wall. When they dragged it away, they found a large wooden box, beautifully made, which was obvious even from a distance in a dim room, several rolls of cloth, one sufficiently long and thick to be a tapestry, and a large scrip.

Owen ran his hand along the wooden box. It was smooth as

silk except where a piece had been gouged out, and had an elegant catch shaped like a swan feather, clearly Robert Dale's work. Within, a felt bag protected the silver plate Dale had described. Taking the splinter from his scrip, Owen fit it into the gouge.

Hempe had been examining the large scrip, which contained several wax tablets.

Alfred carefully undid one of the rolls of cloth and found a large painting of Christine Creswick on a green felt background. Costen had softened her features, a gentle smile playing over her lips and eyes. Perhaps he had not awakened to her cold ambition until too late. Owen shook off the thought. It was conjecture, suspicion. He had no proof. But nor had he ever seen such a look on her face. He guessed from the missing corner that this is what had been torn from the wall near Costen's bed, his love, as she was in his eyes. And in Creswick's? He doubted it.

'We have him,' said Hempe.

'It's enough,' said Owen. 'Alfred, watch the Creswick house while we gather the evidence. If either Rolo or Christine leaves, alert us at once.'

As Alfred departed, Owen fetched the shovel they had used to exhume the body a few hours earlier. Time to see whether Wulf Gifford had told them the truth. Hempe pulled away the pallet, and in a few good shovelfuls Owen hit something. Moving with more care, he unearthed a leather bag. Squatting down, Hempe picked it up and opened it, showing Owen a good handful of gold coins.

'Spying is profitable,' said Hempe.

'I would say the French are keen for information.' Owen glanced towards the door as he heard someone approaching at a run. 'I think we have movement.'

Alfred appeared, panting. 'It's the wife. She just left, heading in the direction of Bootham Bar.

Owen nodded. 'I believe I know where she's headed. I want Creswick in the castle before we follow.'

They had pushed past the maidservant with quiet apologies, checked that the Creswick children were in the kitchen with the cook, and quietly climbed to the solar where Rolo Creswick was stuffing clothing into a leather pack.

Owen walked over and lifted the pack. 'One does not usually take a change of clothing, but you might be there a while. I'll carry this.'

As the taverner had noted, Rolo Creswick was a pretty man, large eyes with long lashes, well-proportioned nose, generous mouth, curly brown hair receding a little with age, but still thick. Yet his permanently petulant expression and eyes half-closed with suspicion ruined the effect.

'What do you mean?' Creswick demanded. 'Why aren't you with Gifford in the castle?'

'We had a little talk with your men Short John and Striper, and we found the goods you took from Costen van Peelt's house and hid in Gifford's kitchen,' said Owen. The well-lashed eyes slowly opened wide. 'Now it's your turn to come with us to the castle. Your cell awaits.'

Owen nodded to Hempe, who caught up Creswick's hands before he could react and bound them behind him.

'I will assist you on the steps if need be,' Hempe said as he nudged him towards them.

'My wife—'

'We will be talking to her as well,' said Owen. 'Shall we go?'

'What exactly do you think I did?'

'You hired Short John and Striper to assist you in torturing and then killing Costen van Peelt, your wife's longtime lover, and stole valuable items from his house,' said Owen. 'All that I know.' Or guessed. 'I believe you also attempted to murder a lad who witnessed your crimes. Fortunate for you, he is alive.' As was the girl who Owen believed actually witnessed one of them.

Now the man looked frightened. Good.

Lucie had returned to the hot work with the wax after Elaine's visit, intent on completing the task before the heat of the afternoon. She had paused to cool her forehead with a damp, lavender-scented cloth when she noticed Brother Michaelo approaching the door she had left open to the garden. He was his usual tidy self, but the companions who came up behind him looked as if they had been in a sweaty brawl, and Rose seemed to be supporting Martin.

As they began to step inside, she said, 'The workshop is too hot. We will talk in the garden.'

Michaelo held out a pair of dented pewter tankards. 'You might wish to take care of this before you join us. Owen asked that you examine the remains of ale in these. He thinks something might have been added to confuse a man's thoughts.'

'I see.' She took them. 'Do you want some supplies to care for your companions' injuries?'

He smiled. 'They have been cared for at the tavern, but Martin might welcome some of your aconite salve on the back of his head.'

'He fell?'

'Pushed down and held there by a large man. It took Stephen to pull him off.'

She handed him a jar of the salve and the basket of bandages and simple physics she kept to hand. 'Is Owen in danger?'

'Not from the men Rose and Martin encountered. They are in the castle. Creswick's hired brutes, it appears. Owen and George Hempe went to the Creswick home to take him. What happens then, I cannot say.'

She nodded. 'I will examine the tankards, then meet you beneath the linden.'

He touched her arm. 'He knows how to defend himself.' His eyes were gentle, as was his voice. This was a different Michaelo than most usually saw. Owen's friend. Her friend.

'I know that, yet I worry.'

'If prayers can protect him, he always has mine.'

She pressed his hand and nodded her thanks.

When he left, she set the tankards in a cleared space on the table and blew out the flame beneath the pot of wax, then fetched a long-handled spoon and scraped the bottom of one tankard, tapping the sticky substance on a small plate. She sniffed it, added a little water, sniffed again, then dabbed a little on her tongue. In such a small amount it should not harm her. She detected nothing but an inferior ale, certainly nothing that would addle a man's thoughts. The other tankard was likewise free of anything damaging.

'I find nothing in the tankards to confuse a man,' she said as she joined the group beneath the linden.

Michaelo was wrapping a cloth round Martin's head despite the man's protests that there was no need.

'So the poor man truly is that sunk into the drink,' said Michaelo as he tucked in the edges of the cloth and stepped back from Martin. 'I will pray for him.'

A breeze shook the linden, sending down yellowed leaves. The heat was lifting. Lucie was grateful. 'I will bring ale. We can enjoy it while you tell me all that has happened since Owen went out.'

'I should hasten to the castle to tell Owen what Martin learned from Robin,' said Michaelo. 'The tavern was not the place to share that information.'

'I am fine now. I can accompany you and tell him myself,' said Martin, 'if I removed this unnecessary bandage.' He plucked at the cloth.

Lucie stayed his hand. She understood his frustration, but she could also see the cold sweat on his brow and neck and observed how frequently he blinked as if to clear his vision. 'You need to rest, my friend. I advise you to accept Brother Michaelo's offer. You, too, Rose.' Her hair had come undone, her gown was dusty, damp with sweat, and torn, and she had clearly suffered several minor injuries, whereas Michaelo looked as if he had spent the day in a cool cloister, his habit impeccably tidy and clean.

'I agree,' said Michaelo. 'You have been a great help today, Martin. You found the gold the spy hid and discovered that Flint witnessed Bolton's murder.'

Martin's white brows came together in a wince. 'And I made it impossible for the boy to tell you what he knows.' He bowed his head. 'Useless old fool.'

'Stop saying that,' said Rose. 'You opened your attacker's cheek without hesitation. He will carry that mark for the rest of his days, and remember you.' Her eyes shone.

Michaelo sat down on the bench beside Martin. 'I know from experience what it is to be useless. You are not that, not at all.'

Martin looked surprised.

'It's true,' said Lucie. 'From the moment you came here you have been a friend to my children and a help to Owen. But the reason you are here is for rest, and that you've not done so well.' She glanced at Michaelo.

'Perhaps, if you rest for some hours, you might go to the children tonight, see whether Robin appears. You might convince her to talk to Owen,' said Michaelo. 'I will be watching for her in the minster yard.'

Martin tilted his head. 'I could do that.'

Rose patted his shoulder.

Lucie wondered whether he noticed how many friends he had made here in a short while.

As Michaelo departed, she asked Martin and Rose to tell her all they knew.

As Owen drew Creswick to the corpse in the castle yard, the man struggled to break away.

'Take a good look at him. I know you've seen him at The Bell. Where else had you seen him? Did you ever speak to him?' When Rolo tried to look away, Owen turned his head back towards the corpse. 'We will stay here until you look at him and answer my questions.'

Rolo tried once more to jerk away, then shouted, 'Yes! I have seen him at The Bell, always watching Gifford. It's Gifford you want, not me.'

'You're here for a separate crime, Creswick. Where else did you see this man?'

'At Gifford's house.'

'Did you talk to him?'

'No. Never.'

'Did he seem friendly with Gifford?'

'No. No, Gifford did not want him there.'

'What is this? And why have you ignored my summons, Captain?' The sheriff, Sir John Constable, stood behind Owen, hands on hips, his face a mask of annoyance.

'I will take him down to the cell,' said Hempe, grasping onto Creswick's shoulder.

Nodding, Owen moved away from the people gathering round them. The sheriff followed.

'I wanted to complete the arrests before reporting to you,' Owen said. 'And now I need to hurry to catch up with Creswick's wife, see whether she's on an errand for her husband.'

'His crime?'

'The torture and murder of Costen van Peelt, with the assistance of two men also brought to the castle.'

'And who was this man?' He glanced at the corpse, grimaced, looked away.

'A French spy being helped by Wulf Gifford.'

'Gifford murdered the spy?'

'He claims Walter Bolton murdered him. Neville's son.'

The eyes widened. 'No. We will not say that.'

'Say what you like, I will give Sir John Neville a full report when he returns this evening.'

'You must not mention any of this until then.'

Owen stayed his retort, nodded to the man, and followed Hempe down into the bowels of the castle.

TWENTY-TWO

A Disappointment

The owner of the stable outside Bootham Bar nodded at Owen's question. 'That sounds like the woman, Captain. She was with Pieter de Bruges.' Her uncle Christian de Bruges's son and heir. Interesting. Owen had wondered who she would find to escort her into Galtres. Her behaviour with him suggested she enjoyed manipulating men to her ends. 'He made much of finding her a gentle mount. They will not move quickly, but the mare is a good one, does not frighten easily. It shouldn't be hard to catch up to them.'

Owen, Stephen, and Hempe were quickly saddled and on the road heading into Galtres. Underneath the warmth of the day Owen sensed change in the strangely still air. His mother would say the sky was holding its breath, storing it up for the big blow. Rain by nightfall, he thought. He smiled at the memory of his sister Gwenllian demonstrating their mother's image of the sky by puffing out her cheeks and holding her breath until her face was as red as her hair, at last blowing it out and collapsing in giggles.

'Smiling about all the men tucked into the castle dungeon?' asked Hempe. 'Or catching Mistress Creswick stealing the golden lion? That's what you're expecting, isn't it?'

Owen snapped back to the present. 'I hope to retrieve the lion, but I was not smiling about that or the men we have detained. I find nothing to smile about in these troubles.'

'Nor I.' Hempe glanced round. 'It's quiet on the road.'

'By this time on a Saturday afternoon most people have headed for home.'

'Only fools like us still sweating on our mounts.'

'Do you think she will expect us, Captain?' Stephen asked.

Did he? She might. And the tears would come easily as she explained that Costen had wanted her to have the means to return to Bruges with the children and make a life away from her husband's shame. He recalled her questions pointing at that, as if teasing Owen with what was to come. Costen might have loved her, but Owen wondered whether he'd realised that Christine Creswick was, in her own way, as conniving as her husband. Remembering the portrait, he thought not. 'I think she might expect us, but she will have rehearsed a story sure to soften our hearts.'

Stephen peered over at him. 'But it won't?'

'No. I would not be following her if I thought she had a right to what I suspect Costen put aside for her.' He ducked beneath a sudden shower of colourful leaves. The weather was turning. Noting where they were, he called them to a halt. 'We'll dismount and lead our horses from here.' They were near a secondary track that would take them close to the cabin, avoiding an encounter on the main track that would give them away. Magda had brought him this way once with her donkey cart, a shorter route to that part of Galtres. 'It's not far this way. We should arrive ahead of them.' The wood was loud with birdsong and the movements of creatures in the underbrush, but they came across no signs of people or horses on this lesser path.

'Are you certain of this?' Hempe asked a few times, unaccustomed to Galtres.

It was shortly after his third query that Owen saw the house through the trees.

'We are here.'

The house and the woodland around it were quiet, no sign of Christine and Pieter. While Hempe searched for a place to tie up their mounts and Stephen looked for a spot from which to watch the trail to the house, Owen opened the door and stepped inside. He knew even before he opened the shutters and looked round that someone had been here since he and Brother Michaelo searched it, a rearrangement of items, the bench moved away from the wall next to the door, a slipper in the middle of the room. Once he opened the shutters he understood his strong sense of intrusion. The bedclothes were torn away from the bed, rolled in a large ball and tossed in a corner, the colourful silk trodden on. The delicate items left on shelves and windowsills were gone. Thrown out the window? He leaned out, but saw nothing.

Hempe stepped in. 'Could use a woman's touch.'

'It was tidy two days ago. Someone came through in a rage,' said Owen.

'Costen's widow?'

'I wonder.' Was this where she had gone after the burial? How had she learned of it? Owen put that aside. 'We don't want Christine Creswick to find us in here. Let's see what Stephen's found.'

He showed them to a space shielded by underbrush with stumps for seats and a good view of the path and the door to the house. They were passing round the last of the wine in the skin Hempe had found in Gifford's kitchen when a horse neighed. Hempe crept to their mounts to keep them calm. In a moment, Christine appeared, Pieter behind her leading two horses. He was a fleshy man with a florid complexion – not ruddy from outdoor work but from an abundance of good food and wine. Christine smiled to herself as she approached the house.

'Who did you say lived here?' Pieter asked.

'A good friend who knew I might have a need to escape Rolo.'

'Escape. You should have said something, Christine. My father would have found a way to release you from the agreement. He'd had his doubts about Creswick.'

'Why don't you see to the horses?' said Christine. 'I will fetch the shovel.'

While Christine moved to the house, Pieter looped the reins to a young oak that looked as if it had been planted to shade one of the windows. Costen had cared for this place. That done, Pieter followed Christine into the house.

'What is wrong?' Pieter asked from within.

'Look at this. Someone tore off the bedding and walked on this beautiful piece of silk.' Christine's voice was icy. 'And all the pretty things on the shelves and sills, where are they?'

She moved towards the window as, crouching low to avoid being seen through it, Stephen took Christine's and Pieter's horses and moved them around the back, to prevent a quick departure.

'Are they what we came for?' Pieter asked.

'No, they're of no importance. But I don't like that someone was here.' She glanced round the room.

'I did not notice a lock,' said Pieter.

'There is none. That's why he buried it.'

The door opened, and Christine appeared holding a small shovel. She paused, glancing to one side, then the other, then counted steps aloud as she paced to her right. Her breath came quick, and she kept glancing round, as if expecting trouble. Owen was ready to move if need be to keep her in sight, but she stopped before rounding the house and began to dig. The ground had been recently disturbed, and she easily lifted a shovelful of dirt, putting it to one side.

Owen motioned to Hempe and Stephen to move to either side of the house.

Pieter stepped through the door. 'Your friend buried it so close to the house?'

'So he said.' She blew up on her hair as if to indicate this was hot work, though she did not seem to struggle.

'Would you like me to help?' Pieter brushed his hands as if readying himself for the work.

With a little bow, she handed him the shovel and stepped away. 'Have a care. It might be delicate.'

Pieter chuckled. 'Coin is hardly fragile, cousin.' He made a show of removing his handsome padded jacket and rolling up his sleeves, then bent to the task in earnest. He had moved but a few shovelfuls when he stopped, then tapped the shovel against something. 'I believe I have found it.'

Christine crouched down and brushed the soil from a flat surface. 'Yes, here it is.' She moved it side to side to loosen it from the soil, then lifted a smooth oak box out of the hole, just the size of the box dropped in Costen's house the night of his murder.

'So small? Not a very generous cache of coin,' said Pieter.

She smiled at him. 'It is more than enough. You recall the golden lion stolen from the goldsmiths?'

'You don't mean this is it?'

Christine gave a little laugh. 'I do.'

'No.' Pieter looked at her now with a slight panic. 'You cannot receive stolen goods, cousin. *I* cannot. This must be returned to Guildmaster Harrigan.'

'What are you saying? This is my freedom. My salvation.' Her voice broke a little.

'No. No, I will not agree to this.'

As he reached for the box in her left hand she revealed a dagger in her right, thrusting it towards his throat.

'You will, cousin, or you will be dead.'

'Christine! Don't be ridiculous, woman.' He reached up to push at her and cried out when she slashed the palm of his hand.

Owen rose up behind her and caught both her upper arms as Pieter bent over his bleeding hand.

'What is this?' Christine cried.

'You have made this worse for yourself by attacking him, Dame Christine.' Owen pressed her wrist until she dropped the dagger, then gently pried the oak box from her other hand as Stephen held her shoulders.

Owen nodded to him. 'Bind her hands in front.'

'How dare you! I've done nothing wrong.'

'You know this is stolen and you intended to keep it.'

She hissed at Stephen as he finished tying her wrists and took her arm. 'And why shouldn't I keep it? I am married to a monster, forced to wed him by Pieter's father, my godfather. Why should I not take the gift my lover hid for me? He wished me to be free of Rolo. Free to take the children to Bruges, away from my husband's ruin. And what was Costen's reward? Rolo murdered him.'

No doubt in her mind.

'I knew nothing of this,' Pieter whined as he wrapped his hand in a linen cloth, the blood soaking through it at once. 'Costen van Peelt? This was his house?'

'And what if it was? He was a good man,' said Christine.

'So those were your things in the cottage,' said Pieter. 'You met him here. How could you do this, Christine? Had you any thought for your family?'

'Had your father any thought for me when he married me to the cur?' Christine dipped her head away, a graceful gesture even with her hands tied. 'Costen and I were children together in Bruges. He always loved me. Your father knew it. He brought us together and then pulled us apart.'

'I knew nothing of this, Captain,' Pieter repeated.

'We will be sending men out to search thoroughly,' said Hempe. 'Is there anything else you care to inform us about, Dame Christine?'

'The furnishings were ours.'

'They will be handed over to Costen's widow,' said Owen.

'They were ours,' she cried. 'Costen would want me to have them.'

'You will have little use for them in the castle,' said Hempe.

Her eyes widened. 'Captain Archer, tell the bailiff I did nothing wrong. If anyone is guilty, it's Costen. He did not mean to kill Neville's man, I believe that, but he knew about us and Costen could not trust him to be silent. And then Costen found the lion in his scrip. He wanted me to have the means to escape. We were to go away together.'

How easily she branded both her husband and her dead lover as murderers. 'How inconvenient that your husband ruined your pretty plan by murdering your lover.' He felt Hempe glance at him sharply, but Owen suspected that it had worked out just as Christine wished. 'I wonder. Did you know that your husband attempted to kill a lad he feared had witnessed what he did to your lover?'

'A child? Why was a child there?' she asked.

It was a good question, one that Owen kept turning round in his mind, remembering a small cushion and pillow, as if for a child, among the items pushed to one side and soiled near the fire. Yes, a curious thing, but not how he had expected Christine to respond.

'It does not bother you that your husband would try to kill a child?'

She blinked rapidly. 'God help me, of course it does. And my uncle forced me to wed him.' She looked at Pieter.

He looked away.

'Will you not help me, Pieter?'

'Do not speak to me,' he said tightly.

'Time to ride back to the city,' said Owen. As he moved towards his mount, he felt something rattle in the box, as if there were more than one piece within. That should not be. He opened it and hissed a curse at the pair of smooth river stones nestled in the velvet. He looked at Christine. 'Where did you put it?'

'Put what?' She peered at the box. 'No. No! He meant that for me. Where is it?'

Owen thought about the state of the house. Someone had

searched for it. 'We need to check for any other disturbed earth. Stephen, Pieter, help me. Hempe, watch her.'

They spent a good hour searching, digging in potential spots, but found nothing.

Darkness shrouded the woods as they drew near the city, clouds hastening the twilight as wind stirred the branches overhead. Pieter had spent the first part of the return journey muttering to himself and calling out to Owen and Hempe about his innocence, his father's good intentions, chastising Christine for her sinful ways, how he never would have agreed to ride out with her had he any notion of her perfidy; but by twilight he was slumped in the saddle, in pain and exhausted. Owen had done his best to bandage the man's hand with a strip of cloth from the bedclothes and an unguent that Christine said was one of Lucie's for bruises. It would do for now. For her part, Christine had said nothing since Owen had lifted her up to ride in front of Stephen, her own mount led behind.

Hempe brought his horse up beside Owen on the right. 'I was not serious about putting her in a castle cell, you know. I meant to frighten her.'

'She does not frighten,' said Owen.

'I underestimated her. Do you think she has the lion elsewhere? That this was a trick?'

Owen had been turning it over in his mind. 'No. It's too elaborate. As for the castle, we could justify it. She withheld information about the golden lion and injured her cousin. But it's weak. We'll send her home with watchers. What do you think of Ned and Rose? They worked well together today.'

Hempe chuckled. 'Ned would like nothing better. But I don't know whether we want him so distracted.'

'Stephen and Ned then. They can take turns sleeping, Stephen first.' Owen raised his head as they rode out from under the trees, feeling a few drops. 'It will be a wet night.'

And indeed the rain came down heavily for a few moments as they rode out into the open, then settled into a chilly drizzle. Owen's clothes were uncomfortably damp by the time he led his horse into the stable outside Bootham Bar, which mercifully still held the heat of the day.

The stablemaster came out to greet the small party. 'I see you caught up with them,' he remarked, watching with interest as Stephen helped Christine from his mount. He glanced at a groom and nodded, upon which signal the lad hurried out.

'Who wants to know when we arrive?' Owen asked.

'Lord Neville. And I've a message for you, Captain. He awaits you at St Mary's, in the hospitium.'

'Boy!' Owen shouted. The groom turned, retraced his steps when Owen waved him back. 'Tell Sir John Neville that I will be with him in an hour.' He gave the lad a halfpenny.

'Sir!' The lad smiled, looked to his master for approval, and receiving it, hurried off.

'That was generous,' said the stablemaster.

'To give him courage. Sir John won't like the delay. But I've more urgent matters to attend to.'

By now he imagined Archdeacon Jehannes overwhelmed with people hoping to make some money on rumours of the golden lion's whereabouts. Then there was Flint, though he doubted the boy was able to talk.

Hempe clapped a hand on Owen's shoulder. 'Stephen and I can escort Dame Christine to her house and set up the watch. Anything else can wait until tomorrow. We've done much this day and deserve a rest.'

'Agreed. I'll see the archdeacon, Flint, Neville, and then I'm for home,' said Owen. At least he hoped so.

TWENTY-THREE

Tales and Consciences

At dusk, Martin set aside the fragments from Costen's house, covering them with a cloth. He suspected it was now a pointless task, Creswick and his hired curs in the castle. He'd learned little but that Costen had focused on Thomas Holme's house and extensive grounds on Castlegate and the gardens of St Mary's Abbey, though there were bits and pieces of Lady Row on Goodramgate, various shopfronts on Stonegate, an elegant little brothel on Grapecunt Lane, and St Mary's Church in Castlegate. The man had given himself over to studying all levels of the city, from the elegant to the tawdry, in remarkable detail. He had been an artist to the bone. Sorrow gripped Martin's heart, though he did not understand why the man's death had taken on such meaning for him. Perhaps it was part of being old. He rose. Time to put this aside and prepare for the evening. Up in his bedchamber he donned the clothes he had worn the previous night to meet the young ones, and while he dressed he thought about how he might honour Costen's memory. He was almost out the door when it came to him – he would approach Geoffrey Gifford with a commission for several paintings based on the remaining sketches, particularly the ones of the Abbey gardens. He smiled at the thought.

When the archdeacon's manservant opened the door, his face was set in a stern frown which quickly relaxed. 'Captain Archer.'

'You were expecting yet another person hoping to collect the ransom?'

'I was. Everyone reporting neighbours sneaking about the night of the theft, as if no one in the city slept. I will tell Dom Jehannes you are here.'

As he withdrew, Owen heard voices beyond the wooden screen

that blocked the draft from the door, Dom Jehannes's and a woman's. In a moment, someone approached with quick steps, and Jehannes appeared, his usually calm face pinched round the eyes and mouth. 'I have come close to cursing you.'

'I don't doubt it. It was a selfish thing to foist on you. I am sorry.'

Jehannes waved away his apology. 'You look too weary for me to scold. And I have guests you will want to see.' He stepped aside for Owen to enter the warm, inviting hall.

Anna van Peelt rose from a chair by the fire. She wore a white coif that hid her lustrous grey hair and seemed to leach colour from her face except for the shadows beneath her eyes. Celia Overton sat stiffly upright in the chair beside Anna's and nodded to Owen, her lips pinched and eyes disapproving.

'I have something for you, Captain.' Anna held out a felt bag. 'I was not about to let that harlot ransom it in exchange for escaping her husband's shame. Costen found it in Walter Bolton's scrip.'

Owen took the bag. It had the right heft. Loosening the draw-string, he pulled out the golden lion, warm from her hands. The firelight danced on its surface, making it seem alive. At last. He tucked it away and motioned for her to sit as he settled across from her. 'The goldsmiths will be grateful, Dame Anna. Did you bring it to Dom Jehannes for the ransom?'

Celia hissed at the insult.

But Anna did not flinch. 'I did not. I first called at your home and was told you were away. When I heard about the ransom, I trusted you would call here on your way home.'

'I take it you went to the house in Galtres after the burial yesterday,' said Owen.

She blinked and glanced over at Celia. 'Yes. You have just come from there?'

'But you waited until this afternoon to hand it over.'

She blushed and averted her eyes. 'It is a wearying journey to the house in Galtres and back,' she said softly.

'How long had you known about the house?'

She straightened and looked at him. 'You have no cause to be so abrupt.'

'I disagree.'

'Captain Archer!' snapped Celia.

'If you would answer my question, Dame Anna.'

Anna glanced at Celia, Jehannes, then, apparently not finding what she had hoped, back to Owen, with a little bow. 'I've known about it for years. Costen and I would meet there before we wed. And we enjoyed it after we were married. It was good between us . . . until *she* came to York.' The venom she put in the word 'she' was sharp and deadly.

'How did you know the lion was there?'

'Costen told me where he had hidden it when he brought it to me.'

'He brought it to you? When?'

Her blush suggested she was beginning to understand why he was not smiling. 'Yes, he brought it the morning he came to apologise. Just before he was murdered.' She caught her breath, bowed her head for a moment. 'He had hidden it for the harlot, and told her where it would be. But a friend suggested to him that the harlot meant to keep it for herself, and the more he considered their argument, he saw that it was likely the truth and he felt a fool. So he brought it to me.'

'You've had it since the day he died?'

'Yes.' She took a deep, shuddering breath. 'I feared his murderer had first tortured him because he thought he had the golden lion. I did not know what to do. . .' Her voice broke and she covered her face with her hands.

'It did not occur to you that you would be safe if you delivered it to me?'

'I was not thinking clearly,' she sobbed.

What was done was done. He now had the lion, and despite her estrangement from Costen, she appeared to have loved him and felt the loss. 'Who was the friend who warned him?' he asked quietly.

She glanced at Celia, who shook her head, her eyes steely. 'I cannot . . .' Anna looked away.

'Did he tell you to keep the lion?' Owen asked.

'He told me to follow my conscience. He admitted that he killed Walter Bolton trying to protect the harlot's honour and stripped him so that no one might identify him as Lord Neville's man. God help me, I do not understand why he did that when he insisted it was a fair fight, that Walter might have won had he not fallen and hit his head on a rock.'

Thinking back to the morning Owen spoke with Costen in the minster, the day of his death, he remembered his haunted eyes. He must have been terrified Owen had discovered his crimes.

'Christine Creswick poisoned his soul,' Celia said. 'I believe she knew about the party at Harrigan's that night and sent Costen to see whether he might steal the lion. That's all she wanted from him.'

'Celia, please, you cannot know what she might have told Costen.'

Celia snorted and added, 'I saw him in the street that night, outside my house, watching the Harrigan shop. So although it is true I do not know what she told him, I believe that he reported that Neville's man had been there first, and she insisted he pursue him.'

'Enough. It is done, Celia,' Anna said. 'More than that, we have been wrong in keeping this to ourselves. We had a duty to inform Captain Archer and return the lion.'

'Anna!' Celia cried.

Ignoring her, Anna faced Owen. 'As for the friend, Costen told me of a child he had grown to care for, a street child, a girl. He had found her sleeping in his woodpile one night and invited her to make a bed near his fire when she needed shelter. He said she was oddly wise for a little thing, and knew what was happening in the city. All the gossip. She warned him against Christine Creswick.'

'You see?' Celia said.

Anna put up a hand to silence her mistress. 'It was this child, Robin, who changed his mind about giving the harlot the golden lion if anything happened to him.'

Things began to fall into place. 'Costen left the rocks for Christine Creswick.'

'Yes.' A small smile. 'I could not find ease after the burial. So we went into Galtres to see whether Christine had discovered what he'd done. I found a sinful pleasure in ruining her things. And I took the collection of treasures from the forest that I had left there.'

'I still don't understand why you didn't come forward when he died,' Owen said.

Anna looked down at her hands. 'I was frightened. But in

truth—' She took a deep breath. 'We expected there would then be no investigation of his murder if the lion were handed over. Costen was of no consequence. A foreigner.'

By 'we', he imagined she meant Celia. 'You did not trust me to investigate?' he asked Celia, who had the good grace to look uneasy.

'I wanted to say something,' said Anna. 'But I could not think clearly, and I let Celia guide me.'

'I take the blame, Captain,' said Celia. She smiled at Jehannes. 'For my sins, I would take in this child, Robin. Employ her as a housemaid.'

'A generous offer,' said Jehannes.

'I do not know whether service would suit her at the moment,' said Owen. Or ever, but he had no right to make that decision for her. 'A friend of hers, a boy, was attacked by one of the men I've taken to the castle. Dame Magda is caring for him at St Leonard's. Robin visits him as much as Dame Magda permits. It will be a long recovery.'

'I see,' said Celia.

'Speaking of the boy, I must be on my way to him, and then Lord Neville.' Owen hoped he might learn whether Flint had indeed witnessed Bolton's death.

'If I might beg a favour, would you not mention my part in this when you deliver the lion to Guildmaster Dale?' Anna asked.

'Robert Dale has been chosen?' Owen smiled. He was glad for his friend. 'As far as your connection to all this, I doubt it can remain a secret. But Robert Dale will not be the one spreading the tale, nor will I.'

'Of course,' she whispered.

Jehannes walked him to the door, where the cook stood ready to fend off people hoping to trade rumours for ransom money.

'I fear the stream of nonsense will continue into the Lord's day,' said Jehannes. 'By the time Michaelo returns from his evening rounds among the poor it will be too late to prepare and send out an announcement to be read in the parish churches tomorrow.'

'Would you like one of my men to guard your door tonight and tomorrow?' Owen asked. 'Tell people that the lion has been recovered?'

'Bless you.'

'I owe it to you.'

'Even so, bless you.'

The solidity of the lion in his scrip brought a modicum of peace. And the murderers were secured in the castle. Little more to do but find out whether Flint had witnessed Bolton's death, and Robin had seen Costen's murder, and assure Neville that justice was being served. He would propose that Neville escort Gifford to the king, along with the Frenchman's corpse. Creswick and his men Owen would entrust to the sheriff, their crimes unrelated to the spying. Might he be shed of this task tonight? That would be a relief.

The children were slow to arrive this night. Martin tended the fire he had begun for them as he waited, wondering whether he had been wrong in thinking they would return for more stories. Enough roof remained to keep the rain off the fire and the wood he'd stacked beside it, but he could feel the damp on his back, a chill that slowly spread. He was thinking about moving on when he heard them calling to one another, 'Pirate's here,' as they trickled in out of the rain and settled round him.

A young boy offered him a cracked bowl and lifted a jug to pour.

'I'm grateful, but I've had plenty tonight.' Martin grinned. 'Any more and I will be snoring before the tale is told.' Not true, but he wanted to keep a clear head.

A girl tugged on his sleeve. 'Is Flint dead?'

'He lives, my friend, and Dame Magda says he is much improved since we found him.' She had sent word in the late afternoon.

'Will he come back to us?'

'He has a good chance. Much is now up to him. Are you all ready for one of the stories I promised you?'

A chorus of voices cheered him on.

A young boy answered Owen's knock at the children's quarters in St Leonard's, his solemn expression shifting to a wide grin when he recognised the caller. 'Milord Captain.' He bowed. 'I want to work for you when I'm old enough.' He lifted an arm as if to flex his muscles, though he wore too many layers of clothing for Owen to see them. 'Dame Magda said she would teach me how to find the right wood for a bow.'

The lad's eyes shone, something Owen never recalled seeing in the eyes of the children at St Leonard's. It seemed Magda was healing more than just Flint. 'That is all very good news, my young man, and I am honoured. But I'm not a lord, just the city captain. And I'm here to see Dame Magda and her patient.'

'Of course. Right this way, milord, I mean, Captain.'

Magda met Owen at the door to Flint's small room. 'Robin was here, glad to see Flint awake and looking about. They had a whispered discussion that did not seem to her liking, and she left.'

'Flint can talk?' That was good news.

'A whisper. Magda does not encourage it.'

Flint lay beneath a mound of covers pulled up to his chin, his head and shoulders propped up by cushions piled in a wedge to lift his head higher than his feet. His eyes were closed. 'He looks so small, so pale,' Owen said.

'Go. Listen to his breathing,' said Magda.

Bending to the lad, Owen heard steady, easy breathing, and his heart lightened. 'You have performed a miracle.'

'Saint Magda?' She chuckled. 'Close care, fresh herbs and roots, and the lad's own strength are at work, not miracles. Sit by him whilst thou dost tell Magda of thy day.'

'I won't disturb him?'

'Magda wishes him to hear, so that he may be drawn back into his life.'

The plain room had little in the way of furniture, so Owen settled on the pallet at Flint's feet. He took a moment to consider what might be of interest to the boy, then began. It was when he mentioned Martin's brief meeting with Robin and how she had disappeared when he asked if Flint had witnessed what happened to Bolton that the boy nudged him with his foot.

'Hast thou something to tell the captain?' Magda asked, leaning close to the boy.

Flint whispered something.

'He says he did see it. Costen killed Neville's son in a fight. A fair fight.' She listened to more. 'Neville's man fell and hit his head on a rock. He did not move after that.'

That was two matching descriptions of Bolton's death. 'I am grateful for your witness,' said Owen.

'Go on with thine account,' said Magda.

The next time Flint reacted was Owen's account of Costen's change of heart, inspired by Robin.

'He says Costen was good to Robin.'

'Was she in the house the night he was murdered, Flint? I ask because I have Rolo Creswick, Short John, and Striper in the castle and I can keep them off the streets if I have a witness who tells me they were the ones who beat and killed Costen.'

Magda bent to him. 'Yes. She was there at the end, too late to help.' As she straightened, Flint reached for her and whispered something more. 'Rolo Creswick thought she was Flint, wearing the hood. Robin fears that is why Creswick tried to kill Flint.'

'He had seen you at the river, with the hood?'

Flint reached for Magda. Whispered something.

'That night, in the house, Creswick told the other two to catch him, to catch Flint. But she escaped them. Flint was glad to take the injury for her.'

'You are a good friend to her,' said Owen.

'Hang them,' Flint hissed.

'Now I can. A question. Had one of them told you to follow Costen?'

Magda bent to the boy, who seemed to have much to say. 'No. Flint was worried that if the rumours of Costen spying were true, Robin might not be safe sleeping in his home. So he watched him, tested him to see whether he would hire him as a spy.'

Well done. 'Who told him where to find Bolton's pack?'

Flint whispered in Magda's ear.

'He watched Costen put it there,' she said.

That did not make sense. 'But you went to the old clothes collectors looking for it.'

Magda smiled as she listened to Flint. 'He feared someone might be watching, hoped he might not need to return to the place in the woods, that someone had already sold the items.'

'But they were too valuable to leave there,' said Owen.

The boy gave a weak nod.

'I am grateful for your help, Flint.'

He bobbed his head, his expression solemn, then pulled Magda close once more.

'He asks whether you found the lion.'

'I did. It is safe.'

At last the boy smiled.

'Thy work is done, Bird-eye.'

'Almost.'

Twilight and rain softened the edges of the abbey walls and turned St Cuthbert's Church just within the gates into a crouching behemoth, ready to spring. Owen pushed away the fancy as he strode along the well-kept paths. He had been tempted to turn towards home after St Leonard's, his work done, but he did not want Neville sending someone to pound on his door in the night, waking the family. The troubles had already touched them more than he liked.

The hospitium was welcoming, the windows glowing with lamplight, and he anticipated that Brother Oswald, the hospitaller, would have provided Lord Neville with good wine. Before knocking on the door Owen lifted his face to the sky, allowing the cool drops to refresh him while he tried to imagine what the sheriff would have told Neville about the men he had rounded up in the castle since they last spoke, and the body in the castle yard. The baron had made his ambition clear, to convince King Richard to use him, his experience at sea, his long engagement with the French in Brest, to lead the naval defence. And despite Owen's dislike of the man, he believed Neville was an asset the young king should employ, and he saw how the capture of the French spy by one of his men could be used to convince the king. But the rest of Owen's discoveries were of interest to Neville only insofar as they explained Walter Bolton's death.

'Archer.'

Owen nodded to the man in the doorway. 'Sir John.'

Unlike his garb earlier, Neville now wore an elegant padded jacket embroidered with silver thread that glittered in the light from a lantern over the doorway. His head was bare, his thick silvered dark hair swept back, enhancing his high forehead. He motioned for Owen to enter.

Brother Oswald was nowhere about, but a novice hurried to open a door to what Owen knew was a pleasant parlour overlooking the river, wasted in the gathering dark. But the room was comfortably furnished, and Owen chose a high-backed chair with plump cushions for the seat and back across from where Neville had been sitting, a bowl of wine on a small table beside it. He stretched out his legs.

'I understand you've had quite a day since we last spoke,' said Neville.

'I have. And you? How was your visit to Sheriff Hutton?'

'I learned little that I had not known, though I heard much praise of your skill as a healer. You are a man of many talents, Archer.'

'While my eye was healing, I assisted the surgeon in the camp. Then I wed an apothecary. The man is recovering?'

'By all accounts. I did not meet him. Wine?' Sir John gestured towards a flagon.

Owen gladly poured himself a bowl and took a handful of spiced nuts, his stomach growling in anticipation. He had eaten nothing since early morning. 'Did you learn more of Walter's movements, whether he was alone here?'

'Colum knew nothing. He cared only to hear who I would send to take Walter's place as his second and how soon. It seems Walter was more trouble than help. He is not mourned.'

'Not an easy thing to hear about your son,' said Owen.

'In his work for me he did not need to be liked.' Neville sat back, pretending indifference as he sipped his wine, but his usually cold eyes were sad. 'I understand you found the corpse of a spy and apprehended the man who had cooperated with him, as well as the Fleming's murderer. I am impressed.'

'You heard much. From the sheriff?'

'Yes. And at the stable outside Bootham I learned that you had ridden into Galtres today with one of your bailiffs. Were you still investigating Walter's murder? Constable said nothing about it, or who murdered the spy.'

Owen was not surprised the sheriff had avoided mentioning their strong suspicion that Costen had murdered Walter Bolton, but it was odd he had not told Neville that his man had murdered the spy. Brother Michaelo was thorough in his reports and would have mentioned that. Perhaps Constable had been uncertain how Neville would react to that news. So it was left to Owen, who simply said, 'Walter caught and killed the spy.'

Neville straightened. 'So he did catch him. Well done.' He smiled to himself. Owen waited, certain that Neville would be quick to make connections. There it was, the slight frown, first in the cold eyes, then the brows coming together. 'But the man you arrested, the one who had buried the spy, what was his part?'

'A witness.'

'The man kept the body?'

'Your son was not aware of Wulf Gifford's presence.'

'Walter left the body for Gifford to dispose of?' Neville tilted his head, thinking.

Owen sipped the wine, ate some of the savoury nuts.

Neville's frown deepened. 'I don't understand why Walter did not alert the sheriff, deliver the body to the castle. He should have been proud.' He leaned forward. 'There is more. I will hear all of it.'

'You will not like it.'

'I don't need to.'

'The spy tried to bargain for his life by offering information that might enrich Walter. He gave him details about a party that very night during which he might steal the golden lion the goldsmiths had created for King Richard. Your son killed the man and availed himself of the information.'

'The golden lion,' Neville whispered, his eyes pained. 'What did he hope to gain? How might that avenge all that happened?'

'Avenge? I don't understand.'

Neville covered his eyes with a carefully manicured hand for a moment, then sat forward to pour more wine. He cleared his throat and sat back. 'I thought you had not found the lion.'

'This morning I had not. I have it now. Costen van Peelt found it on Walter after he fell in a fight, and he handed it over to his estranged wife in case anything happened to him.' No need to mention his first intention, to give it to his mistress.

'The Fleming murdered Walter in a fight.'

'A fair fight, as a witness described it. Walter fell and hit his head on a rock.'

'And the Fleming meant to keep the lion.'

'He left that to his wife's discretion.'

'Such an honourable man,' Neville snarled. 'What did they fight about?'

'Costen wanted Walter's word that he would not reveal to

people in York the identity of a married woman who met him from time to time at a house in Galtres. Apparently he refused, and they fought.'

'Died in a fight. Damn him. But it's murder, no matter the tale. Pity the bastard's dead. Did you find the lion in Galtres?'

'No. Costen's widow handed it over to me.'

'His widow.' A raised brow. 'Yet you seem quite certain that Walter stole it.'

'Even more so since I witnessed your reaction.' Neville said nothing. 'The spy fed him the information and he was seen that night at the goldsmith's party, the night it was stolen, then hurried out of the city the following morning, fought with Costen, fell on a rock. Costen found the lion in his scrip. Believe what you will. That is what I have gleaned. What did the lion mean to Walter? Why would he risk everything?'

Neville looked away. 'I cannot think what he hoped to achieve now, so long after the accusation. The king's mother will have forgotten him.'

This was new. 'He was in the prince's household?'

'He was part of Prince Edward's household guard in the last years in the Aquitaine, one of the men who assisted Princess Joan's ladies in packing their belongings for the voyage home. When the golden lion was not found in the chests on their return, the young prince, now our king, pointed the finger at Walter, swearing that he had last seen the lion in my son's hands, and called him a thief. Walter could not prove otherwise, though they found no lion among his things, and it was his word against the young prince's. He was sent away in disgrace. This mission was his chance to prove himself to me, and the king.'

'Did you ever doubt his story?'

'Not at the time. But then I learned about the gifts he gave his mistress and I did not know what to think.'

'And then he repeated the act.'

'You judge him,' Neville growled, his eyes hard. 'You aren't a baron's bastard. How could you understand?'

'Perhaps.' But he did understand now. The baron knew his son was a thief but did not want to face the truth. Jean had guessed what Bolton wanted more than catching a spy – the gold to buy his freedom from his powerful father.

'You will say nothing of this.'

'Of course not. I asked only so that I might understand, dampen any lingering doubt.'

Neville rose, pacing to the window. 'When I heard what that meddling Lady Carlisle had suggested the goldsmiths of York give the king, I cursed her. She meant to insult me.'

'But she could not know Walter would be here, could she?'

'No. She would have no knowledge of that. It was directed at me. A sly dig.' He returned to his seat. 'Enough of that. Who will take the prisoner and the spy's corpse to the king?'

'Are you offering an escort? I am sure the sheriff would be glad for you to escort the traitor and the dead spy to the king.'

Neville raised a brow. 'You do not want credit?'

'Princess Joan will know my part, and that I believe King Richard should make use of you.'

Two raised brows, and a quiet, 'That is generous of you.'

Not really. He did not wish to make the journey again so soon after the coronation. But if this made peace between them, all the better. 'The realm needs you, my lord.'

Neville frowned, then gave a small bow.

'There is one thing – I promised Wulf Gifford I will ask Princess Joan to intercede on behalf of his family, that they not suffer for his actions.'

'That is not my concern.'

'Of course.' Owen rose. 'I can find my way out.'

But Neville followed him to the door of the room. 'I would like to be with you when you inform Wulf Gifford that I will be escorting him to the king. I want to hear what else he knows.'

That made sense. 'Agreed. He mentioned a group of spies working in Hull.'

'Good. And I want to hear what the other man has to say. The one who murdered the Fleming.'

'Why?'

'Something Constable said made me think Rolo Creswick knew of Gifford's spying and said nothing. That he had in fact hoped to benefit in some way.'

'The king would not find him of use.' Or he might relish executing a pair as traitors. Owen wanted no part of that.

'We shall see.'

'Tomorrow being Sunday, not a day for such work, I will be at the castle at first light Monday,' said Owen.

'I will be there.'

Owen crossed the hall and the novice had opened the outer door for him when Neville called his name. What now? He turned. 'Sir John?'

'If the goldsmiths wish, I would be honoured to escort them south in my travelling party. I will ensure their safe arrival at court.'

A generous offer. For his conscience? 'I will inform the guildmaster.'

'I have misjudged you,' Neville said quietly, his eyes less chilly than usual.

Owen gave him a curt nod and departed before he could tell him how little he cared. He had met his responsibilities before Neville could wreak more havoc. The baron was poison in York. The sooner he headed south, the better.

TWENTY-FOUR

Nighttime Tales and a Lion's Return

Owen found Lucie's account of Harrigan's apprentices entertaining, and though their information came too late for his purposes, it was good to have further detail about the night of the party. They sat at the long table in the hall, opposite the covered mound of debris from Costen's home, a project that would now be abandoned. Lucie had offered to call on Anna van Peelt on Monday morning to ask whether she wanted any of it, otherwise she would arrange for a dustman to haul it away.

Owen did not like to think of a man's work being relegated to the dustman, yet little of it was salvageable. 'I'm not sure what to do with the portrait of Christine Creswick,' he said. 'That, the harbour scene from the house in Galtres, and the large patterned cloth hanging we found in Gifford's kitchen are the few pieces of Costen's art left intact. A pity.' He looked down at the food, spicy and hot, and was puzzled to have little appetite.

Lucie touched his hand. 'What is it? You've delivered his murderer to the sheriff, as well as the traitor, and you've recovered the golden lion. What is left?'

'The spy's partners in Hull. Only when I remove that danger will I be finished. I need to ride there before they hear of Jean's death.'

'So soon.' He heard the disappointment in her voice.

'And I've little doubt Neville will insist on accompanying me.'

'And take the credit.'

'I am not bothered by that.'

'But working with Neville . . .' Lucie touched his cheek.

'That is the rub.' He took her hand and kissed it. 'I have achieved a tentative truce with him. Whether that can hold I cannot say.' He took a long drink of ale. Something else nagged at his heart. 'Robin is still on the run. From me, now. She is not at peace.'

'Martin is out with the children. Perhaps he will talk to her. Or Brother Michaelo might find her in the minster yard.'

'She will do her best to avoid them.'

'As Magda said about Flint, she will not thank you for following her. She has found her way so far. Perhaps it's time to trust her.'

As Martin began the tale of how he lost his right hand, he watched the shadows for Robin. He was well into the immediate aftermath of the brutal cut that had severed his hand from his arm when he saw her hanging back in the shadows, still wearing the pale hood. Doing his best to avoid eye contact that might frighten her away, he continued, doing a poor job of singing one of the songs with which Ambrose, his friend and fellow captive, had serenaded him through his first night of agony. Describing the ordeal in such detail brought back the horror and pain and he wanted to bring the telling to an end, but did not dare. Robin had settled to listen, and all the children were leaning towards him, gasping and wincing as he lingered on the blood and the pain and the brutality of his tormentors.

'Why did they hate you so?' one of the older lads asked when Martin paused to catch his breath.

'I traded in information that was inconvenient for them. But the real brute was a man who liked to cause pain. He had beaten his wife for no other reason than that he could.'

'Beast,' one of the girls growled.

'Yes, he was,' said Martin. 'But you will never guess with what weapon he was killed when Captain Archer and the archbishop came to our rescue.'

'The archbishop's fat,' someone called out, then giggled.

'Not the present archbishop, but John Thoresby, who was quite a different sort of man than Archbishop Neville,' said Martin.

'Well, if it was the captain it was an arrow,' said a boy. 'If Archbishop Thoresby, a sermon.'

A few tittered, but most shushed the boy.

'It wasn't the captain,' said Martin, 'nor the archbishop. But my friend, a musician who protected his hands at all cost. I had no idea he would know how to use what he did, but he had grown up on a farm. Can you guess?' As he dared glance towards Robin he saw someone behind her, tall, moving with care, slipping behind the fallen wall separating the property from the next house. Near Robin, yet hidden. Owen?

'Rebec!' 'Fiddle!' were the first guesses.

'You can't kill someone with those,' said one of the older boys.

'Sword!' 'Dagger!' 'Pike!' The children shouted their guesses as if vying to be the loudest voice, until one of the older boys urged them to be quiet. 'We don't want people to hear and tell us to move on,' he warned.

Martin shook his head to each guess.

'A rock to the forehead!' 'A garrot!' The lad who shouted that had to explain to several what that was. 'A shovel on the head!' said another.

Martin laughed. 'That last one is close.'

'A plough!'

'Are you mad?' one of the lads said. 'How would he lift it up?'

'So what was it?' the oldest boy demanded.

'A pitchfork.' Martin grinned and sat back, watching the effect ripple through the crowd. The gasps and sighs and little shouts were quite satisfying. 'Yes, it was a bloody end to the beast. And I never imagined my friend capable of such a thing.'

'He loved you,' said one of the girls. 'Love makes us strong.'

Some chuckled, and teased her, but most of the crowd quietly talked among themselves.

Martin rose, dusting off his leggings and shrugging off some of the dampness on his back. 'I am off to my bed now.' He glanced over to where only a moment earlier Robin had sat. She was gone. As was her shadow. Bloody balls. She was so slippery. He hoped that had been Owen, and that he had followed her. He motioned for all to be quiet a moment. 'Captain Archer has put the men who tortured and killed the Fleming Costen van Peelt in the castle dungeons. It was Rolo Creswick, and he's likely the one who tried to kill your friend Flint, and a hired pair, Short John and Striper. If any of you have information that could help the captain keep them off the streets, he would be grateful to hear it. You can come to Wilton's apothecary and ask to talk to me, or leave a message with Jasper or Dame Lucie. We will all sleep better if we know they won't be released.'

'Will you be back?' one of the younger boys asked.

'It would be my pleasure.' Martin grinned and bowed, then slowly walked away.

A young girl hurried after him, tugging gently on the sleeve of his handless arm. 'Robin misses Master Costen.'

'Might she be at his house this night?'

'Late, if she is. Just to sleep.'

Another lad fell in step with him. 'Striper's been bragging about some pretty things he stole from a house, offering them to some of the girls for – you know.'

Bloody curs. 'Does he get what he wants?'

'They're smarter than that. And we were all watching him after that. Wondered where he went today.'

Martin patted the lad's shoulder. 'You're like a pirate crew, looking after each other. Good lad.'

As the boy turned back to the fire, Martin headed to Costen's.

There they sat, talking as if old friends, the girl scraping the last of some food from a bowl. Martin settled down beneath the window, the eaves protecting him from the rain, and listened. She was saying that Costen had taught her to mix colours, and then stood her on a stool to paint one of the boats in the harbour scene. He had offered her a safe place to sleep after finding her rolled up in a blanket in the woodpile behind his house.

What had Owen said to gain the child's trust, Martin wondered. His own efforts with the children had gleaned some information, but she'd not come forward. Another proof of his uselessness.

'To sleep in his house took great trust,' said Owen. 'My daughters are wary of strangers, particularly men.'

'Do your daughters trust Pirate?'

'My friend Martin? They do. Because he saved the life of their elder brother. It is a story much told in my home, so when he appeared some months ago they were excited to meet the pirate who was somehow also a kindly man who saved their brother.'

Martin smiled in the dark.

'Why did you trust Costen?' Owen asked.

She did not answer at once. 'He never shouted at me,' she said. A pause. 'He never shooed me away, and he had a soft voice with

me. Not like his usual voice.' Another pause. 'And he promised
never to touch me.'

'And you believed him.'

'I sleep with a knife.'

'That is wise.' Owen said it with respect, not talking down to
her. 'I wish I had known him better. To create such drawings . . .
He looked closely at life.'

'He listened, too,' said Robin, 'and remembered what I said.
He didn't mean to kill the lord's man.'

'I think you're right.'

Tired as Owen must be tonight, he spoke as if he had all the
time in the world for this child. It might be a long night.

Martin crouched as two figures approached, then relaxed when
the light from the window illuminated two of the older lads he'd
been with earlier.

'You take the back,' said one.

'Captain Archer is with her.'

A shrug. 'We'll watch anyway.'

Martin rose from his crouch. 'It's just me, Pirate,' he whispered.
'Heading home.'

They nodded to him as he walked off.

Seeing Lucie on the kitchen settle, Emma asleep on her lap, Martin
was about to back out the door.

'Come in,' Lucie softly called. 'She is now fast asleep, and if
she wakes our voices will comfort her.'

After removing his boots, he poured himself a small bowl of
ale and joined Lucie, lifting Emma's slippered feet to his lap.

'The sleep of angels.' He smiled down on the child. 'I saw
Owen with Robin.'

Lucie stroked her daughter's wavy brown hair, so like her own.
'Then she did not run from him. That is good news.'

'They were talking like old friends. How fares it with him?'

'He has resolved everything he can in York, even to the recovery
of the golden lion.'

'He found it?'

He listened as Lucie told the tale, including Christine Creswick's
humiliation. 'She did not know it was Costen's doing. I don't
know what will become of her. She assaulted her cousin Pieter,

so I doubt he will help her return to Bruges, as she wanted, but she will be shunned in York.'

'Is that Owen's problem?'

'No. Still of concern for him are the French spy's fellows in Hull. He says Neville will insist on joining him there.'

'God help him.'

'I know.' She sighed. 'I fear that while the young king's government is finding its way, Owen will continue to be involved with matters beyond the city, beyond being Princess Joan's ears in the north.'

Martin took that thought up to his bedchamber. Across from his room, Jasper paced in his own.

'Something on your mind?' Martin asked. 'Come talk if you like.'

Jasper joined him, slumping down on the foot of the bed and stretching out his long legs. 'Da isn't home yet.'

'I know. He's with Robin at Costen's house.' Martin shed his wet clothes and crawled under the covers, getting comfortable in case this was a long conversation.

Jasper snorted in frustration. 'So he did go, even after all he did today. And Ma says he'll be going to Hull to catch the spies. Why him? Why doesn't Hull solve its own problems?'

'Finding the spies is part of his service to the king's mother.'

Shifting to sit forward, elbows propped on his thighs, Jasper bowed his head. 'I do know that. But what about our city? Can we be sure there won't be more spies?'

He had come to know Jasper, and it seemed there was more to this than a fear for the city. 'It is difficult for you when he's away?'

Jasper used both hands to scratch his head, leaving his hair standing up in comical peaks for a moment, before it all softly settled. 'I feel responsible for the family.'

'And?'

'As the archbishop's man, and now the captain of the city, and Princess Joan's eye and ears in the north – my father has enemies. And sometimes they look to his family for revenge.'

'I've heard the stories. You fear you might need to defend your family all alone? You don't trust that your father's men, including the bailiffs, watch out for all of you when he's gone?'

'Most of them have their own families.' Jasper yawned. 'I should let you sleep.'

Owen heard Robin rise at dawn and step outside. When she returned, she rolled up the pillow, pallet, and blanket and tied the bundle with cord, stumbling a little as she carried it across the room and set it down beside the door.

'You are moving out?'

'I mean to stay with Flint at St Leonard's until he can come away. You won't need to sleep here tonight.'

'Would you like me to carry the bedding for you? It's a long walk.'

'One of my friends will help.'

Owen had encountered them when he'd taken a walk round the house during the night. He'd not heard them moving in hours.

'I'll carry it until one of your friends relieves me.'

A nod. 'Thank you.'

Owen lifted the bundle. 'Might I ask what you did with the Frenchman's things?'

'The room by the friary?'

'Yes.'

'Sold the clothes and the pack. It was his wine I gave Flint when he was hurt.'

'Did you find any papers?'

'Some. Tossed them in the river. No use to me.'

They headed down the ginnel to Colliergate.

He had slept in his own bed for a few hours after coming home at dawn. The city had been quiet, but Robin had been right, one of the older boys materialised and offered to carry her bedding the rest of the way. Owen had slipped in beside Lucie, grateful for the peace and warmth of his house, the softness of his bed.

Harrigan's hands shook as he lifted the claw-like clasp and opened the box with reverence, breathing out with a sigh of joy. 'Safely returned. I had given up all hope.' He lifted the lion from its velvet bed, turning it about, inspecting for damage. 'Unharmed, God be thanked.' He closed the box and held it out to Owen. 'But no longer my responsibility. You must take this to Guildmaster Dale.'

'I had heard.' Owen would be happy for his friend, in time, but now he saw the devastation on Harrigan's face and could not but regret his downfall. 'But I thought you should be the first to know that it is safely recovered.'

'I am grateful, Captain. I will give thanks at mass this morning. It has been a humbling experience, to be sure. I have much to reflect on. I do not begrudge Robert the honour. He will be a worthy master, though I am not certain how he will make the journey with his sight so poor.'

'Lord Neville has offered to escort him, and anyone he wishes to include in the party.'

'Has he? That is kind.'

Owen walked out into the rainy morning with a full heart. Harrigan had indeed been humbled, in reputation, status, and demeanour, a heavy price to pay for his pride. He crossed over to the Dale house, where he was received with much good cheer.

TWENTY-FIVE

An Unexpected Alliance

After a day of rest and rumination, Owen was ready to complete the interrogations. He had sent word to Neville that he would begin not at the castle but at the Creswick home. Brother Michaelo was just settling himself beneath a window in the chilly Creswick hall to record the proceedings when Sir John arrived. After the introductions, Neville quietly asked Owen why Martin Wirthir was in attendance.

'He is familiar with spying from the other side and offered his expertise,' said Owen.

'And you believe this woman was involved in the spying?'

'We will see.'

A slight smile. 'You have considered what I said about her husband's culpability.'

'Perhaps.'

At first Christine resisted any attempt to incriminate herself, although she had much to say about her husband's greed and jealousy. She assured them that he was capable of such brutality as Costen had suffered, though she suggested that he would have left most of the work to the two men in his employ.

'Have you met Short John and Striper?' Owen asked.

'I have seen them in the yard. I did not permit them in the house.'

'How long have they worked for your husband?'

'Not long. Perhaps three weeks. Rolo said they were helping him in the warehouse.' She shook her head and dabbed at her eyes. 'He has ruined us. I implore you, allow me to take my children to my family in Bruges.'

Before Owen could respond, Neville leaned forward.

'Did your husband ever mention Wulf Gifford's troubles in

Hull, or anything else related to the charges against him?' he asked.

Christine seemed momentarily tongue-tied. 'Only that there had been trouble, nothing more, milord.' She kept her head slightly bowed, looking up through her lashes. 'But I knew from the moment they arrived that Wulf Gifford was no one I wanted in my home.' Neville's cold regard seemed to fluster her, and she added, 'Never realising my own husband was cut from the same cloth.'

'The same cloth? No. As far as I know Wulf Gifford is not a murderer,' Neville said coldly as he rose and wished her a good day.

She gasped. 'You already judge him.'

'You have not?' Neville almost smiled. He enjoyed insulting her.

Seeing her stricken expression, Owen almost pitied her. 'Thank you for your time, Dame Christine.' He nodded to Brother Michaelo and Martin.

As Christine walked them to the door, she touched Owen's arm. 'I am not certain what I should do. Send blankets to Rolo? Food?'

'I will send word later today, when we have a better idea how long he will be here at the castle,' said Owen.

'He might be released?'

'Not that,' said Owen.

'God help him,' she whispered and crossed herself. 'What will happen to us?'

'I cannot say at this time.'

She glanced at Neville, who loomed in the doorway watching her with his cold eyes. 'I have done nothing wrong.'

'Then you should fear nothing,' said Neville.

As they walked towards the castle, Brother Michaelo, walking a little behind Neville and Martin with Owen, asked quietly, 'You offered Dame Christine no comfort. Why?'

'I wager we will learn that she encouraged her husband's crime,' said Owen. 'I cannot otherwise explain his knowing where to dig for the coin in the house.'

'To what end?'

'For just what has happened. He will be executed for murder, and she will be free of him. But she had counted on some wealth.'

'The golden lion.' Michaelo sighed. 'Like Walter Bolton, ruined by her desire for that cursed thing. Might I go to her after we have spoken with her husband and suggest what she might provide him in the castle? And offer to pray for her?'

Michaelo's concern for the woman shamed Owen. 'I was that cruel?'

'That is your role. Mine is the care of souls.' He nodded at Neville and Martin, heads close, discussing the coming interrogation. 'I never foresaw that alliance.'

'Nor did I. I pray Martin is not eaten alive.'

Michaelo sniffed. 'I should think the reverse more likely.'

They escorted Wulf Gifford to one of the more comfortably furnished cells for Sir John Neville's comfort. Owen motioned Gifford towards a bench near an oil lamp and settled between Martin and Michaelo beneath the high window. Neville sat near the lamp in a cushioned, high-backed chair.

Gifford blinked in the lamplight. 'Is this my new cell?'

'Only for the conversation with Lord Neville,' said Owen.

Gifford looked at Martin. 'Why is the Fleming here?'

'He has experience with French spies. He might recognise names, suggest questions,' said Owen.

'Why don't you tell us how you were approached in Hull, and when, Gifford?' Neville began.

A few days in the cells had loosened Gifford's tongue and he was getting hoarse when Martin asked if he might speak. Neville nodded to him.

'You've been helpful. I recognise some of the names,' said Martin. 'Let me tell you how they chose you.'

'How would you know that?'

'Because I've done such work.' He described how the men arrive in a city, sometimes already armed with names, often not. They observe the shippers, the merchants, listen to gossip in the taverns, learn who might be just desperate enough to play with them, or who might hold a grudge against his fellows. And they follow him, befriend him, ask for innocent bits of information, offer a small purse, assure him it is just business, and then the threats begin.

Until this moment, Wulf Gifford had not appeared to understand how serious were his actions. But as Martin talked, Wulf began to fidget and sweat. Neville sat back, seeming fascinated by Martin's quiet description of the trap. In truth, Owen was impressed by his friend's technique.

When Martin paused to drink a little wine, Wulf glanced round the room, his eyes haunted. 'I never meant to betray the king.'

'But you did,' said Neville. 'Many times.'

'When Jean appeared in York, how did that not convince you of your crime?' Martin asked quietly, as if speaking to a child. 'You were their creature. No escaping. Unless you went to someone in authority here – the captain, the sheriff – and exposed the spy. Why did you not do that?'

'I thought—'

'You could outwit them?' Martin chuckled. 'They have manipulated men with far more devious minds than yours, Wulf. You never had a chance.'

'I am a dead man.'

Owen sat forward. 'Remember what I said. If you give us information that helps us find the men in Hull, I will see what I can do about your family's welfare. You have done well with names. Now we need descriptions. Where they lodged. Which taverns they frequented. All that you know.'

Wulf began to talk in earnest.

After the guards collected Gifford, returning him to his cell, Neville sat back, nodding at Martin. 'Well done, Wirthir. I questioned Archer's judgement in including you, but you coaxed more out of him than we might have. I am impressed.'

'You need me in Hull,' Martin said.

Neville grinned. 'I can see that I do. Are you offering?'

'I am, as well as accompanying you when you present the information to the king, if that be your pleasure.'

Neville's smile suddenly faded. He looked to Owen. 'This is your idea. You think to hand your duty over to your friend.'

'On the contrary. I tried to dissuade him.' Martin had insisted on allowing Neville to decide. 'Do you still want to talk to Rolo Creswick?'

'I do. Gifford's confession makes me think Creswick likely heard much, noticed more.'

At first, Rolo Creswick denied any knowledge of Costen's murder, but as he struggled to explain how he had come to possess the stolen items that Alfred had witnessed him moving from his house to Gifford's kitchen, he shifted to outrage.

'He stole my wife's affections. Has a man no right to defend his family?'

'Confront the man, ask him to stay away, that would be reasonable, lawful,' said Owen. 'But torture and murder, no, you have no right to that.'

'I did not torture him.'

'Your men did, while you watched and made suggestions,' said Owen. 'We have their confessions.'

Rolo said nothing to that, but his hand shook as he raised a bowl of watered wine to his mouth.

'How did you learn of your wife's relationship with van Peelt?' Owen asked.

'A costly gift. A silver platter. She forgot to hide it.' He paused after that, frowning at the floor, as if considering that neglect on her part.

Certainly Owen wondered at that, a woman who took such care in manipulating people. 'Go on.'

'When it was gone the next day I asked what had happened and she said she had returned it, begged my forgiveness, said he had pushed himself at her.'

Clever. 'Did your wife tell you where he might hide gold in the house?' Owen asked.

Rolo looked surprised, then tried to hide his reaction. 'What are you saying?'

'How did you know where to dig?'

He stared at the floor. 'How did I— God save me, she meant for this to happen to me.' He looked up at Owen. 'Is it true that my wife thought van Peelt had hidden the golden lion for her?'

'Where did you hear that?' Owen asked.

'The guards. They laugh at me.'

'I will talk to them. But yes, she did think the golden lion was hidden for her.'

His breathing came fast now, his face a dangerous colour. 'She told you, didn't she? Came to you oh so tearfully and told you what I had done? Yes? Of course she did, the bitch. She meant for me to be caught.'

'No, she did not come to me,' said Owen.

'But she has not denied it,' said Martin.

Creswick glanced over at him, frowned as if he had not noticed him before. 'Why is the Fleming here?'

'He is assisting me in my search for spies,' said Neville. 'What did you know about Gifford's friend Jean?'

'What is this? Does she accuse me of spying as well?' He turned to Owen, back to Neville, his eyes wild. 'Does she?'

'What did you know of Jean?' Neville asked again.

Creswick had begun to curl into himself. 'Nothing. Only that Wulf feared him,' he said softly.

'And knowing all you did about his troubles in Hull, you guessed what he wanted,' said Martin. 'Did you not?'

'We know you told others of his troubles,' said Owen. 'That is not the behaviour of a friend.'

'Did I?' Rolo looked haunted.

'Yet you did not report your suspicions,' Neville said in a cold, quiet voice.

And so it went, until Rolo Creswick was weeping and begging for mercy, cursing his wife, cursing all who had disappointed him. When Creswick was removed to his cell, Neville said that King Richard would find the man useful, his execution would serve as a warning to the people. All must be vigilant in defending the kingdom.

'That is a stretch of the law,' said Owen.

'He is for hanging,' said Neville. 'Here or on Tyburn, what does it matter?'

Owen rose. 'Brother Michaelo, Martin, we are finished here.'

'Not Wirthir,' said Neville. 'I would talk with him a while.'

Martin nodded to Owen. 'I will follow shortly.'

Owen and Brother Michaelo said little as they walked away, until the monk broke the silence.

'I do not understand how Martin can stomach the baron.'

'Nor I. But he said he has worked with far worse men. I think he does this to spare me.'

'Then he is a most generous friend.'

He was indeed.

TWENTY-SIX

Departures

Late October

Jasper stood in the doorway, watching Martin pack. 'Will you come back to us?'

The yearning in the question moved Martin. The son he never had. Would he return, or would death take him in the south, far from friends? 'I intend to, Jasper. How could I not?'

'You'll be glad to see Ambrose.'

'I will.' Most of all, he wanted Ambrose to witness his redemption. 'He'll see how my time here has changed me. Given me faith in myself.'

In truth, he was excited to be on the way. In Hull he had been instrumental in trapping the spies for Owen and Neville. Now the men Neville had summoned for the journey to the king were collecting the prisoners from the castle: two French spies, one Spanish – his partner had chosen a watery grave rather than capture, Gifford, Creswick, and Jean's corpse, now packed with scented herbs in a sturdy oak coffin. Accompanying them would be four goldsmiths, Masters Dale, Harrigan, Scardburge, and Goring, each with an apprentice to see to their comfort. And no Owen. This was Martin's gift to the family who had welcomed him, and in whose company he hoped to spend the last of his days. Perhaps. Or perhaps he would find satisfaction in his alliance with Sir John Neville, a cold-hearted, ambitious man who yet grieved for his bastard son. An imperfect man, someone he could understand.

Out in the yard, Emma presented him with a drawing of herself seemingly in a shower of – rose petals? Unusually large snowflakes?

'It's me as the witch who taught the villagers a lesson.'

Of course. 'And I am to remember to befriend all?'

Emma frowned. 'No. I warn you that if you don't come back to us, I will sneak into your room one night and cut up all your belongings.'

His heart melted. He crouched down to embrace her and whisper, 'I promise you I will do all in my power to return to you, my princess.' In a few years, what might she be?

'She was up before dawn working on that,' said Owen, picking her up, offering his free arm to assist Martin in rising. He was grinning, but Martin saw the knowledge in his eye that this might be farewell, considering his gratitude for the steadying hand.

'I intend to return,' he said. It was all he could promise.

The garden echoed with Hugh's earnest explanations and Pippa's giggles and bursts of applause. His hair a fiery cloud in the bright autumn sun, Hugh stood straight and proud as he demonstrated his strength for Pippa Harrigan, and allowed her to touch his upper arm to feel the power required to pull back the strings of his bow. She was a most appreciative audience.

Lucie and Pippa's sister, Elaine, watched from the bench beneath the linden, brushing the last of the crisp yellow leaves from their hair and their clothing now and then. It was a bright afternoon with a sharp breeze. Elaine had brought Pippa to present Hugh with a gift she had made, a stick and string bow and arrow with a tiny piece of feather for the fletching. In return, he'd offered to demonstrate his real bow, finished before Martin left with Sir John Neville for the south.

'She is so grateful to him,' said Elaine. 'And I am grateful to Robert Dale for including my father in the delegation to King Richard. It is an honour he will never forget.'

Lucie had not been surprised when she heard of the gesture. It was what made Robert Dale the wise choice as guildmaster, his respect for all he encountered. He had also included John Scardburge in the party, hoping to smooth any feathers still ruffled by the incident in the schoolroom.

'How did he feel about Scardburge's invitation?'

'Oh, John Scardburge had apologised for his son the very evening of the incident, assuring Da that Edwin had been punished for what he said. He also apologised for angry words thought-lessly spoken in the presence of his children.' Elaine smiled at another round of applause. 'Lord Neville surprised us with his generous offer to escort them, and send them home with an armed escort. But Father says it's because the captain let him claim to have caught the spies in Hull, when we all know it was the captain and Master Martin.'

'My husband has his reasons for offering the glory to the baron.' Lucie turned to Elaine. 'You've heard that Geoffrey Gifford will be attending Oxford, as planned?'

Elaine's eyes sparkled. 'He told me. The Ferribys are so good to make him their ward. Not everyone in York approves.'

'Do not mind them. By the time he returns from Oxford they'll have forgotten his family.'

'My father has a long memory.'

'Time will tell.'

'Master Martin was kind to Geoffrey as well, commissioning the paintings from Costen van Peelt's sketches of St Mary's gardens. He paid him handsomely for the materials and work even before he's begun.'

'Martin is grateful to have a way to ensure that people will see what a gifted artist Costen was.'

'He is a complex man.'

Lucie laughed. 'That he is.'

The pitch of Hugh's voice rose excitedly as he fumbled with the bow.

'Time for cake.' As Lucie gathered the children, she thought of Martin's easy camaraderie with them. He said they had taught him a great deal, and helped him see the world with fresh eyes. And they had restored his faith in himself. *Children see through our masks. They saw through the pirate to the man, and judged him redeemable.*

She smiled as she ushered the children inside.

SEVERN HOUSE

The home of great genre fiction

Discover more must-read stories:
visit severnhouse.com or scan the QR code below

Sign up for monthly updates on our latest books:
severnhouse.com/newsletter

Find us on social media:
@severnhouse
@severnhouseimprint